She is the creator of the Matthew Bartholomew series
of mysteries set in medieval Cambridge and the Thomas
Chaloner adventures in Restoration London, and now
lives in Wales with her husband, who is also a writer.

D0300607

Also by Susanna Gregory

The Matthew Bartholomew series

A Plague on Both Your Houses
An Unholy Alliance
A Bone of Contention
A Deadly Brew
A Wicked Deed
A Masterly Murder
An Order for Death
A Summer of Discontent
A Killer in Winter
The Hand of Justice
The Mark of a Murderer
The Tarnished Chalice
To Kill or Cure
The Devil's Disciples
A Vein of Deceit
The Killer of Pilgrims
Mystery in the Minster
Murder by the Book
The Lost Abbot
Death of a Scholar
A Poisonous Plot
A Grave Concern
The Habit of Murder
The Sanctuary Murders
The Chancellor's Secret

The Thomas Chaloner Series

A Conspiracy of Violence
Blood on the Strand
The Butcher of Smithfield
The Westminster Poisoner
A Murder on London Bridge
The Body in the Thames
The Piccadilly Plot
Death in St James's Park
Murder on High Holborn
The Cheapside Corpse
The Chelsea Strangler
The Executioner of St Paul's
Intrigue in Covent Garden

SUSANNA GREGORY

The Clerkenwell Affair

sphere

SPHERE

First published in Great Britain in 2020 by Sphere
This paperback edition published in 2021 by Sphere

1 3 5 7 9 10 8 6 4 2

A CIP catalogue record for this book is available from the British Library.

ISBN 978-0-7515-6274-3

Typeset in ITC New Baskerville by Palimpsest Book Production Ltd,
Falkirk, Stirlingshire
Printed and bound in Great Britain by Clays Ltd, Elcograf S.p.A.

Papers used by Sphere are from well-managed forests
and other responsible sources.

MIX
Paper from
responsible sources
FSC® C104740

Sphere
An imprint of
Little, Brown Book Group
Carmelite House
50 Victoria Embankment
London
EC4Y 0DZ

An Hachette UK Company
www.hachette.co.uk

www.littlebrown.co.uk

For my lovely 'new' family:
Pat and Martin
Juliette and Hugh
and
Jess and Steve

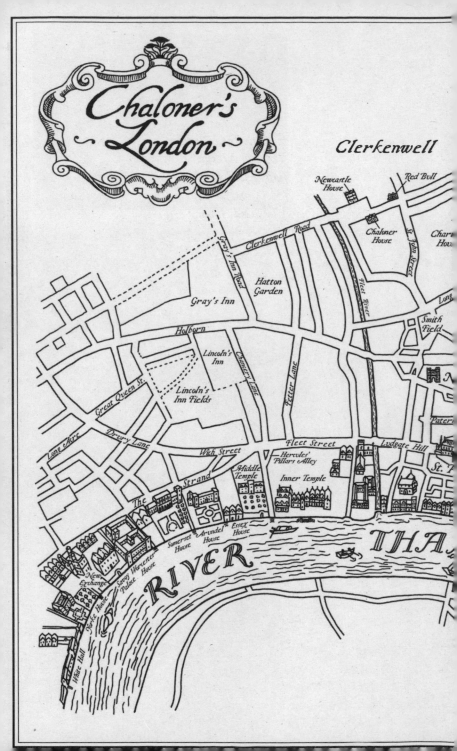

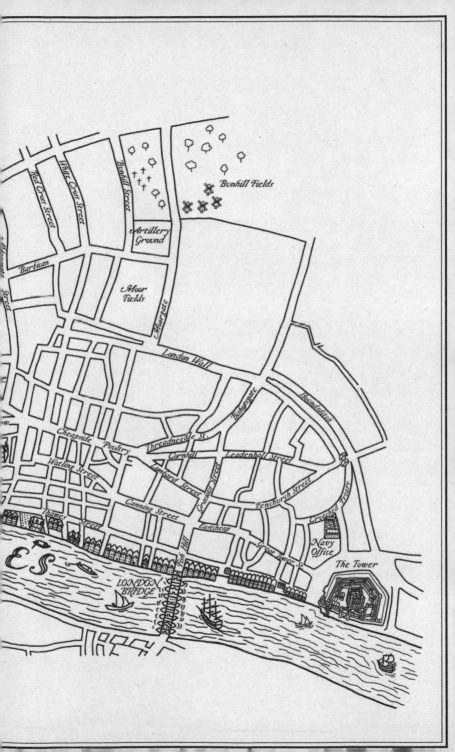

Prologue

Thomas Chiffinch was in an awkward position. He held two important Court posts – Keeper of the Closet and Keeper of the Jewels – and had a reputation for efficiency, refinement and discretion. Unfortunately, the same could not be said of his brother Will, who was one of the worst offenders for shaping the Court's current reputation as a place of debauchery, corruption and greed.

Chiffinch wished Will would behave with more decorum. He might be loved by the King and His Majesty's dissolute friends, but the rest of the country hated him, and there was growing anger at the brazen squandering of public money on courtesans and lavish feasts. Indeed, the King's popularity was at its lowest ebb since he had been restored to his throne six years earlier, and Will's ability to organise spectacularly decadent revels played no small part in this.

Back in January, some Londoners had capitalised on the ill-feeling generated by the moral bankruptcy of courtiers like Will, and had engineered an uprising. Their

1

efforts had come to nothing in the end, but the King stubbornly refused to heed the lesson and rein his favourites in, so resentment continued to fester. The plague had not helped. It had killed the poor in their tens of thousands while the King's response had been to show a clean pair of heels, fetching up in Oxford, where he had continued to frolic as though nothing was wrong. He had come home when the danger was over, but London grieved for its dead, and his merry excesses at White Hall rubbed salt into an open wound.

Chiffinch sat in his sumptuous palace apartments and mulled the problem over. The people were nearing the end of their tether, and the last time a king had made himself this unpopular, he had been executed. Chiffinch was a loyal servant of the Crown, and was not about to stand by and do nothing while a second Charles went about losing his head.

He sighed. Unfortunately, Will and his silly friends – the most flamboyant of whom called themselves the Cockpit Club – were not the only reason why the King was despised by his subjects. His leading ministers did nothing to ease the situation either. They declared war on the Dutch, introduced oppressive taxes, and devised laws to suppress religious freedom. And as for the Earl of Clarendon, his sale of Dunkirk to the French at a ridiculously low price had given rise to the popular belief that he had allowed himself to be bribed. Now the man could not step outside his house without someone howling abuse at him.

Then there was the Duchess of Newcastle, who shocked and unsettled Londoners with her unorthodox behaviour. Her very presence in their city was a source of dissent – some relished her odd ideas, while others found them horrifying. Not only did she hold controversial political and religious opinions, but she questioned the natural order of things. For example, she itched to join the Royal Society, despite the fact that membership was restricted to men, and she wrote books under her own name, instead of having the decorum to use a male pseudonym.

Her antics went against all that was decent, and Chiffinch was terrified of what might happen if she remained unchecked. What if other women followed her example, and brayed *their* opinions to all and sundry? What if she demanded a seat on the Privy Council, on the grounds that she was more intelligent than the current male incumbents? She was, of course, but that was beside the point. And what if she went to the House of Lords and insisted on having a say? Such eventualities would fly against all that was right, just and proper.

Clearly, something had to be done to save the King from his own Court – from the wild licentiousness of Will and the Cockpit Club, from prim old Clarendon with his penchant for bribes, and from the Duchess with her alarming opinions. Chiffinch frowned. But what?

Then the answer came to him, and his once-handsome face broke into a broad grin. He would save his country from anarchy yet! There would be bad feeling and dismay, but it would only be temporary, and the King would thank him for it eventually, while the general populace would rejoice to see their grievances addressed. Still smiling, Chiffinch began to write a letter.

Chapter 1

'Mr Chiffinch cannot be dead, sir,' said Thomas Chaloner, struggling for patience. He disliked the way Court gossip spread like wildfire, growing more ridiculous with every whispered telling. 'I saw him walking around not two hours ago.'

'It was very sudden, apparently,' replied the Earl of Clarendon, a short, fat, fussy man who wore a great yellow wig and shoes with uncomfortable block-heels to make himself taller. 'But I assure you, he is no longer in the world of the living.'

He tried to hide his pleasure in the news, although it was plain for all to see. Chaloner did not blame him: Chiffinch hated the Earl, and who would not be relieved to learn that an implacable enemy was no longer in a position to plot against him?

'Everyone thought it was the plague at first,' the Earl went on. 'But then Timothy Clarke arrived and said that Chiffinch died of an abscess – he called it an impostume – in the breast.'

5

Chaloner raised his eyebrows. Clarke was Physician to the Household, so perhaps the tale *was* true – a medic would know what he was talking about. Or would he? Some of Clarke's colleagues had been rather scathing about his professional abilities in the past. Moreover, if Chiffinch had been suffering from something serious enough to kill him, would he really have been sauntering about a short time before?

The Earl saw Chaloner's bemused expression and misread it. 'Perhaps you are thinking of the wrong Chiffinch. The one who died today is the *older* of the two brothers: Thomas, Keeper of the Closet and Keeper of the Jewels.'

'I know,' said Chaloner shortly. True, he was not as familiar with White Hall as he might have been, because the Earl kept sending him away on missions and errands, but he was not entirely uninformed. He certainly knew the people who meant his employer harm. His official title was Gentleman Usher, but his real remit was to protect the Earl from men such as Chiffinch and others like him.

'As opposed to *Will* Chiffinch, the Pimp-Master General,' the Earl went on, sniggering as he used the title conferred on the younger brother by a contemptuous general public.

'Yes, sir,' said Chaloner, wondering if the Earl would be quite so amused if he knew that, far from being morti-fied, Will considered the title a great compliment and revelled in it.

'The matter will have to be investigated, of course,' the Earl went on. 'We must ascertain that it really was an impostume that carried Chiffinch off. He was not very popular, you know.'

6

Chaloner reviewed his own impressions of the man – a stiff, humourless, proud individual with a firm belief in his own rectitude. Unusually for a King's favourite, Chiffinch was reasonably ethical and genuinely cultured. He was also a devoted Royalist, and had recently expressed concern over the fact that the King was not as well liked as he had been when he had first been restored to his throne.

'Investigated by whom?' he asked, then saw the calculating gleam in his employer's eyes and raised a warning hand. 'It cannot be me, sir. His family will object to any attempt by us to meddle in their affairs, and you may open yourself up to harm if you—'

'I am Lord Chancellor of England,' interrupted the Earl haughtily. 'I have the authority to appoint whomsoever I please to explore a case of foul play among the King's friends.'

'There is nothing to suggest foul play, sir,' objected Chaloner, loath to dabble in such murky waters. And not just for himself – if Chiffinch *had* been murdered, it was sheer madness for his sworn enemy to appoint the investigator. 'A physician has deemed the death natural—'

'But you just told me that Chiffinch was walking around two hours ago,' countered the Earl. '*You* wonder how a man can be alive one minute and dead the next. I can see it in your face.'

Chaloner was suspicious, but that was beside the point. 'Then I will tell Clarke to look at the body again in order to—'

'No, you will arrange for a second opinion,' interrupted the Earl firmly. 'Ask Surgeon Wiseman to examine the corpse at his earliest convenience.'

It was a good idea. Wiseman was not only Chaloner's

friend, but a man who could be trusted to find the truth. He would almost certainly provide a more credible explanation than the one Clarke had offered – an apoplexy or a seizure, perhaps, which might well have carried the victim off in a flash.

'Until Wiseman has given his verdict,' the Earl went on, 'you can determine what happened between the time you saw Chiffinch alive, and the time he dropped dead from "natural causes".'

The way he sneered the last two words made it perfectly clear that he expected the surgeon to declare Chiffinch's end suspicious. Chaloner opened his mouth to repeat that it was not a good idea to interfere, but the Earl overrode him.

'Of course, you will have to hurry if we are to have answers before Chiffinch is laid to rest. He will be buried in Westminster Abbey on Tuesday, just four days hence.'

Chaloner blinked his astonishment. 'Arrangements have been made already? That is fast!'

'Very fast,' agreed the Earl. 'Indeed, one might say *suspiciously* fast.' Then he relented. 'Of course, it may be because the dean is away, so cannot object to such a vile creature being laid to rest in his domain. The family aims to present him with a fait accompli.'

Chaloner remained astounded. 'All this has already been decided, even though Chiffinch was alive two hours ago?'

'It has, so when you compile your list of murder suspects, make sure you put the family at the top. It would suit me very well if you prove that one of them killed him.'

Chaloner was sure it would, as discrediting the Chiffinches would deal a hefty blow to those who had united against him. Of course, he would not have nearly so many detractors if he refrained from scolding the King and his followers like errant schoolboys. Chaloner tried one last time to dissuade the Earl from a course of action that might prove disastrous.

'Even if Chiffinch did die at the hand of another – which I cannot believe he did – it is a mistake for you to get involved. It is better to stay aloof from the entire affair.'

'I disagree. It will show those who hold me in low esteem that I am cognisant of their welfare – that I am an ethical Lord Chancellor, who wants justice for all, even the fools and worthless debauchees who mean me harm. However, you do not have long to discover the truth: *Royal Oak* sails on Easter Sunday, and I want you on her when she goes.'

Since entering the Earl's employ, Chaloner had spent more time away than at home. Indeed, he had only returned from Scotland the previous day – the Earl was a great supporter of the northern bishops, and had sent Chaloner to spy on the Presbyterians who were making life difficult for them. These missions were frustrating, exhausting and prevented him from putting down roots, so he was beginning to resent them. And yet, he thought wryly, the ocean would be a good place to be if he did stir up a hornets' nest by prying into Chiffinch's death.

'What do you want me to do on *Royal Oak*, sir?' he asked curiously.

'Find the sailor who stole a lot of saltpetre while she was moored at Tower Wharf last month. The navy is short of funds, and cannot afford to lose its supplies to light-fingered tars.'

'No,' said Chaloner, although as the navy had decided

not to pay its seamen's wages, he did not blame them for finding other ways to feed their families. 'But saltpetre is used to make gunpowder. Surely it is more important to find the buyer than the thieves?'

'Williamson is doing that as we speak – the trail has taken him to Dover. However *Royal Oak*'s crew is currently on leave, which means he cannot question them about the thieves. Ergo, you will sail on her at Easter and do it.'

He referred to Joseph Williamson, the Spymaster General, who was responsible for matters pertaining to national security. Chaloner neither liked nor trusted Williamson, and was pleased to learn he was seventy miles away, thus eliminating the possibility of a chance encounter in London.

'There will be another great sea-battle when our fleet meets the Dutch,' mused the Earl, when Chaloner made no reply. 'The intelligence you gathered in the United Provinces last year told us that they have built newer, heavier ships, so let us hope you are not blown to pieces while you are gone.'

He did not mean it. Despite Chaloner proving his loyalty on any number of occasions, the Earl was unable to forget that he had not only fought on the 'wrong' side during the civil wars, but had been one of Cromwell's spies into the bargain. Not for the first time, Chaloner wished he could leave the Earl to his enemies, but it was not easy for former Parliamentarian intelligencers to find employment, and he knew he was lucky to have a job at all. He had no choice but to do what the Earl ordered, no matter how asinine, pointless or dangerous.

As Lord Chancellor, the Earl had been allocated a suite of rooms in the Palace of White Hall, but because he suffered from gout and was often immobile, he had taken to working from his home, Clarendon House, instead. This was a glorious new mansion on the semi-rural lane called Piccadilly, although his staff were currently unimpressed with the place, as a sharp downpour the previous morning had flooded the library. His entire household – other than Chaloner – had spent the last twenty-four hours struggling to contain the damage.

Still feeling that probing Chiffinch's death was a mistake, Chaloner left Clarendon House and walked towards White Hall, where the hapless courtier had breathed his last. It was a beautiful day, and warm for the time of year. The hedges along the side of the road were white and pink with blossom, while the scent of new growth was in the air. He inhaled deeply, savouring the heady aroma of fresh leaves. The air did not stay sweet for long though, as a sudden breeze brought a whiff from the city – the stench of ten thousand coal fires, the stink of the laystalls, and the distinctive tang of its tanneries, mills, slaughterhouses and foundries.

Despite London's drawbacks, Chaloner was glad to be back, especially now the plague was in abeyance. Only twenty-six fever deaths had been noted in the previous week's Mortality Bill, compared to seven thousand when it was at its peak. He had lived through some of it in January, when he had investigated a plot centred around Covent Garden, although the Earl had dispatched him to Scotland the moment that matter was resolved.

On his way south again, Chaloner had planned to spend a few days with his family in Buckinghamshire, but an urgent message from the Earl begged him to ride to London with all possible speed. He had made the journey in record time, cognisant of the fact that his employer was never far from disaster. He had arrived the previous afternoon, saddle-sore and anxious, only to learn that there was no emergency, and the Earl could not even recall why the summons had been sent.

Chaloner resented not seeing the family he loved. His clan was a large one, even by the standards of the day. His grandfather had married twice, siring eleven children with his first wife and seven with the second. Most of these aunts and uncles had produced prodigious broods of their own, which meant Chaloner had enough kinsmen to populate a small village. The wars had scattered them, so there were some cousins he had never met, but he was fond of the ones he knew, while his siblings meant the world to him.

He had been blessed with an idyllic childhood, and all his memories were happy right up to the day when one uncle – another Thomas Chaloner – had dragged him off to join Cromwell's New Model Army. Nothing had been the same since, and he felt as though he had spent his entire adult existence leaping from one precarious situation to another, in constant danger and with nowhere to call home. Even his two marriages – both brought to untimely ends by plague – had been unsatisfactory, and at thirty-six years of age, he felt weary and jaded. His brothers and sisters were a much-needed rock in the unsteady, shifting sea of his life.

But dwelling on the matter was doing no good, so he turned his mind to the task the Earl had set him. He began by reviewing what he knew about the dead man, which was not much. Chiffinch was a favourite of the King, and one of his duties had been to buy art for the royal palaces. This he had done extremely well, showing himself to be a man of taste and refinement.

Chaloner thought about his own encounter with Chiffinch earlier that morning. He been strolling down King Street, aiming to break his fast in the Sun tavern in Westminster, when Chiffinch had scuttled out through White Hall's main gate. It had been just as the abbey bells chimed six o'clock. Although Chiffinch disliked the Earl and his household, good manners had compelled him to stop and exchange polite greetings with Chaloner. Then he had shared a bit of gossip about the Duchess of Newcastle, who had evidently gone to the theatre wearing an inappropriate costume. The plump Chiffinch had been flushed and a little breathless, so it was entirely possible that unaccustomed exertion had given him a fatal seizure.

Chaloner would have to find out why Chiffinch had been up at such an hour – whether he had risen early or had not yet been to bed. He suspected it would be the latter: Chiffinch did not indulge in the same wild revelries as his despicable brother, but no successful or ambitious courtier slept while his King was awake and might dispense lucrative favours.

He walked on, enjoying the spirited bustle of the city, although it was still nowhere near as lively as it had been before the plague. Even so, most of the weeds that had grown up between the cobbles around Charing Cross had been trampled away by the returning wheels, feet and hoofs, and although some houses remained boarded up, most showed signs of being inhabited again.

Yet the city was not the cheerful place it had been eighteen months ago. No one had forgotten the fact that the King and his favourites had fled to safety, leaving London to fend for itself, and folk were less willing to overlook their profligate ways now the Court was back. Indeed, most were of the opinion that they were better off without His Majesty and his cronies, especially as there was great resentment over the draconian new taxes levied to fund the royal household.

Moreover, the year was 1666, and it had escaped no one's notice that the combination of three sixes was inauspicious. Soothsayers were predicting a calamity that would make the plague pale by comparison. Worse yet, Good Friday – the day of Jesus's crucifixion – would fall on Friday the thirteenth, a detail that had sent the gloom-merchants into a frenzy. How could something terrible not befall London on such an unlucky date?

As he walked, Chaloner heard people talking about it in low, worried voices. Personally, he thought the chances were that Good Friday would pass without incident. Of course, then the city would be full of anticlimax and disappointment, which would bring its own problems.

'I saw it myself last Sunday,' breathed a laundress. 'A cloud, shaped like Satan himself, hovering over Clerkenwell. His forked tail was perfectly clear.'

'Clerkenwell,' whispered her companion darkly. 'There are tales about Clerkenwell. Courtiers have mansions there, so of course it will be full of wickedness.'

'And do not forget that the new cemetery is nearby,' the laundress went on. 'The Church has agreed not to consecrate it, so that Quakers and other dubious sects can use it to bury their dead. If you ask me, that is a sure way to attract demons and other denizens of hell.'

'Then they will make their presence known on Good Friday,' predicted the friend, pursing her lips. 'And God help us all.'

The Palace of White Hall was vast, boasting more than two thousand rooms. It straggled between the River

Thames and St James's Park, with King Street running through the middle of it. The word 'palace' was a misnomer, as there was no main house, and it comprised a random collection of buildings that had been raised as and when they had been needed, resulting in a peculiar mismatch of styles and sizes. A maze of alleys with unexpected dead-ends, dog-leg turns and crooked yards connected them all, and it had taken Chaloner weeks to learn his way around properly.

The only part that was truly grand was the Banqueting House, a handsome edifice designed by Inigo Jones with a ceiling by Rubens. The rest comprised apartments for the King, his Queen and various princes, nobles and bureaucrats, along with government and Treasury offices, accommodation for servants and retainers, a chapel, and an array of kitchens, laundries, storerooms and stables. Most of these lay to the east of King Street, while to the west were the tennis courts and the cockpit.

Once through the Great Gate, Chaloner paused to look around. He was in a vast cobbled yard, with the Banqueting House on one side and ranges of offices on the others. There was a large fountain in the middle, working for the first time in months. Some wag had been at the statue of Eros in its centre, which now wore a yellow wig, block-heeled shoes and a Lord Chancellor's gown. Servants stood around it, laughing.

Chaloner's first task was to find Surgeon Wiseman and ask him to examine Chiffinch's body. After all, there would be no need to launch a murder inquiry if the courtier had died of natural causes. Unfortunately, he learned that the Queen was ill, and Wiseman had vowed not to leave her side until he had seen some improvement. Chaloner scribbled a note, begging his help for an hour, and paid a page to deliver it. Moments later, the page returned with Wiseman's reply. It was not polite, and accused Chaloner of being callous for putting the needs of the dead above the those of the living. It ended with the curt suggestion that he ask again tomorrow.

With an irritable sigh, Chaloner supposed he would have to start asking questions without the surgeon's verdict, and was just deciding where to begin when he heard someone call his name from the shadows. It was a man who would have been invisible but for his bright white falling band – the square of cloth that covered his chest like a bib; otherwise, he was dressed entirely in black, a colour that suited his sinister demeanour. His name was John Swaddell, and he was one of the deadliest, most disturbing people Chaloner had ever met.

Swaddell worked for Spymaster Williamson, officially as a clerk, although it was common knowledge that he was really an assassin. He was frighteningly good at his work, and Chaloner was always unnerved by the ruthless efficiency with which he dispatched those deemed to be enemies of the state.

He had performed a peculiar blood-mingling ritual the first time he and Chaloner had been ordered to work together, which he claimed had forged an unbreakable bond between them. Chaloner was uncomfortable associating with such a lethal individual, but allies were rare at Court, and not to be lightly dismissed. So, although Swaddell was not a friend, he was at least on Chaloner's side.

'You are back,' said Swaddell, with a grin that was meant to be friendly but that Chaloner thought was unsettling. 'Did you find your annoying Presbyterians? And neutralise them?'

'I warned them about the dangers of fomenting unrest and advised negotiation instead,' replied Chaloner, to make the point that *he* was not in the habit of dispensing his own brand of justice. 'What are you doing here? Something for Williamson?'

'He is in Dover, investigating the theft of some saltpetre from *Royal Oak*. My remit is to lurk in the city and report anything untoward. But it is dull work, and I miss his company.'

'You do?' blurted Chaloner, astonished that anyone should say such a thing about Williamson, who was sly, secretive and unlikeable. Then he supposed that Swaddell was much of an ilk, so the pair would have a lot in common.

Swaddell smiled again, revealing small, pointed teeth and a very red tongue. 'I shall miss him less now that you are home. We must adjourn to a coffee house, so you can tell me about your adventures in more detail.'

'Later,' promised Chaloner, planning to avoid it. 'I have work to do first.'

'I suppose your Earl wants you to look into what happened to Chiffinch,' surmised Swaddell. 'I confess I was astonished to learn he was dead. He seemed hale enough yesterday.'

'Have you heard any rumours or whispers about him?'

Swaddell grimaced. 'People tend to stop talking once they see me listening to their conversations. However, I can tell you that he spent most of last night in the Shield Gallery.'

Chaloner was grateful for the information, as it told him where to start his enquiries. 'Were you there, too?'

A bitter expression suffused Swaddell's face. 'Unlike you, I am no gentleman usher – I was not allowed in. But I know Chiffinch was there, because I overheard his brother Will tell one of their friends as much. Unfortunately, that is all I heard him say, because he spotted me in the shadows and moved away.'

'Pity,' said Chaloner, although he would have done likewise if he had seen an assassin eavesdropping on him, even if the conversation had been entirely innocent.

'However, I do know that Will requested an audience with the King within minutes of learning about his brother's death,' Swaddell went on. 'Apparently, Will accepted the royal condolences, then asked if he might inherit all Chiffinch's titles and duties. The King agreed and invested him on the spot.'

'That is interesting,' mused Chaloner, wondering if the Earl was right to suspect foul play among the dead man's kin after all.

'Not really,' sighed Swaddell. 'Will could have waited a decent interval, but then he would have lost out, because someone else would have rushed to the King and begged to be Chiffinch's successor. White Hall is for the bold and greedy, not the respectfully reticent.'

'How has London been these last few weeks?' asked Chaloner, moving to another subject, as it was one on which he trusted Swaddell's opinion more than anyone else's. 'When I was last home, we only just managed to stop malcontents from blowing half of it up.'

Swaddell lowered his voice. 'I thought the King and his friends might have moderated their revels, given that their bad behaviour was what precipitated that crisis in the first place, but if anything, they are worse. Have you heard of the Cockpit Club?'

Chaloner shook his head. 'What is it?'

'A gaggle of idle, wildly hedonistic courtiers who have declared themselves bored with life at White Hall and who have elected to pursue more "interesting" forms of entertainment, most of which are distasteful and some of which are illegal. Their sole remit is to have fun, and they care nothing for anyone or anything else.'

'Then perhaps someone should tell the King to curb their excesses before they provoke yet another attempt to remove him from power.'

'Your Earl tried, but he refused to listen. Apparently, His Majesty feels that doing what his subjects ask will encourage them to make more demands of him in the future.'

Then he was a fool, thought Chaloner, and if he followed his father to the executioner's block, he had no one to blame but himself. All he hoped was that good men would not die trying to quell the trouble that his arrogance and stupidity might spark. But these were private thoughts, and not ones to be shared with a man in the pay of the Spymaster General.

'Unfortunately,' Swaddell went on, 'when they heard what Clarendon had done, the Cockpit Club declared all-out war on him.'

Chaloner groaned: the Earl had enough enemies already, and did not need more. 'Who is in this society?' he asked, supposing he would have to monitor them as well as all the others.

Swaddell recited thirty or so names, which included the Court's most dissipated rakes. Some were heirs to titles and fortunes, kicking their heels while they waited for their sires to die. Others were penniless aristocrats bent on securing sinecures. Their de facto leader was one Colonel Widdrington, whose family had somehow contrived to hang on to its money during the civil wars and the upheavals that had followed. Widdrington and his wife Bess oozed wealth, superiority and entitlement. Chaloner had always found them unpleasant.

'So these men see my Earl as their enemy,' he sighed, when Swaddell had finished.

'Not just him but his entire household, so take extra care while you are here. I doubt they will risk a physical encounter with you, but they are vengeful, vindictive and petty. And selfish, given that they consider their pleasures more important than the King's standing with his people. They are not good friends to him, no matter what he thinks.'

Chaloner nodded his thanks to Swaddell and went on his way, glad to step out of the shadows and into the bright morning sunshine.

The day had turned hot, with the sun blazing down from a clear blue sky. Usually, fair weather was greeted with delight by Londoners, as persistent rain turned their city's streets into rivers of stinking mud. That year, however, they were inclined to see it as an evil omen, as it had been a long, hot, dry spell that had presaged the plague the previous year.

To avoid arriving in the Shield Gallery drenched in sweat, Chaloner walked slowly across the Great Court, aware of Swaddell's beady black eyes tracking him as he went. He reached the fountain, then wished he had taken another route when he saw who had taken up station on its shady side. Fifteen or so courtiers, all of whom Swaddell had just identified as Cockpit Club members perched on its edge or paddled in its shallows. Some moved to intercept him.

Each was dressed in the height of fashion and moved with the flouncing mince that such people thought showed breeding and refinement. They slathered themselves with face-paints, and the men occasionally donned women's clothing, although Chaloner had never understood why. He could only assume it was something they had picked up in France.

In the vanguard was Colonel Widdrington, whom Swaddell had just identified as their leader. He was a tall, impossibly handsome man with thick brown hair and laughing eyes. By contrast, his wife Bess was plain enough to be ugly, with a snub nose, bad skin and a pugnacious chin. They had married not for love, but because it had been demanded of them by their families. Bess was openly delighted at having landed such a beautiful spouse, but Widdrington felt cheated, and it was common knowledge that he would divorce her if he could. Unfortunately for him, a lot of money was invested in the alliance, so he was stuck with her.

'It is the Lord Chancellor's creature,' Widdrington drawled. 'What errand are you on, Chaloner? Finding him shoes that do not make him waddle like a pregnant sow?'

His cronies guffawed obligingly, Bess the loudest of all.

'You must make sure they are sturdy, to support his great weight,' she put in, casting a sidelong glance at her pretty husband to ensure he noticed her elaborating on his jest.

Widdrington yawned, flapping a lace handkerchief in front of his mouth. 'God, I am bored! If we do not do something interesting soon, I shall turn into stone, like Eros here. Oh, it is not Eros, it is the Lord Chancellor! Do you see, Chaloner? It is your employer who stands so chubby and proud above us.'

'Goodness!' exclaimed Chaloner. 'I thought it was the Duke of York. *He* certainly thinks so, because I heard him complain to his brother the King about it not ten minutes ago.'

It was a lie, but he had the satisfaction of seeing the Cockpit Club monkeys scramble to remove the offending items before there was trouble.

'It is far too hot out here,' Widdrington declared, once the statue had been stripped of its incriminating vestments. 'So let us go to the Shield Gallery, to see the place where Chiffinch spent his last night.'

Bess gave a squeal of appreciation, although the others looked taken aback. The suggestion was in poor taste, even by Court standards.

'An excellent notion!' Bess cried. 'Perhaps *Will* Chiffinch will be there. Then he can tell us what revels he has planned to honour his brother's memory.'

They set off at once, walking with the exaggerated strut of people who thought a great deal of themselves. Chaloner watched in distaste, hoping the King would come to his senses and bring them to heel before their antics did him harm. And if they did? Why should Chaloner defend a regime that he had never wanted, and which had proved itself to be just as corrupt and useless as the one he had fought so hard to overthrow? Then he remembered that his employer was part of that regime, and hoped he would not soon be faced with some difficult choices.

There was no point going to the Shield Gallery if the Cockpit Club men were there, as they would make it impossible for Chaloner to ask questions – either by looming over him and intimidating anyone he tried to talk to, or by driving witnesses away by dint of their objectionable presence. Instead, he went to the kitchens, where he filched a freshly baked knot-biscuit and a cup of cool ale.

When he had finished, he decided to sit in the chapel for half an hour, sure Widdrington and his cronies would have gone to find other 'entertainment' by the time he emerged. But he had not taken many steps before he met two more men whom Swaddell had named as Cockpit Club members. These were not, the assassin had claimed, part of the charmed inner circle, but individuals who lurked on the fringes, hoping to profit from their association with rich and powerful men.

One was Captain Edward Rolt, who was related to Cromwell, but was determined to be seen as a Royalist; his name was a byword for duplicitous sycophancy. The other was eighteen-year-old George Legg, whose father was Master of Armouries, a post he would eventually inherit; until then, his time was his own.

'Have you heard the latest?' Legg asked, all goggling excitement. 'About the Duchess?'

'Which one?' asked Chaloner, aware of at least six who regularly inspired gossip.

'Newcastle, of course,' replied Legg impatiently. 'She has recently arrived from her country estates, and the whole city itches to see her.'

'Really? Why?'

'Because of her reputation,' explained Rolt. 'She is a singular lady. For example, she believes that women are equal to men.' He laughed at this outlandish notion.

'She cannot really think that,' countered Legg with youthful disdain. 'It is just a way to make herself the centre of attention. She is very vain.'

23

'She does like to be noticed,' sniggered Rolt. 'Did you hear what she did when she went to watch *The Humorous Lovers* at the theatre? She wore an antique costume in the classical style, which was cut so low that it revealed her scarlet-trimmed nipples.'

Chiffinch had remarked on this particular incident when he and Chaloner had exchanged greetings earlier that morning. He had been disapproving, on the grounds that noblewomen strutting about in that sort of attire reflected badly on the King.

'I was there,' giggled Legg. 'It caused quite a stir. Apparently, she designed the ensemble herself. I could not take my eyes off her, so I have no idea if the play was any good.'

'It was a serious error of judgement on her part,' declared Rolt. 'She aimed to present herself as a heroic woman of antiquity – bold, strong and romantic. Instead, everyone thinks she is a common strumpet.'

'Other courtiers don that style of dress,' said Chaloner, feeling it was unfair to castigate one woman for what the rest did on a daily basis. 'The King's mistress, for a start.'

'Yes,' acknowledged Legg. 'But *they* do it here in the palace, whereas the Duchess displayed herself for any commoner to see. It was unedifying. Besides, she is forty-three. Ugh! It was like being faced with my mother's naked breasts.'

'Why could you not take your eyes off them, then?' asked Chaloner tartly, and watched the young man blush and flail around for an explanation.

'Rolt has lost a button,' Legg blurted, changing the subject so abruptly that Chaloner could not help but smile. 'Have you seen it?'

'Strangely enough, no. Shall we set the palace guard to hunt for it?'

Rolt regarded Chaloner coolly. 'I do not usually care about trifles, but that belonged to my father – one of a set that I like to wear on my favourite long-coat. But we should not keep you, Chaloner. I am sure you have something important to do – like preventing your Earl from destroying himself with his scolding tongue.'

'Yes, he is his own worst enemy,' agreed Legg pompously. 'You should advise him to be nicer to people, because there are rumours that the devil will visit London on Good Friday, and Satan will certainly snatch the souls of men who sit in judgement of their peers.'

Personally, Chaloner thought there were far blacker souls available at White Hall than the Earl's, and that if Lucifer did drop in, he would be spoiled for choice.

White Hall's chapel was an underused, plain building near the pantries. Chaloner stepped into its cool interior, glad to be on his own for a moment. Inside, it was silent and musty. At first, he assumed it was empty, but then he saw someone sitting at the back. It was the Earl's new clerk, John Barker, a tall, gangling man who always looked shabby, despite his fine clothes: he never managed a close shave, his fingers were invariably inky, and his long hair had a natural tendency to greasiness. But he was efficient and reliable, and the Earl liked him.

'I saw you talking to Legg and Captain Rolt just now,' Barker said admonishingly. 'You do know they are part of a vicious cabal that has sworn to see our employer's head on a block, do you not? And they do not mean figuratively – they actually aim to see him executed.'

'Yes,' acknowledged Chaloner. 'I suspect they do.'

'That Cockpit Club is an abomination,' Barker went on hotly. 'The old King would never have countenanced their vile antics. He would have driven the lot of them out in disgrace.'

Without being asked, Barker told Chaloner how the club had come by its name: because its members used White Hall's cockpit as their headquarters. Then he embarked on a brief history of the building, which had originally been intended for bird fights, but when blood-sports had fallen out of favour under the first Stuart kings, it had been converted into a theatre. The current King preferred his plays in the Banqueting House or on Drury Lane, so the cockpit had lain unloved and forgotten until Widdrington had given it a new lease of life. Barker finished his lecture with an angry question.

'Did you hear what they did there last week?'

'No,' said Chaloner cautiously. 'What?'

'Horse fighting!' Barker pursed his lips in disgust. 'They tethered a mare to a pole in the centre of the arena, then brought in two stallions. The males went wild, flailing at each other with hoofs and necks until the weaker one was killed.'

'Killed?' Chaloner was astonished, as horses were expensive. 'No one stopped the contest sooner?'

'Large sums of money were involved, and the losing animal belonged to Rolt, who dared not end the spectacle while his friends were enjoying it – not when he thinks his future depends on winning their good graces.'

Chaloner grimaced his revulsion. He deplored blood-sports and had been glad when Cromwell had banned them. Technically, they were illegal still, but the government made no effort to enforce the laws prohibiting them.

'News came today that the Queen's mother is dead,'

said Barker, moving to another subject, 'but as Her Majesty remains ill after losing the latest child she was carrying, it has been decided to keep the news from her.'

'Is that wise?' asked Chaloner, sure it was not. 'Someone is bound to let it slip, which would be a cruel way for her to find out.'

'Surgeon Wiseman advocated honesty, too, but Dr Clarke the physician argued against him and won, which is no mean feat if you have ever met Wiseman.' Barker blushed. 'But of course you have – you are his lodger. I mean no disrespect, but . . . well . . . Wiseman is . . .'

Chaloner had not liked Wiseman at first either, considering him arrogant, opinionated and rude. Their association might have ended there and then, but the surgeon had decided that Chaloner was worthy of his company and the two had eventually become friends. Wiseman also rented Chaloner the top floor of his Covent Garden mansion for a very reasonable price.

Embarrassed by his faux pas, Barker changed the subject again. 'Now it is spring and the ocean is calm we shall have a resurgence of hostilities with the Dutch. They are still smarting after our victory at the Battle of Lowestoft last year, and want revenge.'

'They will have it,' predicted Chaloner soberly. 'While our ministers lounged and frolicked all winter, the Dutch forged anti-England alliances with France, Spain, Denmark *and* Brandenburg. They also built themselves heavier ships.'

'So we will lose the next sea-battle?' asked Barker worriedly.

Chaloner nodded, supposing he would be there to witness it if he was on *Royal Oak*. 'The hawks on the Privy Council are wrong to predict victory.'

27

'Perhaps they will come to their senses next week.'

Chaloner frowned. 'Why? What happens then?'

'Good Friday falling on the thirteenth day of the month, in a year containing three sixes. Everyone knows that something terrible will occur, and *I* think it will result in all our ministers abandoning their wicked ways and treading a straighter, more ethical path.'

Chaloner snorted his scepticism. 'Then I am afraid you will be disappointed.'

'Perhaps.' Barker grimaced. 'But I live in hope.'

The Shield Gallery was not a gallery at all, but a long room with views across the river. It had changed since Chaloner had been there last. Then it had been an unwelcoming place, cold, cheerless and hung with drab shields that had been won in jousting tournaments decades before. Now it was cosy, with rugs on the floor, paintings on the walls, and curtains – a new fashion from France – hanging in the windows. There were also small tables and comfortable chairs, provided for those who enjoyed card and board games.

That day it was busy, with courtiers standing in huddles, all speaking in low whispers. Sharp-eyed glances were being directed towards one particular table, leading Chaloner to surmise that it was where Chiffinch had spent his last night.

He examined it, although he was not sure what he expected to find. It was no different from the others, although oily stains on the cloth showed where something had been spilled. He bent to sniff it, and detected a fishy odour. There was nothing else, so he looked around for someone who might be willing to talk to him. The Cockpit Club had already been and gone, as he had

28

predicted, but there were plenty more who disliked the Earl, and there was no point in approaching those.

His eye lit on Sir Alan Brodrick. Although a notorious debauchee, Brodrick was also the Earl's favourite cousin – the Earl steadfastly refused to believe ill of him, and was determined to secure him a good post in government. Fortunately for the country, he had not succeeded, as Brodrick was wholly incapable of holding a responsible position. His only redeeming feature, as far as Chaloner was concerned, was that he loved good music.

Music was Chaloner's greatest delight, and there was little he liked more than playing his viol. As a child, he had longed to be a professional musician, but his father had deemed it an unsuitable occupation for gentlemen. Chaloner often suspected that his sire would have changed his mind if he could have looked into the future, and seen that the alternative was being hired as a henchman for an unpopular Royalist.

'Ah, Chaloner,' said Brodrick as the spy approached; he indicated the man who was standing with him. 'Have you met Baron Lucas? He is the Duchess of Newcastle's brother.'

Lucas was in his sixties, with long grey hair and a soldierly bearing. There were multicoloured stains on his coat, suggesting that he liked to dabble in alchemy. Such pastimes were popular among the wealthy, and those who were good at it were invited to share their findings with the Royal Society – the group of men who began to meet soon after the Restoration with the aim of promoting scientific knowledge.

'I suppose my cousin has told you to find out what happened to poor old Chiffinch,' said Brodrick, after

Chaloner and Lucas had exchanged bows. 'We are all shocked to learn of his death – he was in fine form in here last night.'

'I played a game with him myself,' growled Lucas. 'Backgammon. I lost, and it cost me ten guineas. He smirked horribly as I counted them out.'

'Did he win against anyone else?' asked Chaloner, cognisant of the fact that no one liked a gloat, and courtiers were quick to take offence. Perhaps the Earl was right to suggest that something untoward had befallen Chiffinch.

Brodrick nodded. 'Just about everyone he played – other than the King, of course. His Majesty excels at backgammon, as he excels in all things.'

'Yes,' said Chaloner flatly, aware that only the mad or the reckless defeated a monarch. It was entirely possible that His Majesty was a perfectly gracious loser, but no one had ever been brave enough to find out. 'Who else did Chiffinch play?'

'His brother Will,' began Brodrick, obligingly, 'followed by Timothy Clarke, the physician who examined his body so sensitively today, and Clarke's wife Fanny—'

'You speak as if you like them,' interrupted Lucas, scowling. 'But Clarke is an ass and Fanny is the dullest woman alive. Talking to her is about as interesting as conversing with a bucket, and her idea of high excitement is choosing a needle with which to sew.'

'True,' acknowledged Brodrick. 'Although she did me a good turn when I brought my daughter to Court. That rogue Rolt took an unseemly interest, but Fanny saw him off before there was any trouble. It was kind of her. My daughter did not appreciate it, though, besotted as she was . . .'

30

'You say Clarke examined Chiffinch "sensitively",' said Chaloner. 'So how did he discover the impostume in his breast?'

'By feeling about with gentle hands,' explained Brodrick. 'Although Clarke has been wrong before, and I have never heard of anyone else dying from such a thing. Shall I continue with my list of those who lost to Chiffinch at backgammon last night?' He did so without waiting for a reply. 'Widdrington and his wife Bess—'

'Along with two dozen other rogues from the Cockpit Club,' put in Lucas. 'Did you know they have all enrolled in the Artillery Company – the military unit that will defend London when the Dutch invade?'

Brodrick shuddered. 'I hope the rest of us will not be expected to do likewise. I am not much of a warrior.'

'Nor are they,' spat Lucas contemptuously. 'I would not have them in any regiment of mine.' He turned an appraising eye on Chaloner. 'I might consider you, though.'

'Thank you,' said Chaloner, and turned the subject back to the dead man. 'What did Chiffinch think of the Cockpit Club?'

'He could not abide them,' replied Brodrick promptly. 'Of course, he also hated my cousin the Earl.'

'And my sister the Duchess of Newcastle,' added Lucas. 'He considered one too prim and the other too radical. You could not win with him and I cannot say I liked the fellow.'

'So is that a complete list of everyone he played last night?' pressed Chaloner.

'Well,' hedged Brodrick and glanced at Lucas. 'Yes, except for . . .'

'You can say it, Brodrick,' said Lucas briskly. 'Except for my sister, her husband and her stepson. She won handily, but the other two lost. She is a clever lass.'

'How did Chiffinch seem to you last night?' asked Chaloner. 'Did he complain about feeling unwell?'

'No, which is why his demise is so unsettling,' replied Lucas soberly. 'He seemed to be in excellent health and spirits. Nothing wrong whatsoever.'

'I agree,' said Brodrick. 'The only other thing I can tell you about last night is that he and his brother Will did not part on the best of terms. I recall a dispute over a fifty-pound wager.'

'They quarrelled?' asked Chaloner keenly.

'There was an exchange of words, although I did not pay much attention, and I left not long afterwards – immediately after watching the Duchess defeat Chiffinch – because Lucas invited me to Newcastle House to see his laboratory.'

'I did,' said Lucas, and scowled. 'Although you only accepted because you expected to see lead turned to gold, even though I explained that it is beyond the ability of any man.'

'The Duke came with us,' said Brodrick, ignoring the rebuke. 'But the Duchess and her stepson remained. She wanted to defeat Chiffinch again, while he hoped to see her soundly trounced. He does not like his father's second wife very much. Families, eh?'

Eventually, Brodrick and Lucas wandered away, leaving Chaloner to run through the names they had given him in his mind, supposing he would have to speak to them all if he wanted a full account of Chiffinch's last night. Well, not the King, of course, and probably not the Newcastles either, given that royals and nobles tended not to appreciate being interrogated like criminals. That left the Cockpit Club, the Clarkes and the dead man's family.

He decided to start with the family.

Although Chaloner did not really believe that Will would hurt his brother, he knew the Earl would expect him to speak to the man anyway. In the interests of diplomacy, he decided to disguise the true purpose of his visit by offering his condolences. Of course, Will was not stupid, so Chaloner was going to have to tread with considerable care.

Fortunately, Chaloner had one ally. Will's wife Barbara was a kindly, motherly soul who had befriended him when he had first arrived in White Hall. She had not wanted to marry Will, but her wealthy family had seen the advantages of the connection, so she had had no choice. She accepted her fate stoically, rarely condemning her husband's excesses, but not encouraging them either.

Chaloner had never been to their home, although he knew it was on St Martin's Lane. He also knew that the Pimp-Master General was never there, preferring to sleep in a chamber near the King, lest His Majesty should suddenly find himself in need of a prostitute. Thus Barbara had the house to herself most of the time, which suited them both. Chaloner decided to speak to her first, to see what she had to say about the untimely death of her brother-in-law.

He walked there briskly, taking the longer route across Scotland Yard to avoid Widdrington and his Cockpit Club cronies, who had taken up station by the fountain again. He knocked on Barbara's door, which was answered by a maid who wore a black sash over her apron to denote mourning. She informed him that everyone was at the palace.

'My master is moving into his brother's old quarters,' she explained, 'and my mistress is there to make sure he does not appear too gleeful about it.'

Chaloner smothered a smile, sure Barbara would be mortified if she knew her servants were making that sort of remark to visitors, although he imagined it was true. Will had secured his brother's posts with unseemly haste, so why not seize his White Hall apartments, too?

He retraced his footsteps, and saw the Great Gate was now ringed by a group of yelling people. Such protests were becoming increasingly frequent as the King continued his slide into disfavour. The complaints were myriad, but mostly about tax – the newly imposed ones to pay for the Dutch war and the Royal Household, the recent levy on coal that the poor could not pay, and a butlerage on wine that everyone resented because they felt it went towards funding the Court's debaucheries.

The demonstration that day was unusual, as all the protesters were female. Some looked to be the kin of wealthy merchants, while others were obviously paupers. Indeed, it appeared that some were prostitutes, if the painted faces and low-cut bodices were anything to judge by. Their leader was a striking woman with long red hair and vivid green eyes. The proud way she carried herself suggested that, while not rich, she was certainly not humble.

Anticipating that no one would listen to them, they had taken the precaution of writing their grievances on wooden placards that they waved. Intelligently, their slogans were short, which meant passers-by could not avoid reading them:

SCHOOLS FOR WOMEN.

NO TO HEARTH TAX.

LEARNING FOR ALL.

BANN COK FITES.

He felt a certain sympathy with them all, although the last was closest to his heart. It was being touted by a slack-jawed child whose clothes were dusted in feathers, telling him that she was probably a chicken-keeper in some wealthy household. He liked birds, and failed to understand how people could find pleasure in watching them injure each other.

When various petitioners had first started to take up station outside the palace gates, the guards had responded by moving them on, but demonstrations were now so frequent that this was impractical. Thus an alternative strategy had been devised: closing the affected gate and advising courtiers to use another one. Deprived of relevant ears, it was not usually long before the protesters gave up and drifted away.

Unfortunately, Widdrington and his Cockpit Club friends heard the rumpus and came to investigate. They shoved past the guards, and emerged on King Street. Delighted to be presented with a target for their grievances, the women regaled them with a torrent of noisy abuse. The Cockpit Club bristled with indignation, although Bess prudently scuttled back inside.

Rolt hastened to urge the rest of them to do likewise. As a man determined to win favour from anyone with influence, the slippery captain was in a quandary: he could not afford to be involved in a skirmish, which would besmirch his reputation with the more respectable elements at White Hall, but nor could he abandon his

35

silly friends. Ergo, his only option was to defuse the situation before it did him any harm.

'Please come away,' he begged. 'They are all women.'

'So what?' demanded Widdrington hotly. 'Or do they frighten you?'

Rolt forced a smile. 'Of course not. But it would be demeaning to trounce the fairer sex.'

'It would be fun,' countered a thin, unhealthy-looking courtier named George Ashley, who was a notoriously heavy drinker even by White Hall standards. 'I am game for a spat.'

'How about I trounce you instead?' said Rolt, and gave him a playful shove before dancing away, brandishing an imaginary sword. 'We shall leave these lasses to the guards, because there is no sport in sparring with common folk.'

The courtiers might have withdrawn at that point, as most of them had already lost interest, but Ashley had other ideas. He pushed Rolt away and lurched towards the demonstrators.

'You have no business here,' he slurred belligerently. 'Clear off.'

He lashed out with a wild sweep of his arm. It was a clumsy blow, and anyone should have been able to avoid it. Unfortunately, the chicken girl was slow to duck, and although his hand barely grazed her shoulder, she lost her balance and fell. She burst into tears, and the Cockpit Club brayed derisive laughter.

'Stand up, Molly,' ordered the red-haired woman briskly. 'Do not give these scum the satisfaction of thinking that they have hurt you.'

Ashley stopped cackling and went red-faced with anger. 'This person called us scum. Did you hear that, gentlemen?'

'*Gentlemen?*' The redhead turned to her own supporters. 'They consider themselves gentlemen. Have you ever heard anything more ludicrous?'

It was the women's turn to laugh, which they did long and hard. By now, the commotion had attracted passers-by, who were quick to side with the protesters.

'You dare insult me?' demanded Ashley, trembling with drunken rage. '*I* am a Yeoman of the Larder. I will teach you a lesson, you filthy whore. Come here and—'

'Whore, am I?' snarled the woman, affronted. 'Well, for your information, I have a perfectly respectable occupation. Moreover, I pay my rent and I buy my own food. Can you say the same? No! You are a leech, whose life serves no useful purpose.'

'We should go, Sarah,' said one of her companions haughtily. 'Why waste time bandying words with these asses? They can no more understand what it is to be decent than they can fly to the moon.'

Widdrington gaped his astonishment when he recognised the woman who had spoken. 'Eliza Topp? What are *you* doing in such low company? I cannot imagine your mistress will approve. The Duchess of Newcastle may be a lunatic, but she would never countenance her staff encouraging sedition among the stinking masses.'

'Stinking?' echoed Sarah in disbelief. 'You accuse us of *stinking*?'

Chaloner was not sure what happened next, but suddenly half the Cockpit Club had swords in their hands, while Sarah began swinging her placard about like a battleaxe. A fight was in progress, and he was in the middle of it.

Chapter 2

Chaloner jerked backwards to avoid the placard that was aimed at his head, a move that placed him directly in the path of a wild swipe from the drunken Ashley's rapier. He twisted sideways in the nick of time, then retreated to a safe distance, where he watched the fracas in distaste, feeling both sides were at fault for their short fuses and goading of the opposition.

Fortunately, everyone involved was an indifferent warrior. The courtiers' swords stabbed and swished, but so ineptly that the protesters were easily able to avoid them, and Chaloner found himself thinking that the Artillery Company would be better off without them in the event of a Dutch invasion. Captain Rolt was the only one with any skill, and he did no more than defend himself, staying in the shadows in the hope that no one who mattered would notice his involvement.

The women were not much better, as their placards were too flimsy for walloping and disintegrated the moment they struck home. The exception was Sarah, who had contrived to turn hers into a savagely pointed spear. She wielded it with a ruthless efficiency.

Meanwhile, Molly the chicken girl wept her terror. She had dropped her board and was crouched on the ground, hands over her head as she was buffeted this way and that by milling feet. Unwilling to see her hurt, Chaloner braved the mêlée to haul her out.

'That nasty man *pushed* me!' she sobbed, once she was safe. 'I am going to tell my Duchess and she will chop off his head. Eliza and me, we work for her, see. *I* am her best poultry-keeper.'

'Are you?' asked Chaloner absently, his attention on the skirmish.

'I have chickens, ducks and geese,' Molly chattered on. 'I live in Newcastle House, and the Duchess is very kind to me. Newcastle House is in Clerkenwell, you know.'

Chaloner did not know, but was more interested in watching the whirlwind of red hair and lance that was Sarah, wanting to laugh at the way the Cockpit Club men scattered before her.

'Enough!' came a furious roar from the gate. 'What is wrong with you all?'

It was Baron Lucas, the Duchess's brother, hands on his hips and a scowl on his face. His voice was loud enough to still the skirmishers, although by this time, both sides were aware that a stalemate had been reached. Neither faction was able to advance or willing to retreat, so most were only too glad to end what had become a futile exercise.

'Wine,' announced Widdrington, turning his back on the demonstrators to express his contempt for them. 'To wash away the stench of these harlots.'

'Harlots?' screeched Sarah, bristling with new outrage. She was prevented from racing forward to attack him by her friend Eliza Topp, although not without difficulty.

39

'I am going to tell your Duchess about you,' slurred Ashley, pointing an accusing finger at Eliza. 'She will not want a rabble-rouser in her retinue and she will—'

'Come, Ashley,' interrupted Rolt hastily, grabbing his arm to tug him away before his intemperate tongue could reignite the trouble. 'We have things to do elsewhere.'

'Such as what?' jeered Sarah, still incensed. 'Watching a cockfight? Gorging on syllabub while the city starves? Thinking of new ways to tax us?'

'Such as running the country,' retorted Ashley as he turned to follow his companions, a claim that drew genuine laughter from all those who heard it, including his own side.

'Go on, slink off,' howled Sarah, trying to struggle free. 'Skulk away like whipped curs. You do not even have the courage to stay and listen to our grievances. Cowards!'

But the Cockpit Club had lost interest in the spat, which was fortunate, as further interaction between them and the women was unlikely to be productive. They sauntered away, shoving each other playfully and laughing at some remark made by Rolt.

The excitement over, the spectators began to disperse. The women inspected each other for cuts and bruises, after which Sarah made a short but passionate speech about their rights as Londoners. Her words made them stand a little taller. Confidence restored, they marched away singing a popular song that listed the King's many flaws. People were arrested for less, but the guards prudently elected to overlook it. Eventually, only two were left: the child Molly, who still held Chaloner's hand, and Eliza Topp, who came to collect her.

'I saw what you did, sir,' said Eliza, ruffling the girl's hair affectionately. 'I would have helped Molly myself, but I was too busy protecting Sarah. One of those courtiers would have stabbed her in the back if I had not been there to stop them.'

She was in her mid forties, still beautiful, even though the flush of youth was gone. She wore a peculiar turban on her head, and her dress was made of some heavy material that looked Middle Eastern. Chaloner could only suppose that she had learned her unique fashion sense from the controversial Duchess in whose household she was apparently employed.

'I doubt any of them could have slipped past *her* defences,' said Chaloner drily. 'She is more warrior than the lot of them put together.'

'True,' acknowledged Eliza with a smile, and after she had asked his name and position at Court, described her own. 'My husband is the Duke of Newcastle's steward, and I am the Duchess's companion. She and I grew up together, and she considers me more friend than servant. I owe her everything.'

'I do not suppose you accompanied her to the Shield Gallery last night, did you?' he asked, aiming to see if she had witnessed her mistress playing backgammon with Chiffinch.

'No, I stayed home,' Eliza replied, 'although she did mention today that she was the only one – other than the King – to defeat him. My lady is very clever, and more than a match for any man. Have you met her?'

'Not yet.'

'Well, she has promised to visit the Queen on her sickbed later today. You may see her then, and if you do, you are in for an unforgettable experience.'

Chaloner was beginning to appreciate that this might well be true.

*

As Keeper of the Closet, Chiffinch had been allocated a suite of rooms adjoining the King's. It comprised a parlour with a bay window that overlooked the river, and two smaller L-shaped chambers for sleeping and working; all were linked by a handsome wood-panelled hallway. The apartment was accessed from stairs that led from a tiny but pretty courtyard, and was clearly among the most desirable lodgings in the palace.

Chaloner knocked on the door, and was pleased when it was answered by Barbara rather than her husband. She wore a russet-coloured gown that she would have to change soon, as the current mourning fashion was to dress entirely in black; even buckles and jewels were hidden, lest one should emit an unseemly glitter. Her tense expression softened when she saw Chaloner.

'It has been a trying morning,' she confided unhappily, ushering him into the hall. 'I dare not go home to don more suitable attire lest Will . . . well, you know how it is.'

Chaloner did. She and her husband might not be close, but she was fond of him, and would try to prevent him from doing something that would later cause him problems.

'How is he?' he asked.

Barbara grimaced. 'He has already arranged for his brother to be buried in Westminster Abbey on Tuesday. Now he is here, tossing out things he does not want to keep, and poring over those he does. I am trying my best to persuade him to show more decorum, for appearance's sake, but with scant success.'

'The two of them did not get along?' fished Chaloner.

Barbara shrugged. 'He will grieve later, I am sure, but in White Hall if you do not move at an indecent lick, someone else beats you to it.'

42

At that moment, Chaloner heard the chapel bell strike one o'clock, which meant Will had achieved an impressive amount in the few hours since his sibling had died.

'Is it true that he will inherit Chiffinch's titles and privileges, as well as these rooms?'

Barbara nodded. 'The agreement is already signed and sealed. Poor Thomas never had sons, so it was a straightforward matter to put to the King.'

'Will did well to persuade him to act so quickly,' mused Chaloner. 'His Majesty is not a man for speedy decisions, so he must hold Will in very high esteem.'

'He does love his Pimp-Master General,' said Barbara, acidly for her. 'I suppose I am glad that Will is the one who will profit from our loss, but Thomas's death was so sudden that I fear tongues will wag unless we make some pretence at sorrow.'

'Were you in the Shield Gallery last night?'

'Yes, but I went home early, so all I can tell you is that Thomas and Will played two games of backgammon, both of which Will lost. The first I heard about Thomas being dead was when my maid broke the news to me at about eight o'clock this morning.'

'I have been told that Will and Chiffinch quarrelled.'

'It would not surprise me. They argued all the time, mostly over the fact that Thomas thought Will's pimping brought the Court into disrepute.' Barbara looked Chaloner in the eye. 'I do hope you are not planning to investigate the matter. It would be most unwise.'

'You mean it may harm Will?'

Barbara made an impatient sound. '*He* has nothing to hide. I meant for you and your Earl. If you have been listening to malicious and unfounded tittle-tattle about foul play, then stop. Thomas died of natural causes. It is very sad, but these things happen, and if you meddle, you will anger a lot of important people.'

'You seem very certain that Chiffinch's death was natural.'

'I *am* certain. Dr Clarke diagnosed an impostume, and there is no reason to doubt him. Now, shall I take you to see Will? I am sure he will appreciate your sympathy.'

Chaloner followed Barbara along the hall. Trained to notice such things, he spotted several holes bored in the panelling, allowing the resident to monitor what was going on in the King's chambers next door. These would no doubt prove invaluable to Will, for deciding which prostitutes would best suit His Majesty's particular mood. Then Barbara opened the door to the parlour, which boasted some of the finest artwork Chaloner had ever seen. Clearly, Chiffinch had kept the best for himself when he had been assigned the task of furnishing White Hall.

'What do *you* want?' demanded Will when he saw Chaloner, and scowled at his wife. 'Why did you let him in? You know we do not like each other.'

Although two years younger than his brother, Will looked older, as night after night of carousing had taken their toll. He had removed his wig for comfort, revealing his grey-stubbled pate, and his clothes, although fine, were stained with wine and spilled food from the evening before. His eyes were bloodshot, and he had an impressive paunch.

'I came to express my condolences,' began Chaloner, 'and to—'

'If you are here to say that Clarendon is sorry my brother is dead, you can save your breath,' interrupted Will shortly. 'Because I know he is not.'

'Please, dear,' said Barbara, laying a soothing hand on his arm. 'Tom only came to—'

'I know why he came.' Will's sour expression made him look like an elderly and peevish schoolboy, and Chaloner eyed him in distaste, wondering why the King favoured such people. 'He aims to investigate me for murder.'

'He does not,' said Barbara firmly. 'I have already told him that—'

'I know what people are saying,' snapped Will. 'They saw me argue with Thomas after he defeated me at the gaming table, and they think I dispatched him in a fit of pique. Your Earl will certainly believe such tales, and will claim it is his duty, as Lord Chancellor, to order an inquiry. Am I right?'

'No,' lied Chaloner. 'There is no talk of murder at Clarendon House.'

Will sniffed. 'Well, for your information, I did not see Thomas again after we parted in anger. That was at two o'clock in the morning, and I know for a fact that he played others after me – Physician Clarke and his wife, Widdrington and his Cockpit Club friends, the Duchess of Newcastle and her stepson . . .'

'I understand you lost fifty pounds to your brother,' said Chaloner. 'It is a lot of money.'

It was a veritable fortune, near eight times what a labourer would earn in a year, and far more than Chaloner would ever bet on a game of chance.

Will sneered. 'Not to me. Besides, Thomas would never have made me pay, although as I then won the same amount from the Duchess of Newcastle, he could have had it if he wanted.'

'*You* defeated her, but your brother could not?' asked Chaloner doubtfully.

Will huffed his indignation. 'I am not his second in everything, you know. And I happen to be very good at lanterloo, which is what I played with her. But that is by-the-by. The point is that I had no reason to harm my brother, so any tales to the contrary are malicious slander, and if I learn that your Earl is behind them, I will sue him for every penny he owns.'

'He is not a gossip,' said Chaloner, although this was a brazen falsehood, as the Earl loved derogatory chatter about his enemies. 'And even if he were, he is not acquainted with the kind of people who would regale him with it.'

'True,' conceded Will. 'His friends are mostly prudish dullards, who have no place in a lively court. My brother hated him. Did you know that? He hated anyone who brought White Hall into disrepute, because he felt it damaged the King's standing with his subjects.'

'So he hated you as well?' asked Chaloner, thinking that Will's antics were more harmful to His Majesty than almost everyone else's combined.

'He loved me,' said Will firmly. 'But he was not very keen on my Cockpit Club friends. Or the Duchess of Newcastle, whom he considered the most dangerous person in the country.'

Chaloner was astonished, feeling there were far better candidates for that role. 'All I know about her is that she dresses spectacularly for the theatre.'

Will laughed with genuine amusement. 'It was quite a sight, and the King said later that he could scarce believe his eyes – he kept rubbing them, to see if they deceived him. However, it was not her clothes but her ideas that really alarmed my brother: she thinks women are as clever as men, an eccentric notion that will turn the world upside down if it is encouraged.'

'Yes, because there are dozens of White Hall ladies who are *vastly* superior to him in intellect,' sniffed Barbara. 'And he was terrified of them. Yet Will loved him, despite his shortcomings. Tell him, Will, dear.'

'I did,' said Will obligingly. 'And I rushed to claim his titles and possessions purely to ensure they pass to a *worthy* successor. I did not act out of personal greed or ambition.'

'Of course not,' said Chaloner flatly.

'Yet I do not believe he died of natural causes.' Will raised his hand when Barbara began to object. 'I know you disagree, Babs, but I have been thinking about it, and I am sure I am right. My brother made a lot of enemies by telling folk that their behaviour shamed the King, and I think one of them murdered him.'

'I see,' said Chaloner, while Barbara pursed her lips irritably. 'Do you have any particular suspects in mind?'

'I do,' replied Will. 'The man behind this vicious crime will be his most *deadly* enemy.'

'Not the Duchess?' asked Chaloner warily.

'Of course not. I refer to the one with the blackest heart of all – the Earl of Clarendon.'

'I told you it was a mistake to poke about in Thomas's death,' said Barbara crossly, as she showed Chaloner to the door a few minutes later. 'It was *your* reckless questions that prompted Will to accuse the Earl. Before you came, he was inclined to think the culprit was one of the Cockpit Club. It is your own fault that he settled for your employer instead.'

'Why the Cockpit Club?' asked Chaloner, unruffled. 'I thought Will was a member.'

'He is, but that does not mean he likes them. White Hall is a snakepit, and no friendship or alliance can be relied upon for long.' Barbara sighed. 'You had better warn the Earl to be on his guard, because once Will has a notion in his head, it is very difficult to disabuse him of it.'

'But you will try?'

'Yes, although I doubt he will listen. Of course, if Will *does* start a rumour that the Earl ordered Thomas dispatched, you know who will be charged with doing his bidding.'

'Who?' asked Chaloner stupidly.

'You – the cherished spy who has performed all manner of feats to thwart his enemies.'

'I am not cherished,' said Chaloner, startled. 'Most of the time, the Earl can barely stand to be in the same room as me. I am useful, but that is all.'

'He values you more than you think,' countered Barbara, 'but he does not want you to know it, lest you demand a pay rise – he is a terrible miser. And fingers *will* point at you if he is accused of ordering Thomas's death, because even you must admit that you are sinister.'

Chaloner blinked his disbelief. 'Sinister? *Me?*'

Barbara began to count points on her fingers. 'You wear clothes that mean no one notices you until you are in their midst; you creep up on people when they least expect it; you disappear for weeks on end on business that you then refuse to discuss; and you have dark skills acquired during the wars and in the service of Cromwell's Spymaster. Of course you are sinister!'

Chaloner was horrified to learn what was being said about him, having assumed that no one gave him a second thought. Moreover, it was a shock to learn that his efforts to be unobtrusive seemed to have had the opposite effect. He sincerely hoped that people did not believe that he was to the Earl what Swaddell was to Williamson.

Barbara saw his consternation and patted his arm. 'It has its advantages, dear. It means few will risk taking you on in a fight. However, it does render you vulnerable to a different kind of assault – namely, charges of dispatching your master's enemies. Thomas *did* die of natural causes, but we all know how hard it will be to extinguish rumours to the contrary, once they have taken hold.'

'And it will be difficult to prove my innocence, given that I may have been the last to see him alive,' said Chaloner gloomily. 'I met him in King Street at six o'clock this morning – he gossiped to me about what the Duchess of Newcastle had worn to the theatre. Then he wandered off towards the tennis courts, while I went to the Sun tavern.'

'Not the tennis courts,' said Barbara. 'The *cockpit*. At least, that is where his body was found, exactly an hour after you say you parted from him. I cannot imagine why he went there, as it must have been deserted at that time of the day.'

Chaloner stared at her. He knew Chiffinch had died in White Hall, but he had assumed it was at home. 'Chiffinch breathed his last in a place where no one goes except Widdrington and his monkeys?'

Barbara wagged a cautionary finger. 'He breathed his last in a place that is never locked, and that is open to anyone. Do not confer on it a significance it does not have.'

'Was the cockpit in use last night?'

'I believe there was a bird fight at some point, although it would have been over long before six o'clock in the morning.'

'Have you been to the cockpit lately?' Chaloner had

seen a play there once, but all he could remember was that it had been rather dark and smelled of urine.

'Not since it was commandeered by Widdrington's horde. I do not like them much, and I wish Will would not carouse with them. But to return to Thomas's death, you must have your alibi ready, should anyone make an accusation. I cannot imagine the Sun was busy at that time in the morning. With luck, the landlord will remember you.'

Chaloner shook his head, as he had sat in the shadows and eaten alone, but then he reconsidered. If Barbara thought him sinister, then perhaps the taverner did as well, and would be able to confirm that he had indeed been breaking his fast when Chiffinch had died. Regardless, he hoped that Wiseman would end the speculation when he examined the body. Then no further probing would be necessary and the whole matter could be quietly forgotten.

Barbara sighed. 'People will tell you that Thomas was in good health, so had no reason to drop down dead, but the truth is that he was in his sixty-seventh year and he ate too much, drank too much, and was too fat. He also complained of pains in his chest.'

'From the impostume that Clarke found?'

'Perhaps, although that is a question for a surgeon to answer.'

'Wiseman will do it,' Chaloner told her. 'As soon as the Queen is on the mend.'

'Then you will not have answers today,' said Barbara with the authority of one who knew. 'And perhaps not tomorrow either, unless she rallies overnight, poor lady. The premature end of another pregnancy has all but crushed her.'

Chaloner thanked her for her help and took his leave,

after which he went straight to the Queen's apartments and wrote a second message to Wiseman, asking him to recommend another surgeon because the matter of Chiffinch could not wait. The reply came via a footman who had been ordered to repeat it verbatim. The fellow stood stiffly to attention, and recited the words in a monotone to a spot on the wall above Chaloner's head.

'"Hire another *medicus* at your peril, as none of my colleagues can be trusted to find the truth. I will oblige you at the earliest opportunity, so wait for a man who knows his business or risk the consequences."'

'I did not ask for a full-blown anatomy,' muttered Chaloner irritably. 'A quick examination would have sufficed.'

The footman shrugged and reverted to his normal voice. 'The examination might take a moment, but what of the travelling to and from the Westminster charnel house? It will take Mr Wiseman away from Her Majesty for far too long.' Then he looked around thoughtfully. 'Unless you arrange for the corpse to be brought here . . .'

Chaloner was horrified by the notion. 'I do not think that would be a good idea – on so many different levels!'

Although inclined to think that Barbara had exaggerated when she had told him that he cut an eerie figure, Chaloner nevertheless took more notice of the people he passed as he returned to the Shield Gallery. Was it his imagination, or did they eye him with a combination of unease and curiosity? And if so, was it because they considered him an unsettling presence with an unsavoury past, or because Will was not the only one who thought the Earl might be responsible for the sudden demise of one of his greatest detractors?

Regardless, he decided that the best way to combat

any unpleasant rumours was to conduct his investigation openly, so if anyone did point an accusing finger, he would be able to claim that he would hardly be trying to solve a murder he had committed himself.

His mind made up, he marched to the Shield Gallery, making sure to stay in the sunlight and tipping his hat back so it did not shade his face. It felt contrived, forcing him to wonder if he really had grown too used to living in the shadows. He ran up the stairs, careful to step in the middle of each one – he usually kept to the edges, which were less likely to creak – and threw open the door at the top. It cracked against the wall, causing everyone to turn towards him.

'The Earl of Clarendon, Lord Chancellor of England, is saddened and shocked by the sudden demise of Mr Thomas Chiffinch,' he announced. 'Dr Clarke has determined the cause of death as an impostume in the breast, but the Earl wishes to be certain, so he has ordered an official inquiry. He expects everyone to cooperate.'

'Does he indeed?' murmured the Duke of Buckingham. He was another of the Earl's enemies, and so was the woman who stood at his side – Lady Castlemaine, the King's mistress. 'What does he want us to do? Confess to the murder?'

'He was murdered?' pounced Chaloner. 'How do you know?'

Lady Castlemaine laughed languorously. 'You should watch what you say, Bucks, or the Earl's spy will hang you with your own words. But we have nothing to hide, so let the man do his duty. Come, start with me.'

She undulated towards him. She had donned a very flimsy gown, so it was difficult for Chaloner to concentrate when he asked his questions, and he was acutely aware of her smirking at him all the while. He was relieved when Buckingham sauntered over to join them, and he was able to look somewhere other than at her perfectly proportioned body.

He spent the rest of the afternoon and evening talking to everyone who had been in the Shield Gallery the previous night, along with a lot of people who had not but who admitted to seeing the dead man at other times during the day. As he had anticipated, he learned nothing to suggest that anyone had done Chiffinch harm. Eventually, as the sun began to set, he gave up, and went to stand by a window to think.

Until Barbara had shattered his illusions, Chaloner had prided himself on his ability to blend into the background. Indeed, it was a talent that had allowed him to survive ten years of espionage, which was a long time in such a treacherous profession. He had brown hair, currently covered by a wig, clear grey eyes, and pleasant but unremarkable features. He was neither tall nor short, fat nor thin, and was as comfortable in slums as he was at Court.

But as he stood looking over the grubby ooze of the River Thames, he asked himself whether the skills that had kept him alive in the past might be his downfall in the present and future. It was not a comfortable thought, and he found himself wishing that Cromwell had not died, and that he was still an intelligencer in Holland. It had been perilous work, but at least he had been at ease with it.

Not long after, he bumped into Brodrick again. The Earl's cousin was with three strangers, and Chaloner could tell they had recently arrived in the city because their clothes were newly tailored. Brodrick introduced them with suspicious eagerness, then claimed pressing business elsewhere, scuttling away fast enough to verge on the impolite. It did not take Chaloner long to understand why he had been so keen to escape: the trio were trying company.

Their leader was Viscount Mansfield, the Duke of Newcastle's son and heir from his first marriage. He was small, fair and delicate, with a long nose, pale eyes and a wig that was too showy for the occasion. As his stepmother was forty-three, she had to be less than a decade his senior, and it quickly became apparent that he hated her.

The other two were the Duke's chief stewards: Francis Topp managed the family seat at Welbeck, while Andrew Clayton had charge of the West Country estates. The pair could not have been more different. Topp was short with white hair and an excruciatingly obsequious manner; Clayton was younger, tall and dark, with the hungry air of a man with ambitions.

For a while, Chaloner had no choice but to stand and feign interest while Mansfield made catty remarks about anything that caught his splenetic eye – the dreary artwork, Buckingham's old-fashioned boots, Lady Castlemaine's fading beauty. Topp gushed agreement with every spiteful observation, while Clayton was a dark, brooding presence on Mansfield's other side. Chaloner determined to have words with Brodrick later.

'I met your wife earlier,' he told Topp, the moment he could insert a word into the malicious tirade. 'Outside the Great Gate.'

He chose to mention Eliza because he thought the venomous Viscount would be unlikely to make snide remarks about his retainer's wife – at least, not while Topp was present – and he was keen to put an end to

54

the disagreeable diatribe. Unfortunately, the subject sparked a quarrel between the two stewards.

Topp groaned. 'Oh, Your Honour, *please* do not say she joined those foolish women in their protest! I urged her to stay home, but she is a lady of independent spirit.'

'Only because you allow her to be,' said Clayton, smugly gloating. 'Mine would never venture out once I forbade her. It is a question of establishing who is in charge.'

'*I* am in charge,' averred Topp between gritted teeth. 'However, that does not mean I am a petty tyrant, afraid of a woman who is my intellectual equal.'

'Pah!' sneered Clayton. 'You are a weakling, too frightened to show Eliza her place. Intellect has nothing to do with it.'

'Eliza has fallen under my stepmother's evil spell, Topp,' said Mansfield, all supercilious disdain. 'And has been corrupted with indecent ideas.'

'Please do not speak ill of the Duchess, Your Worshipfulness,' begged Topp unhappily. 'You know I adore her more than any woman alive, save my wife. I live to serve her.'

'Perhaps you should spend less time grovelling and more time controlling Eliza,' put in Clayton with a smirk. 'Then your wife might think twice about fraternising with rebellious commoners, all demanding education for girls and other such nonsense.'

'Eliza does *not* fraternise with commoners,' objected Topp, fixing him with a haughty glance. 'She is a *lady*, not some lowly farmer's lass.'

Judging by the way the blood drained from Clayton's face, this was a low blow. 'At least my Harriet does not embarrass the Duke by brawling in the street,' he retorted tightly.

'My father *would* be mortified if a member of his house-hold was involved in a public spat,' Mansfield informed Topp. 'So, for your sake, I hope Eliza has an explanation.'

Topp began a blustering defence, while Clayton and Mansfield expressed their opinions of his claims with disbelieving snorts and exaggerated drops of the jaw. Chaloner listened in astonishment, amazed that the two stewards should bicker in public – and that the Viscount should join in.

'The Duchess is having a soirée next week,' said Clayton to Chaloner, when Topp's agitated monologue eventually petered out. 'She has charged me with organising the music, and Brodrick said you might advise me. I was thinking of hiring a troupe of flageolet players.'

'Flageolets!' jeered Topp, still livid and looking to retaliate. 'Any fool knows those are for taverns. The Duchess would be mortified if you brought those to Newcastle House. What a peasant you are, Clayton!'

'A consort of violas da gamba might be more appropriate,' put in Chaloner quickly before there was another spat.

'Brodrick thought you would suggest that,' said Clayton, pointedly ignoring Topp's remark. 'He also told me that you own no small talent yourself.'

'Hire him, then,' ordered Mansfield, and looked the spy up and down critically. 'But no drab clothes, if you please. The soirée will be next Wednesday at Newcastle House. Do you know the place?'

'It is in Clerkenwell, Your Worship,' put in Topp helpfully. 'A beautiful spot for a glorious mansion, although no building is too good for our Duke and his Duchess, of course.'

'Are they musicians themselves?' asked Chaloner,

wondering if he had ever met anyone who was more shamelessly servile than Topp.

'*She* is not,' replied Mansfield at once. 'She spent her youth with her nose in a book, and neglected to practise, so she is rubbish.' He sniffed his contempt. 'Of course, all that reading has given her a false sense of her own worth, because now she feels compelled to bray her opinions to all the world. She thinks we should be fascinated by them.'

'We *are* fascinated by them,' averred Topp loyally. 'Her *Philosophical and Physical Opinions* is in its second edition, while *The World's Olio* and *Nature's Pictures* sold more copies than any other book last year.'

'Only because the plague drove all right-thinking people out of the city, leaving only lunatics and radicals to frequent bookshops,' retorted Mansfield. 'And what is an olio anyway?'

'A spicy soup, Your Significance,' supplied Topp obligingly. 'Very tasty.'

'More like a porridge of scraps,' scoffed Clayton. 'Paupers' fare, in other words.'

As the trio seemed to delight in being recklessly indiscreet, Chaloner mentioned the sudden death of Chiffinch, hoping they would gossip about that, too.

'He was younger than my father,' sighed Mansfield, evidently a man who saw everything in terms of himself. 'God knows what will happen when *he* dies. His new wife will see me beggared.'

'She will not, Your Magnificence,' said Topp stoutly. 'She is not interested in money.'

'Perhaps not,' said Clayton slyly. 'But she is interested in the things money can buy – books, microscopes, telescopes, costly scientific instruments . . .'

Mansfield sneered. 'She thinks she will be invited to join the Royal Society – that those learned gentlemen will forget she is female and admit her to their august gatherings. Can you credit the woman? She aims to destroy the proper order of things with her vanity.'

Struggling for patience, Chaloner brought the subject back to Chiffinch, and eventually managed to ascertain that the two stewards had watched Mansfield lose two games of backgammon to him.

'He cheated,' declared Mansfield petulantly. 'I am better at it than my stepmother, so it is impossible that she should have succeeded where I failed.'

'Were you angry about that?' fished Chaloner.

'Furious,' spat Mansfield. 'I wanted a third game, so that Clayton could watch more carefully for sleights of hand, but Chiffinch refused. He gloated that he had taken enough of my money, and did not need any more of it.'

'When did you last see him?'

'At four o'clock, when he stood to leave – I heard the clocks chime the hour as he did so. By then I was tired, but not sleepy, so I went to watch the river for a while. Water always soothes me when my mind is uneasy.'

'Did you go there alone?'

'There would be no point in doing it if someone was with me yammering,' retorted Mansfield unpleasantly. 'So, yes, I was alone. And then I went home, arriving at perhaps seven or eight o'clock. In time for breakfast anyway.'

More questions revealed that Clayton and Topp had left some time before Mansfield, and had alibis in each other, as they had travelled back to Clerkenwell together. They had then sat in the kitchen with other members of the Duke's household until dawn, neither willing to go to bed first, lest the other one said nasty things about him behind his back.

Eventually, Chaloner made his escape, thinking that if Wiseman did discover that Chiffinch had not died a natural death, then Viscount Mansfield's petty malice would put him at the very top of the list of suspects for his murder.

The Shield Gallery grew increasingly hot, as more courtiers crammed themselves inside to see what entertainments had been arranged to honour the dead man. It stank, too, as people perspired in their elegant clothes, and the reek of body odour mingled with an eye-watering combination of perfumes.

The air rang with self-important voices, every one of which had an opinion about Chiffinch. To die of natural causes was far too mundane, so Chaloner was not at all surprised to hear that tales of murder were rather more popular. When he eventually tired of the ghoulish speculation and aimed for the door, he was aware of people watching him. Was it because he was suspected of dispatching Chiffinch on the Earl's orders, because they feared the investigation he had announced, or because he was starting to attract the same kind of nervous interest as Swaddell?

He went to the Spares Gallery, technically a repository for superfluous artwork, but which also served as an informal common room for senior officials. A small pantry was usually stocked with food and wine, and there were comfortable chairs for relaxing. Chaloner drank a cup of ale, savouring the peace of the place after the clamour and press of the noisy courtiers upstairs. He was not alone for long though, as the door opened and Brodrick walked in. The Earl's cousin helped himself to a large goblet of wine, drained it in a single swallow, then poured another.

'I have a bone to pick with you,' began Chaloner coolly.

Brodrick grinned, unrepentant. 'I was stuck with Mansfield for the best part of an hour, so it was high time someone else took a turn. Did he ask you to perform in Newcastle House next week? If so, I shall inveigle an invitation myself. Good music is in short supply these days, as people are still afraid to hire professional players lest they have the plague.'

'The plague is almost gone,' said Chaloner. 'Only twenty-six deaths last week.'

'Which is nine *more* than the seventeen at the end of March,' countered Brodrick, evidently one of those who studied the official figures assiduously when they were released each Thursday. 'So it is still here, as far as I am concerned. And who knows? Perhaps *that* is the dreadful thing that will happen next Friday – a second wave of it. Of course, if so, it will be over by Easter Day.'

Chaloner frowned. 'How did you reach that conclusion?'

'Because that is what the soothsayers predict: a terrible calamity on Good Friday, followed by great rejoicing on Easter Sunday. But you look morose, Chaloner. Are you having trouble with the Chiffinch affair? I did recommend that my cousin keep his nose out of it, but he refused to listen.'

Chaloner regarded him coolly. 'I wish you had made your case more forcefully.'

'I did my best, but I had a terrible headache this morning, and it was hard to string two words together.'

Brodrick grinned again. 'Last night was a lot of fun. I do not play backgammon, but there were plenty of card games on the go – maw, lanterloo, quinze. . .'

'But you left early to go to Newcastle House,' recalled Chaloner.

'At roughly half past three, which shows how drunk I was, because I am not remotely interested in laboratories. Incidentally, I asked a few questions on your behalf today – fellows who will talk to me, but not to you. They say Chiffinch left the Shield Gallery at four o'clock precisely, and they were under the impression that he was off to do some work.'

'Where? In his apartments?'

'They thought so, but I have been unable to find anyone who can say with certainty. The next time he was seen was almost two hours later, when he walked across the Great Court with members of the Cockpit Club – Widdrington and a few others.'

'Really?' asked Chaloner, thinking immediately of frantic attempts to avoid debts incurred by losses at backgammon. 'Was their conversation amiable?'

'My friends could not tell, so you will have to ask Widdrington's cabal yourself. That will not be pleasant! And an hour later, at seven, the corpse was found. Naturally, I went to see it when the alarm was raised.'

'How?' asked Chaloner. 'You were in Newcastle House.'

Brodrick waved a dismissive hand. 'Oh, I had escaped Lucas's smelly pots and bubbling cauldrons by then. I heard the commotion, and my curiosity was piqued, so I went to see what was happening. Do not look so disapproving, Chaloner. Only a fool does not keep abreast of happenings in the place where he intends to flourish.'

'And your friends are certain of all these times?

61

Chiffinch left the Shield Gallery at four, disappeared for two hours, and was last seen walking across the Great Court just before six?'

'And found dead in the cockpit at seven,' finished Brodrick. 'Yes, quite sure.'

Which meant, Chaloner thought uneasily, that he himself probably *had* been the last person to see Chiffinch alive, as the courtier had been alone by the time he was in King Street.

'What was he doing in the cockpit?' he asked. 'Have you heard any suggestions?'

'There was a bird fight, but it had been over for hours by then. Try asking Fanny Clarke – you know her; she is married to the Physician of the Household. It was she who discovered the body. Of course, you have to wonder what *she* was doing there at such an hour, too.'

'Where does she live?' Chaloner set down his cup and stood.

Brodrick laughed. 'You cannot interrogate her now, man! It is late, and she, being a respectable lady, will be asleep in bed. You will have to wait until tomorrow. But if Chiffinch does transpire to have been murdered, I hope one of the Cockpit Club is the culprit. It will discredit the whole cabal, which will please my cousin. They mean him serious harm.'

'What can you tell me about them?'

'That Widdrington is a mean-spirited elitist who cares for nothing except his pleasures. That his wife Bess is an ugly, spiteful harpy, who aims to win her husband's love by aping his vileness. That Ashley is a drunkard and—'

'Not so loud!' warned Chaloner, aware that Brodrick's voice had risen in its passion.

'That Captain Rolt is a sycophant, who is all things

to all men. And that the rest are detestable dullards with no redeeming qualities.'

'So they are destined for top posts in government then,' said Chaloner drily.

'Fortune always favours the unworthy,' agreed Brodrick bitterly. 'Or rather, the King does. But the whole vile coven is united by its hatred of my cousin, and they do not want him disgraced – they want him executed. It is deadly stuff, Chaloner.'

'Then perhaps you should persuade him to leave London and live quietly in the country. There is only so much I can do to protect him against this level of malice.'

'I have tried, believe me, but he will not listen. Incidentally, Widdrington has organised a cockfight for tonight – it will be starting as we speak. You should go and watch these rogues in their natural habitat, as you will learn more about them there than from listening to me.'

Chaloner baulked – he detested bloodsports. But then he supposed that Brodrick had a point, and if the Cockpit Club really did mean his Earl harm, then it was his duty to learn as much as he could about them, so as to be ready to fight them off.

The Cockpit was a square building lined with steeply pitched rows of benches and a central, circular arena. It was very luxuriously appointed, with ornate mouldings on the walls and a glass turret that allowed light to flood in during the day. At night, it was lit with torches, which flickered and smoked, lending the place a rather insalubrious atmosphere.

Cockfights were noisy occasions, especially ones in White Hall. There were agitated crows from birds awaiting their turn in the ring, but most of the racket came from the courtly spectators, who cheered, booed, hissed and howled. Chaloner climbed the stairs to the stalls, wrinkling his nose at the stench of overheated people, spilled wine and chicken droppings.

He reached the top tier and surveyed the scene below. The benches were packed with important, wealthy and influential people – the Cockpit Club had invited Members of Parliament, Treasury officials, half the Privy Council, several prominent churchmen and a lot of high-ranking lawyers. Although they were predominantly men, there were some ladies present, most notably Bess Widdrington, Lady Castlemaine and a bevy of *filles de joie* from the infamous 'gentleman's club' in Hercules' Pillars Alley – the establishment that was owned and run by Wiseman's lover.

A fight was in progress, with a big white cockerel launching itself at a smaller blue-black one. There was something peculiar about their heads, and Chaloner saw that their combs and wattles had been sliced off, to prevent opposing birds from fastening on to them. Neither had been fitted with metal spurs, as they would have been in Spain, although their natural ones were still sharp enough to cause serious injury.

Chaloner looked around again, thinking it was here that Chiffinch had died. Had the courtier breathed his last down in the arena or on one of the benches? And why had he visited the place at such an hour? For a meeting perhaps? Chaloner wished he had come sooner, as any clues would be long gone by now.

He took up station in a shadowy corner and studied the people he still wanted to question – unless the Earl came to his senses and ordered him to leave the matter well alone. Or better yet, Wiseman pronounced Chiffinch's death natural and ended the speculation.

About twenty members of the Cockpit Club were there. They included the rich and arrogant Colonel Widdrington, the wife he did not love, the poor but ambitious Captain Rolt, and the drunken Ashley. Viscount Mansfield was there, too, trying to look jolly, but clearly ill at ease in such boisterous company. Young Legg was fast asleep, leading Chaloner to wonder if he was old enough to handle the late nights that his cronies kept.

Bess Widdrington screeched abuse at the black cockerel when it limped away in defeat, suggesting she had lost a lot of money. Her husband sidled away from her with a moue of distaste. When the exhausted birds had been whisked away, two more were produced. Widdrington presided over the betting, and Chaloner noticed that while Rolt was very free with advice regarding which combatant to back, he kept his own purse securely in his pocket.

At that point, a Cockpit Club member, whom Chaloner knew was named Thomas Cobbe, stood up. Like Rolt, Cobbe was a penniless nobody, but he elected to win his peers' notice by being outrageous – that night he wore a scarlet suit with pink lace. With careless aplomb, he placed a wager so huge that a stunned silence descended over the entire gathering.

'Are you sure?' breathed Widdrington, shocked. 'On the *brown* one?'

'It reminds me of my grandfather,' drawled Cobbe, revelling in the attention, 'and with his sainted soul smiling down on me, how can I lose?'

When Widdrington laughed and the others clapped their appreciation, Mansfield bet an identical sum on the opposing bird.

'It looks like my stepmother,' he quipped, 'and that woman wins at everything.'

He grinned, expecting people to applaud his wit, too, but no one did because it lacked originality. Then Cobbe's chicken won, earning him enthusiastic cheers, whereas Mansfield received nothing but a smile of sympathy from Rolt, who never missed an opportunity to curry favour with a nobleman. Mansfield might be a member of the Cockpit Club, thought Chaloner, but he was not really one of them.

Eventually, there was a break in the 'entertainment', while servants came to sprinkle the bloodied arena with fresh sand. Desultory conversation broke out, so Chaloner eased closer to the Cockpit Club contingent to eavesdrop.

'Perhaps I should have betted on the outcome of the skirmish between you lot and Eliza Topp's whores,' said Mansfield sulkily, still smarting after his defeat. 'The one you had outside the palace gates today.'

'If you had been with us, we would have won handily,' declared Cobbe, draping an elegant arm around the Viscount's narrow shoulders. The others guffawed, although Mansfield blinked uncertainly, not sure what to make of the remark.

'Those women should have been at home, cooking and cleaning for their menfolk,' declared Bess, glancing at Widdrington in the expectation that he would agree. 'It is a woman's duty to support her husband in all things, not prance about screeching rebellious slogans.'

'Is that why you are here tonight, Bess?' slurred Ashley. 'To support Widdrington? You did not come to win a few pennies on the birds?'

'To serve him is my sacred duty as a wife,' retorted Bess loftily, and would have added more, but Widdrington had started talking to Mansfield, and was not listening to her. She flushed with disappointment and fell silent.

At that moment, young Legg woke himself up with an undignified snort. Embarrassed, he blurted the first thing that entered his mind.

'Did you find your button, Rolt? The one you lost here last night?'

'You have been looking for a *button*?' Cobbe's voice dripped laconic astonishment. 'Is it made of diamonds then? Or has it been blessed by the Archbishop of Canterbury?'

The captain forced a smile. 'Its value is sentimental – it belonged to my father. Obviously, I would not demean myself hunting for it otherwise.'

'Speaking of fathers, Chiffinch is not much mourned by his daughter,' piped Legg, refreshed by his nap and ready to make up for lost time by providing some gossip. 'He thought her only use was to marry someone who could benefit him, but she believes she is worth more.'

'Then she is mistaken,' declared Ashley, all tipsy indignation. 'Women were put on Earth to be useful to *men*. I do not want females making decisions for themselves – it would result in anarchy! Incidentally, did you know that Chiffinch died right in the centre of our arena?'

'How do you know?' asked Cobbe curiously.

'Because Fanny Clarke – the physician's wife – told me,' replied Ashley. 'Although I cannot imagine what *she* was doing in here at such an hour.'

'The same is true of Chiffinch himself,' said Widdrington, willing to rejoin the discussion now that Bess had left it. 'This building is ours – the place where we have fun. I hope he did not come with the intention of sabotage.'

'Well, if he did, he died before he could do anything,' shrugged Cobbe. 'Nothing has happened to us, and all is well with the world.'

He performed an elegant twirl that made his coat-tails fly, revealing their beautiful pink silk lining. There were murmurs of admiration from anyone with an eye for fashion. Unfortunately, it was looking at Cobbe that caused Bess to spot Chaloner in the shadows beyond. Her square, homely face broke into a scowl that turned it uglier than ever.

'Why are *you* here?' she demanded in a voice that was shrill with indignation. 'I do not recall members of Clarendon House being invited.'

The Cockpit Club surged to their feet as one, and hands dropped to the hilts of rapiers. Chaloner was not unduly concerned about a fight, having seen their martial abilities outside the palace earlier that day. Even so, he was loath for everyone to think he had come to spy, so he flailed around for an excuse to explain why he was there.

'I came to say that you owe Chiffinch money,' he blustered. 'The debts incurred at the tables last night did not die with him, and the family still expect you to pay.'

It was not a complete lie, as he was sure Will would be delighted to be handed some free cash, while there were laws governing the settling of posthumous financial obligations.

'Do they?' gulped Rolt in dismay. 'That is damned unfortunate!'

It was impossible to eavesdrop once he had been exposed, so Chaloner decided to go home. Perhaps the Queen would have rallied, releasing Wiseman from his bedside vigil, and the surgeon could be persuaded to examine

Chiffinch at once. But he had taken no more than two or three steps towards the door when someone stalked through it, barring his way.

The Duchess of Newcastle was immediately identifiable by her eccentric appearance. She wore a riding coat with breeches and bucket-topped boots, and she carried a brace of pistols, although they were only wooden replicas. Black face-patches had been stuck over the smattering of pimples around her mouth, and she had adopted a feminine hairstyle with curls forming a fringe across her forehead.

She was accompanied by Eliza Topp and twenty pages, each of whom was dressed in identical white satin long-coats. There was not really enough room for them all, resulting in a noisy commotion as they tried to cram themselves inside anyway.

Mansfield scowled his outrage that his stepmother should foist herself on what he considered to be his territory, and he made a point of standing to leave in a huff. No one noticed, because all eyes were on her.

'I have long wanted to see this place,' she declared, looking around appraisingly. 'But it is disappointing. I thought it would be bigger – and not so full of smelly people.'

It was hardly a remark to win friends, and there was an offended silence. Then she gave a disdainful sniff before turning to walk out. Her retinue followed close on her heels, so when she stopped suddenly, they all ploughed unceremoniously into the back of each other.

'I almost forgot,' she announced loudly, 'is Edward Chaloner here? Or was it *William* Chaloner? Everyone I meet these days is an Edward or a William or a John. It is difficult to keep them all straight.'

She cackled, amused by her observation, although Rolt was the only one who laughed with her. He desisted hurriedly when he realised it was doing him no favours, and hastened to deflect any hostile attention away from himself.

'Here is *Thomas* Chaloner, Your Grace,' he said, jabbing a finger at the spy. 'Will he do?'

'He will have to,' drawled Widdrington slyly. 'Because the only other Chaloner of our acquaintance was the regicide. He is dead, thank God, but this fellow is his nephew.'

Chaloner wished the floor would open and swallow him up. It was bad enough belonging to a family of dedicated Parliamentarians, but far worse to have had an uncle who had signed the old King's death warrant. The older Thomas Chaloner had died shortly after the Restoration, but the Royalists had not forgiven his crime and never would. Chaloner glanced around quickly, looking for another exit to use, should the situation turn even more awkward.

To his surprise, Eliza Topp came to his defence, which he supposed was in return for him rescuing Molly the chicken girl earlier that day.

'You cannot visit the sins of the fathers on their children,' she said firmly. 'We are all responsible for ourselves, and it is on our own lives that we shall be judged.'

'I disagree,' countered Widdrington, his eyes cold and hard. 'I will *never* forget the role the Chaloners played in the old King's murder. They are—'

'I deplore cruelty to animals,' interrupted the Duchess, pointing to where a servant was ready with the next pair of cockerels. 'And anyone who disagrees with me is a fool.'

'I beg to differ, ma'am,' countered Widdrington shortly. 'It is a—'

'Just because they cannot speak does not mean they have no feelings,' the Duchess blared on. 'Cromwell was right to ban bloodsports.'

A murmur of shock rippled through the gathering, not just for her condemnation of something they happened to enjoy, but that she should express approval of the hated Cromwell. Widdrington opened his mouth to argue, but the words died in his throat when she fingered the handguns in her belt. He was evidently unaware that they were incapable of doing him harm.

'I have had enough fun for one night anyway,' he declared, indicating that the servant was to take the birds away. 'And finishing our revels early is a sign of respect for poor Chiffinch. We grieve deeply for him after all.'

'Do you?' asked the Duchess, with what seemed to be genuine bemusement. 'Because he considered *you* to be a worthless idler and a bad influence on the King. If it had been you who had died, he would be dancing for joy.'

Widdrington gaped at her. 'I hardly think—'

'Of course, he did not like me either,' she went on blithely. 'Although I fail to understand why. I am no vile, bird-torturing debauchee.'

'Chiffinch did not approve of anyone,' said Cobbe soothingly, evidently aiming to defuse the situation before there was trouble. 'He could not help it – it was in his nature.'

'He was a scoundrel,' stated the Duchess haughtily. 'With dreadful taste in poetry.'

At that point, Widdrington decided he had had enough of her, and led his entourage away without another word. Everyone else waited to see what the eccentric Duchess would do next. She gazed around with an imperious eye, then strode towards Chaloner.

'Surgeon Wiseman mentioned you when his path crossed mine at the Queen's bedside an hour ago,' she said, peering at him as she might some exotic insect.

'How is Her Majesty?' asked Chaloner, not liking the notion that his friend talked about him, especially to the likes of the Duchess.

'Recovering, thank the good Lord, although Wiseman says he will not leave her until tomorrow afternoon at the earliest, just to be sure. However, he told me that he aims to be at the Westminster Charnel House at three o'clock to inspect Chiffinch, and that he expects you to be there. I shall accompany you.'

Chaloner blinked. The examination of a courtier's body was hardly something to be conducted in front of an audience, and he was sure Wiseman would never allow it.

'It will not be—' he began.

The Duchess cut across him. 'Wiseman believes that Chiffinch was unlawfully killed, so I *insist* on watching him work. I have never seen a murder victim dissected before. Well, I have never seen anyone dissected before, if you want the truth. However, I predict it will be very interesting from a scientific viewpoint.'

Chaloner stared at her, sure she must have misunderstood. 'How can Wiseman have reached that conclusion? He has been nowhere near the body – not if he has been at the Queen's bedside all day.'

The Duchess shrugged. 'All I can say is that he seemed very certain that he would unveil a case of foul play tomorrow. We shall both have to wait for his explanation.'

Chapter 3

Unfortunately for Chaloner, Wiseman remained with the Queen all night, and refused to step outside, even for a moment, to explain why he had decided that Chiffinch's death had not been a natural one. Chaloner loitered until the small hours, hoping the surgeon might spare him a few minutes, but eventually gave up and went home.

He woke at six o'clock the following morning, roused by the clatter of the market that was establishing itself in the piazza outside. He glanced out of the window to see bakers and grocers setting out their wares on make-shift stalls. The fresh bread, pies and vegetables were quickly snapped up by servants from the nearby houses, who were glad to be spared the trek to the larger markets around Smithfield and Leadenhall.

He turned his back on the bustle and looked at the place he now called home. It comprised a sparsely furnished parlour, a bedchamber, and a tiny pantry for foodstuffs, although it rarely held more than a jug of wine and some cheese. It was considerably cleaner and neater than the rest of Wiseman's domain, because Chaloner did his own housework – the surgeon's footman, whose duties included dusting and sweeping, was an indifferent domestic and Wiseman did not care enough to make a fuss about it.

Chaloner washed and shaved, then donned a blue long-coat and matching breeches that one of his sisters had made for him. It was a brighter shade than he normally favoured, and he wondered if it might help dispel the image of Swaddell-like menace he seemed to have acquired.

Wiseman's lazy servants were making the most of their employer's absence by having a lie-in, so Chaloner was obliged to make his own breakfast. He ate a piece of bread, then collected a bowl of grain and went to the henhouse. He opened the pop-hole, and stood back so the feathered residents could flow out into the early morning sunshine. He had acquired five chickens the previous winter, but had bought more because they reminded him of his happy childhood in Buckinghamshire, where his duties had included care of the family poultry. He had always liked birds, and found much that was comforting and restful in hen-keeping.

He collected the eggs, then scattered the grain. Suddenly, there was a commotion, and several birds screeched their alarm. He looked around to see what had startled them and glimpsed a flicker of movement near the gate. The gate had a faulty latch, and a ginger cat had contrived to slip through it. Chaloner began to herd the animal out, and was doing well until his largest chicken, Ada, darted forward in a flurry of angry wings and claws. Terrified, the cat shot through the gate like a cannonball.

'Was that a *fox*?'

Chaloner turned to see the question had come from Wiseman's cook, who was rubbing his eyes with his one remaining hand – all the servants were missing body parts, but Chaloner could never bring himself to ask whether the surgeon was responsible.

'A cat,' he explained. 'Will you hire a smith to mend the latch? Leaving it broken is an invitation to burglars.'

'No, it was a *fox* and Ada saw it off,' breathed the cook. 'I saw it with my own eyes.'

Before Chaloner could tell him he was mistaken, the cook had raced away to tell the groom and the footman. Chaloner could have followed and attempted to put him right, but he knew from experience that he was unlikely to succeed. All Wiseman's retainers were men of unbending convictions, and once their minds were made up, nothing could change them. Instead, he sat on a bench to enjoy the contented chatter of hens while he planned his day.

His most important task was to meet Wiseman at the charnel house at three o'clock, where he would learn the truth about Chiffinch's premature demise. He hoped it would be without the Duchess looming over his shoulder. In the meantime, he decided to assume that Wiseman was right about Chiffinch being murdered, which meant he should start hunting seriously for the killer. After all, the best way to protect himself and the Earl from damaging accusations would be to produce the real culprit.

The first thing to do was speak to Timothy and Fanny Clarke, both of whom had played Chiffinch at backgammon and lost. Chaloner also needed to know why one had diagnosed an impostume, and why the other had been in the cockpit at such a peculiar hour.

Next, he would turn his attention to the others Chiffinch had defeated. He ran through a list of them in his mind. The Duke of Newcastle and Baron Lucas could be eliminated as suspects, because they had gone home with Brodrick while the victim was still alive. The Duchess had won the backgammon, so Chaloner was inclined to cross her off the list, too. That left Mansfield, her malcontent stepson, who thought Chiffinch must have cheated.

Also on the list was Will, who had gained so much from his brother's death and who had quarrelled with him. His name was followed by various members of the Cockpit Club, who also may have felt that the older courtier had been less than honest – which would certainly matter to them if large sums of money had been wagered.

But before he interviewed suspects, he had two other matters to attend. First, he should report to the Earl, and second, he wanted to visit his old friend John Thurloe in Lincoln's Inn, to see what advice he might have to give on exploring the death of an important courtier.

He stood, brushed himself down, and set off for Piccadilly.

It was another glorious day, although he heard many muttered concerns about five days without a drop of rain. A drought had preceded the devastating plague the previous year, and Londoners were naturally afraid that history was about to repeat itself. Chaloner revelled in the sunshine, though, and once he was striding along Piccadilly, he breathed in deeply, savouring the scent of clean air from the fields that lay to the north.

As he walked, he looked at the houses that were sprouting up on what had recently been farmland. The Earl was not alone in wanting to live away from the city's noxious airs, so several areas were being turned from meadows to suburban sprawl. These included Clerkenwell and Hatton Garden, as well as Piccadilly.

He reached Clarendon House to see that anti-Earl slogans had been daubed on the surrounding walls during the night, most pertaining to the unpopular sale of Dunkirk. They would be washed off later, but were always back within a few hours, no matter how many guards were hired to prevent it. Chaloner suspected the sentries sympathised with the protesters, something that would never be remedied as long as their employer treated them like dirt.

He nodded a greeting to the soldier on the gate, then walked up the gravelled drive. As a gentlemen usher, he could have used the grand front door, but instead he walked to the back. He entered via the kitchens, which were a chaos of noise and steam as the cook and his assistants prepared to feed the Earl, his family, and their army of staff and officials – more than a hundred people in all. It was a major undertaking, so Chaloner was surprised when they stopped working to exchange pleasantries with him. All smiled and some even bowed.

Bemused by the unusually friendly reception, he moved on to the formal rooms beyond – the domain of the Earl and his more senior retainers. The first person he met was Barker the clerk, who eyed him approvingly.

'You are very handsomely dressed today, Tom. Are you meeting a lady? I am glad. It has been ten months since Hannah died, so it is time you found yourself a replacement. Besides, no one should board with Wiseman for too long, as his company must be very tiresome.'

Chaloner was astonished that the clerk should offer

such intimate advice to a man he barely knew, especially as Hannah's death remained painful to him, despite the passage of time, and he was far from ready for a 'replacement'.

'My other coat seemed a little drab,' he said, aiming to keep the conversation brief if Barker was going to be personal.

'More than "a little",' said Barker bluntly. 'But if you want to attract the lasses, a pretty outfit is a good place to start. I can introduce you to some suitable candidates if you want. I have several nieces you might like. All are young, intelligent and polite. Of course, none have a dowry worth speaking of, but I do not believe you to be a pecuniary man.'

'I shall not marry again,' vowed Chaloner firmly, aiming to stop Barker from doing something both of them might regret. 'Twice is enough.'

'I am on my fourth,' confided Barker, and winked. 'Rich old widows, who are the easiest way to supplement one's income. But never mind that. I have some good news for you. Have you heard the rumour that Chiffinch was dispatched on the orders of our Earl?'

Chaloner nodded. 'Why is that good news?'

'Because I have witnesses who will swear that you are not the one who carried out the order.'

'You do?' asked Chaloner warily.

'I went to the Sun tavern to break my fast this morning, and all the talk was about the murder. Then Colonel Widdrington – the fellow who heads the Cockpit Club – piped up to bray that the Earl told *you* to do it, but the landlord and his regulars remember you. They swore that you were in the Sun from six o'clock until half-past seven, thus proving your innocence.'

Chaloner frowned his mystification. 'Why would they remember me?'

'Because you unnerved them and they were glad when you left.' Barker looked apologetic. 'It is your own fault, Tom. You insist on wearing anonymous clothes and you scowl a lot. Moreover, it is obvious from the way you move that you are an old soldier. You cannot help it, I suppose. It is what the wars made of us.'

Chaloner was grateful for the Sun's patrons' testimony, but was not sure it helped. The truth was that he had entered the tavern a few minutes *after* six o'clock, so would have had ample time to follow Chiffinch to the cockpit and kill him before going to eat his breakfast.

'You are safe from accusations,' finished Barker when Chaloner made no reply. 'But the rest of us are not, and nor is our Earl, so please find the culprit as quick as you can. Until then, you are the only member of Clarendon House who cannot be blamed.'

'So that was why the kitchen staff went out of their way to greet me this morning,' mused Chaloner. 'It was not friendliness or civility, but brazen self-interest.'

'So?' shrugged Barker. 'What is wrong with that?'

Clarendon House had been designed for show, and was not a pleasant place to live. It was full of marble, and its large function rooms were impractical for a middle-aged couple with children who had mainly flown the nest. The most obvious example of this was the chamber known as My Lord's Lobby, a vast, chilly mausoleum that the Earl used as an office. Even on warm days, it was cold, despite the fire burning in the hearth.

The Earl was huddled close to the blaze, his gouty

foot on a stool in front of him. There were black smudges under his eyes – he had slept badly.

'Have you heard?' he whispered as Chaloner walked in. 'There are tales that I ordered Chiffinch's murder, and aim to disguise the fact by setting you to investigate.'

Chaloner felt like saying 'I told you so', but prudently held his tongue.

'The only way to prove them wrong is by exposing the real culprit,' the Earl went on shakily. 'Today, before the gossip does me serious harm. Who are your suspects?'

'None I am ready to list, sir,' said Chaloner, afraid that if he did, the Earl would bandy the names about in an effort to silence the whispers about himself, which would likely land him in more trouble than ever. 'Although I have several leads to follow.'

'Then do it quickly,' urged the Earl, ashen-faced. 'Barker tells me that *you* have an alibi, but what about the rest of us? When you became unavailable as a scapegoat, people started to murmur that my cousin was responsible.'

'*Brodrick?*' Chaloner started to laugh, amazed that anyone should think the Earl's lazy, dissipated kinsman capable of anything as energetic as murder.

'Yes, Brodrick,' said the Earl, fixing him with a baleful eye. 'He is the only member of my staff – other than you – who was not rescuing books from my flooded library. My enemies were quick to pounce on the fact. Of course, I imagine they will accuse us all in time, regardless of whether we can prove our whereabouts when the crime occurred.'

'Probably,' agreed Chaloner.

The Earl winced at his bluntness. 'I received an urgent dispatch from Spymaster Williamson in Dover earlier. *He* wants the matter resolved before there is trouble, too, and suggests pooling our resources. He has detailed his man Swaddell to investigate, and recommends a joint inquiry to expedite matters.'

'You want me to work with Swaddell?' asked Chaloner uneasily, aware that such an alliance would convince even more people that he and the assassin were of an ilk. His reputation might never recover!

'I do. Of course, if you had done your job and resolved the matter yesterday, we would not be in this terrible position today.'

Chaloner itched to suggest that *he* should try solving a murder in a couple of hours if he thought it was so easy, but opted to maintain a dignified silence instead. It stretched out until the Earl spoke again.

'My plan misfired,' he said bitterly. 'When I ordered you to investigate, it was to cast shadows over *Chiffinch's* reputation, not my own. You should have warned me.'

'That is why you asked me to look into his death?' asked Chaloner, startled. 'You told me it was because you wanted your enemies to think you care about their welfare.'

The Earl released a derisive snort. 'What I care about is seeing them all banished to some rural backwater where they can do me no more harm – a place where they can reflect on their evil deeds before they are judged by God.'

'I see,' said Chaloner, who had scant faith in divine justice. In his experience, unless he organised it himself, it tended not to happen, allowing the undeserving to prosper and leaving their hapless victims to make the best of it.

'So you must work fast,' the Earl went on. 'It is in

your own interests to do as I say, because no one else will hire a man with your dubious past, and if I fall from grace, you will tumble with me.'

Chaloner did not need to be reminded. 'I will do my best.'

'I want more than that, Chaloner. This time, I think we might need a miracle.'

Chaloner was in a sullen frame of mind as he left My Lord's Lobby. He resented having Swaddell foisted on him, not just because he preferred working alone, but because he did not want to be associated with the Spymaster's favourite assassin. Then he brightened. The Earl had not specified *when* he and Swaddell should start collaborating, so he decided to begin without him. Perhaps he would solve the case before their paths crossed, and they would both be spared the experience.

He met Brodrick by the front door. The Earl's cousin was pale and there were shadows under his eyes, which Chaloner attributed to being up at a time when he would normally be in bed. Maliciously, he wondered how Brodrick would fare if people really did think that he had dispatched Chiffinch. It would certainly put a dent in his social life, as no one would invite a suspected killer to their homes, and the Earl was not noted for scintillating entertainment.

'I know you will do your best for me, Chaloner,' Brodrick said miserably. 'But please hurry. I do not want to be beheaded or whatever it is they do to murderers these days.'

'They are usually hanged,' supplied Chaloner, a piece of information that made Brodrick blanch. 'But you can help yourself by staying out of the public eye. Either remain here quietly, or better yet, leave the city altogether. Out of sight, out of mind.'

'I considered that, but Barker told me that if I disappear, folk will assume that I have fled the scene of my crime. He advises me to be my normal self and pretend that nothing is wrong. But I do not know if I can do it, Chaloner. I am not very good at dissembling.'

And the likes of Widdrington would make mincemeat of such an easy target, thought Chaloner, sorry for him. 'Then perhaps you should pretend to have the plague. That will keep visitors away and the forty-day quarantine will allow everyone to forget about you.'

'It is tempting, believe me. Court is not what it was, and I dislike the "entertainments" offered by the Cockpit Club. Barker told me that after they left White Hall last night, they went to the Bear Garden in Southwark and spent the rest of the night watching dogs getting killed. I do not mind the occasional dab of blood, but that is sickening.'

Chaloner fully agreed.

As Chaloner left Clarendon House, he saw the unmistakable figure of Swaddell hurrying along Piccadilly towards him. Hoping his new blue suit would render him unrecognisable, Chaloner turned in the opposite direction, then cut across the building site that was St James's Fields. He glanced behind and heaved a sigh of relief when Swaddell continued towards Clarendon House. He had escaped – for now, at least.

He trotted on until he reached St James's Park, and rather than waste time convincing the guard that he did indeed have right of access – it was a royal park, so the general public were not allowed inside – he scaled the back wall and walked through a small copse until he met the footpath that ran east.

Although trees and shrubs were bursting into life, the aviaries were empty and no water-fowl graced the banks of the man-made lake known as the Canal. Those birds rash enough to overwinter there had long since been snared and eaten by people struggling to stave off starvation – there had been a dearth of food because farmers had refused to trade with plague-ravaged London. A solitary mallard preened on an empty patch of mud, but it flew off when Chaloner approached. He wondered how long it would be before the wildlife recovered.

As one of the park gates exited near the cockpit, Chaloner decided to stop there and look at the place where Chiffinch had died while the building was empty. He did not expect to find or learn anything useful, but it was something he felt he should do.

He arrived to discover that the Cockpit Club had not been content with the carnage at the Bear Garden, and had returned to resume the cockfighting that the Duchess had interrupted. The games had finished at dawn, but a hardy few had lingered to finish off the remains of the wine. These included the outrageous Cobbe and Will Chiffinch, who were just lurching out through the door. Will was drunk, and Cobbe was struggling to hold him upright.

'You missed a good night, Chaloner,' slurred Will, a greeting that suggested he was too inebriated to remember the accusations levelled the day before.

'So did your brother,' retorted Chaloner pointedly.

'Thomas did not like cockfighting,' said Will, the barb missing its mark completely. 'He preferred backgammon. He was a bit stupid in that respect.'

'*Is* it stupid to prefer an intellectual challenge over watching two birds claw each other to death?' asked Chaloner coolly.

'Yes, I think so,' replied Will, after a moment of serious consideration. 'But perhaps you prefer bull-baiting?' He smirked. 'Or are dancing fleas and slug-racing more to your taste?'

'Wit-spotting,' retorted Chaloner, and when Will frowned his incomprehension, he elaborated. 'You put two courtiers in a room and bet on the first one to say something intelligent. Sadly, the match usually ends in a draw, with neither participant able to oblige.'

Will was far too drunk to appreciate what Chaloner was saying, which was probably just as well. He frowned his bemusement for a moment, then spoke in a pensive voice.

'Yet the bear-baiting bothered me. Black Ursus was supposed to be invib . . . invis . . . *invincible*, but one little dog saw him in his grave. Nothing can be taken for granted these days. Small hounds kill great big bears, while my whores claim they have purer souls than their customers. Our world is turning upside down yet again.'

Just then, Bess Widdrington emerged from the cockpit. Captain Rolt was behind her, struggling to support a crony named James Tooley, a hulking young man whose elegant clothes could not disguise the fact that he looked like an ape: he had a backward-sloping forehead, thick lips and peculiarly elongated arms There was no sign of Bess's husband, and her face fell when she realised that he had selfishly taken their carriage, leaving her stranded. Then her eye lit on Will, who was also wealthy enough to keep his own coach and four.

'Of course you may borrow Will's conveyance,' gushed Rolt, anticipating her need, and hastening to spare her the ignominy of admitting that she had been abandoned by the man she loved. 'Now he has taken up residence in his brother's old quarters, it will take but a moment to drop him off. Then his driver will take you anywhere you would like to go.'

'I am not sure I want to ride with him while he is in that state,' said Bess, eyeing Will in distaste. 'He might be sick over me.'

'I will not allow that to happen,' said Rolt gallantly. 'You can trust me.'

'Well, hold him upright, then,' ordered Bess, after considering her options and deciding they were painfully limited. 'Then Cobbe can run and tell Will's driver that we are waiting.'

Chaloner watched in amusement as Cobbe shoved the listing Will at Rolt, who then had two drunken friends to support. While the captain struggled under their combined weight, Cobbe sauntered away, clearly having no intention of 'running' anywhere. To pass the time Bess regaled Rolt with gossip, pointedly ignoring Chaloner as a person of no consequence.

'Did you hear about the devil visiting the Red Bull tavern in Clerkenwell the other night?' she asked. 'Apparently, he just strolled in and ordered a drink.'

'Did he pay for it?' asked Rolt, snatching at Will as he reeled sideways. He shot Chaloner a pleading glance for help, which the spy ignored.

'I cannot tell you that,' replied Bess, 'but Satan appearing so brazenly is a warning for the evil that will befall the city on Good Friday.'

'The Red Bull,' mused Rolt thoughtfully. 'A place you

know well, of course. I followed you and Fanny Clarke there a few days ago, all the way from White Hall.'

'You did what?' demanded Bess indignantly.

'You were in disguise, so my interest was piqued,' explained Rolt, fighting to prevent Tooley from sliding out of his grasp. 'However, while it started out as fun on my part, I was worried when you entered Clerkenwell. Some of that area is not very safe for respectable ladies, so I watched you very closely, lest you needed my assistance.'

'You are mistaken,' said Bess coldly. 'First, I have never donned a disguise in my life. Second, if I did embark on some wild venture, I would certainly not do it with Fanny Clarke, who is too staid for japes. And third, I would *never* visit the Red Bull – it is a brothel.'

'We are going to a brothel?' slurred Will. 'Excellent! Lead on.'

He lurched away from Rolt, lost his balance and collapsed in a heap. He giggled foolishly for a moment, then closed his eyes and began to snore.

'I suppose it must have been someone else I saw then,' said Rolt, propping Tooley against a wall, and wiping his sweaty brow on his sleeve. 'Because you are right about Fanny being too staid for japes. She is the dullest woman I have ever met.'

Bess's eyebrows shot up. 'But you think *I* visit brothels?'

Rolt was appalled that he had offended a lady who might do him future favours, even if it had been inadvertently. 'You mistake me, ma'am,' he gushed. 'The Red Bull must have stopped being a brothel and become respectable. Indeed, I imagine it is now . . .'

His flustered apology was interrupted by Cobbe, who arrived with Will's carriage.

'Did I just hear you call the Red Bull a brothel?' he asked, jumping down next to them. 'Because it is actually a common kind of theatre. The Duke of Newcastle's latest play – *The Humorous Lovers* – was performed there recently.'

'Was it?' asked Bess in distaste. 'I saw it in the rather more salubrious surroundings of Drury Lane.' Her ugly features twisted into a malicious smirk. 'As did the Duchess of Newcastle, who was virtually topless. It was embarrassing in a woman of her age.'

'And Fanny Clarke flounced out in protest,' recalled Cobbe, laughing. 'You should not associate with her, Bess. She is a bore, always telling us what we should and should not do.'

'She is all right,' shrugged Bess. 'And she is only thinking of the King. She worries about anything that might damage his reputation as an upright, virtuous man.'

Chaloner struggled not to smirk – or to point out that the King had never been considered upright and virtuous, even by his most blinkered admirers.

'Well, the only good things *I* can say about Fanny is that first, she is an excellent judge of lemons, and second . . .' Cobbe trailed off, leaving everyone to surmise that the lemons were it.

'Lemons?' slurred Tooley, coming to and joining the conversation. 'They are nice squeezed over shellfish, but they are difficult to come by at this time of year. I am an expert on them, though, because I am a Yeoman of the Larder. Indeed, it is . . .'

He faltered, too drunk to pin down the thought that had sprung into his mind. After a moment, he closed his eyes and began to slide down the wall, forcing Rolt to catch him before he landed on Will. Bess flounced towards the carriage, climbed in and banged on the ceiling to tell the driver to go. Rolt gaped as it rattled away.

'I did not mean her to make off with it on her own! How are we going to get this pair home now? Tooley is heavy.'

'Poor old Bess,' said Cobbe softly. 'She aims to win her husband's love by being as decadent as he is, yet she also craves the respect of prissy old birds like Fanny Clarke. She thinks she can have both, but will end up with neither.'

'Is this why I came to London?' muttered Rolt, as he heaved the semi-conscious Tooley upright. 'To haul drunks around?'

Cobbe made no effort to help. 'Perhaps this is how you lost your button, Rolt – it was ripped off while you lugged insensible friends to their beds.'

Rolt scowled. 'That damned button! I wish I had never mentioned the thing. Is either of you going to help me, by the way, or am I to struggle with this great oaf alone?'

'He is all yours,' said Cobbe cheerfully. 'I have Will to see home. Or would you rather he learned that not only did you give away his private carriage, but you left him to sleep off his excesses in the dirt?'

Fuming, Rolt staggered away with his burden. Since they were alone – the somnolent Will did not count – Chaloner took the opportunity to ask Cobbe some questions.

'Were you in White Hall the night Chiffinch died?' he began.

Cobbe shook his head. 'I was in Chelsea all last week, and only returned yesterday morning. I can provide witnesses, should you doubt my word as a gentleman.'

Chaloner tended to doubt anyone who expected him

to believe that gentlemen never lied, but he had better suspects to pursue than Cobbe, so he decided not to ask for the witnesses' names just yet.

'Have you heard any rumours that might explain what happened to Chiffinch? Other than the ones that claim my Earl killed him, which we both know is a nonsense.'

'It is a nonsense,' agreed Cobbe, much to Chaloner's surprise. 'Clarendon would never murder his enemies, although I imagine he is sorely tempted on occasion. However, the only rumours I heard have nothing to do with Chiffinch, but are about the Duchess of Newcastle. Have you met her simpering steward Topp? I cannot abide that man. He is so greasily servile that it is difficult to take him seriously. Do you think he and the Duchess are lovers?'

'What?' blurted Chaloner, startled.

Cobbe winked as he podded Will awake with his foot. 'Well, who can blame him? She is a remarkable lady, and if you do not believe it, ask her.'

It did not take many minutes in the cockpit for Chaloner to see he was wasting his time. Too many feet had trampled in and out since Chiffinch had died. He did learn that it would be a good place to kill, though. It was tucked away in a remote corner of the palace, so any cries for help from the victim were unlikely to be heard by anyone else if the cockpit was empty.

Aware that more time had passed than he had intended, Chaloner took a hackney carriage to Lincoln's Inn, flagging one down just outside the Holbein Gate. There followed a hair-raising journey as the driver demonstrated his intimate knowledge of shortcuts, some of which were barely wide enough for his coach and that

Chaloner would never have attempted at such high speeds. While he drove, the man regaled his fare with gossip.

'I am going to Ratcliff on Thursday,' he bellowed, struggling to make himself heard over the furious clatter of his wheels. 'To avoid the terrible calamity that will hit London the following day. After all, how can disaster *not* strike the city, when Good Friday falls on the thirteenth day of the month in the year with three sixes in it?'

'How indeed?' gulped Chaloner, as the man twisted around for an answer. He breathed his relief when the fellow turned his attention back to the road.

'Mother Broughton has ideas about what form the crisis will take,' the driver went on. 'Have you heard of her? She is the famous seer who lives in Clerkenwell. All her prophecies come to pass. Every one of them.'

'What does she think will happen?' asked Chaloner, then held on tight as they took a corner so fast that the right-hand wheels lifted off the ground.

'That Good Friday will see a lot of weeping and gnashing of teeth, and that a great darkness will cover the city. It will not lift until Easter Day.'

'Goodness,' murmured Chaloner. 'And this seer hails from Clerkenwell?'

'Near Newcastle House, home of that peculiar Duchess. Mother Broughton can often be found in its local taverns of an evening.'

'Drinking?' asked Chaloner pointedly, but they had just reached the Temple Bar, where the Strand met Fleet Street and all traffic was obliged to pass through a very narrow entrance. There was a queue, forcing the driver to haul on his reins to prevent his horse from ploughing into the back of the vehicle in front.

The near-collision precipitated a lot of bad-tempered swearing, during which Chaloner's driver somehow contrived to hurtle through the gate ahead of everyone in front of him, and there was another stomach-wrenching lurch as he took a sharp left into Chancery Lane. Chaloner clambered out unsteadily and paid. Then the driver was off again, belting along as if the devil was on his tail, scattering everything and anyone who went before him. Chaloner pitied his hapless horse.

Lincoln's Inn was one of the four legal foundations that licensed lawyers, and owned not only several ranges of buildings along Chancery Lane, but also the large open space to its west called Lincoln's Inn Fields, an area worth a fortune, given the current demand for more houses. The Inn itself was encircled by walls that granted its residents privacy and security, and encompassed a chapel, a splendid hall, living quarters for its 'benchers', and extensive gardens.

The youthful porter recognised Chaloner from previous visits. He waved him inside, and exhorted him to enjoy the next six days, as they might be his last. London's wicked, he informed Chaloner soberly, would not make it to Easter. Then he promised to pray for Chaloner's soul, the implication being that he considered himself one of the godly few who would survive, whereas the spy stood no chance whatsoever. Normally, Chaloner would have laughed, but he was still smarting from the news that he was sinister.

The man he was going to see lived in Dial Court, although Chaloner knew his friend would be walking in the grounds at that hour of the day. He hurried there at once, barely noticing the bright green of new growth in the trees, or that the Inn's gardeners would soon have to do something about the weeds sprouting up in the rose beds.

John Thurloe had been powerful during the Commonwealth. He had been Cromwell's Spymaster General and sole Secretary of State, and it was often said that the Lord Protector could not have clung to power for as long as he had, if it had not been for his brilliant first minister. Chaloner did not know if it was true, but there was no question that Thurloe was one of a kind. He was slightly built, and resisted the current fashion for wigs, although there was more lace at his throat and cuffs than he had worn when the Puritans were in power. The most remarkable thing about him were his large blue eyes, which gave the appearance of soulful innocence, although he had a core of steel that had seen more than one would-be traitor sent to the gallows.

'Tom!' he cried in delight. 'I heard you had returned from Scotland, although I am horrified that you took so little time before immersing yourself in trouble.'

Despite the fact that he no longer had dozens of intelligencers reporting to him every day, a number of old agents still kept Thurloe up to date with events, and he was far better informed than the current Spymaster. Thus Chaloner was not surprised that he already knew about the investigation into Chiffinch's death. He gave him a brief account of what he had learned about it, including Wiseman's contention that he was murdered.

'Chiffinch was a man of rigid opinions,' mused Thurloe. 'And devoted to the King. He deplored anything that he felt damaged His Majesty or the reputation of his Court.'

'Such as the Cockpit Club,' surmised Chaloner.

Thurloe nodded. 'He hated the way its antics made White Hall the subject of gossip and disgust. Its members objected to his censure, so if he *was* murdered, you should certainly look among them for the culprit, and that includes his silly brother. However, his disapproval was not restricted to debauchees. He was very outspoken about the Duchess of Newcastle as well.'

'He certainly complained to me about the costume she wore to the theatre.'

'He also deplored her radical ideas, which he felt threatened the established order of things – the books written under her own name, her belief that women are as clever as men, her controversial views on religion. He hated your Earl, too, for selling Dunkirk and for being so prudish that people mock him.'

'And he was the perfect courtier, I suppose,' said Chaloner acidly. 'Neither too prim nor too licentious, and all his opinions were a credit to his King.'

'Naturally,' said Thurloe. 'It is very possible that he plotted to remove anyone he considered to be a danger or a nuisance, so any list of suspects must include Newcastle House and your Earl's household, not just the Cockpit Club.'

'There are rumours that the Earl ordered his death, and until Barker proved otherwise, there were whispers that I obliged him.' Chaloner hesitated for a moment, then blurted, 'Do you consider me sinister?'

'Of course! Why do you think I recruited you to work for me?'

Chaloner was not very pleased to hear this. 'So I am of an ilk with Swaddell?'

'To a degree. But do not look so dismayed. It is part

94

of what has kept you alive all these years – and part of what stands between your Earl and the scaffold. He would be dead by now if his enemies were not afraid of what you might do if they contrive to see him beheaded.'

Although Chaloner usually respected Thurloe's opinion, he was sure the ex-Spymaster was wrong about this. 'They barely know I exist.'

'Oh, they know,' averred Thurloe. 'But your friends appreciate your good heart, and there is nothing wrong with being considered strong and resourceful by your enemies. Besides, why does it matter what folk at White Hall think? Most are beneath our contempt.'

Chaloner regarded him in surprise. Thurloe rarely voiced an opinion about the current regime, given that to do so might see him arrested for treason. Chaloner was touched by his friend's trust, but also alarmed, revealing as it did that the Court's antics were trying even Thurloe's dogged patience.

'I can tell you that no one at Clarendon House killed Chiffinch,' Chaloner said, tactfully changing the subject. 'First, they were too busy with a flood in the Earl's library to sneak off and murder anyone; and second, none of them are capable of doing it without being caught.'

'Your word is good enough for me, but I doubt the Earl's enemies will accept it.'

'No,' sighed Chaloner. 'I have to speak to Timothy and Fanny Clarke when I leave here: he claims Chiffinch died of natural causes and she found the body. Do you happen to know where they live?'

'They have taken up residence in the mansion your grandfather built, and that your Uncle James inherited: Chaloner Court in Clerkenwell.'

Chaloner winced. He was unfortunate in having not one but two kinsmen associated with the regime that had executed the old King. Uncle Thomas was the one everyone remembered, because he had signed the death warrant and was a flamboyant supporter of Cromwell. But there was also Uncle James, who had spent much of the Commonwealth governing the Isle of Man. Both had been condemned as traitors at the Restoration, and all their goods – including Chaloner Court – were confiscated. Chaloner had barely known James, recalling him only as a quiet man with a passionate devotion to 'godly religion'. Both were now dead, but their ghosts kept returning to haunt him.

'Is it still standing?' he asked. 'I thought it would have been demolished by now.'

'Clarke bought it for a very reasonable price,' replied Thurloe, 'but he lives in fear that His Majesty will pardon the regicides and return all property to their heirs.'

'There is no danger of that,' said Chaloner ruefully. 'The King will never forgive them.'

'No,' agreed Thurloe. 'He will not, but Clarke is uneasy even so, especially as James's widow lives in very reduced circumstances on the Isle of Man. James's son – a vicar – has a small income from a country parish, but his daughters are wholly unprovided for.'

'How do you know?' asked Chaloner. He had not been aware of their predicament, although he was not surprised by it: his own branch of the family was struggling under a massive burden of penalties, and they had had nothing to do with the old King's death.

'Because James's son wrote to me recently, and asked if anything could be done to get some of his father's holdings back. I advised him to be grateful for what he had, and not to draw attention to himself with requests that will never be granted.'

'Goodness!' muttered Chaloner in alarm. 'Will he listen to you?'

'I believe so. But we digress. The point is that you will have to go to Chaloner Court if you want to speak to Clarke and his wife. While you are there, will you take a moment to look around Clerkenwell and assess it for me?'

'Why? Because it is where the Duchess of Newcastle lives with her revolutionary ideas? Because a Satan-shaped cloud was spotted there last week? Because it has a tavern called the Red Bull, where its landlord served Lucifer a drink? Or because a seer named Mother Broughton resides there?'

'All these reasons,' replied Thurloe. 'Something unsavoury is brewing in the area – something that should be stopped before it does any harm.'

But Chaloner felt that if Thurloe could voice dissatisfaction with White Hall, then so could he. 'And what if the "something unsavoury" only harms the current regime? God knows, I do not want another civil war, but our country is being dealt a poor hand by these Royalists. They make no pretence at justice and decency, and all the promises they made when they returned to power have been broken.'

Thurloe regarded him lugubriously. 'Perhaps so, but please dispel any hopes of another glorious revolution, Thomas. We have no Cromwell to lead us, so it would fail, and we have seen enough turmoil for a while. See what you can learn in Clerkenwell, and report back to me.'

Chaloner said that he would.

Chapter 4

It was not far from Chancery Lane to Clerkenwell – just up to Holborn, through Hatton Garden, and across the bridge that spanned the reeking Fleet River.

Chaloner enjoyed the walk, although reminders of the plague were everywhere. He saw a number of houses with fading red crosses on the doors, marking where the sickness had been identified within. Some had been reoccupied and the owners had not yet scoured the marks off, but others remained empty and boarded over. A few had notices nailed to them, saying they were subject to legal proceedings as rival heirs competed over the spoils from the dead.

Much of Clerkenwell was a very desirable place to live. It was close enough to the city to be convenient, but still retained a spacious, slightly rural air. It boasted a number of impressive mansions, not least of which was the Charterhouse, once a religious foundation, now a school set in extensive gardens. Further to the east were the wide open spaces of the Artillery Ground and Bunhill Fields, the latter of which had recently been set aside for use as a cemetery.

The centre of Clerkenwell was its green, an expanse of grass bordered by handsome houses on all four sides, although the ones at the western end trailed off into hovels and slums. As in Covent Garden, the prospect of easy sales to wealthy residents had encouraged a small market to develop. His eye was caught by a handcart piled high with shellfish. Or rather, by the woman who was selling them, as it was Sarah, the woman with the flaming red hair who had led the protest outside White Hall the previous day. He was amused to note that she even managed to make that innocuous activity appear radical, and the manner in which she yelled her prices was more challenging than informational.

Dominating the north side of the green was Newcastle House. This was a perfectly symmetrical H-plan building, with quarters for the Duke on one side and the Duchess on the other. In between were the grand reception rooms where the couple entertained guests.

Diagonally opposite Newcastle House was a mansion that was simultaneously familiar and different. Chaloner Court was a blocky house with a forest of Tudor chimneys. In his youth it had been soot-stained and forbidding, but its current owners had lavished so much money on it that it was now bright, clean and boasted gaily painted window shutters. Chaloner had expected to experience a flood of memories when he saw it, but all he could think was that the slate slabs used to retile the roof looked a little too heavy for the house's foundations.

'I thought I might catch you here,' came a low voice from behind him. Chaloner spun around in alarm to see Swaddell standing at his shoulder. 'Although I expected you sooner. I have been waiting for over an hour.'

'Have you?' Chaloner cursed himself for not antici-pating that the assassin might try to hunt him down. Worse, he had been so preoccupied with looking at Chaloner Court that he had failed to pay attention to his surround-ings, which was an unforgivable lapse in his line of work.

'We are to explore the Chiffinch affair together,' explained Swaddell, brushing invisible dust from his spot-less black long-coat. 'Did the Earl not mention it? He promised he would.'

'I did not know where to find you,' lied Chaloner. 'How did you know I would be here?'

'By reasoning that you would want to speak to the person who discovered Chiffinch's body. Discreet enqui-ries revealed that you did not do it yesterday.'

Swaddell smiled, revealing his sharp little teeth and red tongue. Chaloner was irked that the assassin had read him so easily. How was he going to convince everyone that they were different if Swaddell knew him well enough to predict his movements?

'We have had reports of something dangerous brewing in this area,' Swaddell went on, looking around him. 'Although none of our spies have been specific. They just say that there are worrisome rumblings.'

'Probably because of a local seer who has predicted a dreadful calamity for Good Friday,' said Chaloner. 'Her name is Mother Broughton. Perhaps you should set someone to watch her, as it would not be the first time that a prophet cheats to make sure a "foretelling" comes true.'

'Unfortunately, all our spies are busy. Dutch-loving traitors supply the enemy with information about our ships and defences, and Williamson says rousting them out must take precedence.'

'Can he not hire more men?' asked Chaloner, exasperated. 'There is no point preserving our shores from foreign invaders if there is rebellion at home.'

'Money,' explained Swaddell tersely. 'We do not have any, and our politicians refuse to allocate more. And they should, because it is not only Mother Broughton who warns of imminent disaster. It was predicted in the tailed star that blazed across the sky last winter, along with the plague, eclipses of the Moon, the position of Saturn in relation to the Sun . . .'

'Superstition and coincidence,' interrupted Chaloner dismissively.

'And the date,' finished Swaddell. 'How can there *not* be trouble when Good Friday falls on the thirteenth day of the month, in a year containing three sixes? Of course there will be a calamity of monumental proportion.'

His words sent a shiver down Chaloner's spine, despite the warmth of the day. To take his mind off it, he looked at the shellfish-seller, admiring her slender figure and the defiant angle of her head. She wore a shawl over her hair, although one red tendril escaped to curl at the side of her face. Her apron was white and her clothes spotless, even though hers was not the cleanest of trades. She stood with her hands on her hips, scowling at passers-by so that he wondered how she expected to win any customers.

'She is splendid, is she not?' Swaddell's low voice cut into his ruminations. 'Sarah Shawe is a person of interest to the intelligence services, because she has opinions.'

'Opinions about what?' asked Chaloner, irked that Swaddell had caught him ogling.

'Women,' replied Swaddell darkly, 'and what she considers to be their rights. For example, she thinks they

101

should be able to divorce men who prove to be unsatisfactory. Can you imagine anything more disturbing? Half the men in the country would find themselves solo if women were allowed to decide what is best for themselves.'

'Would that be such a bad thing?' asked Chaloner provocatively.

'Not for them, but it would be a disaster for us. Well, not for me, as I would never give a lady cause to get rid of me. Should I ever win myself a female companion, I would do all I could to ensure she thought she was the luckiest woman alive.'

'Good luck with that,' said Chaloner, sure Swaddell would never be in a position to put his plan into force, as no woman would be stupid enough to let him get anywhere near her. 'But I do not see why Sarah's opinions should unsettle the intelligence services.'

'She also believes that women are as intelligent as men, that they should be paid the same as their male counterparts, and that the country would be better governed by a Privy Council of ladies. She considers men too violent and rash, and says that if females were in charge, we would have fewer wars, less corruption, and a kinder, more ethical society.'

'She might be right,' said Chaloner. 'And an all-female Privy Council cannot possibly be worse than the one we have already.'

'Do not let anyone else hear you say that, Tom,' advised Swaddell, glancing around uneasily. 'It is radical stuff. But your subversive thoughts are safe with me, because we are blood brothers, tied by an unbreakable bond of loyalty.'

'Right,' said Chaloner uncomfortably, and changed

the subject. 'I am told that Chiffinch disliked the Cockpit Club, the Duchess of Newcastle and my Earl, and that he may have gone beyond angry words to actual plots against them. Have you heard anything about this?'

Swaddell shook his head. 'He *was* vocal in his disdain for people he disliked. I heard him grumbling myself. However, I doubt he did anything more than rail against them.'

'We should bear it in mind anyway,' said Chaloner. 'Perhaps you should return to White Hall and make enquiries there, while I speak to the Clarkes.'

'No, we should stick together,' countered Swaddell. 'However, first, we must pool all the information we have, which will allow us to work more efficiently. Come to Myddleton's Coffee House with me. We shall do it there.'

Coffee houses were where men – never women – went to discuss religion, politics and other contentious subjects over a dish of the beverage that had been unknown a few years before, but that was now very popular. The government considered them sources of sedition, and longed to close them down, although that would likely ignite the very trouble it aimed to avoid. In theory, anyone was welcome to speak his mind in a coffee house, be he an earl or a scullion. In practice, some establishments catered to the wealthy elite, while others were for ordinary folk.

Myddleton's was one of the latter. It was a shabby building near where the elegant homes around Clerkenwell Green gave way to the hovels that lined the Fleet River. It had benches that had been polished to a bright sheen by the rumps of pontificating customers, and tables that were ring-stained from spillages.

Coffee-house etiquette was that arriving patrons sat next to whoever was already there, but Swaddell chose an empty table in the window. His dark, menacing presence was such that no one objected to him breaking the rules. Myddleton scurried forward with a long-spouted jug, filled two dishes with an aromatic brown sludge, and retreated to his regulars, where they conferred in low voices about the two disquieting strangers in their domain.

Swaddell sipped his coffee, gave a nod of appreciation, and began to talk about Chiffinch. He knew little that Chaloner had not already learned, other than the fact that the courtier had been outspokenly critical of a number of people at Court, not just the Cockpit Club, the Duchess and the Earl. All had earned his enmity for doing or saying something that he felt reflected badly on the King.

Reluctantly, as it went against his nature to share information, Chaloner outlined what he had found out. Then he recited his preliminary list of suspects and confided his hope that Wiseman would provide a definitive explanation that afternoon in the charnel house for the courtier's sudden death.

'So the Duchess wants to see Chiffinch anatomised,' mused Swaddell, when Chaloner had finished. 'And she is on your roll of people who may have done him harm.'

'I did not include her at first, on the grounds that she defeated Chiffinch at backgammon, so had no cause to resent him. However, now we know that he openly condemned her eccentricities, she is certainly a suspect. However, even if she is innocent, I will not allow her to watch him dissected, even if it is only for scientific curiosity. It would not be right.'

Swaddell chuckled. 'If you do succeed in keeping her out, you will be inundated with demands from people wanting to know how you did it. She is not a woman easily dissuaded from a particular course of action once she has set her mind to it.'

Before either could add more, there was a commotion outside as a flock of people marched on to the green. At their head was a large person who carried herself with great authority. She wore a sugarloaf hat of the kind that had once been popular with Puritans, but a velvet doublet and skirt of a style that was currently favoured by Royalists. There was a plain white apron around her waist, and her hands were big, red and competent.

'I suspect this horde has just come from the Red Bull,' muttered Swaddell, watching through narrowed eyes. 'Once a theatre, then a brothel, now a place where malcontents gather.'

When the procession reached the centre of the green, the woman waited while two men hurried forward with a wooden box. They set it down and helped her to stand on it. When she was up, she folded her arms and looked around imperiously. Immediately, her followers fell silent.

'I have had another vision,' she declared in such a loud voice that she was perfectly audible from inside the coffee house, especially as the other customers had stopped muttering about Chaloner and Swaddell, and had opened the door to listen to her.

'Mother Broughton, I presume,' murmured Chaloner.

'It must be,' Swaddell whispered back, 'and we should take heed of what she is about to announce, because you are right to say that some seers are not above making sure their predictions come true – and I do not like the sound of the wailing, gnashing of teeth and darkness that she claims will afflict London on Good Friday.'

'The dead will walk on Tuesday,' declared Mother Broughton in sepulchral tones, which caused a frisson of fear to ripple through her listeners, the ranks of which were rapidly swelling with folk who lived around the green. Among them were Eliza Topp and Molly the chicken girl from Newcastle House. Sarah Shawe had abandoned her wares and also stood nearby.

'What dead?' called someone uneasily. 'Not plague victims?'

'If they lived godly lives, those will rest in peace,' replied Mother Broughton grandly. 'But if they were evil, they will rise to move amongst us, clad in long black cloaks to hide their mouldering bones. In their hands, they will hold red lights – not lamps to illuminate their way, but the vessels that contain their tainted souls.'

'Crikey!' breathed Myddleton, turning to regard his customers with frightened eyes. 'I do not like the sound of that!'

'The first sighting will be in Bunhill,' Mother Broughton boomed on, 'where too many Quakers and Baptists are being buried. The second will be in Westminster Abbey.'

'I have an uncle interred in Westminster Abbey,' Swaddell told Chaloner conversationally. 'It will be interesting to meet him again.'

Chaloner regarded him askance, but then his attention was caught by a remark from Eliza Topp, who was speaking anxiously from the back of the crowd.

'But if only the *wicked* dead will have their eternal rest disturbed, we shall we inundated with nasty people: wife-beaters, religious fanatics, bullies, thieves, killers, courtiers—'

106

'Courtiers!' spat Sarah in disgust. 'Scoundrels to a man! God forbid that they should make an honest living. Or engage in something that might tax their intellects, like devising ways to end this stupid Dutch war or to help the downtrodden poor.'

'You cannot tax something you do not have,' put in Eliza, an assessment that drew a snigger of appreciation from the crowd.

'The government taxes *us* on what we do not have all the time,' countered Sarah. 'They take our hard-earned wages to support a palace that is full of expensive, worthless toadies.'

'Goodness!' muttered Chaloner, wondering if she would be so frank if she knew the Spymaster's favourite assassin was listening. 'She is bold.'

'She is,' agreed Swaddell worriedly. 'Our informants are right to say that something worrisome is bubbling in Clerkenwell. The whole area is ripe for insurrection, and Sarah Shawe will be at the heart of it.'

'But the dead will not stay among us,' Mother Broughton went on, eager to reclaim the attention. 'They will return to the soil. Then I predict that three things will come to pass.'

'Why are there always *three* things with seers?' muttered Swaddell. 'Never two or four?'

'Just be thankful she did not say thirteen,' quipped Chaloner, 'or we would be here all day.'

'The first will be on Maundy Thursday,' Mother Broughton announced. 'Five days hence. There will be a death, which will cause much sorrow.'

'Of course there will,' spat Swaddell. 'We live in the biggest city in the world. Someone will also die today, Sunday, Monday, Tuesday, Wednesday and Friday.'

'Who?' called Eliza, alarmed. 'Did you see that in your vision?'

'Naturally,' replied Mother Broughton loftily. 'It will be an important messenger – someone who carries vital news and makes it public. A diplomat, perhaps.'

'George Downing is due home next week,' gulped Swaddell. 'Our ambassador in the United Provinces. We are expecting him to bring detailed intelligence on the enemy, and there will be much sorrow if *he* dies, because we are desperate for the military advantages his report will provide. I had better send word for him to be on his guard.'

Chaloner would not be sorry if Downing met an untimely end. The man was selfish, duplicitous, greedy and unreliable, and it was largely because of him that England had declared war on the Dutch in the first place.

'The second will be on Good Friday,' Mother Broughton went on, and dropped her voice to make her next words full of dark foreboding, 'which falls on the thirteenth day of the month in the year sixteen sixty-six.'

'She is a charlatan,' scoffed Chaloner, as the crowd exchanged fearful glances. 'How can people not see through these clumsy theatrics?'

'There will be a rain of fire, which will destroy the wicked,' Mother Broughton informed everyone confidently. 'It will be followed by a darkness that will cover the entire city. I have already told you that there will be wailing and gnashing of teeth on Good Friday. This is why.'

'Her predictions are vague enough to mean anything, yet contain enough detail to make them seem convincing,' observed Chaloner contemptuously. 'She is crafty.'

'Yes, damn her,' muttered Swaddell. 'Which means

my colleagues must squander precious time keeping an eye on her. What is wrong with the woman? Can she not see that we should be concentrating on the Dutch, not wasting our time on the likes of her?'

'The third thing I foresaw will happen on Easter Sunday,' Mother Broughton finished. 'And it is this: the wicked will be gone and the righteous will take their places. There will be such happiness that even the Sun will dance for joy.'

'That will be a sight, Tom,' said Swaddell, as the seer was helped off her box to tumultuous applause. 'Let us hope you and I will be in a position to appreciate it.'

As Swaddell was worried by the notion that Ambassador Downing might be assassinated, he asked Chaloner to wait an hour before tackling the Clarkes, while he mingled with the crowd to see if he could learn anything else of use. Chaloner agreed, as all the window shutters at Chaloner Court were closed, suggesting the Clarkes were still abed. Moreover, the delay provided an opportunity for him to survey Newcastle House without Swaddell at his side.

There was nothing much to see at the front of the ducal residence, so he did a circuit around the outside. The grounds were extensive and surrounded by high walls. On one side was a large gate leading to the stables, which were a glorious creation of honey-coloured stone, set prettily around a cobbled yard. Chaloner recalled that horses were the Duke's passion, and that they were said to live in greater luxury than most Londoners.

The gate was open, so Chaloner stepped through it, aiming to strike up a conversation with one of the many grooms, after which he hoped he would have a clearer picture of the Duchess and her husband. He was just deciding which lad to waylay when four men emerged from one of the stalls. He recognised two. The first was Baron Lucas, the Duchess's curmudgeonly brother. The second was Andrew Clayton, the younger and more sullen of the Duke's two stewards.

'I do not understand why it failed to work,' Lucas was grumbling angrily. 'You must have done something wrong.'

'I followed your instructions to the letter,' countered Clayton, and indicated the other two men with a curt wave of his hand. 'If you do not believe me, ask Booth and Liddell here.'

'They are your lickspittles,' said Lucas, regarding them with haughty disdain. 'Ergo, they will say whatever you want me to hear. Their testimony means nothing.'

'You insult two good men,' objected Clayton, incensed. 'Booth is vicar of St Quentin's near Nottingham, while Liddell is a respected horse-trader. Their integrity is beyond question.'

'Humph!' spat Lucas, before turning and stamping away.

Chaloner thought the Baron was right to be sceptical, as neither Booth nor Liddell looked trustworthy. The cleric was small, shabby and devious-eyed, while the horse-trader positively oozed guile. In the hope that their spat with Lucas might dispose them to indiscreet gossip, Chaloner strolled up to them.

'Baron Lucas is a difficult man,' he began, all friendly sympathy. 'Nothing seems to please him, so it cannot be easy to work in Newcastle House.'

'He is a fool,' growled Clayton, recognising Chaloner from White Hall and greeting him with a bow. 'He bought a bay horse last month, but the Duke said her coat is too dark. Instead of accepting the fact, Lucas thinks to lighten her colour by feeding her white food.'

'He is in the Royal Society,' put in Vicar Booth, making it sound sinister, 'and is of the opinion that anything can be achieved through science, even changing the hue of a horse's fur.'

'Hair,' corrected Liddell. 'The poor beast has been eating bleached oats ever since.'

'Why did you agree to do it?' asked Chaloner, feeling they should have refused for the horse's sake.

'Because if we had not, his grumbles would have driven his sister – the Duchess – to buy him another,' explained Clayton. 'And that would be unfair on Viscount Mansfield. She spends money like water, but it is not hers to waste – it is Mansfield's inheritance. The poor man will have nothing left if she is permitted to squander it as she pleases.'

'I see,' said Chaloner, recalling from the encounter in White Hall that Clayton was firmly Mansfield's man. 'Are the Duke's finances so precarious then?'

If they were, he thought, glancing around at the beautiful stables, then he should not be splashing out on fancy new accommodations for his equine friends.

'He still has massive debts from the wars,' explained Clayton. 'Mansfield wants his father to pay them off, so the estate will be in credit when the old man dies.'

'It is all Steward Topp's fault,' sniffed Vicar Booth. 'He encourages the Duchess to spend money on things she does not need, just to hurt poor Mansfield.'

'Well, Topp does hail from merchant stock,' said Clayton cattily. 'So what do you expect? I imagine he siphons off a percentage of all her purchases for himself.

111

The man is a rogue, and I fail to understand why she trusts him.'

'She trusts him because he is married to Eliza,' growled Liddell. 'And Eliza is her closest and most valued friend. I liked Eliza until she came to London, but living here has turned her opinionated.'

'She listens too much to Sarah Shawe,' put in Clayton, pursing his lips, 'who thinks women should have the same rights as men. She should not be permitted to say such things in public. It is dangerous, and a direct challenge to God's authority.'

'Of course, Sarah Shawe is not nearly as bad an influence on Eliza as the Duchess is,' gossiped Booth. '*She* should be in Bedlam. I read her books, and I was appalled. They are the rantings of a lunatic, and should never have been published.'

'I read one of them, too,' said Liddell. 'It was mostly gibberish to me, but I did understand that she wants the world turned upside down again, this time by having women at the top and us men at the bottom.'

'I do not suppose you have heard her mention Thomas Chiffinch, have you?' asked Chaloner, the moment he could insert a question into their venomous tirades.

'Only to remark that she disliked him,' replied Clayton. 'Well, of course she did! He told his friends that it is wrong for women to publish books for public consumption. She was livid.'

'Was she?' fished Chaloner.

'Oh, yes! I imagine she is delighted that he is no longer in a position to insult her.'

'She is not the only one,' said Booth. 'Mansfield is sure that Chiffinch cheated him of fifty pounds when they played backgammon on Thursday night, and he hates parting with money. And who can blame him when the Duke keeps him on such a meagre allowance?'

'Then why did he risk fifty pounds of it on a bet?' asked Chaloner pointedly.

'Because of the Duchess,' explained Clayton. 'She won against Chiffinch, and Mansfield is a better player than her. He assumed he would emerge victorious, with a tidy sum to supplement his income. Poor Mansfield. She injures him at every turn.'

They returned to the subject of the overly dark horse at that point, so Chaloner took his leave, his mind full of questions. Would a middle-aged Duchess really dispatch a man who disparaged her? Or would her feeble stepson kill a cheat? Suddenly, he was glad Swaddell would be working with him. The assassin could share the blame if they found answers that might not be to the authorities' liking.

By the time Chaloner returned to the green, Swaddell had finished his eavesdropping, but before either could tell the other what he had learned, Newcastle House's front door opened, and a number of people filed out. All began to walk towards a waiting coach. The Duke was in the lead, but went to examine the horses first. Behind him were the Duchess and her stepson Mansfield, quarrelling, while the obsequious Topp scurried at their heels.

She stretched out a hand to touch Mansfield's arm, an attempt at affection that he killed dead by knocking it away. The expression of contempt on his face made her bristle. In revenge, she shouted something to her husband, who turned and laughed. Fuming, Mansfield shoved past her, jumped into the coach and ordered the driver to take him to White Hall immediately. Clearly, if this command was followed, his father and stepmother would be left without transport. The driver glanced nervously at the Duke.

'Go, you damned fool!' Mansfield screeched. 'Or look for another post.'

The Duke rolled his eyes and nodded at the driver, who flicked his reins to urge the horses into a trot. The Duchess murmured something to Topp, who hurried off towards the stables. The steward returned a few moments later with Liddell and two prancing stallions. With a whoop of joy, the Duke dashed towards them, and there followed a lot of serious discussion as he contemplated which one to ride. The Duchess watched with an indulgent smile.

'He has an affliction,' Swaddell explained to Chaloner. 'An uncontrolled trembling in his limbs. His physicians have forbidden riding, which is a cruel blow to a man born in the saddle. The Duchess has made him very happy by allowing him to ignore their strictures for once.'

'Then let us hope he does not topple off,' said Chaloner. 'Or Mansfield will accuse her of trying to kill him.'

'Of course, Mansfield did himself no favours by hogging the family coach,' Swaddell went on. 'His father is unlikely to forget such selfishness, and the Duchess certainly will not.'

Eventually, the Duke made his selection, climbed into the saddle and showed off with a series of fancy manoeuvres. His lady cooed and clapped appreciatively, causing him to flush with pleasure. Then, with Liddell on the second horse, he cantered away, yelling over his shoulder that the spare coach would not be long, and that he would wait for her at the other end.

As the spare carriage did not materialise immediately, Chaloner took the opportunity to go and pay his respects to the Duchess, aiming to dissuade her from visiting the charnel house later – assuming she had not seen sense and reconsidered already, of course. She was talking to Eliza Topp, who had come to keep her company while she waited. As he approached, he heard they were talking about the Red Bull tavern.

'Eliza has established a school there,' the Duchess informed Chaloner, although he had not asked. Indeed, he had not even had time to bow or utter even the briefest of greetings. 'For intelligent ladies.'

Eliza smiled, and took her arm in a gesture of easy familiarity, which showed they really were friends rather than mistress and servant. 'And the Duchess is generous with money for books. Perhaps you would care to visit, Mr Chaloner, and see our good work for yourself. Come tomorrow. You are sure to learn a great deal, as all our students have very keen minds.'

Before Chaloner could respond, there came a wail of anguish. A woman was walking past carrying a cloth-covered basket over her arm. Hot on her heels was Molly. Sobbing in distress, the chicken girl tried to grab the basket, to which the woman responded by kicking at her. Chaloner went to intervene before the child was hurt. Unwilling to do battle with someone who might kick back, the woman backed off, although she did not relinquish the basket. She tried to stalk off with it, but was forced to stop when the Duchess herself barred her way.

'I have warned you before,' the Duchess said coldly. 'Molly is simple, and responds to kindness, not abuse, so why are you—'

'Dutch Jane has *stolen* Audrey, lady,' wept Molly,

distraught as she pointed an accusing finger. 'My best chicken. She is going to sell her and keep all the money for herself.'

'I am not!' declared Dutch Jane indignantly. 'The little half-wit is mistaken, as usual.'

An avian cluck from inside the basket made a liar of her. Molly lunged and pulled off the cloth. Underneath sat a pretty brown hen, which the girl retrieved to cuddle protectively.

'She put it there herself, to get me into trouble,' declared Dutch Jane defiantly.

The Duchess regarded her in distaste. 'Molly is incapable of implementing such a sly scheme. Nor would she risk harming one of her birds.'

Dutch Jane shrugged carelessly. 'Then you explain how it got there.'

The Duchess blinked her astonishment at the impudent response, but then her expression hardened. 'You are dismissed from my service with immediate effect.'

Dutch Jane was not expecting this, and her jaw dropped. 'But—'

'I do not tolerate thieves and liars,' the Duchess went on crisply. 'Or disobedience. I issued an express order that none of our poultry were to be harmed until I have ascertained whether they are capable of intelligent thought.'

'They are, lady,' Molly assured her. 'They are all very clever. Not like Dutch Jane, who thinks I will not notice if she filches one of them.'

'Yes, Molly,' said Eliza kindly. 'Now take Audrey back to her friends.'

Molly scurried away, leaving Dutch Jane standing with her fists clenched and her face as black as thunder. Eliza

116

clearly thought the woman represented a danger to the Duchess, because she stepped forward protectively.

'You cannot dismiss me,' snarled Dutch Jane. 'You brought me to this country, so you are morally obliged to look after me. You cannot expect me to find my own way home.'

'You should have thought of that before stealing birds and ignoring orders,' retorted the Duchess, unmoved. 'Now, be gone before I have you thrown in gaol. Hah! Here is our transport. Eliza, your husband is a treasure. I shall see *you* at three o'clock.'

The last remark was addressed to Chaloner, and was accompanied by a meaningful wink.

'You have an appointment with him, Your Loveliness?' asked Topp, overhearing. 'Then you cannot keep it. You promised to spend all afternoon with the Queen.'

'She will not miss me for an hour,' averred the Duchess. 'And my assignation with him is a matter of great scientific import. I shall include any discoveries in the next edition of my *Philosophical and Physical Opinions*.'

'That would distress the dead man's family,' said Chaloner quickly. 'So stay with the Queen today, Your Grace, and I will see that Wiseman writes you a full report of his—'

'No,' interrupted the Duchess, in a tone that told him further argument would be futile. 'I *will* watch the surgeon at work. Topp, assist me into the carriage.'

Topp hastened to oblige, then handed Eliza in beside her. He scrambled in last, although not before shooting Chaloner a sympathetic glance – the kind that suggested he was used to his mistress making up her own mind and then not being budged from it.

'She is insane,' spat Dutch Jane furiously, as the carriage rattled away. 'No low deed is beneath her, despite her pretensions to being a great lady. And what does she expect us to eat if we are no longer allowed to slaughter chickens?'

'Try bread and cheese,' suggested Chaloner. 'But what will you do now you are dismissed? Return to the United Provinces?'

'That is none of your business,' snapped Dutch Jane unpleasantly. 'However, I can tell you one thing for sure: I am not going anywhere until I get revenge for this outrage. The Duchess will regret treating *me* like scum.'

Chaloner hoped the Duchess's staff would be on their guard.

The bells in nearby St James's Church were ringing for the noonday service by the time Chaloner and Swaddell arrived at the Clarkes' house. They walked up its short drive, through a neatly manicured garden that was unrecognisable as the tangled wilderness Chaloner remembered from his youth. The door was opened by a liveried maid, who ushered them inside and asked them to wait while she went to see if her employers were receiving visitors.

'So this is your ancestral home,' said Swaddell, looking around enviously. 'You must have been devastated when you lost it at the Restoration.'

'Not at all,' said Chaloner firmly, unwilling for Swaddell to report *that* to Williamson. 'First, it was never owned by my branch of the family, and second, it has been years since I was last here – so many years that virtually none of it is familiar.'

It was the truth: the house was so different that it might have been another building. Gone were the dark wooden panels, and in their place were fresh white walls.

The heavy oak stairs had been removed to make way for an elegant French creation, while the rough flagstone floors had been replaced with modern tiles. Absently, Chaloner noticed that several of the tiles were already chipped, while the plaster was flaking in one or two places – the Clarkes had replaced substance with style, and although the improvements looked pretty, they were inferior and would not survive the test of time.

The maid reappeared and indicated that they were to follow her to a reception room at the rear of the house. This was a handsome chamber with windows that overlooked the main garden. Chaloner was bemused to note that all the original portraits still adorned the walls, but the identifying plaques at the bottom had been amended, so that his ancestors were now those of the new owners. He smothered a smile, wondering what his stuffy old grandfather would have thought about being passed off as 'Sir Ignatius Clarke'.

The physician was sitting at a table in the window, pretending to read a medical tome. He was a nondescript man with mousy features, who had attempted to render himself more interesting by donning glorious clothes and an impressive wig. It had not worked, and he looked as though he had been at someone else's wardrobe, as well as someone else's forebears.

'Mr Swaddell from the office of the Spymaster General, and Mr Chaloner, Gentleman Usher to the Lord Chancellor,' announced the maid, before backing out and closing the door behind her. The way she intoned the introductions suggested that she was impressed by their credentials, although the blood drained from her master's face.

'Chaloner?' he gulped. 'With the Spymaster's assassin?

Please! I have done nothing wrong! I bought this house perfectly legally. You cannot demand it back!'

'I know,' Chaloner assured him hastily. 'My family has no claim on it now.' He flailed around for a compliment, to put him at ease. 'You have made it very attractive.'

Clarke relaxed slightly. 'Thank you. We spent a fortune on repairs, especially the roof. It leaked horribly, but the new one keeps us lovely and dry.'

'I should like to live in a house like this,' said Swaddell wistfully. 'Perhaps my future wife will provide me with one.'

'You are betrothed?' asked Clarke politely.

'Not yet,' replied Swaddell. 'But I am always on the lookout for suitable candidates, so if you happen to know any, send them my way.'

Clarke was patently horrified by the notion of Swaddell on the marriage market, so Chaloner tried to change the subject before they were thrown out.

'We are here to talk about—' he began.

'You aim to question my decision regarding the Queen,' interrupted Clarke, eyes narrowing angrily. 'But it is *right* to keep her mother's death a secret. She is fragile after yet another failed pregnancy, and it would be cruel to heap more misery upon her. Besides, it is not for the Lord Chancellor and Williamson to meddle in medical matters.'

'We shall tell them you said so,' drawled Swaddell, much to the physician's alarm, while Chaloner was tempted to point out that the Queen was likely to hear the news anyway, given White Hall's propensity for loose-tongued gossip, and in a way that would cause her a lot more pain than if broken gently. But it really was none of his business, and time was passing.

120

'We want to ask you about Chiffinch, not the Queen,' he said briskly. 'I understand you inspected the body.'

Clarke nodded as he struggled to regain his composure. 'Yesterday morning. I was in the Shield Gallery, handing out remedies for overindulgence, when I heard that Chiffinch was in need of medical attention. I ran to the cockpit, and arrived to see a large number of people already there. None had dared go near him, though. They were afraid of the plague.'

'Chiffinch was alive and well an hour earlier,' said Swaddell. 'Surely they know the disease does not strike that quickly?'

Chaloner doubted they were aware of any such thing, given that they had all raced to safer pastures at the first mention of buboes.

'Of course it can,' countered Clarke, thus proving that he had been one of them, despite the fact that, as a *medicus*, he should have been better informed. 'However, Chiffinch died of an impostume in the breast. I felt it under my fingers as I examined his corpse. He must have known it was there, but he neglected to seek my help, so it killed him.'

'What kind of—' began Swaddell, but Clarke cut across him.

'When I finished my inspection, I sent one of the onlookers to carry the news to the King, and arranged for the body to be removed to the charnel house. Then I returned to my duties in the Shield Gallery.'

'You played backgammon with Chiffinch the night before he died,' said Chaloner. 'How did he seem then?'

Panic showed in Clarke's face as it dawned on him that this question had no good answer. If he admitted that he had failed to spot a serious ailment hours before

121

it killed a man, he would appear incompetent, but if he declared that Chiffinch was fit and well, it would make his diagnosis of a deadly impostume unlikely.

'He was a politician,' he said eventually, 'and thus a skilled dissembler. He could convince anyone of anything, so, naturally, he was careful to conceal symptoms that might have aroused my professional attention.'

'He deliberately withheld evidence of ill health?' Swaddell's voice dripped disbelief. 'Why would he do such a thing?'

Clarke shrugged uncomfortably. 'Perhaps he did not want to be forcibly retired, so that a younger, fitter man could be appointed in his place. And he was right to be uneasy, because that is exactly what *did* happen, within minutes of me declaring him dead.'

'Are you suggesting that we arrest Will for bringing about his brother's death?' asked Swaddell keenly.

Clarke eyed him with dislike. 'You twist my words. I do *not* accuse Will. He is a good man, who loved his sibling dearly.'

'Can you tell us anything about Chiffinch's last evening?' asked Chaloner, after a short silence, during which all three men reflected on the fact that Will was as far from being 'a good man' as it was possible to be, and that he probably had not loved his brother either. 'For example, did you witness any quarrels or hot words?'

'No, but all my attention was on Baron Lucas – a florid man of a certain age who might soon require medical expertise. I am always looking for new clients . . . I mean, people to help.'

Chaloner moved to another subject. 'We have been told that your wife found the body. What was she doing in the cockpit at seven o'clock in the morning?'

Clarke regarded him coolly. 'That is her business and none of yours. However, I hope you do not intend to pester her for answers. You will leave her be, if you are gentlemen.'

'Chaloner is a gentleman,' said Swaddell with one of his crocodilian smiles. 'But I am not, so *I* have no objection to pestering women. Where is she?'

'I refuse to say,' declared Clarke stoutly. 'It is my duty to protect her.'

Swaddell took a menacing step towards him. 'Then perhaps I shall pester you instead.'

'In that case,' gulped Clarke, 'she will be in the orangery. Follow me.'

There had not been an orangery when the previous owners had been in residence, and Chaloner was not sure there should be one now. It looked odd, tacked on to the rear of the house, like a very long lean-to with a plethora of windows. Access was via a door from another reception room, although judging by the way the lintel sagged, the builders had chosen to punch through a load-bearing wall. He eased under it quickly, wondering how long it would be before the Clarkes experienced structural problems with their so-called improvements.

Inside, the orangery was crammed with exotic plants in pots. The large windows allowed the light to flood in, while the air was moist, and filled with the aroma of lemons. Chaloner recalled the outrageous Cobbe declaring Fanny to be an excellent judge of the fruit, and if she grew them, that was likely to be true. He thought he heard the chunter of chickens from deeper in the foliage, but told himself that this was unlikely.

Fanny Clarke was fast asleep in the sunshine when

123

they arrived, slumped on a bench with her mouth hanging open. She wore a blue silk mantua – a kind of dressing-gown – and her hair fell loose down her back, brown and plentiful. Some embroidery sat neglected in her lap.

When she did not wake at once, her husband poked her. Her initial confusion turned to horror when she saw she had visitors, and she immediately began to berate him for showing them in while she was improperly attired. Clarke interrupted her curtly.

'They want to know why you were in the cockpit yesterday morning,' he said, glaring at her. 'I told you to stay away from the place, and you should have listened to me. Now you have landed yourself in trouble. Tell them why you were there.'

Fanny blushed and her hands began to tremble. 'I would rather not say.'

'You must,' said Swaddell sternly. 'Or we shall conclude that *you* killed Chiffinch.'

Fanny gaped her shock. 'That is a terrible thing to say! Why would I do him harm? Besides, no one killed him. He died of an impostume. Ask Timothy.'

'His death *was* natural,' said Clarke between gritted teeth. 'As I have already told you.'

'So why were you in the cockpit?' demanded Swaddell, ignoring Clarke and concentrating on Fanny so intently that she looked frightened. Chaloner felt sorry for her.

'If I say, you will think me deranged,' she whispered wretchedly. 'Worse, you will tell everyone and I shall be a laughing stock. My reputation as a respectable lady . . .'

'Better that than the alternative,' said Swaddell menacingly. 'Which is that we arrest you for refusing to cooperate with an official inquiry.'

124

'For God's sake, Fanny,' snapped Clarke, 'just tell them. And in future, perhaps you will accept that your husband knows best when he forbids you to do something.'

Fanny hung her head. 'I went to see if there were any injured birds to rescue,' she mumbled uncomfortably, 'from the fighting the night before. Their keepers do not bother with the damaged ones, you see. They just leave them to suffer.'

As if on cue, a cockerel strutted out from among the potted foliage. It was limping, missing an eye, and wore a bandage around its middle. It gave the humans an appraising look, before disappearing back to its tropical foraging grounds.

'She brings them to me for medical care,' explained Clarke with a long-suffering sigh. 'I succeed with some, but others are beyond even my superior skills. She is upset when they die, but I am a physician, not a bird-healer. A very good *royal* physician.'

Wiseman also bragged about his abilities, leading Chaloner to wonder if instruction in brazen boasting was included in the medical curriculum, perhaps to disguise the fact that most practitioners had no idea what they were doing.

'I hate cockfighting,' said Fanny with a small spurt of defiance. 'It is disgusting and so are the people who enjoy it. If I were a man, I would campaign to see it stopped.'

Chaloner felt himself warm to her. 'Do you visit the cockpit after every fight?'

She winced. 'Unfortunately, there are too many of them, and I can only go when my Court duties allow.'

'She sews for the Queen,' put in Clarke, pride in his voice as he indicated the embroidery in her lap. 'As you can see, no one else can make such beautiful stitches.

125

And it is, of course, a far more genteel pastime than rescuing wounded birds.'

He shot her a pointed look, but she did not see it, because a different cockerel had appeared through the leaves, and was pecking at her feet in the hope of treats.

'You were in the Shield Gallery the night that Chiffinch died,' said Chaloner, watching her feed the bird raisins, an expensive import from Spain that most Londoners would never taste. 'And you played backgammon with him. How did he seem to you at the time?'

'She cannot answer that,' said Clarke at once. 'She is not a physician.'

'We do not want a medical opinion,' said Swaddell, eyeing Clarke with such venom that the man took an involuntary step back. 'We want her observations.'

Fanny considered the question carefully. 'Well, he spent most of our game denigrating the Duchess of Newcastle. He disliked her intensely – her dangerous views on religion, politics and philosophy, her outrageous clothes, her outlandish behaviour. If she ever heard half of what he said about her, she would never appear in decent society again.'

'Did you speak to him after that exchange?' asked Chaloner.

'Yes, when he came to demand five pounds from me, which he claimed I owed for losing to him.' Fanny gave a brief smile of satisfaction. 'But I disapprove of gambling and would never stake money on the outcome of a game. He swore and argued, but eventually conceded that I was in the right.'

'So he was angry with you?'

'A little, but he had the last word, because he was able to inform me that he had already wrested twenty pounds from my husband, who *had* agreed to wager with him.' She gave Clarke an arch stare.

'I had no choice,' said Clarke defensively. 'I cannot take a moral stance on gambling, because I rely on men like Chiffinch for business. It would be foolish to alienate them by denouncing what they love. Besides, the King enjoys betting, and if he likes it, then so must I.'

'His Majesty likes breaking his marriage vows with harlots as well,' retorted Fanny acidly. 'But I sincerely hope you do not intend to follow *that* example.'

'Of course not,' gulped Clarke. 'Harlots indeed!'

Fanny gave him another cool glance, then picked up her sewing. Her rapidly flying needle revealed so much skill that Chaloner was momentarily mesmerised by it.

'I dislike the immorality that abounds at Court,' she confided as she worked. 'I fear it will lead to trouble. The only courtier with decent principles is the Earl of Clarendon.'

Much good it did him, thought Chaloner caustically, given that it rendered him no more popular with Londoners than the debauched monkeys of the Cockpit Club.

'Were there any further exchanges between you and Chiffinch that night?' he asked.

'No, and I spent the rest of the evening with Lucy Bodvil and Mary Robartes, discussing how we would rather be at home in bed. None of us enjoy these riotous late nights.'

Chaloner knew Lucy Bodvil and Mary Robartes would not. They were the staid, middle-aged wives of ambitious officials, who were obliged to accompany their spouses to courtly functions but who usually found some quiet corner where they sewed and talked. They were an exception to the rule that all courtiers were dedicated hedonists with no redeeming qualities. Behind his wife's back, Clarke grimaced his disdain for such uninteresting company.

'They are your friends?' asked Chaloner.

Fanny nodded. 'There are half a dozen of us who deplore drinking and gambling; we always seek each other out on occasions like the one on Thursday.' She went on to name four or five other worthy matrons, all of whom tended to be mocked for their lack of conversation and devotion to the mundane. 'Then yesterday morning, I rose early and went to the chapel for my morning devotions Afterwards, I hurried to the cockpit to see about the birds.'

'Alone?' asked Chaloner.

Fanny winced. 'Yes, unfortunately. My friends do not share my fondness for poultry.'

'Nor does your husband,' put in Clarke pointedly.

'I thought the cockpit was empty,' continued Fanny, 'but then I saw someone lying in the middle of the arena. It was Mr Chiffinch. I was so shocked that I forgot my errand of mercy and fled. On my way out, I collided with Captain Rolt, who had come to look for a lost button. He bade me sit down and take some deep breaths while he went inside to look for himself. Moments later, he dashed out and ordered a passing servant to fetch a *medicus*.'

'Did he indeed?' mused Chaloner. 'He did not mention any of this to us.'

Which was curious, as Rolt loved recognition and would have gained a lot of it by declaring that he had taken control of the situation when Fanny had emerged in a fluster. Had *he* killed Chiffinch, then realised a button had been torn off in the struggle, so had gone back to retrieve it before it incriminated him? Or was his silence that of a gentleman aiming to protect a lady from being mocked for panicking at the sight of a corpse? Regardless, Chaloner decided to speak to Rolt again at the first opportunity.

'Before you bolted, did you notice if Chiffinch was breathing?' he asked.

Fanny shook her head. 'It was obvious that he was dead.' She shuddered. 'It was a terrible thing . . . A man I had seen alive a few hours before, suddenly all cold and still and . . .'

'You can rescue injured birds, but corpses unnerve you?' asked Swaddell sceptically.

Fanny's expression was bleak. '*Human* corpses do. And Mr Chiffinch . . . well, he . . . he made a *noise*. My husband says escaping air . . .'

'Corpses release some awful sounds,' explained Clarke with an amused smirk. 'Fanny understands that now, but she did not at the time. Hence her alarm.'

Perhaps Rolt *had* been sparing her blushes then, thought Chaloner, because this was certainly a tale that would be repeated with relish by White Hall's prurient inhabitants. As she was looking mortified, he moved to another matter.

'Rolt tells me that you and Bess Widdrington went to the Red Bull the other day. It—'

'Did you, Fanny?' interrupted Clarke, startled. 'I wish you had not.'

'Captain Rolt is mistaken,' said Fanny firmly. 'It would be most improper for me to visit a common tavern. But if you want someone who does not care about such things, talk to the Duchess of Newcastle. *She* would have no qualms about frequenting that sort of establishment. Indeed, last week, she expressed a wish to watch the Cockpit Club at their revels.' She shuddered again.

'Well, she got her wish last night,' said Chaloner. 'She appeared with her retinue.'

Fanny looked astonished, then thoughtful, and Chaloner could almost see her mind at work. Clearly, the Duchess appearing at the murder scene was suspicious in her eyes.

'Perhaps your Earl should teach the woman how to behave,' said Clarke, pursing his lips. 'She is a menace to decent society with her peculiar opinions. For example, she told me that women should abandon their homes to work like men; that they should endeavour to be as vain, ambitious and greedy as men; and that telling lies is good, because it sparks debate.'

'I have had enough of revolutionary ideas,' said Fanny tiredly. 'We have suffered far too many of them over the last thirty years, and all I want now is a country that is stable, safe and decent, where everyone knows his or her place.'

'Quite,' said Clarke tersely. 'Which is *not* in the cockpit looking for injured cockerels.'

'Yes, dear,' said Fanny, contrite.

They had taken longer in Clerkenwell than Chaloner had anticipated, and he saw he was going to be late for his appointment at the charnel house. He hurried to John Street, where there were usually hackney carriages for hire. Swaddell fell in at his side.

'I did not take to the Clarkes,' the assassin declared. 'He is a pompous fool with an inflated sense of his own worth, while she is a prim bore with inflexible ideas.'

130

'True, but Fanny has one thing in her favour,' said Chaloner. 'She saves injured birds.'

'I suppose,' conceded Swaddell. 'Now, tell me what you make of the tale Captain Rolt told us – that Fanny and Bess Widdrington visited the Red Bull together. I cannot see that pair being comfortable in each other's company: one is a rake, the other is a dullard.'

'They have both denied it, so I am not sure what to believe. We will ask Rolt about it again when we next see him, although I doubt it is relevant to Chiffinch's death.'

'If it is, I shall prise the truth out of him. I shall just threaten to slit his throat unless he cooperates.' Swaddell saw Chaloner's expression of distaste and hastened to defend himself. 'I am not saying that I *will* slit his throat, but most folk confess if they believe it is a possibility.'

'You can try, but Rolt earned his captaincy by taking part in battles, unlike most courtiers. He may not be so easily intimidated.'

'He will,' averred Swaddell confidently. 'I shall do it now in fact, when I shall also demand to know why he did not mention being at the cockpit when Fanny hurtled out. It is suspicious that he neglected to mention the central role he played in the incident.'

'I agree. There is something distasteful about him. Brodrick said he is all things to all men, and it was an astute observation. With him, I always have the feeling that he is waiting to see which way the wind blows before committing himself to anything.'

Swaddell's eyes narrowed. 'His association with Widdrington has already cost him a horse, so he will be looking to make good on his losses. I do not trust him an inch. But what about you, Tom? Where are you going in such haste?'

131

'To the charnel house, to learn once and for all if Chiffinch was murdered. Wiseman expects the answer to be yes, but I have been unable to corner him to ask why.'

Swaddell looked more interested than was nice. 'Perhaps I should do that. You can corner Rolt instead.'

It was tempting, but Wiseman would never countenance such an arrangement because he disliked Swaddell and would baulk at being in his company. Reluctantly, Chaloner decided he had no choice but to endure the ordeal himself.

Chapter 5

The Westminster Charnel House had once been an unprepossessing place, situated at the end of a narrow alley and sandwiched between a coal-merchant's warehouse and a granary. The plague had changed all that, as its owner, Mr Kersey, had grown fabulously rich by accepting property that no one else dared touch.

He had bought the granary and converted it into a museum for all the artefacts he had collected from the dead over the years. More recently, he had purchased the warehouse, too, which he had demolished and replaced with a pretty cobbled yard, complete with ornamental trees and tethering for horses – his charnel house was a popular attraction for London's wealthy elite, who paid a fortune to go in and look around.

The main building had two elegant rooms at the front. The smaller one was an office, where Kersey recorded all the 'guests' who passed through his hands. The larger one was a parlour where he received grieving friends and relations; Chaloner had always been impressed that the same gentle courtesy was extended to paupers and nobles alike. Behind these was the mortuary proper, a long, low-ceilinged chamber crammed with wooden tables. Each body was respectfully covered with a clean grey blanket.

Kersey was a neat, dapper little man, always impeccably dressed. There was gold thread in his handsome mauve long-coat, while French lace frothed at his throat and wrists. He was plumper than the last time Chaloner had met him, and his cheeks were pink with rude health and vitality. Business was good.

'I am glad to see you home,' he said warmly, gripping Chaloner's hand. 'Although I hope you will not be crushing any more rebellions. The one in January promised to teach our cowardly rulers a lesson, and I was sorry when you thwarted it.'

Uncomfortably, Chaloner recalled that Kersey was one of those who had been particularly outraged by the fact that the King and his Court had fled the moment the plague had started to take hold in London. He could not imagine what the charnel house had been like when the disease was at its peak, so did not blame Kersey for resenting the fact that his city had been so selfishly abandoned by those whose duty it was to protect it.

'I have visitors at the moment,' the charnel-house keeper went on, and grimaced his distaste. 'Courtiers. I despise them all, but I like the colour of their gold, so I avenge myself on their spinelessness during the plague by charging them a fortune for guided tours.'

Chaloner glanced past him into the parlour, and saw he had been taking a glass of wine – which he knew from experience would be of excellent quality – with three men from the Cockpit Club: Colonel Widdrington, the drunken Ashley and the massive, apelike Tooley. He started to back away, having no wish to exchange words with them, but they had seen him.

'Have you come to view the corpse?' called Widdrington, yawning as he stood. 'Good luck with that! This fellow refuses to let us anywhere near it.'

'Which is unfair,' growled Ashley, who had to be helped to his feet by Tooley, suggesting he had swallowed more of Kersey's wine than was polite. 'We offered him good money.'

'And it is not as if we are ghouls,' put in Tooley indignantly. 'We came because we want to join the Royal Society, and assessing cadavers will show us to be men with enquiring minds.'

'I am sure the Royal Society will be delighted to enrol such dedicated students,' said Kersey smoothly, although Chaloner heard the disdain behind the words. 'But as I have already explained, Mr Chiffinch's family has requested privacy.'

'So what?' demanded Widdrington petulantly. 'I shall not mind people admiring *my* corpse when the time comes, so why let them keep Chiffinch to themselves? It is hardly reasonable.'

'We always accede to the family's wishes,' said Kersey, although Chaloner did not know how he kept his calm with the man. 'I am afraid my hands are tied.'

'Perhaps Will dispatched his brother,' slurred Ashley slyly, 'and he aims to conceal his guilt by preventing anyone from seeing his victim's body. After all, he did leap into his shoes with unseemly haste, before the rest of us could even *consider* doing it ourselves.'

'I would not have minded one of those posts,' sighed Tooley, although Chaloner suspected that even the King, no great judge of character, would have had reservations about appointing *him* as Keeper of the Jewels. 'And if Will *is* a killer, perhaps we should be more picky about

135

who we enrol in the Cockpit Club from now on. For example, Rolt is not really our kind of fellow. He—'

'We should leave,' interrupted Widdrington with a bored yawn. 'The King promised to come to our wrestling tournament tonight, so we had better ensure that everything is ready.'

'Just one question before you go,' said Chaloner. 'You were seen walking across the Great Court with Chiffinch shortly before he died. How did that come about?'

'It is none of your damned business!' declared Tooley angrily. 'How dare you try to quiz us like common criminals. You have no right!'

Widdrington raised a soft, white hand. 'Steady now, Tooley. We have nothing to hide, and we do not want the Earl's rat to go away thinking we are responsible for giving Chiffinch his impostume. I say we let him ask his questions.'

Chaloner took him at his word, and launched into an interrogation that had Tooley and Ashley huffing their outrage at its sharp, discourteous tone, although Widdrington stubbornly declined to be ruffled.

'Why were you with Chiffinch in the Great Court just before he died?' he asked again.

'Our paths crossed,' shrugged Widdrington. 'By accident, not design. We kept company with him until he trotted through the gate towards King Street, and we went to the Banqueting House.'

'What did you talk about? The money you owed for losing to him at backgammon?'

Widdrington smiled pleasantly. 'Yes, he did mention our debts. We promised to settle them, and schedules for payment have since been negotiated with his next of kin.'

'What else did you discuss?'

136

Widdrington's grin did not waver. 'The weather, the King's new horse, the fact that a mutual friend is about to give birth, even though she has not seen her husband in a year.'

'How did Chiffinch seem to you?'

'As he always was,' put in Tooley sourly. 'Smug, boring and quick to give his opinions.'

'His opinions about what?'

'All the people he deplored,' replied Tooley. 'Radicals, prudes, pacifists, women who want schools for girls, Puritan divines, female writers, merrymakers – even though his own brother is the biggest merrymaker of all.'

'He and Will were on bad terms?'

'We would not know,' said Widdrington. 'We rarely saw them together, and when we did, it was Will whose company we preferred.'

'Where were you when news came that Chiffinch was dead?'

'Still in the Banqueting House. We shall stage one of Lord Rochester's plays there soon, and we were discussing the scenery. When we heard what had happened, we hurried to the cockpit to see if we could be of assistance.'

'Our motives were honourable, not ghoulish,' put in Ashley unconvincingly.

'What did you see when you arrived?'

'Chiffinch lying on the floor, surrounded by spectators,' replied Widdrington. 'Although none stood too close, lest he had died of the plague. Then Clarke arrived, diagnosed an impostume, and arranged for the corpse to be brought here.'

Chaloner was learning nothing he did not already know, and had the distinct sense that Widdrington was

137

laughing at his efforts to catch him out in a lie or an inconsistency.

'You may go,' he said, aiming to annoy the man with a summary dismissal. 'Naturally, I shall be verifying your claims with your wives and friends.'

Widdrington laughed. 'I doubt Bess will give you the time of day, but you are welcome to try. Poor Bess! She tries so hard to fit in at Court, but the task is entirely beyond her. I shall send her to the country soon, where she will be much happier.'

'I rather think she is happy here,' said Chaloner, not surprised that Widdrington wanted to be rid of her, but sure he would never have the courage to do it. 'With you.'

Widdrington smirked. 'No woman knows what is best for her, which is why we have marriage – so she will have a man to look after her interests.'

Chaloner found himself imagining what most females of his acquaintance would say to this remark, and suspected it would be nothing polite.

'Besides,' put in Tooley, 'it is unseemly for Bess to trail at his heels all day. Some of our activities are more suitable for men than for ladies.'

The way he leered made Chaloner suspect they were suitable for neither sex.

When the three courtiers had gone, Kersey invited Chaloner to wait for Wiseman in his office, where he provided not only a goblet of his fine wine, but a plate of pastries. Chaloner was hungry, and devoured the lot while the charnel-house keeper regaled him with his own news and gossip, none of which was pertinent to Chiffinch. It was now well past three o'clock, and as the

Duchess had not put in an appearance, he dared hope that she had had second thoughts.

'Wiseman is late,' he said, wishing the surgeon would hurry up so he could leave.

'Good,' said Kersey. 'It was been too long since you and I had a decent natter.'

'I suppose so,' said Chaloner, although there were places he would far rather do it than the charnel house.

'Widdrington and his ghouls are not the first I have sent off empty-handed,' said Kersey with a satisfied grin. 'Dozens of courtiers have come, and it has given me great pleasure to refuse them all – although only *after* they have paid an exorbitant entry fee, naturally.'

'Why does Chiffinch's family want him kept from prying eyes?' asked Chaloner.

'The instruction came from his sister-in-law Barbara,' replied Kersey. 'She is that most rare of specimens – an honourable courtier. She said that Chiffinch was a proud, private man, who would not have wanted to be paraded as a spectacle.'

'Does this mean that Wiseman will be unable to perform?' asked Chaloner worriedly.

'As Surgeon to the Person, he has the right to examine anyone he chooses, whether the family agree or not,' said Kersey. 'Barbara was indignant when I told her, as she is sure Clarke's diagnosis is correct and rejects Wiseman's cries of foul play.'

'Then let us hope she is right,' said Chaloner. 'Incidentally, the Duchess of Newcastle expressed a desire to watch Wiseman at work. Will you repel her, too?'

'I shall. However, I am willing to make an exception for you, as you come in search of the truth, not to amass grisly tales with which to entertain a lot of idle fools.'

Just then, they heard the rattle of wheels outside. Chaloner glanced out of the window, and his heart sank when he recognised the coach. It was the Duchess, arriving fashionably late in the arrogant expectation that Wiseman would not have dared start without her. Steward Topp jumped out first. He helped his wife and the Duchess to alight, escorted them to the door, then darted back to the coach. He climbed in and drew the curtains, making it clear that this was the full extent of *his* participation in the unpalatable venture.

Kersey went to escort them into his parlour. The Duchess held out her hand for Chaloner to kiss, then ignored him, inspecting the room with an interest that bordered on the invasive. Eliza stood anxiously by the door, leaving Chaloner to surmise that it would take very little for her to dash out and join her husband. Loyalty to one's employer and friend had its limits.

'So this is where all the plague victims were brought,' mused the Duchess, a remark that did nothing to soothe Eliza's obviously raddled nerves. 'You must have been very busy.'

'We handled but a fraction,' replied Kersey soberly. 'Most went straight into the pits.'

'How many died, in your opinion?' asked the Duchess. 'I have heard wildly divergent estimates, although I know the official figure stands at sixty-eight thousand.'

'Unfortunately, the old women hired to determine causes of death were easily bribed and often wrong,' explained the charnel-house keeper. 'Then there were those who declined to notify the authorities at all, like Quakers, Anabaptists and Jews. All told, I suspect the toll was nearer a hundred thousand – one in every three souls who lived in the city and its environs.'

140

'Shocking,' breathed the Duchess. 'I am glad I was safely in the country.'

Kersey's mouth tightened into a hard, straight line at this bald admission of self-interest, so Chaloner hastened to change the subject. He liked Kersey, and did not want him in trouble for speaking his mind to someone powerful enough to harm him. Eliza helped by mentioning that Newcastle House had just been completely refurbished, which allowed the Duchess to brag about a special glass ceiling she had designed, so that its hall and ballroom were now flooded with natural light.

'Unfortunately, it is difficult to clean and has started to leak,' she admitted ruefully. 'It was also *very* expensive to install. But I am proud of it, even so.'

When she told them what it had cost, Chaloner struggled not to gape, although Kersey, a wealthy man himself, was unmoved. However, the gleam of malice in her prominent blue eyes led Chaloner to suspect that at least some of her delight in the venture derived from the fact that such a massive outlay would have sent her stepson into paroxysms of impotent rage.

'I am afraid you have had a wasted journey, ma'am,' said Kersey, when the subject of transparent ceilings had been exhausted. 'Mr Chiffinch is not available for inspection. However, I can show you some other corpses, if you are interested.'

'I am,' declared the Duchess. 'So I shall view them while we wait for Mr Wiseman to appear. Then I will watch his examination of Chiffinch – I have made up my mind to do it, which means no one can stop me. Is that wine on the cabinet? Good. You may pour me a glass, and when I have had it, we shall begin the tour.'

Wrong-footed by her supreme self-confidence, Kersey

did as he was told, and while he busied himself with his beautiful crystal goblets, the Duchess sat on the bench recently vacated by Widdrington. Chaloner was becoming worried, wondering why Wiseman had failed to appear. Had the Queen taken a turn for the worse?

'No,' replied the Duchess, when he asked the question aloud. 'She is on the mend, although she might have a relapse unless we finish here soon. I promised to read to her from one of my books, and she will be getting desperately impatient with the delay.'

She was not the only one, and Chaloner chafed at the passing time. He was on the verge of going to do something more useful when the Duchess began to talk about the morning when Chiffinch's body was discovered.

'I was nowhere near White Hall when the alarm was raised,' she said, 'so I missed viewing the body then. I only heard about it hours later, when my stepson came to tell me.'

'When did you arrive home exactly?' asked Chaloner, keeping his voice casual, so she would not guess he was trying to establish if she had an alibi.

Unfortunately, her sharp gaze revealed that she knew exactly what he was doing, although she did not seem to take umbrage. 'I cannot recall specifically when I left the palace, but I travelled in a hackney carriage. I had never been inside one before, and I was in the mood for an adventure. However, I shall not do it again, because it stank of onions.'

'You rode a hackney on your own?' breathed Eliza, aghast. 'My Lady! You should not have taken such a risk. London is full of undesirable characters—'

'Pah!' interrupted the Duchess. 'I was perfectly safe. The driver was a charming fellow, and did not mind at all when I remunerated him with a gold ring instead of coins. I did not have any money with me, you see, and I could not be bothered to go in the house to fetch some.'

Chaloner was sure the man had been delighted, given that it sounded as though he had been seriously overpaid. 'Who greeted you when you rolled up?'

'No one,' replied the Duchess. 'They were all still abed. Is that not so, Eliza?'

'Yes,' replied Eliza, who had gulped her claret down in a single swallow and looked as though she wished she was somewhere else; she smiled gratefully when Kersey poured her a refill. 'You later said that you let yourself in, then curled up with *Paradise Lost*.'

'By John Milton, who is our neighbour,' nodded the Duchess. 'Although he is completely blind now, and his circumstances are very reduced. I tried to visit him on Thursday evening, but he was out. I waited an age in his parlour before I gave up and went to White Hall instead.'

Eliza blinked. 'Was someone else with you, My Lady? It was not me, because I was in Newcastle House all day, sorting through your old clothes.'

'I need no chaperone for Milton,' averred the Duchess. 'He is a poet.'

'Did you like Chiffinch?' fished Chaloner, feeling they were ranging too far from what he wanted to know.

'Not particularly. When I defeated him at back-gammon, he pouted like a spoiled brat. He reminded me of Mansfield, who also cannot accept the fact that I am cleverer than him.'

'Were you aware that Chiffinch disapproved of your . . .' Chaloner faltered, suspecting that while she was happy using pejorative words to describe other people's views, she would be rather less tolerant if the same rule was applied to hers.

Eliza came to his rescue. 'Your philosophical and intellectual opinions.'

The Duchess sniffed. 'Yes, but he was a dim-witted, self-satisfied hypocrite, who had no time for anyone's views but his own. Yet I bear him no ill will, especially now he is dead. But where *is* Wiseman? I thought he said three o'clock.'

'Perhaps you should go back to the palace,' suggested Chaloner hopefully. 'Wiseman might be delayed for ages yet.'

The Duchess grimaced. 'Unfortunately, the opportunity to watch a vicious critic dissected does not come along every day, and I shall never forgive myself if I miss it. In the interim, Mr Kersey can show me his best corpses.'

For the next hour, Chaloner trailed after the Duchess, Eliza and Kersey, viewing all manner of 'interesting' cases, while time ticked past relentlessly. Fortunately, nothing too gruesome was in residence, the bloodiest being a man who had died from a blow to the head the previous Wednesday.

'It damaged his brain irreparably,' explained Kersey. 'But he still managed to stagger to the River Fleet, where he died. Wiseman says he was as good as dead as soon as he was struck, but his limbs continued to function anyway. It must have been an eerie sight.'

The thought of it was too much for Eliza, who raced out with her hand over her mouth. Chaloner followed, partly to see if she needed help, but mostly because she was not the only one who needed some fresh air.

'There is no need for you to miss the rest of that . . . unusual tour, Mr Chaloner,' she said unsteadily, wiping her mouth with the back of her hand. 'I shall sit with my husband in the coach until Her Grace comes out.'

'I do not mind missing it, believe me,' said Chaloner fervently. 'I have seen enough death and violence in my life.'

He had not intended to make such an intimate confession, and was surprised at himself, although Eliza gave his arm a sympathetic squeeze. 'Have you decided whether to accept my invitation to the Red Bull tomorrow? I should like you to meet our talented pupils.'

'I will come if I can.'

'Good. Hopefully, you will be so impressed that you will donate some money for books and the like. We are always short of funds, although the Duchess is generous. And who knows? Maybe you will learn something. We women have much to say that is worth hearing.'

'I know,' said Chaloner, aiming to stem the tirade he sensed was coming. 'It is—'

'Do you?' interrupted Eliza, her eyes bright with the strength of her convictions. 'Then when did you last listen to one, and I mean *really* listen? Moreover, I know what you were thinking in there – that my Duchess is a lunatic who should be locked in Bedlam.'

'I thought nothing of the kind,' he objected.

She regarded him intently, then relented with an apologetic smile. 'Perhaps I misspoke. However, you do consider my lady to be an oddity. I could tell by the way you looked at her.'

'Well, she *is* an oddity,' retorted Chaloner, thinking Eliza should be used to it, given that everyone else thought the same. 'But that does not mean she is mad.'

'I will lend you some of her books, and when you read them, you will see that she is a great visionary,' Eliza went on with some passion. 'Her brother, Baron Lucas, agrees, and *he* is a member of the Royal Society.'

Chaloner was not sure that being in the Royal Society proved anything. So was the Duke of York, set to become King James II unless the Queen provided an heir, and he had never had a rational thought in his life.

Once Chaloner had deposited Eliza in the coach, he returned to the tour. The Duchess had finished looking at bodies, and was in the museum. The vast pair of drawers that had enjoyed pride of place for years had been relegated to an antechamber, and the star attraction was now Kersey's huge collection of false teeth. Lying on a table nearby was an eclectic assortment of objects waiting to be catalogued – some oddly shaped shillings, letters and a book.

'All these belonged to the man who walked around while he was effectively dead,' Kersey explained, and smiled. 'However, I doubt his kin will come to claim them.'

'Why not?' asked the Duchess, agog.

It was Chaloner who answered. 'Because of the coins. Some of the silver has been clipped from their edges, and that is a capital crime. To claim them will risk being implicated, and the government takes a dim view of people who devalue the national currency.'

The Duchess poked the money with a plump forefinger, then picked up the book. 'Coin-clipping was not the rogue's only capital crime,' she declared, her voice suddenly harsh with anger. 'The wretch has been through this tome and made some very unpleasant annotations.'

146

'I was not aware that defacing—' began Kersey, bemused.

'It is one of mine,' interrupted the Duchess coldly. '*The World's Olio*. And his inane scribbles show him to have been a man of very limited intellect. Regardless, I hope you do not intend to put this on display, Mr Kersey. It insults me.'

'It will never see the light of day again,' promised Kersey diplomatically. 'And you must forgive me for leaving it out. I have had scant time to assess—'

'Do the letters reveal the rogue's identity?' asked the Duchess, making a grab for them. 'If so, I shall visit his kin, and put them right about his asinine remarks.' Then she frowned. 'I cannot make head nor tail of them, and none are signed. Are they in code? And what is this symbol that looks like a broken wheel? What does it mean?'

'I do not know,' replied Kersey. 'However, I shall send them to the Spymaster when I have a spare moment. I suspect our dead friend was embroiled in some very dark business, which is probably why he met his untimely end.'

Wiseman arrived eventually, so Chaloner went outside to meet him. Unrepentantly, the surgeon explained that his lateness was due to an emergency with the courtier who would soon give birth to the child she had claimed to have carried for the past twelve months. He already knew that the Duchess aimed to watch him at work, and was delighted that his expertise was about to be witnessed by a high-ranking noblewoman.

'Perhaps you are, but you cannot allow it,' said Chaloner, while Kersey nodded fervently at his side. 'First, it would not be seemly, and second, she might

147

march up to Chiffinch's family and tell them what she has done. It will distress them and cause trouble for you.'

'Nonsense,' argued Wiseman. 'I am Surgeon to the Person, and who I invite to admire my skills are for me to decide. Not Chiffinch's family and not you either.'

Wiseman possessed an impressive physique to go with his larger-than-life personality. He was tall and muscular, and kept himself fit by lifting heavy stones each morning. He always dressed entirely in red, right down to his boots, and as his own auburn locks had started to lose their lustre, he had bought a massive wig made from fiery ginger hair. He was in one of his belligerent moods, almost certainly because staying with the Queen had deprived him of sleep. It meant he would be trying company until he had rested.

'You have not seen the body, so why are you so sure that Chiffinch was murdered?' Chaloner asked. 'Clarke thought it was natural causes.'

'And *that* is why,' replied Wiseman loftily. 'Clarke is an ass, and any diagnosis he makes is bound to be wrong. Ergo, I took the opposing view.'

Chaloner regarded him askance. 'You had me hunting a killer on that basis alone?'

Wiseman gave a superior smile. 'Along with some clever deductions that I shall explain after I have examined the body. Now, I shall partake of a small cup of wine and then begin.'

'How is the Queen?' asked Chaloner, knowing there was no point in urging him to hurry, so following him into the parlour where the Duchess was idly flicking through the ledger where Kersey wrote the names of all his guests.

Wiseman's expression softened. 'Past the worst, thank

148

God. Now she must rest, to allow her body to mend. Fortunately, that is no problem, because the poor lady sleeps all the time.'

'If you have finished drinking, Mr Wiseman, let us begin,' said the Duchess, speaking almost before the surgeon had taken his first sip. 'Time waits for no woman, and I have been here too long already. The Queen will be missing me.'

'She will not,' averred Wiseman, nettled. 'Indeed, she barely notices *me* keeping vigil at her bedside because she is so deeply asleep. But you are right in that time passes. Come.'

He led the way to the mortuary, the Duchess sweeping along imperiously at his heels. Eliza and Chaloner followed more reluctantly. They arrived to find that Kersey's assistant had prepared Chiffinch for the ordeal – clothes removed, surgical implements set out, and a bucket of clean water set ready to sluice away any mess. Wiseman donned a leather apron, warned everyone to stand well back, and began. Chaloner kept his eyes fixed on the dead man's face so he would not have to see what was happening further down, thinking that the Keeper of Jewels looked smaller, older and more insignificant now he was stripped of his worldly finery.

While Wiseman worked, the Duchess kept up a non-stop monologue about her plans to write a play featuring surgeons. To his credit, Wiseman did not allow it to distract him, and his replies were little more than grunts as he concentrated on the task at hand.

Chaloner was not squeamish, having seen more of death, battle and violence than most men, but there was something about the cold act of dissection that repelled him deeply. He glanced away, and saw the Duchess staring fixedly at a spot on the wall above Wiseman's head. He realised then that the self-serving chatter was her way of dealing with what was happening in front of her – that she was appalled, but did not know how to escape without losing face.

'Shall we go now, Your Grace?' he asked gently. 'Wiseman has almost finished.'

'Yes, I think I have seen enough,' said the Duchess, struggling for insouciance. 'I expected the art of anatomy would be . . . well, an art. Not all this hacking and yanking.'

'Hacking and yanking?' echoed Wiseman, looking up, affronted. 'I assure you, madam, that my dissections entail great finesse, and you will find me a far more elegant operator than all the other butchers in my profession.'

'What did you find?' asked Chaloner quickly, before there was a spat.

Wiseman straightened from the gore that had once been a living, breathing person. 'That I was right to claim Clarke was mistaken. Of course, it was not easy to discover the truth, and no other surgeon would have found it, but there *is* evidence of foul play. This man was murdered – by the most ingenious means I have ever encountered.'

Wiseman would say no more until he had sewn his subject back together and dabbled his fingers in a bucket of water. It immediately turned red, as did the cloth on which he then dried his hands. Kersey pursed his lips at the stains, although Chaloner thought he should have known better than to provide a white towel for the purpose. Then, with blood still encrusting his fingernails, Wiseman led the way back to Kersey's parlour.

They arrived to find Eliza and Topp there, having

grown tired of sitting in the carriage. Eliza hastened to see the Duchess comfortably seated, while Topp and Kersey fussed around her with cushions and wine.

'I did warn you, Your Loveliness,' said Topp, all paternal concern. 'I witnessed an anatomy myself when we were in Holland, and I have been unable to eat sausages ever since.'

'I never liked sausages anyway,' said the Duchess, and gave a wan smile. 'But I am glad I came, as I now have plenty of material for my play. I shall call it *The Bloody Barber*.'

'An excellent title, Your Grace,' gushed Topp, although Wiseman looked ready to argue.

Chaloner wanted the Duchess to leave, so that Wiseman could tell him what he had learned about Chiffinch in confidence. Unfortunately, she had other ideas. She indicated that Topp and Eliza were to sit next to her, and ordered Wiseman to begin his report. The surgeon took a sip of claret, then began to pontificate. He loved showing off.

'When I first heard that Chiffinch was alive and well at six o'clock, but dead by seven,' he began, 'I assumed an apoplexy or a seizure had carried him off. He was, after all, old, fat and unhealthy. However, I changed my mind the moment I heard Clarke burbling about impostumes. He is a buffoon, and how he was appointed Physician Royal, I shall never know.'

'So there was no impostume?' asked Chaloner, before he could embark on a diatribe.

'Chiffinch was wearing this locket,' said Wiseman, tossing it on the table; it contained a miniature portrait of one of the King's ex-mistresses, suggesting a degree of hypocrisy when Chiffinch had condemned others for

151

breaking their marriage vows. 'And it was this that Clarke's questing fingers detected – that he mistook for an abscess. As I said, the man is an ass, who should not be trusted to tend Chaloner's chickens, let alone the King.'

'Are you suggesting that chickens deserve an ass to oversee their welfare?' asked the Duchess coolly. 'They are intelligent beings. As intelligent as us, in fact, although they lack the means to communicate their political and philosophical ideas.'

'Chaloner's hens are not intelligent,' quipped Wiseman. 'When I stopped off at home on the way here, my servants told me that one of them challenged a fox this morning, which was hardly sensible.'

Chaloner shot him an unpleasant look. Covent Garden was not 'on the way' to Westminster from White Hall, and he resented the surgeon taking detours while he himself had been left kicking his heels.

The Duchess sniffed. 'As you would not have bothered to mention the incident if the fox had won, I deduce that the hen did, so my point is proven: this bird saw a problem, assessed it critically, and devised a solution based on logic. Ergo, she *is* intelligent.'

'Chiffinch,' prompted Chaloner, before the discussion could range any further into the bizarre. 'You were telling us how he was murdered.'

'No,' corrected Wiseman pedantically. 'I was explaining how I knew that Clarke was wrong before I had proof of it in the locket that the fool mistook for an abscess. In short, there would have been specific symptoms if Clarke's diagnosis had been correct. I reflected on all my recent encounters with Chiffinch, and concluded that there were no such signs.'

'Very well,' said Chaloner. 'But it is a big leap from suspecting that Clarke made a mistake to saying that Chiffinch was unlawfully killed.'

'Yes,' acknowledged Wiseman. 'But by then, I was in possession of a second piece of information – one I had from Captain Rolt.'

'Which was?' prompted Chaloner impatiently when Wiseman paused for dramatic effect.

'That Chiffinch ate nothing all night except a large plate of oysters, which he had ordered in specially and that he did not share with anyone else. They were delivered to him at around midnight, and he swallowed them in fits and starts, until the last one slid down his throat at four o'clock, just before he took his leave.'

Irritably, Chaloner struggled to understand what the surgeon was saying. 'So he died from a surfeit? Or because one of these shellfish was bad?'

Wiseman shot him an arch glance. 'If that had been the case, there would have been vomiting and pain, and we all would have known about his discomfort.'

Chaloner controlled his exasperation with difficulty, although Wiseman was revelling in his role of shrewd detective. The Duchess was spellbound by his analysis, while Topp, Eliza and even Kersey hung on his every world.

'So what, then?' Chaloner demanded. 'Poison?'

'Yes, and the way it was administered was very clever. The killer must have known not only that his victim was a glutton for this particular dish, but also that he never chewed them.'

Using his hand, Wiseman mimicked someone tipping a shell and propelling a hapless crustacean straight down his throat.

153

'How do you know how he ate?' asked Chaloner, bemused. 'You were not there.'

'Because all twenty-four oysters were still whole – or virtually so – inside his stomach,' explained Wiseman. 'Unfortunately for him, each had been implanted with a little capsule of poison. Most of these pods are still intact, but a couple had ruptured, which was why he died. Death was inevitable with two or three doses, but with twenty-four . . .'

Chaloner glanced at the Duchess. *She* would be familiar with Chiffinch's eating habits, given that they met at Court. Moreover, the oysters must have been poisoned *before* they were delivered to him at midnight, as he would have noticed someone meddling with them once they were in his possession. And he recalled that the Duchess's alibi for that particular time was waiting – alone – in the parlour of a poet she had never met.

But surely she could not be so macabre as to want to see her victim anatomised? Or had she foisted herself on the procedure in the hope of preventing Wiseman from finding out what she had done? Or was she just an innocent but very peculiar lady with odd notions of what was acceptable behaviour?

'So I was right to predict foul play,' finished Wiseman with great satisfaction. 'And I was right to inform you of my suspicions before I had examined the corpse, so you could begin your hunt for the killer at once. I imagine it has given you an edge.'

'Not as much as if you had told me all this yesterday,' said Chaloner ungraciously.

'I considered the Queen's health more important,' said Wiseman loftily. 'Besides, my word alone should have been enough. Surely you trust my remarkable abilities by now? You have relied on them often enough in the past.'

'What was the poison?' asked Chaloner, declining to pander to his vanity.

'One containing henbane, probably. But do not expect to find the killer by tracing the apothecary who made it. Anyone with a modicum of medical knowledge could have thrown the ingredients together, and none are difficult to acquire.'

'But if Chiffinch ate the oysters between midnight and four o'clock, why was he still walking around – seemingly well – at six?' asked Chaloner, thinking about the man who had gossiped so disapprovingly to him about the Duchess and her preferred theatre-wear.

'The capsules are made of a substance that takes time to dissolve,' explained Wiseman, 'allowing the culprit to be well away from his victim when the toxin is released. Once that happened, death would have been fairly quick – less than an hour.'

'So who prepared the capsules?' asked Chaloner. 'From what you say, you have never encountered such a thing before, so the maker should not be too difficult to identify.'

'It is the *idea* that is clever, not the capsules themselves. Anyone could fashion them from the intestines of a rabbit and some weak glue.'

Chaloner considered the information, thoughts tumbling. How had the killer managed to insert the capsules into the oysters? And when? Clearly, a visit to White Hall's kitchens was required as a matter of urgency. He decided to go as soon as he left the charnel house.

'If I were investigating this crime,' said the Duchess,

'I would start by looking at those people he defeated at backgammon on the night he died. I won, of course, so I am exonerated.'

'No one would suspect you anyway, Your Sweetness,' Topp assured her. 'Everyone knows you are good, gentle and kind, even if your reading has taught you a lot about toxins.'

'Knowing and using are hardly the same,' said Eliza, shooting her husband a sharp look.

The Duchess stood to leave, thanking Wiseman for indulging her scientific curiosity. Then she swept out, Eliza at her side and Topp scurrying at their heels.

'Eliza is the more intelligent of those two women,' remarked Wiseman, when they had gone. 'I detect a sharp mind behind that modest façade, whereas the Duchess is not as clever as she thinks she is.'

'Should I include Eliza on my list of suspects then?' asked Chaloner. 'You did say the killer was ingenious.'

'I did, but I doubt Eliza is the guilty party. She cannot have known Chiffinch well, if at all. You would do better to concentrate your enquiries on Will, who has inherited some very lucrative posts and some lovely accommodation. Incidentally, there are visitors waiting for you at home. Two pretty young ladies.'

'For me? Are you sure?'

Wiseman nodded. 'I asked what they wanted, but they refused to say. I recommend you race home and find out what they want before they give up on you and leave. It would be a pity to miss them.'

'I will,' said Chaloner. 'But not before I have visited White Hall's kitchens to find out how Chiffinch's food came to be poisoned.'

*

The kitchens were less impressive than might have been expected for a palace with hundreds of residents needing to be fed. They comprised a sprawl of buildings, many of which were very inconveniently placed. Thus the bakery was some distance from the cellars where the flour was kept, while the buttery was nowhere near where the milk was delivered each day.

The kitchens were busy, as a veritable army of cooks, their assistants, scullions and children scurried about preparing the feast that would be served to the King and his Court later. When that was done, more food would be needed for the dozens of courtiers, footmen, maids and underlings who had served it and cleaned up afterwards. The rooms were hot, steamy, noisy and full of delicious smells.

The Master Cook was William Austen, a plump, red-faced man who looked as though he tasted each of his culinary creations personally before allowing them to be served. He gaped in horror when Chaloner explained what had happened to Chiffinch's oysters.

'But I have prepared thousands of them for him over the years, and nothing like this has ever happened before. Are you certain? There is no mistake?'

'None,' replied Chaloner. 'Did anyone other than Chiffinch eat oysters on Thursday?'

'No – most courtiers consider them vulgar, because they are so plentiful in season that paupers gorge on them. No White Hall resident wants to eat beggars' fare.'

'But Chiffinch did not mind?'

'He was unusual in that respect. He ate them live, with a sprinkling of lemon and salt.'

'Who supplies them to you?'

'The fish market in Lower Thames Street, where we

buy all our seafood. We have been using them for years, and I trust them implicitly. We were a little late ordering Chiffinch's repast that day, because his request slipped my mind until late afternoon. They did not arrive until about six in the evening.'

'What happened to them then?'

Austen wrung his chubby hands, frightened and defensive in equal measure. 'Like all perishable goods, they went directly to the larder, which is underground and thus cool. Oysters always go into a bucket of cold water, which keeps them fresh until they are needed.'

'Who has access to the larder?'

Austen indicated the labouring throng around them. 'Anyone who needs the ingredients that are stored in it. There are guards, who are meant to prevent theft, but their task is nigh on impossible, given that so many of us are in and out all day and night.'

'I see,' said Chaloner, realising with resignation that identifying the poisoner by tracking the oysters from the fish market to Chiffinch's plate would likely be hopeless. He persisted anyway. 'So what happened to them once they were in the bucket?'

'They remained there until just before midnight, when I sent one of the kitchen boys to fetch them. When they arrived, I arranged them on a platter, and added the lemon juice and salt. Then a page took them to Mr Chiffinch.'

'He did not want them sooner?'

'No – he had dined with the King at seven, so was not peckish again until later.'

The page was summoned, but all he could add was that he had taken the oysters straight to the Shield Gallery, and that Chiffinch had devoured five or six at

158

once. The rest he had eaten at intervals through the night, with the last couple disappearing just before four o'clock, when he had retired to his apartments.

Chaloner was thoughtful. 'So the oysters were left unattended from six o'clock, when they arrived at the palace, until just before midnight?'

Austen nodded. 'Yes, so if Wiseman is right, these poisoned capsules must have been inserted between those two times. The responsibility lies with the larder, not the kitchens.'

'How do you know the toxin was not there when you bought them from the market?'

'Because we always rinse them thoroughly before putting them in the bucket of water. Anything nasty would have been washed out then.'

'Fair enough,' said Chaloner. 'Do you have any thoughts about the murder?'

'Only that the intended victim was definitely Chiffinch. It was common knowledge that he always had oysters when he spent the evening in the Shield Gallery.'

He took Chaloner to the larder, which comprised a series of cool cellars with thick walls, designed to keep perishable foodstuffs fresh. There Chaloner learned that although the door was always guarded, Austen was right to say that security was very lax. The sentries tended to admit anyone claiming to be on kitchen business, because the palace cooks were notoriously irascible and reacted with fury if their underlings failed to bring them what they wanted. Worse, some guards were rumoured to let anyone inside for a few pennies.

'No wonder it costs so much to keep White Hall in victuals,' said Chaloner, disgusted. 'Half of London can come in and load up.'

'Yes,' agreed Austen. 'So is there anything you would like, since you are here?'

Chaloner was so appalled by the dismal security that he marched straight to the guards' quarters and announced that their ineptitude and corruption might have allowed the killer to poison the King and his entire Court. His censure fell on deaf ears, and he was curtly informed that they did not need an old Parliamentarian to teach them how to do their jobs. He continued to argue, but gave up in disgust when they returned to their card game, clearly with no intention of listening to anything he had to say.

To take his mind off their criminal complacency, he turned his mind to the 'pretty young ladies' who had called on him at home. He wondered if they were still there, or if they had despaired of him ever returning and had left. He walked a little more quickly, but had only reached the end of King Street when he was intercepted by Swaddell. He grimaced. Was the assassin stalking him? He seemed to be everywhere.

'I could not find Rolt,' explained Swaddell. 'But it is evening now, so I imagine he will be preparing for another night of fun in the cockpit. Shall we go there together?'

But Chaloner had had enough for one day. 'I must return home. Wiseman says there are some ladies waiting to see me.'

Swaddell looked interested. 'In that case, I shall come to hear what they have to say. Perhaps they know who killed Chiffinch. And while we walk, you can describe what happened in the charnel house – and why you then went to White Hall.'

Chaloner did not mind telling him what Wiseman had

discovered, or about the shoddy practices among the palace guards, but he was not about to take the assassin home with him. Thus, while he spoke, most of his mind was devising ways to escape without causing offence.

'Chiffinch was better than most of the King's favourites,' mused Swaddell, when Chaloner had finished. 'He was not particularly underhand, all the bribes he took were modest, and he furnished White Hall with some lovely paintings.'

'Is that what will go on his epitaph?' asked Chaloner, amused. 'Not especially dishonest, only moderately corrupt, and had good taste in art?'

'I can think of worse – such as that he cheated at backgammon and was a judgemental hypocrite.' Swaddell cleared his throat. 'I have a list of suspects. Do you want to hear it?'

'Very well.'

'At the top are his brother and the Cockpit Club, all of whom he despised for being dissipated, which he felt damaged His Majesty's reputation. All bitterly resented his criticism.'

'Resented it enough to kill him?'

Swaddell shrugged. 'Perhaps, although I would have thought they would do it with political intrigue rather than murder, but . . .'

'The Cockpit Club has about thirty members. Are they all on your list?'

Swaddell nodded. 'But some names are higher up it than others. Such as Colonel Widdrington, because he is in charge; the outrageous Cobbe, because he loves to shock and Chiffinch's death has certainly done that—'

'Cobbe was not in London when Chiffinch died, and he says he has alibis to prove it.'

Swaddell continued as if he had not spoken. 'Captain Rolt, because he was first on the scene, using the pretext of a lost button; young Legg, because he is desperate to make an impression among his older, more urbane cronies; Ashley, because he is a drunk; and Tooley, because he is a mindless lout.'

'I see,' said Chaloner. 'Anyone else?'

'Yes – Dr Clarke. He is not in the Cockpit Club, although I think he would like to be. He is on my list for insisting that Chiffinch died of an impostume when he did not. I wonder what he will say once the truth emerges. It will reveal him either as incompetent or a liar, neither of which will do his reputation any good. Now tell me who you want to include.'

'The same people as you. However, two more Cockpit Club members deserve a specific mention: Bess Widdrington, because Chiffinch hated the husband she loves; and Viscount Mansfield, because he is weak, jealous and spiteful. I would also include his stepmother the Duchess of Newcastle, and Fanny Clarke.'

'I understand why you include the Duchess – it is hardly normal to want to see someone you know anatomised – but why Fanny?'

'Because Rolt did not find Chiffinch's body. *She* did.'

'Very well,' acknowledged Swaddell. 'Anyone else?'

Chaloner nodded. 'White Hall is a dangerous place, where ambition runs fierce, hot and deep. Any courtier with power will accrue enemies, so we shall have to identify all those that Chiffinch has made since he was appointed six years ago.'

'That will include your Earl,' warned Swaddell, then eyed him appraisingly. '*You* did not dispatch Chiffinch, did you? I will understand if you did – an order is an order – but it would be awkward if I uncover proof that sees you in trouble.'

Chaloner regarded him askance. 'I would never poison anyone!'

'Nor would I,' agreed Swaddell earnestly. 'There is always a danger of killing the wrong target. A blade is much more reliable.' He removed one from his belt. 'This is Florentine steel, very expensive. There is nothing quite like it for slitting a throat. Would you like me to procure one for you?'

'No, thank you,' said Chaloner firmly, feeling the discussion was sliding into very dark waters. 'I am not an assassin, and the Earl would never ask such a thing of me.'

Unfortunately, the same could not be said of other nobles and courtiers, and Chaloner realised with a sense of despair that he would also have to find out which of Chiffinch's enemies were the kind of people to hire others to do their dirty work. That would not be easy.

'I must see what these ladies want,' he said tiredly, 'so will you go back to White Hall and look for Rolt?'

Swaddell shook his head. 'I should see these women, too. Perhaps they are the two who fought each other earlier – Dutch Jane and Chicken Molly. Maybe they have intelligence for us about our suspects at Newcastle House.'

Chaloner blinked. 'How on Earth did you reach that conclusion? And even if you are right, why would they visit me? They cannot possibly know where I live.'

'It would be easy enough to find out, and Dutch Jane has some experience in matters of espionage. She is a spy.'

'One of yours?'

'One of the enemy's. The clue is in the name, Tom – *Dutch* Jane. She tells the United Provinces' ambassador things she has learned from snooping about in Newcastle House.'

'What ambassador?' asked Chaloner. 'Michiel van Goch went home in January, when his government decided there was no hope of peace.'

'He is back, much against his will,' replied Swaddell. 'Ambassador Downing spies for us in The Hague, and the Hollanders realised that recalling van Goch had put them at a disadvantage. So they ordered him to return, and Dutch Jane is one of his informants.'

'You let her remain at large?'

Swaddell smiled superiorly. 'We use her: we write letters to the Duke about our war plans and ships, which we know she will see. All are false.'

'So she betrays her employers. Why? For money?'

Swaddell smirked. 'She thinks van Goch arranges for cash to be deposited with a goldsmith in Antwerp, but he "forgets", so her account is empty. Such is the lot of the spy – an unsavoury profession begets unsavoury liaisons. Present company excepted, of course.'

'She will find out soon. The Duchess has dismissed her, so she will be going home.'

'We heard,' said Swaddell, and grinned again. 'Dutch Jane will be livid when she finds out she has been working for free all these years.'

As it happened, Chaloner and Swaddell bumped into Rolt on King Street. The captain was walking from the direction of the cockpit. At first glance, his clothes appeared to be the height of fashion, but a closer inspection showed that the elbows in his coat were worn, while his shirt was made of rougher linen than courtiers usually favoured. Chaloner wondered if his failure to secure a Court sinecure meant he was getting desperate, and had dispatched a critic in order to improve his chances.

'We understand that you found Chiffinch's body,' he said, launching into an interrogation with a brusqueness that made his victim start in surprise.

'Then you understand wrong,' said Rolt indignantly. 'Fanny Clarke found the body. I just happened to be passing when she came reeling out, wailing for help.'

'Passing the cockpit?' echoed Swaddell incredulously. 'At seven o'clock in the morning?'

'I was searching for my lost button,' replied Rolt irritably. 'As I have already explained. I expected the place to be empty, so it seemed a good time to hunt.'

'Is that what you have been doing this evening?' probed Swaddell. 'Having another look for it? You must really want to locate the thing.'

Rolt shrugged. 'It belonged to my father and I am a sentimental fool. And yes, I thought I would have one final ferret about before the wrestling tonight. But I could not find it, so I must put it out of my mind.'

'Why did you not mention that you played such an important role in the discovery of Chiffinch's body?' demanded Chaloner. 'Helping Fanny Clarke to recover, going to inspect him for yourself, sending a servant for a *medicus*. All very heroic.'

Rolt shrugged again. 'All I did was sit her down and make sure she had not mistaken what she claimed to have seen. My actions were hardly worth alluding to. Besides, at the time, we thought he might have the plague, and I did not want to be shut away for forty days.'

'Chiffinch despised the Cockpit Club,' said Swaddell.

'He thought your wild carousing would harm the King. Indeed, I learned today that he aimed to see your cabal disbanded. What do you say to that?'

'He did advise us to moderate our behaviour,' acknowledged Rolt, 'but he could never have crushed us. We have too many powerful members and the support of the King.'

'Did you see him eating the night before he died?' asked Chaloner.

Rolt nodded. 'I have already told Surgeon Wiseman all this. Chiffinch had a plate of oysters, which arrived around midnight. He scoffed the lot over the course of the evening, and left at around four, saying he had business to attend to. I assumed he went to his rooms, so I was surprised when Fanny said he was in the cockpit.'

'On a different note,' said Swaddell, before Chaloner could press him further, 'Fanny and Bess deny going to the Red Bull. Are you sure it was them?'

'Fairly sure. But of course they deny it – the place is frequented by whores and rebels.'

Did this mean Eliza was educating prostitutes and insurgents with the Duchess's money? Chaloner supposed he would have to accept her invitation and find out. He bade Rolt good night, then hurried on to Covent Garden, Swaddell sticking to his heels like glue.

The parlour that Wiseman used for entertaining was eye-catching. It had been decorated by his lover, Temperance North, who ran a brothel off Fleet Street, and reflected her tastes as well as his own. There were scarlet-frilled curtains, comfortable chairs, and shelves along the walls that displayed his favourite anatomical specimens. He believed his grisly collection would be conversation pieces for visitors, although there were very few of these, as Chaloner and Temperance were his only friends.

'My goodness!' breathed Swaddell, looking around in distaste. 'No wonder you were reluctant to bring me home. It is a chamber of horrors!'

Standing in the middle of the room, obviously uneasy and full of trepidation, were two young women. Both were pretty, with fair curls and grey eyes, and although their clothes were of good quality, they were unfashionable and much mended. The elder of the pair was politely demure, but the younger had a very mischievous grin.

'May I help you?' asked Chaloner, beginning to be suspicious. Wiseman and Temperance thought he should remarry, and were always suggesting 'suitable' candidates. Had they encouraged these women to visit, in the hope that one would take his fancy?

'Which of you is Thomas Chaloner?' asked the elder, her eyes flicking between him and Swaddell. 'Or are you just colleagues of the man who was here earlier? We thought he was the devil when he exploded in on us, dressed all in red and leering like a pirate.'

'Wiseman has that effect on people,' acknowledged Chaloner, aware of Swaddell chortling under his breath. 'But he is no demon. Just Surgeon to the Person.'

'What person?' asked the younger woman, intrigued. 'Yours?'

'The King's,' explained Chaloner, supposing the title would sound peculiar to those unfamiliar with it. 'Wiseman tends His Majesty and the Court.'

'Is he married?' she asked keenly.

Chaloner blinked, taken aback. Wiseman's wife had been incurably insane for years, but had fallen prey to the plague the previous year, despite the surgeon's best efforts to keep her safe. Everyone who had met her thought her death was a blessed relief from the tormented hell of her ruined mind, although Wiseman disagreed and felt he had failed her. Chaloner admired the fact that his friend had never given up on her, and had consistently put her welfare above his own convenience and happiness.

'Not any more,' he replied, deciding not to mention Temperance until he knew more about who was asking. 'Why do you want to know?'

'Never mind,' replied the girl, and smiled in a way that was vaguely predatory. 'I am sure there are others who will suit our needs. Preferably ones who are younger and more handsome. Rich is important, obviously, but it should not be our only consideration.'

Chaloner looked from one to the other, and saw there was something familiar about their eyes: they were the same shade of grey as his father's. And his own, for that matter.

'Do I know you?' he asked curiously.

'We have never met,' replied the older with quiet dignity, 'but you will have heard of us. We are your cousins, Ursula and Veriana, daughters of your Uncle James.'

Chaloner was aware of an uncomfortable feeling growing in the pit of his stomach. He was usually pleased to meet other members of his enormous clan, but he sensed trouble would follow if he began to associate with the progeny of Uncle James – the fervent Parliamentarian, whose wife and children had remained on the Isle of Man after the Restoration, shunning all contact with the rest of the family.

'*James* Chaloner?' asked Swaddell, his usually flat black

eyes bright with interest. 'Is that the fellow who was arrested for supporting Cromwell's rogue government? Word is that he deliberately swallowed poison when he was in prison, to avoid being tried for treason.'

Veriana, the older girl, glared at him. 'That is a lie put about by spiteful Royalists who were disappointed because he passed away before they had finished hounding him. Our father departed this life because he caught a sickness in their horrible gaol.'

'It must have been difficult for you,' said Chaloner hastily, before she could quarrel with a man who might report the discussion to the Spymaster. 'But why are you here? I hope it is nothing to do with reclaiming Chaloner Court from its current owners.'

'Unfortunately, our lawyers say the government's seizure of that house cannot be challenged,' said Veriana bitterly. 'It is lost to us for ever, along with everything else we once owned. They even took Ursula's dolls.'

'Although I do not play with those any more,' put in Ursula hastily. 'I am eighteen now, and too old for such nonsense. Indeed, I am ready for a husband, which is why we are here.'

'You are to be married?' asked Chaloner politely. 'Congratulations.'

'Thank you,' said Veriana briskly. 'But your felicitations are premature, because first, you must find us suitable partners.'

'*I* must?' blurted Chaloner, startled. 'I hardly think—'

'Our family is destitute,' interrupted Veriana. 'Our mother survives by mending shirts, and our brother Edmund is an impoverished country parson. Ergo, Ursula and I must make good marriages. Ones that will restore the family fortune.'

'I appreciate that,' said Chaloner. 'But I cannot—'

'You are a courtier with important connections,' cut in Veriana. 'And our mother wants you to use them on our behalf.'

'I am sure she does,' said Chaloner coolly, 'but it is out of the question.'

'But if you refuse,' cried Ursula, distraught, 'we shall be condemned to wed tenant farmers with no prospects, and our branch of the family will be doomed to penury for ever. *Everything* depends on you.'

'So no pressure, Tom,' muttered Swaddell, smirking his amusement.

'But I have no idea how to go about organising such matters,' objected Chaloner, sure it would be a lot harder than it sounded, given that some matches were rumoured to be years in the making. 'You will be better off applying to—'

'So who will you choose for me?' asked Ursula eagerly. 'Rich *and* handsome, remember. And preferably young.'

Veriana shot her a warning glance. 'Rich will suffice. We are prepared to sacrifice our happiness for family honour, so you are free to choose whomsoever you please. Neither of us will question your decisions.'

'Even so, I cannot help,' said Chaloner firmly. 'Our name is not one people are willing to associate with these days. You should go home and—'

'There is nothing for us at home,' blurted Ursula, tears starting in her eyes. 'All the eligible rich men are taken. You are our only hope.'

'I will help,' offered Swaddell, and smiled, revealing his sharp little teeth and red tongue. Chaloner saw both women take a step back, unsettled. 'Do not worry about a thing.'

170

Ursula and Veriana were not the only ones unnerved by this offer. So was Chaloner, who did not want Swaddell's assistance in such a personal matter. Indeed, he did not want the task at all, so it was with considerable misgiving that he even agreed to let the girls stay the night. Before they could thank him, he warned them that they would be on the first coach home in the morning, although it would not be with spouses in tow. He was powerless to do anything about that.

'I will see *you* tomorrow,' he told Swaddell curtly when the assassin started to accompany them upstairs. 'White Hall kitchens at noon, where we will see if we can learn any more about how these oysters came to be poisoned. Someone must have seen something useful.'

Swaddell did not look convinced, and Chaloner did not blame him, suspecting they had gone as far as they could go with that particular line of enquiry.

'Good evening, then, ladies,' said the assassin, effecting a bow that was all thin black legs and sharp elbows. 'And welcome to our fine city. You will like it here, I promise.'

When he left, he was humming and there was a definite spring in his step.

Chaloner inspected and rejected several bedrooms before he found one that met his approval, which essentially meant one that was not filled with alarming medical specimens or piles of risqué spare clothing from Temperance's brothel. It was, however, thick with cobwebs, although the women were too well-mannered – or too desperate – to complain.

'We will unpack tomorrow,' said Ursula, plumping herself down on the bed and then coughing as dust billowed around her. 'Although you must buy us some new clothes, or people at Court will think that we are fortune hunters.'

Well, you are, thought Chaloner, aware that her words showed she had no intention of being sent home the next day.

'We will pay you back,' promised Veriana. 'Once we have rich husbands.'

'It is not the money,' said Chaloner, although equipping two young ladies for White Hall would use up funds he had set aside for his own family. 'It is that I do not know how to begin.'

Ursula smiled rather wolfishly. 'Oh, do not worry about that. All you need do is introduce us to any wealthy man in need of a wife, and we will manage the rest.'

She and Veriana went to the window, and began to scrub away the grime so they could look out, chatting excitedly as they peered down at the piazza below. Watching them, Chaloner tried to think of anyone he knew who was in the market for a spouse. There were two ancient clerks at the Treasury, although he doubted his cousins would be thrilled by those. Then there were several single Cockpit Club men – Cobbe, Legg, Ashley and Tooley, for example – but they would do nothing to restore family honour, and would never agree to allying themselves with a family of Parliamentarians anyway.

Just when he was beginning to despair, two names popped into his mind. First, there was his friend Will Leybourn, the mathematician–surveyor; he was a good man who earned a respectable wage. And second was Captain Salathiel Lester, currently at sea fighting the Dutch.

He decided to write to them as soon as he had caught Chiffinch's killer.

172

Chapter 6

The next day was Palm Sunday, and as registers were kept of those attending church — anyone who stayed away was suspected of that most heinous of crimes, religious dissension — Chaloner had no choice but to put in an appearance at St Paul's, Covent Garden. However, the service was not until mid-morning, and as he had risen shortly after three o'clock, woken by a churning unease about his cousins, he had plenty of time to pursue the matter of Chiffinch's murder first.

He donned his grey long-coat and breeches, but recalling what the Earl's clerk had said about his dowdy clothes making him sinister, he tied a blue ribbon around his hat. Then he crept down the stairs and left via the back door. He could hardly call on witnesses or ask questions about Chiffinch's death at such an ungodly hour, so he took a hackney carriage to the Red Bull in Clerkenwell, to determine what manner of place it was — if it was still open to revellers or respectably closed.

It was not a pleasant night, with rain hissing down in sheets. The roads were already muddy rivers, and one or two drenched early-risers tried to hail his carriage as it rattled past, keen to share his ride. The driver ignored them, for which Chaloner was grateful, as he wanted to be alone with his thoughts and concerns.

The Red Bull was a timber-framed tavern on John Street, east of the green. It had a number of spacious public rooms, and a large courtyard. It had once been a famous theatre, but had since been surpassed by the richer, bigger, purpose-built playhouses in Drury Lane. It was closed, but Chaloner picked the lock on a side door, and spent half an hour exploring. When he had finished, he could state with certainty that it was not a brothel, and that Eliza's school had a large number of pupils, judging by the great piles of books stacked in every corner.

He slipped away when women began to arrive for pre-dawn classes, all heavy-eyed from lack of sleep, but determined to study before their daily rounds. Then he prowled the surrounding area, fulfilling his promise to Thurloe to monitor it for signs of trouble.

There was certainly an atmosphere. Resentment still festered that the King had abandoned Londoners to the plague, then strolled back in the expectation that everyone would be pleased to see him. Worse, there was a consensus that his immorality had brought the disaster down on them in the first place, so anti-monarchist sentiment was rife. But there was also hope, inspired by Mother Broughton's prophecies, that the city was heading for a brighter, kinder, fairer future. Chaloner wondered what would happen when Easter Day arrived and folk woke up to find that nothing had changed.

He wandered deeper into the overcrowded slums between Smithfield and the Fleet River, an area that never slept, and heard the seer's name on many lips.

Most talked about her predictions concerning the dead rising from their graves, and there was a widespread belief that it would be wise to avoid cemeteries for the next few days. Alehouses were abuzz with activity – workers fortifying themselves for the day ahead, or revellers still enjoying the night before. Cheers and angry squawks from one told him that courtiers were not the only ones who liked cockfighting.

He was about to leave when he saw someone slinking along so furtively that he could not help but stop to watch. The man wore a hooded cloak, and kept glancing behind him, to see if he was being followed. He was so intent on staying invisible that he did not watch where he was going, and stumbled in a pothole. The curse that followed was in a voice Chaloner knew.

'Barker?' he called, watching the Earl's clerk jump in alarm. 'What are you doing here?'

'I might ask you the same thing,' retorted Barker sharply. 'It is not nice to jump out on people in the dark. Did no one ever tell you that?'

'I am on the Earl's business,' replied Chaloner, honestly enough.

Barker peered at him. 'You mean Chiffinch's murder? His killer lives *here*?'

'I am following a number of leads,' replied Chaloner, not about to be specific lest Barker told the Earl, who was notoriously indiscreet. 'But speaking of Chiffinch, what can you tell me about him? I barely knew the man, and would value your opinion.'

Barker pondered. 'Well, he loved the King, and deplored anything that might hurt him or his reputation – which included the antics of his brother, the Cockpit Club, the Duchess of Newcastle, and, on occasion, our

175

Earl. He was fairly honest, and neither prim nor debauched.'

Chaloner knew all this. 'Have you heard anything about him moving from grumbles to actual plots against those he had taken against?'

'Not specifically, but he was a courtier, so I would not be surprised if he had. I would say his death is good news for our Earl, but enemies are like sewage leaking into a cellar – you scoop away one foul bucket, but more oozes in to take its place.'

'True,' agreed Chaloner, and changed the subject. 'So why are you here at such an hour?'

'My mother lives in John Street, and the only time I can visit her is when the Earl is asleep. When he is awake, his demands on me are constant.'

'I am sure they are,' said Chaloner. 'But your mother died last summer.'

'She got better,' replied Barker shortly. 'But I must return to Clarendon House before the Earl misses me. Nice hat-ribbon, by the way. The lasses will love it.'

He shot away, leaving Chaloner to watch him uneasily. Why was the clerk lying about his reason for being in Clerkenwell? Did he have a lover, and wanted to keep her existence from his latest elderly wife? Or had he been there for a darker reason, perhaps relating to whatever trouble was brewing in the area? After all, it was not just Londoners who deplored White Hall's excesses – so did many palace servants, who were exposed to them on a daily basis. It was entirely possible that Barker was one of these, and Chaloner saw he would have to be alert for rebellious rumblings in Clarendon House if he wanted to keep his employer safe.

*

On his way home, Chaloner passed the Duke and Duchess of Newcastle's residence. All the upstairs windows were shuttered, but lamps blazed in the stables. He went to find out why, and discovered a rumpus concerning a colicky mare. Clayton, the sullen steward, was walking the ailing animal around the yard, while the Duke shouted anxious advice. His voice was loud, and had woken the other servants, who had come to watch. They included Clayton's two disagreeable friends – Liddell the horse-trader and Vicar Booth. Chaloner went to talk to them.

'These nags have better accommodations than I do,' said Booth, glowering around with open envy. 'And the Duke prefers that mare to his own son. Poor Mansfield would be better loved if he had pointed ears and a tail.'

'So would we,' growled Liddell, while Chaloner marvelled anew at their indiscreet grumbles. 'Although I am glad he is taking such pains to save Henrietta Florence. She is a fabulous beast, and it would be a crying shame to lose her.'

'Your "fabulous beast" sympathises with criminals,' retorted Booth darkly. 'A thief stole my purse last Wednesday, and I chased him into her stall. She would not let me get near him – every time I tried, she feinted at me. The rogue escaped in the end, thanks to her antics.'

'Was it a very full purse?' asked Liddell sympathetically.

'No, but I cannot afford to lose a penny, given my recent misfortunes.' Booth elaborated for Chaloner's benefit. 'My church, St Quentin's, was struck by lightning and caught fire. The year of three sixes is certainly unlucky for me, because that disaster came hot on the heels of a flood in my house and my father being struck down with a palsy.'

'I have had some vile luck myself,' sighed Liddell unhappily. 'My stables were damaged in a storm and I lost a foal to fever. Then there is the rent I pay the Duke. It used to be a fair sum, but the Duchess said it was too low and insisted on doubling it. It was unkindly done.'

'She does not care about tenants and servants,' averred Booth bitterly. 'Just about her books and how many copies she can sell. Did you hear what she did to Dutch Jane? Cast out without a penny? And her a foreigner in a strange land! I cannot say I liked Dutch Jane, but that was just plain cruel.'

'It is Topp's fault for always telling the Duchess that she is the best philosopher and playwright in the world,' put in Liddell acidly. 'She believes him and now thinks that whatever drivel oozes from her pen will rival that of Plato and Aristotle.'

At that point, Clayton called for Liddell to take over walking the sick horse. Once the steward had handed over the bridle, he came to stand with Chaloner and Booth, wiping his sweaty face with his sleeve.

'I think we are winning the battle,' he reported, although Booth was not very interested. 'Poor Henrietta Florence. She *will* bolt her food.'

'Liddell and I were talking about Topp,' Booth told him. 'And how he encourages the Duchess to write, even though she is not very good at it.'

'Topp!' spat Clayton. 'Always telling people what they most want to hear. And I am sure he steals from the mistress he claims to adore. Did you hear about the silver ship-shaped brooch that went missing? I am sure *he* took it. He does not really love her – just her money.'

'Eliza loves her, though,' conceded Booth, albeit reluctantly. 'They are more like sisters than mistress and

178

servant.' Then his spiteful little face hardened. 'I cannot abide Eliza or her silly ideas about teaching women their rights. What rights? I tell my wife to sit at home and give me heirs, which is all she should expect from life.'

But Clayton was already thinking about something else. 'There were ghosts abroad in Bunhill cemetery last night. Did you hear?'

'No, but I am not surprised,' replied Booth. 'Mother Broughton predicted it. She said the dead would rise from their graves: Bunhill first, then Westminster Abbey.'

Chaloner started to ask for details, but more people had poured into the yard to see what was going on, and there were now so many that he was jostled away from the gossiping pair. One of the new arrivals was Molly, who gave him a shy smile. Then she was almost knocked from her feet as Viscount Mansfield bulled roughly past her. She was saved from a tumble by Baron Lucas, who was walking behind the younger man.

'Have a care, boy!' he bawled. 'Only oafs ride rough-shod over their servants.'

Mansfield whipped around to regard his step-uncle challengingly. 'Tell that to your sister, who dismissed Dutch Jane over some trivial nonsense. I was shocked by her callousness.'

Lucas opened his mouth to reply, but at that moment, the Duke released a great whoop of joy, jabbing an excited finger at a steaming pile of horse dung. Henrietta Florence was on the mend. Everyone surged forward to express their delight. Mansfield was first, but his good wishes were so obviously insincere that his father only inclined his head in polite acknowledgement. Then others crowded around and the Duke's face split into a grin as he accepted their more genuine felicitations.

'Be a man,' Chaloner heard Lucas inform the resentful Viscount. 'If you want him to love you, do something to deserve it.'

'I should not have to,' snapped Mansfield petulantly. 'He should take me as I am. Why should I have to fight for what should be freely given?'

Chaloner did not want to be caught listening to that sort of conversation, and slipped away before either of them noticed him.

As dawn was still only a yellow smear of promise in the night sky, Chaloner decided to go to Bunhill cemetery, to find out exactly what had happened there the previous night. It had nothing to do with Chiffinch, but Thurloe would appreciate a report, given his concerns about the area.

He walked briskly, aware of smoke belching from chimneys as thousands of Londoners heated water for washing, cleaning and cooking. Church bells tolled all over the city, advertising the first of their Sunday services, a bright sound over the deeper rumble of the many feet, hoofs and wheels on cobbles. He hurried past the Charterhouse with its towering walls, then skirted the Artillery Ground, where musketeers drilled, reminding all who saw them that England was currently at war.

Beyond the Artillery Ground was Bunhill Fields, part of which had been set aside for a burial ground during the plague, when the city graveyards began to overflow. The disease had relinquished its hold before any pits could be dug there, but a man named Mr Tyndal had paid for the designated area to be enclosed by walls anyway, anticipating that there would always be a demand for graves, and that money could be made from it.

Chaloner arrived to find Tyndal supervising a funeral. The mourners wore the kind of clothes that revealed them to be nonconformists, for whom the Bunhill cemetery was perfect – most of it was unconsecrated, so Quakers, Baptists and their ilk could use it without compromising their religious beliefs. All carried lanterns, indicating that the deceased had been a person of substance – lamp fuel was expensive, so burying someone in the dark was a public statement of wealth.

Tyndal was a thin, cadaverous individual with long bony limbs, who was forever wringing his oversized hands. He twisted and rubbed them obsequiously until the last mourner had filed past him through the gate, then heaved a sigh of relief.

'Thank God that is over! Mr Bagshaw was meant to be buried at midnight, but *things* were seen, so we had to delay until they had gone. His family expressed an immediate desire to take him somewhere else, so I had to bribe them to stay with a hefty discount.'

Chaloner introduced himself as an envoy of the Lord Chancellor, then said, '"Things"?'

'The walking dead,' elaborated Tyndal hoarsely. 'Of course, we knew they were coming, because Mother Broughton mentioned it. Is that not so, boys?'

The last question was aimed at four men who stood nearby, all larger, younger versions of himself. In the gloom of approaching dawn, they looked vaguely eerie, and Chaloner had noticed a number of the departing funeral party shoot them wary glances as they passed.

'Did you see these mobile corpses yourselves?' Chaloner asked. 'Or did someone just tell you about them?'

'Oh, we saw them,' replied Tyndal grimly. 'At first, we thought they were grave-robbers. Surgeons pay handsomely for fresh specimens, you see, and some are not too picky about where they come from.'

'So what did you see exactly?'

'Well,' began Tyndal, 'we were over by the wood, trimming the turf around Edward Bagshaw's new-dug grave . . . Have you heard of him? He was a famous Puritan divine.'

'Of course.' Chaloner struggled for patience. 'But you were by the wood and you saw . . .'

'The dead,' replied Tyndal in an unsteady voice. 'They wore long black cloaks to conceal their mouldering bones, and they carried their red-glowing souls in little pots.'

'It is true,' put in the biggest son. 'I did not believe Mother Broughton's prophecy before last night. You cannot afford to be superstitious in our line of work, so I usually treat such claims with a healthy scepticism. But now I have seen those terrible figures . . .'

'We fled,' finished Tyndal. 'As fast as our legs could carry us.'

'How do you know it was not a prank?' asked Chaloner, thinking it sounded ludicrous enough to be risible. 'Or one of Mother Broughton's disciples, aiming to add credence to her prophecies by ensuring that one "came true"?'

'Because we know a cadaver when we see one,' replied Tyndal firmly. 'I ran straight to the nearest church and begged the vicar to come and recite some dead-banishing prayers. Only when he pronounced our cemetery safe again did we allow the Bagshaw ceremony to proceed.'

182

Chaloner asked exactly where the 'dead' had been seen, and went to investigate. None of the Tyndals offered to accompany him.

The cemetery was enormous, but as it had only been operational for a few months, it was mostly devoid of graves. The rest was undulating pasture broken by an occasional scrap of woodland. The 'dead' had been spotted inside the largest copse, near the westernmost wall. Chaloner explored it carefully, and found a rope that someone had used to scale the wall, along with footprints in the mud at the bottom. As he had thought, there had been no walking corpses – just people using Bunhill for reasons of their own.

The only other thing of interest was something that was almost invisible in the long grass, evidently having been dropped by mistake. It was a bonnet of an unusual style. He had seen it, or one very similar, on Dutch Jane. He picked it up and saw that a brooch had been pinned to the inside, to keep it out of sight. It was silver and in the shape of a ship. He recalled that Clayton had mentioned something of the kind going missing from Newcastle House and had accused Topp of stealing it. Clearly, the surly steward owed his rival an apology.

As his route home took him past Newcastle House, Chaloner stopped to return the brooch and ask if anyone knew why Dutch Jane had been in Bunhill the previous evening, possibly pretending to be a walking corpse. He entered the yard, and saw Topp and Eliza there, watching servants wash the coach that would take the Duke and Duchess to church later.

'They intend to ride there?' asked Chaloner, startled.

'But the church abuts their house. Surely it would be quicker to walk?'

Eliza shot him a mock-stern look. 'Walk? Perish the thought!'

'Besides, I would sooner carry my beloved Duchess on my back than let her sully her feet in London's filth,' declared Topp stoutly, then reconsidered. 'Although she may be a little too heavy for me these days.'

'If such heroics are necessary, we shall ask Clayton to do it,' said Eliza acidly. 'He is good at lugging hefty burdens about – far more so than the delicate business of estate management.'

'True,' agreed Topp, and smiled at Chaloner, revealing cracked yellow teeth. 'I am pleased you offered to bow your viol for us on Wednesday, Your Honour. It will be much nicer than the flageolets he had intended to hire.'

Chaloner had 'offered' nothing of the kind, and had no intention of playing in Newcastle House, sure he would be too busy. He flailed around for an excuse to decline.

'I am afraid my cousins arrived unexpectedly last night, so I am needed at home.'

He did not bother to say that the girls would be gone long before Wednesday.

'Bring them, Your Worship,' gushed Topp. 'The Duchess will not mind, especially if they can sing or play an instrument.'

'Although she will think more of them if they have some *useful* skills,' put in Eliza. 'Like reading and knowing their own minds. Any ape can bow a jig.'

'But not any ape can make it sound pleasant,' retorted Chaloner, thinking the remark revealed her as a barbarian.

'Men use music to keep women in their place,' announced Eliza pompously, 'by forcing them to practise,

184

so they have no time for more worthy pursuits. I thank God daily for my own dear husband. *He* is not afraid of clever ladies.'

Chaloner glanced at Topp, and decided it was not progressive thinking that prompted the man to grant Eliza her freedom, but fear of what she might do to him if he stood in her way.

'So bring these cousins, Your Honour,' said the steward, speaking to bring an end to the sparring. 'They will be most welcome.'

Chaloner declined again, but Topp was insistent, claiming first that the Duchess would be disappointed to lose a decent violist, and then that she would want to meet two talented young ladies. The second point prompted Chaloner to reflect that he did not know if the girls *had* any talents, and if they did, whether they were socially acceptable ones. What if they took after him, and had an aptitude for spying or swordplay?

'You are kind,' he said briskly, 'but I do not—'

'Good, it is settled then, Your Nobleness,' said Topp. 'There is no need to bring your own viol, because we have hired a set. The Duchess cannot abide instruments that do not match, and says that the look of them is much more important than the way they sound.'

'Does she indeed?' murmured Chaloner, thinking the occasion was sounding worse and worse. He hastened to ask his questions so that he could leave before he was bludgeoned into something else against his will. 'Clayton mentioned a missing brooch earlier—'

'The silver ship,' interrupted Topp wearily. 'He thinks I took it, but I never did. Why would I would steal from the mistress I love? And why would I risk losing a nice job with a large salary and free accommodation?'

185

Chaloner rummaged in his pocket. 'Is this it?'

Topp snatched it from him. 'Where did you find it? *Please* tell me that Clayton sold it to you. I should love to see him disgraced.'

'It was pinned inside this.' Chaloner presented the hat.

Eliza frowned. 'That is Dutch Jane's cap. Are you saying *she* stole the Duchess's jewellery? I suppose she might have done. She *was* caught red-handed with a pilfered hen.'

'Have you seen her since she was dismissed?'

'No, but I cannot say I miss her,' replied Eliza. 'She had developed a nasty habit of listening at keyholes and pawing through personal documents. She never did it when we lived in Holland, but the moment we arrived in England . . . I wondered if she was a spy, to be frank.'

Topp scoffed. 'My lady is only interested in academic pursuits, while my Duke is only concerned with horses. I cannot see the enemy learning anything of value from them.'

'So Dutch Jane has not been back, begging to be reinstated?' asked Chaloner.

'Just once, Your Brilliance,' said Topp. 'But she was more indignant than contrite, so I gave her some money and sent her on her way.'

'Enough for her to buy passage home?'

'No, but more than she deserved – and more than the Duchess would have wanted me to give. My lady was furious with her, because her antics hurt Molly, who is a simple child. Moreover, the Duchess had decreed that all our poultry were under her personal protection, so the theft of a chicken was a deliberate affront to her authority.'

'Why all these questions?' asked Eliza curiously. 'And why do you have Jane's bonnet?'

'I found it in Bunhill cemetery. Do you know why she might have been there?'

Eliza raised her eyebrows in astonishment. 'I cannot see her – or anyone from Newcastle House – frequenting such a place. She would have been afraid of meeting its walking corpses.'

'And those *have* been out and about,' put in Topp. 'Our milkmaid told us this morning. Apparently, cloaked skeletons were seen carrying their bloodied souls in glowing cauldrons.'

'Pranksters,' said Chaloner dismissively. 'Or cronies of Mother Broughton, who want everyone to think her predictions are coming true. Dutch Jane was probably one of them, given that her hat was found where these so-called bodies were seen.'

'You are wrong,' stated Eliza firmly. 'First, Dutch Jane would never pretend to be a corpse – she is far too dour for japes, not to mention far too superstitious. And second, Mother Broughton is a great seer whose prophecies are always accurate. Have you met her?'

'No,' acknowledged Chaloner. 'But she is—'

'Then come with me now. I shall introduce you, and you can judge her for yourself.'

Chaloner followed Eliza to the maze of alleys between Clerkenwell Green and the Fleet River, where Mother Broughton occupied a small, mean cottage at the end of a row. Eliza rapped on the door, which was answered by a woman whom she introduced as Joan Cole the tobacco-seller. Joan smiled at her, but regarded Chaloner with such rank suspicion that he supposed his attempt to render himself less sinister with a gay hat ribbon had not been entirely successful.

The house was tiny, comprising a downstairs parlour and an attic for sleeping. The floor was of beaten earth, yet was very respectably furnished: new stools around a handsome table, a gleaming set of copper pots hanging over the hearth, and some clean, bright cushions. They all looked like recent acquisitions, so he supposed they were gifts from admirers.

Mother Broughton sat in a throne-like chair by the fire, smoking her pipe. The room was hot to the point of stifling, and Chaloner, whose clothes were still damp from poking around the cemetery, began to steam. Predictably, the seer was offended when Eliza told her that there was some doubt over the authenticity of Bunhill's ambling cadavers.

'I am a genuine soothsayer; I have no need for deceit,' she snapped. 'My prophecies *will* come true, so I do not need anyone to help them along. Perhaps Dutch Jane went to the cemetery to *watch* the walking corpses, and fled when she saw they were real, dropping her bonnet in the process.'

Eliza looked doubtful. 'I do not see her visiting a cemetery in the dark.'

Mother Broughton sniffed. 'I do. She is a nasty piece, and took against me after I foretold that she would come to a bad end – one entailing a vat of milk and a sausage.'

'Goodness!' muttered Chaloner, trying to envisage how that could possibly come about. Then he thought about the rest of Mother Broughton's testimony. If she and Dutch Jane had fallen out, then it was unlikely that Jane would go to Bunhill and put on a show on her behalf,

188

so what *had* she been doing in a place that must have been eerie at night, especially for someone who Eliza said was superstitious?

'Do you know where I might find her?' he asked.

The women shook their heads. 'But I will ask around,' offered Eliza. 'And if I track her down, I will say that you will pay for her time. Greed will bring her running to your door.'

'Then do it quickly,' advised Mother Broughton. 'I told you: her days are numbered.'

'I heard your predictions for the coming week,' said Chaloner, supposing he had better learn more about them for Thurloe's benefit. 'Walking corpses in Westminster on Tuesday, the death of a messenger on Thursday, and weeping and wailing on Good Friday, along with a covering of darkness.'

'It will all come to pass, just as I say,' declared Mother Broughton comfortably. 'However, you left out the best bit – the joy of Easter Day, when all sin and evil will be wiped away, leaving the righteous in charge. I shall be one of them, of course, and I am looking forward to having a bit of power.'

'I am sure you are,' said Chaloner. 'So what happens to the rest of us?'

'The wicked will die, but do not worry, because you will not be among them. I predict that you will leave London and devote your life to cheese.'

Chaloner blinked, wrong-footed. 'To *cheese?*'

Mother Broughton smiled enigmatically. 'You will see.'

Outside, a bell began to chime the hour, and Eliza cocked her head. 'I must go. My lady will be waiting for me to accompany her to church. Now, do not forget,

Mr Chaloner – the Red Bull tonight. Your eyes will be opened in ways that you cannot possibly imagine.'

Chaloner was not sure he liked the sound of that.

As there were no coaches travelling west that day, Chaloner took his cousins to the Palm Sunday service in the Covent Garden church, although he doubted the wisdom of this decision when Wiseman accompanied them, and it transpired that Ursula had a provocatively swaying gait of which any prostitute would be proud. Thus it appeared as though he and the surgeon had secured themselves a couple of harlots.

'They are my cousins,' he informed a smirking Dr Clarke, knowing exactly what the Court physician was thinking.

'Of course they are,' replied Clarke with a man-of-the-world wink. 'I have a "cousin", too. Her frolicking company is always a delightful change from my dull old wife.'

'How can you frolic with a cousin, yet have a wife as well?' asked Veriana guilelessly.

'Lord!' muttered Chaloner, while Wiseman smothered a snort of laughter.

'I take it you are new to London, my dear,' said Clarke with an indulgent leer. 'So allow me to explain. Men are—'

'Why are you here, Clarke?' interrupted Chaloner hastily, not about to stand by while a courtier corrupted his cousins, although he suspected that the younger but more world-wise Ursula would learn nothing she did not already know. 'What is wrong with your own parish church in Clerkenwell?'

Clarke pulled a disagreeable face. 'Its services never

start on time, because the vicar is obliged to wait for the Newcastles, who turn up when the fancy takes them. I cannot afford to waste hours sitting around doing nothing. I am a busy man.'

'I see,' said Chaloner, wondering if other parishioners thought the same, and if so, whether it was yet another grievance that Londoners could bring against the nobility.

'Besides, this is a better place to meet new patients,' Clarke went on. 'In Clerkenwell, too many mansions have their own chapels, whereas most rich Covent Garden folk worship here.'

'They do,' agreed Wiseman. 'Why do you think I bought a house on the piazza? Incidentally, did you hear that I examined Chiffinch yesterday and revealed you to be a fool of the first order?'

Clarke scowled. 'You had no right! It shows a lack of professional courtesy.'

'He discovered the truth about Chiffinch's death,' countered Chaloner, before Wiseman could respond with something more forceful. 'Namely that he did not die of an impostume, but was murdered. Your diagnosis would have allowed a killer to go free.'

Clarke eyed him coolly. 'I suppose you think that *I* did something to harm him, then gave a verdict of natural causes to conceal my crime. But you are wrong. I liked Chiffinch. Indeed, he was one of my wealthiest – and thus most valued – clients. Believe me, he was worth far more to me alive than dead, and his demise is a serious financial blow.'

He turned and stalked away before Chaloner could ask him any more.

'I pity his wife,' declared Ursula, watching him go. 'She married an arse.'

191

'That sort of language will not encourage respectable suitors,' warned Chaloner, although he was aware that the rebuke made him sound like a stuffy old matron.

Ursula winked roguishly. 'Then I will have to settle for the other sort. As we said yesterday, it does not really matter, as long as they are rich.'

'Of course it matters,' said Chaloner primly. 'Your mother would not condone you marrying . . .'

'An arse?' asked Ursula innocently when he faltered.

Wiseman roared with laughter.

As it was Palm Sunday, the service was longer than usual, and the vicar, for reasons known only to himself, delivered a rambling homily on the perils of home-brewing, which was irrelevant to most of his congregation, who either had servants to do it for them or could afford to buy from reputable dealers. Veriana sat with her eyes closed, so that Chaloner wondered if she was asleep, while Ursula flirted with two young men in the pew behind. As the vicar droned, Chaloner pondered what the girls had asked him to do.

He began by reflecting on family obligations, trying to guess what his father's position would have been. He kept coming back to the same conclusion: that his cousins had lost everything through no fault of their own, and that it would be unkind to send them home with nothing. He imagined his own sisters in the same predicament, and the sorrow and anger *he* would feel if a kinsman refused to help them.

Of course, the favour they wanted was no small order. It would not be easy to secure wealthy spouses, because no matter how charming, intelligent and pretty they were, they were still the penniless offspring of a man

192

named as a traitor, and no Royalist would consider them a good match. Again, he considered Leybourn and Lester, but neither was in London, and he had a feeling that unless he acted quickly, the girls would take matters into their own hands – which might be disastrous if Ursula's behaviour that morning was anything to go by.

He had asked Wiseman's opinion the previous night, but the surgeon's solution was to set them to work for Temperance, on the grounds that her high-class courtesans were showered with money from besotted customers. Unfortunately, Chaloner doubted his family would approve of him apprenticing his cousins to a house of ill repute, no matter how fabulous the financial returns.

The more he reflected, the more he realised he was massively ill-equipped to handle such a matter. First, he had no idea how to go about it, although he did know that arranged marriages were complex and took weeks, months and sometimes years before mutually satisfactory agreements were hammered out. Second, he was too busy to chaperone two young women, and it was obvious that Ursula in particular should not be allowed out alone. And third, he was unpopular at Court – not only did people remember his past and consider him sinister, but he worked for an earl who tottered nearer to disaster with every passing day. No one would want an alliance with him or his relatives.

Then, with a flash of inspiration, he remembered Thurloe, a man to whom family meant everything. The ex-Spymaster had arranged good marriages for his own kin, and there was no one whose advice Chaloner respected more. The ex-Spymaster might even know some suitable bachelors. Relieved to see light at the end of the tunnel, Chaloner turned his attention back to the dangers of home-fermentation.

The moment the vicar intoned the final grace, Chaloner stood to leave. Usually, he was among the first out through the door, but his cousins had other ideas, and decided to use the opportunity to their advantage. Murmuring that the more people they met, the easier it would be to achieve their objective, they smiled at and curtsied to anyone who glanced in their direction. When Chaloner looked around for Wiseman, aiming to beg his help in prising them away, he saw the surgeon had been cornered by an angry Fanny Clarke.

'You should have been more circumspect,' she was informing him tightly.

'Circumspect?' echoed Wiseman indignantly. 'I reported the facts, madam. It is not in my nature to cover up the ineptitude of incompetent colleagues.'

'My Timothy is not incompetent!' cried Fanny, distressed. 'And while I appreciate that you had to make your findings known, did you *have* to do it in a way that hurt him so?'

Chaloner backed away, unwilling to be drawn into their spat. Then he heard a sibilant voice behind him, and turned to see Swaddell.

'There you are, Tom,' beamed the assassin. 'I have been looking for you.'

'Why?' asked Chaloner uneasily. 'Has something else happened at White Hall?'

'No,' replied Swaddell, and Chaloner saw with alarm that his beady black eyes were fixed unblinkingly on Ursula. 'Although I did go back there after we parted last night, in the hope of cornering one or two suspects.

But most were at a private gathering in the King's apartments, to which I was not invited.'

Chaloner blinked his surprise. 'His Majesty held a party so soon after the death of one of his favourites?'

'Yes, and a good time was had by all, judging by the racket they made. It led me to question whether Chiffinch was as popular as his so-called friends claim.'

'It is something to bear in mind. So why are you here? I thought we had agreed to meet in the White Hall kitchens at noon, to ask about the oysters.'

'We did,' replied Swaddell, still gazing at Ursula. 'But you already followed that trail and it took you nowhere. Besides, I felt obliged to come and warn you about the palace – it is not a safe place for you to be at the moment because of the ill-feeling towards your Earl.'

'I know,' said Chaloner drily. 'He has not been popular for some time.'

This was an understatement.

'But it is much worse now that everyone knows Chiffinch was murdered,' said Swaddell, and looked at Chaloner for the first time. 'People really do suspect him of ordering the death.'

'Then tell them he had nothing to do with it. Not only would he never resort to such tactics, but his entire household was struggling to save his library from a flood when Chiffinch's oysters were poisoned. Well, other than Brodrick, but anyone who thinks *him* capable of clever plots is seriously deluded.'

'I will try, but folk believe what suits them, not what is true. Regardless, there is an *atmosphere* in White Hall. I did not want you strolling into it without due warning.'

'Thank you, but you could have sent a message. You did not need to come in person.'

'It was no trouble,' said Swaddell airily, his eyes back on Ursula. 'Besides, I am not averse to attending my devotions occasionally, and this is a nice place to do it.'

'What about your own church?' Chaloner realised he had no idea where Swaddell was currently living.

'The last time I went, there happened to be a clap of thunder, a flash of lightning, and a gust of wind that blew out all the candles. The vicar had the temerity to suggest that it was God objecting to my presence.'

Swaddell's vicar was not the only one who was uncomfortable with the assassin being in a holy place. Some of the Covent Garden congregation had formed a knot by the altar, as if for safety, while those nearest the door had already scuttled through it.

Sincerely hoping that Swaddell's appearance had not permanently ruined his standing with his neighbours, Chaloner hastened to draw his cousins outside. He paused to ensure that the parish clerk had recorded his name in the attendance register, although he had a feeling that everyone would remember that particular visit anyway, then led the way at a rapid clip across the piazza, aiming to be out of sight as quickly as possible. He was irked but not surprised when Swaddell followed, offering Ursula his arm. She took it, and Chaloner supposed he would have to advise her to be more particular.

When they arrived home, they discovered that Wiseman's servants had been busy, and had produced a fairly normal meal – the surgeon had peculiar dietary theories, and had trained his people to produce all manner of 'delicacies' that rational folk would never allow past their lips. However, the presence of two young ladies had prompted them to do something special, so Chaloner, his cousins and Swaddell were presented with fresh bread, eggs from Chaloner's chickens, and a venison pastry. For Wiseman, there was boiled cabbage and raw liver, which he maintained strengthened the blood and improved virility.

'Then I shall share them with you,' declared Swaddell, after listening to the surgeon pontificate on the matter. 'There is nothing wrong with improving virility, as you never know when it might come in handy.' He beamed at Ursula, who grinned back.

Chaloner had not expected Swaddell to dine with them, but the assassin had declared himself available, and Ursula's come-hither smile had seen him shoot through the front door like an arrow. Wiseman had not been very pleased, loath for his reputation at Court to be tarnished by dint of him entertaining state-sanctioned killers in his home.

'You do not consider yourself virile enough already?' the surgeon asked, making no effort to disguise his antipathy. 'Perhaps Williamson should recruit another assassin then.'

'I am not an assassin,' objected Swaddell sharply, although the dangerous gleam in his eye belied the claim. 'I am a clerk. His *favourite* clerk, which means I own the respect and admiration of many people.'

'Do you?' breathed Ursula, patently fascinated by him.

'No!' cried Chaloner, suddenly recalling with awful, heart-stopping clarity that Swaddell had expressed a desire for a wife, and here were two young women in want of husbands. Everyone looked askance at him, so he hastened to conceal his consternation before Swaddell guessed what had caused it. 'I mean, of course you are well regarded, but—'

'You should take Ursula and Veriana to the soirée in Newcastle House on Wednesday,' said Wiseman, coming to his rescue by changing the subject. '*I* shall be at Temperance's club, of course, but as you tell me that place is not good enough for your superior kin, I shall not extend an invitation for them to accompany me there.'

'God help me!' muttered Chaloner, realising he would have to see Thurloe before either Wiseman saw his cousins enrolled as prostitutes or one accepted an offer of marriage from Swaddell.

'Oh, please let us go to Newcastle House, Thomas,' begged Ursula. 'I can sing and Veriana plays the viol.'

'We shall all go together,' determined Swaddell happily. 'You two can entertain the ducal couple, while Tom and I conduct some important business.'

'What important business?' asked Veriana keenly. 'Our marriages?'

'Matters pertaining to the security of a nation,' replied Swaddell grandly and not very truthfully. 'We are influential men, you know.'

'Are you?' gushed Ursula, simpering in a way that made Swaddell beam back rather inanely. 'I thought you must be. You have that air about you.'

At that point, Chaloner saw he could not wait to talk to Thurloe – he had to act now. 'I have given the matter some serious thought,' he said briskly. 'And I have decided upon two good suitors for you. You can go home to the Isle of Man tomorrow, while I begin negotiations on your behalf. Their names are Salathiel Lester and Will Leybourn.'

'Lester is a fine man,' said Wiseman, 'although as a sea-captain in wartime, his chances of survival are slim. However, you should not consider Leybourn. He is too . . . second-hand.'

'What do you mean?' asked Chaloner, offended on his friend's behalf.

'I mean he has tried many times for a happy alliance, and every one of them has failed,' explained Wiseman. 'The common factor in all these romantic disasters is Leybourn himself.'

'That is unfair,' objected Chaloner. 'It is hardly his fault that circumstances have conspired against him.'

'He is not rich either,' put in Swaddell smugly. 'Surveyors are badly paid and their prospects are poor. You should widen the search to include other men. Clerks, for example.'

'I agree,' said Veriana. 'So we shall go to Newcastle House and—'

'No,' interrupted Chaloner sharply. 'I have no intention of going there myself. And if I change my mind, I shall be working and thus too busy for escort duties.'

'Do not let that trouble you, Tom,' said Swaddell smoothly. 'I can mind the ladies, while you see to . . . the vital issues that have been entrusted to us.'

'It is settled then,' said Veriana, pleased, and Chaloner saw he had been outmanoeuvred on all fronts. 'But do not fear that we might disgrace you, Thomas. Ursula and I are accomplished musicians.'

'Then show me,' said Chaloner, partly to see if they were telling the truth, but more because it had been a while since he had had time to play, and if he ever needed the peace his viol could bring, it was that day.

He was pleasantly surprised to discover that they had not exaggerated their skills. Veriana was a solid violist, while Ursula was a sweet, clear soprano. He played duets with one and sang with the other, and although he knew he should be thinking about Chiffinch, he was enjoying

199

himself too much to stop. The only negative was that Swaddell declined to leave.

'I do not relax very often,' the assassin confided, 'but I find your cousins' company a delight. Besides, there is no point going to White Hall today, because the Cockpit Club has organised some fox-tossing in the Privy Garden. Decent people will have gone home, while the rest will be too interested in the resulting blood and gore to talk to us.'

Chaloner grimaced his distaste. Fox-tossing entailed driving the animals across canvas slings that people would then haul on, to see who could flip the hapless creatures highest into the air. Injury was inevitable and death frequent.

'You disapprove?' asked Swaddell, seeing his reaction. 'But foxes kill chickens, and given your affection for birds . . .'

'That does not mean I want to see them tortured,' retorted Chaloner shortly.

'I dislike any sport involving cruelty to animals,' said Swaddell, a confidence that surprised Chaloner, given the assassin's fondness for bloodshed. 'I always sense their longing to be somewhere else, which is how I feel, most of the time.'

Chaloner softened. The admission did not mean he wanted the assassin to marry one of his cousins, but it had certainly rendered him a little more human in his eyes. Perhaps it would not be such a trial to work with him after all, he thought.

Chapter 7

At six o'clock, Veriana and Ursula declared themselves too tired to perform more, although Chaloner could have continued longer. He set down his bow with considerable reluctance, and woke Swaddell, who had fallen asleep on Wiseman's velvet-upholstered 'Knole' sofa. This was a fashionable but acutely uncomfortable piece of furniture, so nodding off on it revealed just how bored he had been. The assassin left soon after, promising to take the ladies for a walk in St James's Park as soon as his duties allowed.

'What a charming man,' declared Ursula, when she returned from seeing him to the door. 'Much nicer than that terrifying surgeon.'

Chaloner saw he would have to supervise her closely, given that she was obviously not a very good judge of character. He asked the footman to bring cake and watered wine, ignoring Veriana's claim that she preferred French brandy, ate quickly, then set off towards Lincoln's Inn. He needed to tell Thurloe about his foray to Clerkenwell, not to mention begging his advice regarding his cousins, and after that, he decided to accept Eliza's invitation to the Red Bull, in the expectation that it would allow him to make casual enquiries about what was brewing in the area. He felt simultaneously energised and relaxed from his musical interlude, and his head was full of melodies by his favourite composers.

He reached Lincoln's Inn, and was told that Thurloe was in his Dial Court chambers. The yard was named for the scientific instrument that graced its middle, although this had been broken and no longer worked properly. It did not matter much, though, as the device was so complicated that no one knew how to use it anyway.

Chaloner climbed the stairs to Chamber XIII and knocked, but there was no answer. He was just wondering where his friend might have gone when he heard his name called. He stifled a sigh of annoyance when he saw Thurloe's fellow bencher, William Prynne, approaching.

Prynne was a pamphleteer, who penned poisonous discourses on anything that drew his disapproval. Most things did, so Londoners were regularly regaled with diatribes on the wrongs of long hair, women's fashion, maypoles, dancing, bishops and politics to name but a few of his bugbears. He had been outrageously vocal in his criticism of the government, and had lost his ears for calling the old Queen a whore. Then the King, in an inspired and uncharacteristic act of genius, had appointed him Keeper of Records. Flattered, Prynne had become an instant Royalist.

'Have you heard?' he began, delighted to find someone to rant at. 'A thousand robins descended on Clerkenwell last week. It means the area will soon suffer a terrible calamity.'

'Did Mother Broughton tell you that?' asked Chaloner warily.

'Mother Broughton!' spat Prynne. 'She is a woman, and I put no store in what *they* have to say. No, this information comes from *me*. I saw the birds myself.'

Chaloner raised his eyebrows. 'If there were that many birds in one place, why has no one else reported it?'

'Because they were only seen by the godly and pure in heart,' replied Prynne loftily. 'Obviously, I was the only one who met the criteria.'

'A *thousand* robins? How did you count them all?'

'Well, it was only six, if you are going to be pedantic, but the point is that I sensed great evil there, especially around the Red Bull. That place encourages women in the dreadful and epidemical vanities of our age – like reading and writing.'

Chaloner blinked. 'Those are not vanities! Indeed, you make your living from them.'

Prynne waved a dismissive hand. 'Yes, but I am a man. It is different.'

'Is it, indeed?' muttered Chaloner, half amused and half repelled by the man's bigotry.

'Clerkenwell is a pit of abomination,' declared Prynne. 'It heaves with mischievous sinners, heretics, idolaters, harlots, blasphemers, mahometans, heathens, unbelievers and other miscreants that by their words and acts dare to pour scorn upon the holy gospel of Jesus Christ. I have seen them cavorting in the Red Bull, that notorious hub of filth and debauchery.'

'You have been inside it?'

'Of course not! It is a playhouse, and they stand on the broad, beaten, pleasant road that leads to hell. I watched from a distance, and I witnessed the wicked flocking there for capering wantonness, incontinency and profanity. Every one of them aims to turn the world upside down – to set women over men, the wicked over the just, and promote vice over decency.'

'I do not suppose you noticed Bess Widdrington or Fanny Clarke among the throng, did you? Captain Rolt claims to have followed them there, but they deny it.'

'Fanny Clarke would never enter such a place,' declared Prynne, 'and even that foolish Bess would know better than to step over its idolatrous and epidemical threshold.'

'Oh,' said Chaloner. 'Then—'

'Unless they were led astray by their husbands, of course. Clarke has a vile and iniquitous soul, while Widdrington has no soul at all. Neither should be allowed near His Majesty. Did you hear what they did on this most holy of Sabbaths? The filthy and pestilential entertainment they staged?'

'The fox-tossing?'

'Yes! On Palm Sunday! Widdrington's creature Tooley – the gross, hulking one who looks like an ape – won the game by hurling one fox so high that it is said to have seen Lambeth before it crashed to its death.'

'Perhaps you should write a pamphlet about it,' suggested Chaloner, thinking it was high time that Prynne's vicious pen did something worthwhile.

Prynne smirked. 'There is no need, because vengeance has already been visited upon Tooley – he died shortly afterwards. His demise is blamed on a fever, but I know it was God.'

'Tooley is dead?' asked Chaloner, startled. 'Are you sure?'

Prynne nodded with great satisfaction. 'I shall pray for

his soul, although not even the petitions of a godly man like myself can save *him* from eternal damnation. But speaking of godly men, are you here to see Mr Thurloe?'

Prynne admired Thurloe and was always trying to win his favour. Chaloner was glad of it, as Prynne would make a vexatious enemy with his penchant for libellous diatribes.

'He is in the chapel,' Prynne went on. 'It is Palm Sunday, so of course that saintly soul will be at his devotions. I have been at mine all day . . . well, other than the times I went to White Hall, Clerkenwell, Bunhill Fields, the Tower, and my coffee house.'

'Your knees must ache with all that kneeling.'

Chaloner's sarcasm was lost on Prynne. 'They do, so I must fortify myself with medicinal claret. I deplore strong drink as a vice of Satan, but on occasions such as this, it cannot be avoided.'

Lincoln's Inn's chapel was a pretty building with large windows that allowed sunlight to flood in. At night it was quietly serene, lit by lamps that turned its pale stone to dark gold. It stood above an open undercroft, where the benchers were buried when they died. Thurloe had expressed a desire to lie there one day, although the prospect of a world without the ex-Spymaster was one that Chaloner refused to contemplate.

'There you are at last,' said Thurloe, as Chaloner came to sit on the pew next to him. 'I expected you sooner than this.'

'You did?' asked Chaloner warily. 'Why?'

'Because two of James Chaloner's daughters arrived in the city yesterday, which caused no mean stir among those who still consider him a hero. I informed them that your cousins did not come to lead a new rebellion, but I would have liked confirmation of it before now.'

Chaloner bowed an apology, but was not about to confess that the delay had been because he had been enjoying himself with music. 'Mischief was not their reason for coming. However, they do resent their father's treatment by vengeful Royalists, and grudges are easily tapped by the unscrupulous.'

'They are,' agreed Thurloe. 'So you must find something to keep them busy while they are here. A courtship, perhaps.'

'I am glad you suggested that. Do you know anyone who wants a wife? They say it does not matter if he is old and ugly, but he must be rich.'

Thurloe laughed. 'I am afraid respectable men with large fortunes are in short supply these days. Is that why they came? I should have guessed.'

Chaloner scrubbed his face with his hands. 'What am I to do? They will refuse to leave as long as they are single, and I cannot think of any suitable candidates. I thought Lester and Leybourn might do, but Wiseman raised some concerns about them both . . .'

'I love Leybourn dearly, but I would not want him as a husband for any kinswoman of mine. He is fickle in his affections, and there would be a constant danger that he would tire of her and fix his gaze on someone else.'

'And Lester?'

'He has chosen too dangerous an occupation. War will resume now that winter is over, and ships will batter each other until one side concedes defeat. Lester cannot provide for a wife if he is dead.'

Chaloner was silent. Of all his friends, he liked Lester the most, because he was honest, decent and lacked the eccentricities of the others. He hated the thought of him killed in a senseless conflict that should never have been started in the first place.

'I suppose there is always Kersey,' he said after a while. 'He is wealthy.'

Thurloe laughed a second time. 'He is married already, not to one lady, but to two. He spends Mondays, Wednesdays and Fridays with the first; Tuesdays, Thursdays and Saturdays with the second; and he takes Sundays off.'

Chaloner gaped at him. 'Kersey is a bigamist?'

Thurloe nodded. 'And may be willing to take both your cousins off your hands, too, but I would not recommend it.'

Chaloner was astounded. He had always known that there was more to the quiet, dapper little charnel-house keeper than met the eye – he had once virtually confessed to killing his predecessor, for a start – but he could not see him as an alluring lothario. Then he reconsidered: Kersey was rich, and that was all that mattered, according to Ursula and Veriana.

Thurloe read his thoughts. 'Do not judge your cousins too harshly. Life is harder for gentlewomen than men. You thought you were in a difficult position after the Restoration, but you could work, and now you are a valued member of a noble household.'

'Hardly valued,' muttered Chaloner.

'But Veriana and Ursula's only hope is to make decent marriages. I appreciate that you are busy with Chiffinch's killer, but the lives and happiness of two people are at stake here. You must find the time to do what is right.'

'Yes,' conceded Chaloner. 'Will you help me?'

'Of course. However, first, you must find them more suitable lodgings. They cannot live with you and Wiseman for more than a few days, or people will talk and their reputations will be tarnished. Until you have them respectably housed, you must provide a chaperone. Do you know any virtuous ladies who might oblige?'

'Barbara Chiffinch,' suggested Chaloner. 'She would do it.'

Thurloe raised his eyebrows. 'Taking them to the Pimp-Master General's home is hardly wise, Thomas. Think of someone else.'

But Chaloner shook his head helplessly. There was no one.

'Then you had better acquire some new friends – fast,' advised Thurloe. 'In the interim, I recommend making them your wards, which will give you the legal authority to negotiate marriages on their behalf. I can draw up the document in my chambers now, if you like. And as we walk there, you can tell me all you have learned since we last met.'

The Inn was silent as Chaloner and Thurloe strolled towards Dial Court, its tall walls muting the sounds from outside. Chaloner breathed in deeply, relishing the scent of soil dampened by spring rain, and the sense of ancient solidity from the venerable buildings.

'The peace is deceptive,' said Thurloe, as they crunched along the gravel paths. 'While the city sleeps, a serpent stirs in Clerkenwell.'

'You sound like Mother Broughton. She believes that something terrible will happen on Good Friday, but that anyone who survives until Easter Day will enjoy a glorious Utopia with her and all the other righteous souls. I was taken to meet her this morning.'

'Tell me about her,' ordered Thurloe.

Chaloner obliged, then described what had happened with Bunhill's 'walking corpses', finishing with, 'I do not know if Dutch Jane was involved or just an innocent bystander. Regardless, the dead were *not* up and about – unless they need ropes to climb over walls.'

'So have you discovered any more about what is brewing in the area?'

'Not really, although I plan to visit Eliza's school in the Red Bull when I leave here. Perhaps I will learn something useful there.'

'Then be careful, because the courtier who died this afternoon – Tooley – is rumoured to have caught his fatal fever in that particular tavern.'

'Prynne thinks it was divine punishment for him winning the fox-tossing contest.'

'Fox-tossing?' Thurloe grimaced his revulsion. 'Oh, for a military dictatorship again! Cromwell would not have countenanced such disgusting pastimes.'

'Tooley's death is so untimely that I want Wiseman to look at him. Of course, if it does transpire that he died by sly means, I am not sure what I can do about it. It is not for me to explore the murder of everyone who hated the Earl.'

'It will be if Tooley was poisoned, like Chiffinch,' Thurloe pointed out. 'But tell me about your investigation so far.'

Chaloner did, aware as he spoke that his findings were disgracefully meagre. Then they reached Chamber XIII, where Thurloe sat at his table to draw up the promised contract. Before he began, he reached inside his coat and withdrew a sheet of paper.

'While I work, read this. You can tell me your thoughts when I have finished.'

Chaloner sat by the fire and unfolded the page. It was an anonymous letter addressed to the Duke of Newcastle. The sender began by declaring that he was sorry to cause such a fine, honourable man pain, but His Grace was likely to lose his good name unless he took his wife in hand. It went on to claim that the Duchess was having an affair with Steward Topp.

Chaloner studied the letter carefully. The handwriting was inconsistent, suggesting that the writer had tried to disguise it, although he was only partially successful, as he had failed to change the way he styled his letter *f*s. These were so distinctive that it would be easy to match them to samples taken from suspects. Moreover, Chaloner was sure he had seen them before, although he could not recall where, no matter how hard he tried.

'An unpleasant piece of malice,' he said eventually, when Thurloe set down his pen and scattered sand on the document he had just completed. 'But why do you have it? Was it intercepted by your spies?'

'I have no spies, Thomas,' said Thurloe mildly. 'I have friends who send me news. However, this letter has nothing to do with them. The Duke gave it to me himself.'

'Did he?' asked Chaloner, surprised. 'Why?'

'Because he wants me to find out who sent it. He approached Prynne first. He thought *he* might recognise the handwriting, given that he sees so many different documents in his capacity as Keeper of Records. But Prynne could not help, so he brought the Duke to me. I agreed to look into the matter, because the Duchess once did me a great kindness and I am in her debt.'

Chaloner waited for an explanation, but none came, and he knew better than to pry. 'Does the Duke believe this claim about his wife and Topp?'

'He does not, and is outraged by it. He assures me that the Duchess is more interested in books than amours, and that if she did have an affair, it would not be with Topp.'

'What is wrong with Topp, other than being oily, old and unattractive?'

'First, she loves her Duke, who is a poet, equestrian, war hero and fellow intellectual, whereas Topp is a former coal merchant. And second, when the Duke is away or indisposed, the Duchess always shares her bedchamber with Eliza. Ergo, an illicit liaison would be impossible, because the Duchess is never alone.'

'So the Duke wants to prosecute the writer of this letter for libel? That is why he wants you to hunt the culprit down?'

Thurloe nodded. 'The Bishop-mark shows that it was mailed in Grantham, so I shall go there tomorrow, to see if the postmaster remembers who sent it.'

'Is there any connection between Grantham and the Newcastles?

'None whatsoever, which tells me that the sender thought he was being clever by choosing it. However, he has miscalculated, because the postmaster will not see many missives addressed to nobles, and he will almost certainly recall who handed it to him. I am confident of a good description, after which I may require your help in apprehending the culprit.'

Chaloner inclined his head. 'It should not be difficult to identify him. I already know several people who dislike the Duchess, starting with her stepson.'

'Poor Mansfield does not have the courage to launch such a scheme – he would be too frightened of being caught and losing the last vestiges of his father's affection.

But perhaps you will keep your eyes and ears open as you go about your business. Any clues will be gratefully received, and in return, I shall think about husbands for your cousins.'

It was not far from Chancery Lane to the Red Bull, although Chaloner was aware of a very peculiar atmosphere as he crossed the Fleet River and entered Clerkenwell. Some folk walked with a bounce in their step, while others skulked furtively. He supposed Mother Broughton's prophecies were responsible, and people's responses to them depended on whether they considered themselves godly or sinful.

He was just approaching John Street when he saw the Earl's clerk scuttling along. Barker started to duck down an alley when he recognised Chaloner, but thought better of it when he realised he had been spotted. With obvious reluctance, he came to talk.

'I have just delivered letters to Newcastle House,' he gabbled, although his eyes were furtive and Chaloner knew he was lying; for a start, he had been coming from entirely the wrong direction. 'Now I am on my way back to Piccadilly.'

Chaloner regarded him appraisingly. 'Have you been in the Red Bull?'

Barker stared at him. 'Of course not! Bess Widdrington says that is where Tooley caught the fever that carried him to his grave.'

'His death is odd,' mused Chaloner. 'I heard he won the fox-tossing contest, but if he was well enough for that – and I imagine it was strenuous – how can he have been dying?'

'These sicknesses strike very fast, as I am sure you know.'

212

'Not that fast,' averred Chaloner. 'But Wiseman will find the truth. I will ask him to examine Tooley tomorrow.'

'Very wise,' said Barker, and bowed. 'Now, if you will excuse me, I must return to Clarendon House.'

He hurried away, and Chaloner continued towards the Red Bull. He arrived to find all its window shutters closed, and two men minding the door, ready to repel undesirables. It did not take a genius to guess that something illicit was going on within, and he wondered if it was wise for him to enter openly – that it might be better to pick the lock on the side door again and slip in unnoticed. But the sentries had seen him, and it would look suspicious to walk away now.

He took a deep breath and approached them, a little surprised when the guardsmen transpired to be guardswomen. One was the beefy tobacco-seller from Mother Broughton's house – he recalled her being introduced as Joan Cole.

'Name?' she demanded. 'I know we met before, but I cannot remember what you called yourself. Our seer gets so many visitors, see.'

He told her, and she ran a thick forefinger down a visitor list that she tugged from her pocket. Chaloner was evidently on it, because she opened the door and indicated that he was to enter. He did, then gazed around in astonishment.

The main room had been rendered warm and welcoming, with clean rushes on the floor and a fire in the hearth. Its atmosphere was quietly civilised, with none of the rowdy bawling that usually characterised taverns when they were full. And the Red Bull *was* full – there was scarcely room to move between the packed tables. Eliza hurried to greet him.

213

'I did not think you would come,' she exclaimed, smiling. 'You seemed very unenthusiastic when I invited you, but I am glad your curiosity won out.'

Chaloner was still scanning his surroundings. Most of the tavern's clientele were women, but there was also a smattering of men. These included some of Clerkenwell's literati – poor blind John Milton, once the darling of the Puritans but now living in quiet poverty; Dr Goddard, whose cure-all drops were world-famous; Erasmus Smith, the wealthy Parliamentarian, who had founded an educational trust to prevent Royalists from prying too deeply into his financial affairs; and Izaak Walton, author of *The Compleat Angler*.

There were other familiar faces, too. Gruff Baron Lucas was talking to red-haired Sarah Shawe, both wearing the earnest expressions of people engrossed in intense intellectual debate – Chaloner overheard enough to tell him that it was regarding some element of combustion developed by the Royal Society. Dr Clarke sat nearby, ogling Sarah, and Chaloner was sure he would be punched if she noticed.

'Walk around,' invited Eliza with a gracious wave of her hand. 'Or join any group.'

Chaloner took her at her word and began to reconnoitre. Some women were learning to read, supervised by a few of the merchant-class protesters he had seen outside White Hall a few days earlier. Molly the chicken girl was there, frowning in concentration as she struggled to write her name. Others were more advanced, and debated philosophy and science – the Duchess's books were piled on every table, and each copy was very well thumbed.

Eventually, he reached Lucas, Sarah and Clarke. The

two debaters did not notice him, but the physician greeted him with a wary grin.

'Do not tell the wife, eh?' he said, treating Chaloner to one of his man-of-the-world winks. 'Fanny does not approve of this place. She thinks it is a brothel.'

'Then tell her that it is not. She may even like to come herself, as there is clearly a need for more teachers.'

'She would refuse because she thinks educating women is cruel. She is cognisant of the fact that no amount of learning will turn them into physicians, bankers or bishops, so all it does is make them discontented.'

'Do you agree with her?'

Clarke lowered his voice. 'I do, actually. These lasses want to better themselves, but what good will it do? They will still be whores, milkmaids and laundresses, taking orders from men.'

'So why are you here, if not to help them?'

'Because Fanny is a dull old hen, and I prefer more lively company on occasion.' Clarke nudged Chaloner in the ribs and nodded at Sarah. 'Like her. I would not mind giving *her* a complete medical examination!'

Chaloner changed the subject before Clarke could see his distaste, not just for lusting after women who had gone to the Red Bull to escape that sort of thing, but for being ready to cheat on his wife. Perhaps Fanny was a 'dull old hen', but that was a poor excuse for betraying her.

'I understand Tooley died today,' he said. 'Were you in White Hall when it happened?'

Clarke nodded. 'I was the one who diagnosed his cause of death as a fever. However, do not ask Wiseman for a second opinion if you have any affection for him. It has since occurred to me that it might have been the plague.'

'I heard a rumour that he was infected here. Is it—'

'Here?' gulped Clarke in alarm. 'Lord! No one told me *that*!'

He leapt up and bolted for the door, slamming it behind him so hard that the window shutters rattled and several people jumped to their feet in alarm.

'Did I hear you say that Tooley caught some sickness here, Chaloner?' growled Lucas, tearing himself away from Sarah with obvious reluctance. 'Because he did not. If that ape had tried to come in, I would have torn his head off. There is no room for his sort in the Red Bull. It is for *civilised* company.'

'So I see,' said Chaloner, and looked around. 'But where is your sister? I understand she has been generous in her support for this venture.'

'She has,' said Lucas, 'but she is conscious of being married to a duke and declines to mix with what she calls "common society". But *I* do not care about all that nonsense. I would rather debate philosophy with a clever beggar than a stupid fox-tossing nobleman.'

Eliza came to join them at that point, and explained that the Duchess herself had chosen the subject for that evening's debate, which was: *There is little difference between man and beast, but what ambition and glory makes*. Animal intelligence was, Eliza explained, something about which her mistress felt very strongly.

'She will include it in the novel she is writing,' she elaborated, eyes shining with pride. 'Which is a story about a perfect society – one that contains only women.'

'Then it will be a very short-lived perfect society,' quipped Chaloner, 'if there are no men to help provide future generations.'

'She does not address that sort of issue.' Eliza sounded

216

shocked. 'She is too genteel to raise vulgar matters like procreation.'

'Your pupils are not,' said Chaloner, aware that the table nearest to them had embarked on a very ribald detour, which had the participants howling with coarse laughter.

'Sarah!' snapped Eliza crossly. 'Your seamstresses need you to keep them on track.'

Sarah obliged, although she was obviously sorry to abandon her intellectual sparring partner. Lucas was just as disappointed, and when she had gone, he informed Chaloner that her mind was far superior to most of those in the Royal Society. Chaloner was inclined to believe him, given that its membership included the King and the Duke of York.

As Sarah passed Eliza, their fingers touched briefly, and the glance they exchanged told him that their relationship was rather more than just two friends who shared common interests. He hoped they were discreet, as the Duchess would not appreciate her staff being at the centre of a scandal, especially if the contents of the anonymous letter ever became public. It would be said that Topp had leapt into the Duchess's bed because his wife preferred women.

Then someone pulled on Chaloner's sleeve, and he looked down to see Molly.

'Come to see Mother Broughton,' she piped. 'I am sure she will want you to admire her.'

She led Chaloner to the hearth, where the seer smoked her pipe and repeated her predictions to anyone who would listen. The women she had cornered slithered away with relief when Molly arrived with fresh prey.

'You came to my house earlier,' said Mother Broughton,

217

eyeing Chaloner closely. 'Although I cannot recall your name. I get so many visitors, see, all wanting my wise words.'

'You told me I had a future in cheese.'

'Ah, I remember now. But I have had another vision since then – of the Fleet River running red with blood. This will happen on Maundy Thursday, and is just one of the terrible things that will come to pass in our fine city before a just, gentle new kingdom is ushered in.'

Chaloner suspected it ran with blood every day, given the number of slaughterhouses along its banks. 'London is the only place these things will happen?'

'Oh, yes! No other city boasts so many wicked sinners.'

Eventually, Eliza brought the evening to a close by thanking everyone for coming. The participants took their leave, laughing and joking until they reached the door. Then they raised their hoods or covered their faces with scarves, and slipped away into the night. Chaloner understood their reluctance to be recognised when he stepped outside and saw that a group of men had gathered there to hurl abuse. They were masked as well, and anonymity made them bold in spouting their opinions.

'Not again!' muttered John Milton, tilting his head to hear what his ruined eyes could not see. 'Have they nothing better to do?'

'They are frightened of us,' declared Sarah with great satisfaction. 'Afraid that if we continue to gain strength by meeting, we will rock their comfortable existences.'

'Or they just want to cause mischief,' countered Chaloner, noting that although the protesters wore shabby cloaks, they had neglected to change their footwear, where silver buckles shone like beacons. Moreover, he recognised

Widdrington's lazy drawl, and suspected that the one with the functional sword was Rolt, although the captain was careful to stay in the shadows. Cobbe was there, too, identifiable by wearing an eye-catching puce cape.

But more interesting yet was a small man with three friends. His voice was shrill as he spewed his vitriol, and Chaloner heard one of his companions urge caution, lest the tirade attracted too much attention. It was Viscount Mansfield with his favourite servants – Steward Clayton, Liddell the horse-trader and Vicar Booth – aiming to make trouble for the charitable scheme that his step-mother funded.

'Go away,' Mother Broughton ordered him when she emerged. 'You stupid oaf.'

'Stupid?' echoed Mansfield indignantly. 'It is *you* who is stupid, madam!'

'Hold me up, Eliza,' cried Sarah, pretending to swoon. 'I am so dazzled by this fellow's wit that I might faint at its sheer acerbity.'

'Its sheer what?' asked Mansfield suspiciously.

'She is calling you an ass,' translated Lucas, who had trailed out on Mother Broughton's heels. 'Which you are. And a cowardly one into the bargain – too timorous to show your face.'

'Ignore them, Baron,' said Eliza haughtily. 'They are beneath our contempt. And as the Duchess always says, a better future will come if we bide our time.'

'Yes, it will come on Sunday,' put in Mother Broughton confidentially. 'It is all foretold.'

'I hope it will take longer than that,' countered Lucas. 'I would love to see things improve, but rapid change is dangerous. That is why the Commonwealth failed: it was imposed too fast, and people baulked.'

219

At that point, a stone flew through the air. It sailed between Chicken Molly and Sarah, and cracked into the wall behind them. Sarah's eyes narrowed as she scanned the mob for the culprit, and her fingers went to her belt, where she carried a long knife.

'No, Sarah,' warned Eliza. 'The Duchess said she would withdraw funding if there is any hint of impropriety or violence here. Take no notice of them. They are not worth it.'

'Hey, you!' roared Baron Lucas suddenly, stabbing an angry finger towards Mansfield. 'Yes, I am talking to *you* – the stinking weasel holding the handful of mud. Call yourself a man, lobbing missiles at defenceless women? Come here, you snivelling little rat, and fight *me!*'

Mansfield took to his heels when Lucas drew his sword, and his three companions were quick to follow. The Baron then proceeded to bawl such apposite insults that Chaloner suspected that he, too, had seen beneath the disguises, and knew exactly who was on the sharp end of his tongue.

'Now go home, all of you,' ordered Eliza, standing with her hands on her hips to glower at the remaining protesters. 'You have made your point.'

Unnerved by Mansfield's flight and unwilling to risk a tongue-lashing from Lucas, the men began to melt away. Chaloner set off after the one who had thrown the rock. *He* had seen the guilty arm go back, even if no one else had noticed. The culprit saw him following and ran, zigzagging through alleys and yards in a desperate attempt to throw him off.

The pair of them hurtled by the Charterhouse, at which point Chaloner lost his quarry. He stood still, listening intently, then heard footsteps. He set off after them, past Red Cross Street and the silent Artillery Ground. Then he glimpsed a shadow climbing over the cemetery wall. He raced towards it and managed to grab the hem of a cloak as its owner ascended.

'*Godverdamme!*' swore the shadow, and the material snapped out of his hand.

Chaloner scrambled over the wall, too, now in possession of two pieces of information: the culprit's native tongue was Dutch, and 'he' was a she. He made a guess at her identity.

'Jane, please stop!' he called in her own language. 'I only want to talk.'

He reached the ground on the other side, but Dutch Jane had disappeared. Then he saw a shadow by the grave of the Puritan divine who had recently been buried. He set off towards it, stumbling over ground that was uneven with molehills and rabbit holes. Red lights bobbed ahead. Jane had company. The dagger Chaloner always carried in his sleeve slipped into his hand.

'Wait!' he called again. 'I only want to—'

He ducked instinctively at a flicker of movement, and thus avoided the hacking blow aimed at his head by someone with a rapier. He drew his own sword, and engaged in a fast and furious exchange of blows before others came running to his assailant's aid.

'Stop!' hissed Jane, just when Chaloner thought he was going to meet an ignominious end at the hands of people whose faces he could not see. 'Tyndal is coming. Run! Quickly!'

The swordsmen promptly broke off the fight and the red lights danced away. Chaloner tried to follow, but the night was pitch black, and it was impossible to see where he was going. Suddenly, the ground disappeared beneath his feet. He fell and landed with a jarring thump – he had plunged into an open grave. Pain speared through the leg that had been injured at the Battle of Naseby and had never fully healed. As he put out his hands to push himself to his feet, he felt a face, cold and dead. He jerked them back in revulsion.

Then the grave was filled with light, and silhouettes appeared above him. It was Tyndal and his four sons, all carrying lanterns.

'What are you doing down there?' he asked. 'That is the hole we dug for the courtier who died today – Mr Tooley. His own vicar refused to take him, because he was a fever case.'

Chaloner glared crossly up at him. 'You should have covered the hole with planks, not left it wide open for people to fall down.'

'The only ones at risk of that are trespassers,' said Tyndal tartly. 'And they get what they deserve. Is your friend all right, by the way? He is very pale.'

The lamps illuminated the dead face that Chaloner had felt. He recognised it with a shock It was the Cockpit Club member who was always drunk.

'Ashley!'

Chapter 8

Monday dawned bright and sunny, although Chaloner felt sluggish and heavy-eyed after his fraught and very late night at the Red Bull and Bunhill cemetery. When a vigorous wash in cold water and a spell in the garden with his hens did not refresh him, he decided the only remedy was a dish of coffee.

Although his years as an intelligencer had taught him that it was unwise to have regular haunts, he set off for the Rainbow on Fleet Street anyway, feeling the need for something familiar and constant. Home did not count, not with Veriana and Ursula rearranging all his furniture to suit themselves. He had nearly broken his neck the previous night, flopping exhaustedly on to his bed in the dark, only to discover it was no longer where he had left it.

He walked briskly, trying to clear his muddy wits for the day that lay ahead. The streets shone wetly from recent rain, and steam rose in places, while all the potholes were full of mucky water. They were a serious hazard to pedestrians, who risked either being deluged by the carts that splashed through them, or of coming to grief in one that was deeper than it looked.

The city was awake, but sombre, and the churches he passed were busy. Holy Week – the days between Palm Sunday and Easter Day – was a quiet period for the faithful, a time of fasting, reflection and prayer.

The Rainbow was near Temple Bar, and did a roaring trade with those who needed something to calm their nerves after battling through it. Not many months ago, the coffee house had been closed with the plague, and Chaloner feared that its regulars had died. But all had survived, and he opened the door to see the same old faces sitting around the same worn table, amid the familiar reek of tobacco smoke and burned beans. As usual, they were discussing the latest government newsbook – now called *The London Gazette* – hot off the presses that day.

'What news?' called Farr, the owner, in the traditional coffee house greeting. He wore an apron that had once been white, but that was now brown and greasy from the smoke that curled from his stinking beans. 'Oh, it is you, Chaloner. Where have you been these last few weeks?'

'That is a fine welcome for an old friend,' chided Rector Thompson, coming to take Chaloner's hand in a genuine expression of friendship; no one else moved. 'We are pleased to see you home. So what is new at White Hall these days?'

'Do not look to him for information,' said Farr sourly. 'He never has anything interesting to report, even though he has access to the most intimate Court secrets. He must walk around with his eyes closed and his hands clapped over his ears.'

'I might be tempted to do the same,' averred Thompson prudishly. 'White Hall is no place for a decent man, and I admire his fortitude in working there.'

224

This was why Chaloner liked the Rainbow. Accusations might be levelled, but no one was ever obliged to defend himself, as everyone else wanted to do the talking.

'I agree with Farr,' said Stedman, the youthful printer. 'Chaloner is the least observant man I have ever met. If I spent *my* days at the palace, I would have a wealth of fascinating snippets to share.'

'Perhaps he does not have time for that sort of thing,' said Thompson, watching Farr pour Chaloner a dish of his famous viscous brown sludge. 'He may have duties and responsibilities.'

'In *White Hall?*' demanded Farr incredulously. 'A place where no one ever does anything except have fun?'

'Other than the King,' put in Stedman, who was a passionate Royalist, and would hear no word spoken against His Majesty. This had once extended to his Court as well, but the past three or four years had taught him prudence in this respect.

'Have you heard the latest news from Clerkenwell?' asked Farr, changing the subject to one he liked better. 'Corpses with red souls were seen in the cemetery for a second night running, and the man who witnessed the phenomenon was so terrified that he toppled into an open grave, stone dead.'

Chaloner marvelled at the speed with which garbled versions of the truth could spread through the city. It had only been a few hours since he had chased Dutch Jane and found Ashley's body, but already people had put their own slant on events.

'Speaking of mysterious happenings, there are reports of a hen killing a fox in Covent Garden,' said Stedman. 'All are signs that our world order is wobbling once again.'

'I disagree,' said Thompson. 'It is Holy Week. Hens killing a fox is a symbol of Easter.'

'You equate Jesus with a fox?' asked Farr, bemused. 'I cannot see it myself, but . . . Hah! Here comes Speed from the bookshop. Perhaps *he* will have something interesting to share.'

Speed's contribution was to embark on a detailed analysis of Mother Broughton's prophecies, leaving Chaloner to wonder if there was anyone in the city capable of telling the truth without twisting it to suit himself. According to Speed, the glorious event promised for Easter Sunday would be a relaxing of the Sabbath trading laws, so that shop owners like him could open whenever they pleased.

'That is not my idea of a glorious new order,' said Thompson doubtfully. 'I was hoping for something a little more religious.'

'Well, I suppose you would,' said Speed disdainfully. 'You are a clergyman.'

Chaloner arrived back in Covent Garden just as the sun was chasing the last of the night's shadows away. Aware that he would have to go to White Hall that day, he donned his best coat and breeches, then raided Wiseman's wardrobe for some accessories to liven them up – a pair of crimson gloves and a cherry-red band around his hat.

'Very smart,' said Wiseman approvingly. 'Although an all-red ensemble would have been better.'

'Have you heard that two members of the Cockpit Club died yesterday?' asked Chaloner. 'James Tooley and George Ashley.'

Wiseman nodded. 'But if you want me to look at them, it will have to wait until this afternoon. I must bleed the

Queen this morning. Some stupid oaf let slip that her mother is dead, and the shock has played havoc with her humours.'

'It was Clarke's idea to keep the news from her,' recalled Chaloner. 'You argued for her to be told, so it could be done gently.'

Wiseman grimaced. 'I knew some loose-tongued fool would blurt it out in a way that would prove harmful, and I was right. Clarke is as useless at dealing with the living as he is at assessing the dead. Do not believe anything he says about Tooley and Ashley. I will provide you with an *informed* opinion this afternoon.'

Before he left the house, Chaloner went to check on his cousins, and was appalled to find them in the parlour with Swaddell. He glared at the footman for allowing the assassin in, but the man only glared back, silently telling him that repelling such a deadly invader went well beyond his job description.

'There you are, Tom,' the assassin said, and when he turned to smile a greeting, his usually pallid face was flushed; having two unattached females hanging on his every word was much to his liking. 'Do not worry about being late. Your cousins have entertained me royally.'

'Late?' echoed Chaloner indignantly. 'It is nowhere near noon, and my home is not White Hall's kitchens – which is where we agreed to meet last night.'

Swaddell's smile became rather less amiable. 'Yes, but we cannot afford to lose a minute now there are *three* courtiers crying out for justice. Besides, I went to the larder this morning and made my own enquiries. There was nothing to learn that you have not already uncovered.'

'This morning?' asked Ursula, wide-eyed. 'You must

have started work very early, Mr Swaddell. The city is fortunate to have such a dedicated servant.'

Chaloner glanced sharply at her, suspecting mockery, which would be rash to practise on Swaddell, but she seemed sincere. Swaddell preened, flattered.

'Did you hear anything about Tooley and Ashley while you were in White Hall?' Chaloner asked, disliking the way Swaddell and Ursula were looking at each other.

'Apparently, both were well at the fox-tossing yesterday,' replied Swaddell, not tearing his eyes from the object of his fancy, 'and they celebrated Tooley's win with a drinking contest. He perished of a fever an hour or so after the party broke up. Wild with grief, Ashley went to sit by his tomb in Bunhill, but he died of fright when he encountered the walking corpses. At least, that is the tale on everyone's lips.'

Chaloner raised his eyebrows. 'But Tooley has no tomb – he has not been buried yet. And who goes to mourn at an empty grave?'

'Quite,' said Swaddell. 'It is suspicious, is it not? I had hoped Wiseman would examine both bodies at once, but he says we must wait until he has tended the Queen.'

Chaloner was about to suggest that he and Swaddell left, when the footman arrived with platters of food. The cook had gone to considerable trouble, and the eggs, smoked pork and fresh bread smelled delicious. Suddenly hungry, he decided to stay and break his fast. So did Swaddell, who proceeded to ignore Chaloner entirely while he regaled the young women with descriptions of the exotic goods that could be bought from the city's many markets.

'Oranges?' breathed Ursula. 'I have never tasted one of those.'

'I eat them most days,' said Swaddell casually, the sophisticated man-of-the-world. 'I shall bring you one later. With your guardian's permission, of course.'

Chaloner supposed the girls had mentioned the recently signed deed making them his wards, and was glad. It would make his task easier when he told the assassin that he was not in the running to marry either of them. To change the subject, he told Swaddell what had happened at the Red Bull the previous night. Ursula gave a shrill squeal of excitement.

'Please take us there, Thomas! *We* could teach these ladies to read, and we could learn a lot from listening to erudite men like John Milton, Baron Lucas and Izaak Walton.'

But Chaloner recalled what Thurloe had said about the anticipation generated by the arrival of two of James Chaloner's brood, and was not about to compound Clerkenwell's problems by introducing two people who might act as magnets for would-be revolutionaries.

'I am afraid you must stay here until I find a suitable chaperone,' he said.

Both cousins regarded him with a distinct lack of affection, but it could not be helped.

'Have you borrowed some of Mr Wiseman's things in the hope of making yourself look more courtly?' asked Ursula sulkily. 'Because if so, it has not really worked.'

'It might do for a gathering of Parliamentarians,' put in Veriana cuttingly, while Swaddell sniggered into his napkin, 'but Royalists will consider you gauche.'

Before he could object, they began fussing around him, exchanging the gloves in his belt for a lace handkerchief, and adorning his hat with a sprig of flowers instead of the band. By the time they had finished, even he was forced to admit that the result did look less contrived.

The moment they were outside, Swaddell began to bombard Chaloner with questions about the girls and their family. Loath to arm him with anything that might be used to snag their affections, Chaloner turned the discussion back to Chiffinch, Tooley and Ashley, making the point that they should do all they could to prevent a fourth death. Swaddell frowned.

'You think there will be another?'

Chaloner shrugged. 'It is impossible to know until Wiseman tells us how Tooley and Ashley died. If they were poisoned – and the suddenness of their departures suggests it is a distinct possibility – we need to find out why. And what links them to Chiffinch.'

Swaddell moved to another subject. 'I am still not clear about Dutch Jane's role last night. You say she was among the protesters outside the Red Bull, but why would she throw her lot in with them?'

'Probably because its school is funded by the Duchess who dismissed her. What better way to retaliate than by provoking a violent scene outside it? She threw the first stone, turning a vocal protest into one where blood might have been spilled.'

'Especially as you say the Cockpit Club men were there with swords,' mused Swaddell. 'We must ask them why they went.'

'We know why: the rumour is that Tooley caught a fever there, so I imagine they went for revenge. Fortunately, they lacked the courage to act. Mansfield tried to follow Dutch Jane's stone with a handful of mud, but he slunk off when Baron Lucas challenged him.'

'So why did Dutch Jane flee to the cemetery? Do you think she is connected to these so-called walking corpses?'

'Well, she knew exactly where to climb over the wall, which suggests she has done it before. We will have to track her down and ask.'

'Very well, but . . .' Swaddell stopped walking in confusion when Chaloner turned west. 'Where are you going? White Hall is this way.'

'I should visit Clarendon House first, to report to the Earl.'

'Oh, I nearly forgot.' Swaddell's expression was suddenly sheepish. 'His clerk gave me a message for you: the Earl wants you to report to him at once.'

Chaloner increased his pace. 'Then I will go to Clarendon House, while you speak to the Cockpit Club about Tooley and Ashley.'

'No,' said Swaddell, skipping a few steps to keep up with him. 'We were ordered to work side by side, so that is what we are going to do. I will wait outside while you are with Clarendon, after which we shall tackle these courtiers *together*.'

Chaloner nodded agreement, but determined to ditch the assassin at the first opportunity. As far as he was concerned, the less they were seen in each other's company, the better. They walked in silence for a while, then Swaddell remarked that he had secured an invitation to the Duchess's soirée on Wednesday.

'Did Williamson's office arrange it for you?' asked Chaloner curiously.

'The Bishop of Winchester did. He mentioned that he was going, so I asked him to take me as his guest. He said he would be delighted.'

'Did he?' Chaloner was astonished. Bishop Morley

231

was a friend of the Earl, an intelligent, shrewd, ethical man who was unlikely to associate with killers. 'Why?'

'Because he owes me a favour. When one's trade is rooting out treachery, one makes many acquaintances among the wealthy and powerful, as I am sure you have discovered yourself.'

'Unfortunately, most of the wealthy and powerful I meet tend to end up as enemies,' said Chaloner ruefully.

Swaddell changed the subject. 'Can your cousins cook?' he asked casually.

'I have no idea, but I had better find out, as their suitors will want to know.'

'What suitors?' demanded Swaddell, narrowing his eyes.

Chaloner smiled enigmatically. 'Negotiations are at an early stage, but they will be completed soon, even so.'

Swaddell blew out his cheeks in a sigh. 'Then I must stake my claim before you parcel them off to someone inappropriate.'

Chaloner was about to inform the assassin that *he* was inappropriate when it occurred to him that there was no need to offend such a deadly individual. No woman in her right mind would accept romantic overtures from the assassin, and while Veriana and Ursula might enjoy his company when no one else was available, they would never consider him a serious contender for marriage.

Relieved, he increased his stride towards Clarendon House.

Chaloner's reception was cooler than it had been the last time he had visited, and Brodrick explained why: the Cockpit Club had openly accused the Earl's staff of causing Chiffinch's death. Ergo, Chaloner's failure to solve the case meant that no one from Clarendon House dared step outside, lest they were on the receiving end of any unpleasantness.

'We are under attack from all sides,' said Brodrick unhappily. 'I popped my head into the Shield Gallery this morning, and the Cockpit Club men accused me of murder. I have never been so frightened in my life. They clustered around me with their hands on their swords, and I was lucky the King intervened, or I would not be standing here now.'

'Then stay home,' suggested Chaloner. 'If you do not go out, no one can bully you.'

'I shall,' vowed Brodrick. 'Except for Wednesday, when I will attend the Duchess of Newcastle's soirée. She will not invite the Cockpit Club, so I shall be safe there.'

'How do you know she will not invite them?' asked Chaloner, thinking that if bishops and assassins were being included, then God only knew who else might be on her guest list.

'Because she clashed with them over yesterday's fox-tossing. She wrote letters to every courtier in the palace, claiming that decent folk would shun such monstrous cruelty. The Cockpit Club men were livid, because it meant the King decided not to go. He does not usually heed such things, but that lunatic Duchess apparently unsettled him with her forceful opinions.'

Chaloner went on his way, and saw Barker in the hall. The clerk tried to slip away without being seen, but Chaloner caught up with him and grabbed his arm.

'Why were you really in Clerkenwell last night?' he demanded. 'I know it was not delivering letters to Newcastle House.'

Barker glared at him. 'I suppose you base your charge

233

on the fact that I was walking in the wrong direction. Well, for your information, I *did* take a bundle of missives to the Duke, but I stopped off on the way back to visit my mother.'

'Your dead mother?'

Barker scowled. 'I told you: she is alive. However, the Earl ordered me to hurry home, so I am naturally reluctant for him to find out that I disobeyed him. It is a pity Ma needs me, because I would never venture into such a dangerous area otherwise.'

'It is not dangerous! The Duchess of Newcastle lives there.'

'So do a lot of radicals and Puritan poets,' said Barker. 'It is no place for respectable men, so I advise you to keep your distance. You will be much safer if you do.'

He walked away, leaving Chaloner staring after him, not sure what to think. Were the clerk's parting words a friendly warning or a threat?

A few minutes later, Chaloner knocked on the door to My Lord's Lobby. His employer looked pale and tired, and the hope that filled his eyes when Chaloner first walked in faded once he had heard his report.

'But it has been *days* since Chiffinch died,' he whispered, 'and accusations and insinuations grow by the hour. They have reached the point where I dare not show my face anywhere. Nor do my staff. You *must* find the killer. Our future – our lives – depend on it.'

'I will do my best,' promised Chaloner, although the Earl did not seem much comforted. 'Incidentally, did you send Barker to Newcastle House with letters last night?'

'I might have done. Why?'

'Because it may help me understand what is happening

in Clerkenwell,' hedged Chaloner, unwilling to elaborate until he had more information. Barker might have been telling some version of the truth, and he did not want to cost an innocent man his livelihood.

'I do not care about Clerkenwell,' snapped the Earl. 'I care about White Hall – about being accused of killing debauchees.'

'They may be connected, sir. Some of my suspects live in Clerkenwell; Tooley is alleged to have caught a fatal fever there; he will be buried in its cemetery; and Ashley's body was in Tooley's grave. So *did* you send letters to Newcastle House?'

'I cannot recall, but Barker will know, as I always use him to take them. He is the only servant I trust not to go about his own business on the way home.'

'I see,' said Chaloner. 'But why do you communicate with the Duke so often? I thought he no longer concerned himself with affairs of state.'

'I am advising him on a legal matter pertaining to his estate. All I can tell you is that he wants to provide for his wife after his death – to prevent his son from leaving her penniless.'

'What is your impression of Viscount Mansfield, sir?'

The Earl regarded him narrowly. 'I hope you are not about to claim that *he* is involved in these murders. The Duke would be devastated.'

'I did warn you that exploring Chiffinch's demise might lead to uncomfortable truths.' Chaloner realised that this sounded insolent, so he asked his question again before the Earl could berate him for it. 'Is there anything about Mansfield that I should know?'

'Well, the Duke considers him a disappointment. He is a weak nonentity, but he is also greedy, and blanches every time the Duke opens his purse. And he hates his stepmother. Poor Mansfield would have been happier born as an ordinary man, because inheriting a dukedom is quite beyond him. But none of us can choose our kin.'

'No,' sighed Chaloner wryly.

The Earl smiled suddenly. 'Speaking of kin, Wiseman tells me that you have two young cousins wanting husbands. You are honoured to be entrusted with so important a task, and it is an opportunity to secure alliances that will benefit yourself.'

Chaloner struggled not to show distaste at the notion that he would be so selfish as to use other people's happiness for personal gain. 'I hardly know where to begin,' he replied ambiguously.

'By finding suitable lodgings, because you cannot keep them in Covent Garden with you and Wiseman. It is vaguely indecent. Bring them here: my wife will look after them.'

It was a generous offer, and living in the home of a staunchly Royalist family would help with the small matter of Veriana and Ursula's father being charged with treason. Of course, Chaloner would definitely have to ensure that the Earl was not then accused of murder.

'Thank you, sir.'

'Well, I cannot send you away on *Royal Oak* next Sunday if you have women to look after,' said the Earl, thus revealing that it was not kindness that had prompted him to intervene, but self-interest. 'My wife is away until Easter, so someone else must mind them until then. I suggest Fanny Clarke, the physician's wife.'

'Do you?' asked Chaloner, surprised. 'Why?'

'Because she is modest, respectable and *very* dull – a woman you want your cousins to emulate. It will be easier to secure good matches if they are malleable, demure and stupid. After all, no man wants a wife who is too clever.'

Chaloner laughed, then realised the Earl was serious. 'But surely he will appreciate one who can manage his household and provide intelligent conversation of an evening?'

'His servants can provide one and his friends the other,' replied the Earl. 'Besides, the Duke of Newcastle married a lady with spirit, and look at how *she* is regarded in decent society. Take it from me, Chaloner, Fanny Clarke is the woman you need until my wife can take your cousins. Of course, even she can be unorthodox. Yesterday, she tried to stop the fox-tossing.'

'But she did not succeed, and nor did the Duchess. It went ahead anyway.'

'It did, much to White Hall's lasting shame. It attracted a very large audience, although not all onlookers were approving. It was a pity Cobbe's ploy was unsuccessful.'

Chaloner frowned. 'What ploy?'

'He let the foxes out of their cages. He claims it was an accident, but he is intelligent, and understood that such a spectacle might turn Londoners against us. Unfortunately, the foxes failed to find their way out of the palace, and so they were rounded up again.'

'Pity,' said Chaloner. 'For the foxes and for White Hall.'

He emerged from Clarendon House to see Swaddell sitting on a horse trough outside the gate. The assassin seemed uncharacteristically happy, chewing on a blade of grass and humming. Chaloner hoped it was not because he saw the prospect of a bride on the horizon.

'I have just learned that the whole Court is in St

237

James's Park,' Swaddell said, standing and indicating that Chaloner should walk there with him. 'As it is a nice day, Bess Widdrington has organised some dog-races. Her husband is none too pleased, apparently, as he would rather she stayed at home, doing wifely things.'

'Who told you that?' asked Chaloner, falling in at his side.

'Captain Rolt. He lives in Kensington, so he walks along Piccadilly most days. He stopped to chat when he saw me.'

'He was on foot?' asked Chaloner, thinking this was a low mode of transport for a man who aimed to make an impression and win himself a lucrative post.

'He lost his horse in a fight, as you know, and says he has not had time to buy another. I wonder why he lives in Kensington. It is full of hovels and farmyards. He also mentioned that Widdrington aims to send Bess to Ireland soon, because she is becoming an embarrassment.'

'Why Ireland? Does his family have connections there?'

'No, he chose it so she will be separated from him by a wide, very rough stretch of water.'

Chaloner let the tittle-tattle wash over him as they entered the park, enjoying the pretty day with its soft spring light. Birds sang, and the air was full of the scent of blossom and clean, fresh earth. Then he saw the crowds near the Canal, and thought the entire palace must have turned out. A big black wig at the heart of the throng explained why it was busy: the King had chosen to attend, and where he went, his sycophants followed.

The dogs were being raced down one side of the lake, but they did not understand what they were supposed to do, so instead of running in a straight line, they trotted where they pleased, stopping to sniff and cock their legs along the way. Widdrington led the derisive laughter, while Bess's face was a mask of dismay.

'This will cost her money,' murmured Swaddell. 'Fortunes are wagered at these events, but no one will bet on this debacle, which means she will not recoup her expenses. Worse, it was organised to impress Widdrington, but he mocks her the loudest. And now the King has tired of the commotion and is leaving early.'

Sure enough, His Majesty was preparing to go. His senior courtiers rallied around him, although some of the younger ones held back, loath to exchange fresh air for a stuffy gallery. The Cockpit Club men were among the latter, watching Bess vent her disappointment by beating a dog with a stick. It yelped and bit her, which made her husband cackle anew. Cobbe, even more outrageous than usual in lime-green silk, hastened to rescue it.

Meanwhile, the ambitious Rolt was trying to decide whether it would be more advantageous to follow the King who did not know him, or stay with the 'friends' who did. In the end, he compromised by choosing a spot near the end of the Canal, which the King would have to pass on his way back to the palace, but that was close enough to the Cockpit Club men to ensure he was included in any plans they might make for later.

'Widdrington's rabble do not seem unduly disturbed by the deaths of two of their number,' remarked Swaddell. 'Shall we ask them why?'

He and Chaloner walked towards them. Most reeked of wine, suggesting that the morning's races were a continuation of the previous night's entertainment.

Young Legg had been sick down himself, which meant that no one wanted to stand too close, while the rest looked seedy and stained. Rolt was alone in being freshly shaved and clean.

'Here comes the Earl's assassin and the Spymaster's creature,' drawled Widdrington. 'Do you see this pair, Pamphlin? One of them dispatched Chiffinch, then accused us of the crime.'

The man he addressed was a thin, spotty courtier whom Chaloner had seen with the Cockpit Club before. He was dressed almost as decadently as Cobbe, and had affected an insouciant pose that entailed leaning on Mansfield's shoulder. The Viscount was trying not to mind, although it was obvious that he was uncomfortable with the familiarity.

'You are lucky Tooley is dead,' said Bess to Chaloner and Swaddell, her face an ugly mask of frustration, bitterness and spite. 'He was big and strong, and would not have tolerated your loathsome presence here today.'

'No,' agreed Mansfield, eager to play his part. 'Nor would Ashley.'

'We can see you are grieving,' said Chaloner, looking pointedly at the makeshift racecourse, 'so we shall be brief. What—'

'Stop right there,' ordered Pamphlin sharply. 'We do not answer to you.'

'Oh, I think you can make an exception, just this once,' said Swaddell with such soft menace that the courtier blanched. 'So tell us about the deaths of your two friends.'

'What do you want to know?' asked Widdrington, also unsettled by the assassin, but struggling not to show it. 'I can tell you that we will miss them. They were lively company.'

240

'Begin with Tooley,' instructed Chaloner. 'Did he seem unwell yesterday?'

'He was in fine fettle when he celebrated his win at the fox-tossing,' shrugged Widdrington. 'We had a drinking game after, and he won that, too.'

'And Ashley? When did you last see him?'

'Just after Tooley died,' supplied Widdrington. 'He was distraught, and said he was going to pray over the body.'

'Then why was he in Bunhill?' pounced Swaddell. 'Tooley was – and still is – lying in the chapel at White Hall.'

'Perhaps he craved peace for his devotions,' suggested Pamphlin slyly. 'And the chapel was busy yesterday because it was Palm Sunday. Ashley was a devout man, who needed tranquillity for his holy contemplations.'

The others sniggered at this claim.

'I thought Ashley and Tooley were your friends,' said Chaloner, shaking his head in incomprehension. 'Why do you make light of their deaths?'

'They would not want us to be miserable on their account,' averred Widdrington carelessly. 'The Cockpit Club is about having fun and living for today. Our only rules are that we do not dwell on what happened yesterday and we do not fear what might happen tomorrow.'

'Well, perhaps you should,' retorted Chaloner, 'because I doubt the sudden deaths of two healthy young men are natural.'

With a dismissive sneer, Widdrington swaggered away. The others followed, but Chaloner did not try to stop them, knowing he would have no answers as long as they were in a pack and too drunk to know when to be sensible. Eventually, the only ones left were Rolt, still nodding and smiling at anyone important who happened past him,

241

and Cobbe, who was playing with the dog he had rescued.

'Perhaps one of those two will be more helpful,' said Swaddell. 'Shall we find out?'

With no audience to entertain with shocking remarks and mincing manners, Cobbe was just an ordinary young man in outlandish clothes. He smiled warily as Chaloner and Swaddell approached and stood hastily, dog forgotten.

'I heard you tried to free some foxes yesterday,' began Chaloner.

'I cannot abide the things,' declared Cobbe with a shudder that convinced no one. 'Unfortunately, they declined to leave, so were killed anyway. But never mind them. I have information for you, Swaddell. Did you know I took refuge in the United Provinces when Cromwell was in power? I have always been a Royalist.'

He shot Chaloner the kind of glance that suggested he did not approve of men who flopped from side to side as occasion demanded.

'Did you like it?' asked Chaloner, declining to be baited.

'Not particularly, although it did allow me to learn Hollandish, so when I heard the Dutch ambassador chatting to his minions in White Hall the other night, I understood every word they spoke. They had no idea, of course, and blathered on obliviously.'

'What did they say?' asked Swaddell keenly.

'That they use the Bunhill cemetery to meet their spies. And that they have devised a simple system of communication, which entails lamps and red cloths. The light is kept white if all is well, but will glow scarlet if there is reason to be cautious.'

'Hah!' exclaimed Swaddell. 'Mother Broughton must have seen these lanterns and decided to include them in her prophecy. Corpses carrying tainted souls indeed!'

'They also mentioned the name of an informant: Janneke.'

'Which is Dutch for Jane,' mused Chaloner. 'So now we know why she ran to Bunhill when I chased her. It is a place where she thought she might get some help.'

'Keep this information to yourself, Cobbe,' Swaddell ordered. 'Then we can place our own people in the cemetery and catch these traitors red-handed.'

'Anything for King and country,' said Cobbe, and yawned exaggeratedly. 'And when you have them under lock and key, I shall be a hero.'

'Unlike last night then,' retorted Chaloner. 'When you and your friends tried to intimidate unarmed women outside the Red Bull. Why did you do it? For Tooley, because someone told you that he caught his fatal fever there?'

'Well, he did,' declared Rolt, overhearing and coming to join them. 'Bess said so.'

'Oh, then it must be true,' said Swaddell flatly. 'She would *never* twist the truth in the hope of winning her husband's good graces.'

Rolt regarded him with dislike. 'Do you mean to investigate his demise as well as Chiffinch's? And Ashley's, too?'

'If they do, we had better provide alibis, Rolt,' said Cobbe with a pleasant grin.

Rolt scowled, but answered anyway. 'We were with our Cockpit Club friends all day.'

'*Most* of the day,' corrected Cobbe. 'We all had personal errands to run on occasion, and there is not a

243

man among us who did not slip out for an hour or two.' He smiled again at Chaloner and Swaddell. 'I imagine the same is true of you two.'

'Actually,' countered Swaddell, 'I can prove my whereabouts for every moment.'

Chaloner doubted it was true, but was not about to challenge him in front of two men who might be killers themselves – and he was suspicious of both of them. Rolt was ruthless enough to commit murder if he thought it would further his ambitions, while Cobbe was an enigma, whom Chaloner did not understand at all.

'Then perhaps we should narrow the field by establishing exactly when Ashley and Tooley died,' he said. 'Begin with Tooley.'

'Between six and seven o'clock last night,' replied Cobbe promptly. 'In other words, between the end of the drinking game and the time when his servant found his body.'

By Chaloner's reckoning, he and Swaddell had only his cousins as witnesses to their whereabouts at that time, and no one was likely to believe the testimony of two country girls who would lose everything if their guardian was arrested for murder.

'What about Ashley?' he asked. 'When did he die?'

'All I can tell you about him is that he was alive just after ten o'clock,' replied Cobbe. 'I know, because I heard the Clerkenwell church clock chime the hour, and we parted company a few moments afterwards. His body was found at some point during the night.'

'Was he with you when you made a nuisance of yourselves outside the Red Bull?' asked Swaddell, although Chaloner knew he was not – he had been dead by then, lying at the bottom of Tooley's empty grave.

Rolt raised his hands defensively. '*I* did not go there to make trouble – it was not me who threw the stone. And we all left when Baron Lucas ordered us away.'

'You have not answered my question,' said Swaddell sharply. 'Was Ashley with you?'

'No, he was not,' replied Cobbe. 'He had already disappeared on business of his own. He did not tell us where he was going or what his errand entailed. He just left.'

'Perhaps he went to sell information to the Dutch,' suggested Chaloner.

Cobbe blinked in genuine shock. 'Ashley? Never! He may have been a drunk, but he was a patriotic one.'

Rolt grinned wolfishly. 'So where were you two when Ashley was killed?'

Swaddell smiled back, although it was not a nice expression. 'With the Bishop of Winchester. Then Tom went to the Red Bull – its patrons will confirm it.'

Swaddell's claim was so outlandish that Cobbe and Rolt exchanged a glance of disbelief, and Chaloner silently cursed him. It was simply *asking* to be accused of the crime.

'I see,' said Cobbe keenly. 'And the Bishop will corroborate this tale, will he?'

'Of course!' Swaddell sounded genuinely indignant. 'It is the truth.'

'Do *you* have any idea who killed Tooley and Ashley?' asked Chaloner, eager to move away from the subject of alibis before Swaddell's wild claims landed them in trouble. 'We all know they *were* murdered – that the tales of fever and grief are a nonsense.'

'Well, my first choice of culprits was you two,' replied Cobbe. 'But if you have a Bishop to vouch for you, I shall give you the benefit of the doubt. Now, I have been more than generous with information, so how about some reciprocation? Who do you suspect?'

'Other than you?' asked Swaddell archly. 'A number of your fellow Cockpit Club friends, several courtiers, a servant or two. Why do you want to know?'

Cobbe flapped his handkerchief. 'Oh, just idle curiosity.'

'I neither like nor trust him,' muttered Swaddell as Cobbe minced away, Rolt fawning at his heels. 'There is something very dangerous beneath that smooth exterior.'

Coming from the assassin, this was damning indeed.

Chapter 9

As he felt national security was at risk, Swaddell insisted on travelling to Bunhill at once, to assess the danger posed by the traitors. Chaloner agreed to accompany him, thinking the journey would give him time to think about what they had learned in the park, although it did not take him many moments in the swaying hackney to conclude that it had actually been very little. They had approximate times of death for Ashley and Tooley, but Cobbe had made it clear that any of the Cockpit Club could have slipped away to commit murder, and the lack of grief displayed by the entire pack was suspicious to say the least.

'You should not have used Bishop Morley as an alibi,' he told Swaddell, wishing he had not been ordered to work with the man. 'Prelates do not lie, and we will be in trouble if anyone asks him about his movements last night.'

Swaddell looked hurt. 'But I *was* with Bishop Morley – we took a glass of wine together. You know he has a house in Clerkenwell, do you not?'

'I know he has one in Southwark,' said Chaloner tartly.

'It is called Winchester Palace, and has been the London residence of his ecclesiastical predecessors for centuries.'

'Well, he does not like it, so he bought another,' flashed Swaddell, equally curt. 'It is just down the green from Newcastle House. I thought you would have noticed, given that it has a cross on the roof and stained-glass windows.'

Chaloner supposed he was telling the truth, as it was something that could easily be checked. However, he simply could not imagine Morley and Swaddell enjoying a cosy evening together, and was sure that Swaddell was exaggerating the intimacy of the association.

'Even so,' he continued, 'Morley will not say that *I* was with him last night.'

'He will if I ask. I told you: he owes me a favour.'

Chaloner regarded him uneasily. 'You mean you will blackmail him into lying?'

'He would do it willingly,' said Swaddell, affronted. 'And you should be thanking me, not insulting me. If this is how you treat your friends, I am surprised you have any.'

They rode in silence the rest of the way and reached the cemetery during a downpour. Swaddell told the driver to wait, and they hurried through the deluge, calling for Tyndal. There was a guardhouse by the gates, and Tyndal and his sons were crammed inside it, waiting for the rain to stop. They invited their visitors to join them, which made for a very tight squeeze.

'Those walking corpses will see us beggared,' said Tyndal glumly. 'No one wants their loved ones buried in a place where they might get up and leave.'

'Well, you will have work tonight,' said Swaddell, 'because you are going to help us catch a coven of traitors. It will prove beyond doubt that your "walking corpses" are nothing of the kind, and you will have served your country into the bargain.'

Needless to say, the Tyndals were not very keen on tackling potentially dangerous spies, but Swaddell fixed them with a glower, which had them promising to do whatever he asked. While he issued a stream of instructions, Chaloner walked to the wood where he had found Dutch Jane's bonnet. In the middle of it was an ancient oak with a hole in its trunk. He would never have used it as a 'drop' – a place to exchange secret communiqués – because it was far too obvious. Thus he was astonished when he slipped his hand inside it and found a letter.

It was a report in Dutch, and Jane had even signed it, presumably to ensure that she was paid. It contained a lot of trivial chatter: the Queen's illness, Chiffinch's untimely end, and the Bishop of London being booked to preach in White Hall on Easter Sunday. Then there was some idle gossip: the King had a new mistress, and the Royal Society wanted to expel Baron Lucas before he offended *all* its less-gifted members by calling them stupid.

Captain Rolt merited a paragraph of his own, as it transpired that he was the son of a Puritan divine who had disowned him for becoming a Royalist. There was an account of him losing the only valuable thing he owned – the horse killed during the fight in the cockpit – concluding with the recommendation that he be offered the traitor's shilling, because he was in such desperate straits that he would almost certainly accept it.

Jane also wrote that Rolt intended to blackmail Bess Widdrington for visiting a Clerkenwell tavern without her husband's permission, although how she had discovered this was beyond Chaloner. He could only assume she had overheard Rolt telling someone else. Regardless, it suggested that the captain had been telling the truth, while Bess had lied.

The final paragraph was about Mother Broughton's prophecies, which Jane claimed would definitely come true: Good Friday would see a rain of holy fire, which would set Clerkenwell ablaze and wreak vengeance on the wicked. She ended by informing her reader that she aimed to be gone before that happened, lest she was among the casualties.

Swaddell approached at that point, and read the report with a dismissive sneer. 'Ambassador van Goch will be disappointed with this! She had a lot more to convey when we fed her misinformation via the Duke. The enemy will not care about tittle-tattle, while Mother Broughton's ramblings are irrelevant.'

Chaloner was about to return to the waiting hackney when he spotted something white in the grass. Curious, he went to investigate, and found himself staring at a familiar face, although one that was pale and waxy in death, eyes gazing sightlessly up at the clouds.

It was Dutch Jane, and her throat had been cut. He examined her quickly, recalling Mother Broughton's prediction about sausages and vats of milk, but there was no evidence of either.

He glanced at Swaddell. 'Throat-cutting is your favourite method of execution.'

Swaddell was deeply offended. 'My incisions are works of art, Tom, whereas this is pure butchery. I would *never* make such a mess.'

It did not escape Chaloner's notice that Swaddell was more indignant at being accused of an untidy assassination than he was of being considered guilty of murder.

*

While Swaddell went to inform Tyndal that he had a customer for his funerary services, Chaloner had the uncomfortable sense that events were beginning to spiral out of control, but he understood virtually nothing of what was going on. Who had killed Jane? Someone who knew she was a spy – the execution of a traitor? Or one of her countrymen, for leading a pursuer to Bunhill, forcing them to fight and then flee?

He leaned against the cemetery wall, thinking that he was no further forward with finding Chiffinch's killer than he had been when he had started his enquiries three days ago. Worse, he now had two more victims to investigate – three, if he included Dutch Jane – so he sincerely hoped Wiseman would tell him something useful when he examined Ashley and Tooley. He recalled the Earl's fear and the unease of his staff, with no one daring to go out lest it occasioned an accusation. Chaloner needed to solve the case soon, or irreparable harm was going to be done to Clarendon House.

Eventually, Swaddell finished making arrangements with Tyndal, and he and Chaloner climbed into the waiting hackney, where the driver began to regale them with what he knew about Bunhill's walking dead. He claimed to have seen them with his own eyes, their red souls glowing like hot embers. At first, Chaloner assumed he had seen the Dutch spies, but when he reported decaying legs, arms and jaws, along with trailing grave clothes, it became obvious that the testimony was pure fabrication.

Although Chaloner itched to race to White Hall and beg Wiseman to inspect Tooley and Ashley at once, Swaddell wanted to stop at Newcastle House first, and ask about Dutch Jane.

'Her death is a serious blow to the intelligence services,'

he sighed, 'because now it will be impossible to lay hold of her accomplices. I had planned to use her as bait to trap them.'

'You go to Newcastle House,' suggested Chaloner. 'I will visit White Hall and—'

'We will stick together,' interrupted Swaddell firmly. 'Here we are. Ready?'

He marched up to Newcastle House's front door and hammered imperiously. It was answered by a liveried butler, who took one look at his grim face and stood aside for him to enter. Chaloner followed reluctantly. It was the first time he had been inside, and he was surprised to find the hall unusually bright. He glanced up and saw the high ceiling was made of glass, which allowed daylight to flood in.

'The Duchess mentioned her transparent roof,' he recalled.

'It is a nice idea, but it leaks,' said the butler, and indicated several strategically placed buckets. 'Worse, the rain pools on the glass above, which encourages seagulls to come and paddle. You should see the mess they make.'

At that moment, a maid arrived to report that the Duke and Duchess were still abed, but would be ready to receive visitors in an hour.

'An hour?' echoed Chaloner in agitation. 'We must come back later.'

'Nonsense,' said the butler soothingly. 'Mr Clayton, one of the Duke's stewards, does a lovely tour of our unusual roof for a very reasonable price. The views are lovely. When you are up there, the time will just fly past.'

That was what Chaloner was afraid of.

*

The sullen steward appeared with impressive speed, delighted to make a little money on the side. Chaloner deplored the wasted time, but Swaddell was eager to see a part of the house that was normally off-limits to visitors.

The moment the fee was in his pocket, Clayton led them to a servants' staircase, the entrance of which was discreetly concealed behind a statue of a horse. They began to climb, past the grand reception rooms on the ground floor, then the bedchambers and finally the attics in the wings. Eventually, they reached a small, low door that opened on to the roof. He stepped through it, then ducked as wings flapped around his head.

'Damned seagulls,' he snapped, picking feathers from his coat. 'They attack me every time I come up here. I shall have to start bringing a musket.'

Because the house was in the shape of a stubby H – a fat arm at either end with a longer, lower block joining them together – the roof was in three sections, too. There was a 'pyramid hip' over each of the two wings, while the middle part of the roof was flat, with knee-high balustrades running along both edges – one overlooking the street at the front, and the other overlooking the garden at the back. The central section had originally been tiled, but these had been removed – other than a wide 'walkway' immediately outside the door – and replaced with panes of glass, so as to illuminate the hall and the ballroom below. There were dozens of panels, each one in a lead frame. Unfortunately, lead was not very rigid, so the whole structure had started to sag.

The problem had been resolved by installing a massive iron brace, which spanned the flat part of the roof from right to left, dividing it neatly in half. It was impossible to see over its top, so Chaloner could only assume that the far side was a mirror image of the one on which he stood. The warped frames had then been fastened to the brace with smaller supports. Even so, some bits remained lower than others, and as there was no mechanism to let water drain away, it meant that every time it rained, the Newcastles had a series of ponds on their roof.

'Ugly, is it not?' said Clayton with superior disdain. 'She should have given up when the lead startled to buckle, as anyone with half a brain could see that a glass roof will never work.'

'But it *has* worked,' countered Swaddell. 'The hall below is lovely and light, and I imagine the ballroom is, too.'

'Oh, they are light,' sneered Clayton. 'But you may as well have no roof at all in inclement weather, because the ceiling leaks. Surely you noticed the buckets, set ready to catch drips? Worse, there is no way to clean the inside of the glass, so in a few years, it will be coated in soot from the lamps. Then our hall and ballroom will be as dark as ever.'

'Why does the glass not crack under the weight of the water?' asked Swaddell, gripping Chaloner's arm for balance while he tested the depth of one pool with his foot. He withdrew it quickly when it transpired to be higher than his boot.

'Baron Lucas devised a way to strengthen the panes,' explained Clayton, 'although his experiments cost a fortune, and poor Viscount Mansfield's inheritance was used for the whole process. The Royal Society got fat on his tests though, damn them.'

'The central brace is unattractive,' mused Chaloner, eyeing it critically; it comprised a wall of iron plates that stood taller than the height of two men. 'Yet I did not notice it when I looked at the house from the street.'

Clayton sniffed. 'You will now you know it is here. It spoils the look of the place in my opinion. Moreover, the wretched thing is so tall that I cannot climb over it.'

Chaloner regarded him askance. 'Why would you want to do that?'

'The gulls,' explained Clayton between gritted teeth. 'They love it up here, but as soon as I chase them off this side, they fly to the other. That means I have to run all the way down the stairs to the ground floor, then all the way up the opposite stairs – at which point the damned things fly back over here again.'

Chaloner could tell from the noise that the birds had indeed landed on the other side of the structure, and supposed that shooing them off would present a challenge.

'The views are nice, though,' said Swaddell appreciatively. 'It would be a fine place to bring a young lady for an unusual jaunt.'

'Not my cousins,' said Chaloner, knowing exactly what he was thinking. 'It is starting to rain again. Can we go now?'

Back in the hall, the butler was waiting to say the ducal pair was still unavailable, but Eliza Topp was in the ballroom and wanted to see them. Chaloner started to object, loath to waste more time, but the man was insistent. They followed him across the hall and through a huge pair of gilded doors, where Chaloner stopped to gaze around in awe. The ballroom was huge, and no expense had been spared on its renovation – so recent that it still reeked of paint and freshly oiled wood. He began to understand why Mansfield was worried that his father might have no money left to bequeath him.

Eliza was by one of the great windows, red-eyed and

clutching a sodden handkerchief. Perched next to her, looking out of place but defiant, was Sarah Shawe.

'My husband,' whispered Eliza. 'Have you seen him?'

Chaloner frowned. 'No, why?'

Sarah took her friend's hand and chafed it comfortingly as she replied. 'He went out last night and did not return. Eliza is worried that something bad has happened to him.'

'He has enemies, you see,' elaborated Eliza shakily. 'Clayton is jealous of the trust the Duke and Duchess place in him, and is always trying to besmirch his good name. And a few days ago, Clayton's horrible friends arrived in the city . . .'

'Liddell the horse-trader and Vicar Booth,' put in Sarah. 'Both are rogues, and we are concerned that Clayton has tired of trying to harm Topp with words and insinuations, and has resorted to actual violence.'

Chaloner thought about the anonymous letter that the Duke had asked Thurloe to investigate – the one accusing the Duchess of having an affair with Topp. Had Clayton sent it, not so much to hurt her as to destroy his enemy? But if so, Clayton would hardly have dispatched his victim before the letter had had a chance to work its mischief.

'Do you have any evidence that Clayton might hurt Topp?' he asked. 'I accept that he and Topp dislike each other, but colleague rivalry does not usually result in physical harm.'

'No,' admitted Eliza, tears coursing down her cheeks. 'But my husband has never disappeared like this before. He knows I worry . . .'

'Were you up on the roof with Clayton just now?' asked Sarah. 'You cannot make out much from down here, with all that thick glass and water, but we thought we saw shadows. Did he mention Topp at all?'

'No,' replied Swaddell. 'But—'

'Then that *proves* he has done something untoward,' declared Sarah. 'Normally, he cannot utter two words without maligning Topp. His silence is suspicious.'

'Not necessarily,' said Chaloner, thinking that Clayton had not had time to talk about Topp, because he had been too busy disparaging the Duchess and her ceiling.

'Perhaps Topp found out about you,' said Swaddell to Sarah. 'No husband wants to share his wife with someone else, and it is clear that he has a challenger for Eliza's affections.'

'He knows my friendship with Sarah does not threaten my love for him,' said Eliza firmly. 'He is my husband – he will always be first in my heart. Him and my Duchess.'

This was clearly news to Sarah, and hurt flashed in her eyes, although it was quickly masked. She forced a smile. 'Besides, if he had gone on a journey, he would have taken his travelling bag with him, but Eliza tells me it is still here.'

'I shall ask my people to keep an eye out for him,' promised Swaddell. 'But I am afraid we are here to bring you other sad news. Dutch Jane is dead.'

Eliza gaped as he outlined what they had learned about the Duchess's former maid, then began to weep afresh, although Sarah's expression hardened.

'*I* am not sorry. She tormented poor little Molly, tried to disrupt our school, and now we learn she was a traitor, too. Well, as far as I am concerned, she got what she deserved.'

Eliza was kinder. 'She was lonely. We should have tried harder to befriend her.'

'But I did not want to befriend her,' objected Sarah. 'Of course, we should not be surprised by the news – Mother Broughton foretold it.'

'She also foretold that it would involve sausages and a vat of milk,' said Chaloner wryly. 'Neither of which were in evidence around the body.'

'Sausages would have been,' countered Sarah. 'Dutch Jane loved them, and always had one secreted somewhere on her person.'

'Then seeing one in her future was not very impressive, was it?' said Chaloner. 'Your so-called soothsayer just took some commonly known fact and included it in—'

'You say there was no sausage with Jane's body?' interrupted Sarah, and raised a triumphant finger. 'Then *that* is its relevance! She *always* had one with her, but on the night of her death, she did not. It was the unusual *absence* of a sausage that Mother Broughton foretold.'

'You are twisting the facts to suit—'

'I am proving that Mother Broughton is a genuine prophet,' argued Sarah. 'And nasty old Jane should have listened to her. It is a good thing I have an alibi for the woman's murder, or those with suspicious minds might think I did it.'

'What alibi?' asked Swaddell, showing his thoughts had indeed run in that direction, while Chaloner resolved not to mention the vat of milk again, sure Sarah would find a way to 'prove' one of those featured in Dutch Jane's demise, too, and he did not have time to listen to more nonsense.

'I was with Joan Cole and a dozen others pickling cockles all last night. Then I came here at dawn, when Eliza sent for me. And do not accuse her of the crime either, because she read with the Duchess until sunrise, then raced around this place searching for Topp.'

Eliza blushed uncomfortably. 'They do not think we hurt Jane, Sarah. And I am sorry she is dead. I hoped she would get another post in the city. She makes . . . *made* lovely marchpanes.'

Sarah turned to Chaloner and Swaddell with a sneer. 'So there is a summary of Dutch Jane's character for you: spiteful, cruel and ignorant, but a virtuoso with sweetmeats.'

When the butler appeared to announce that the Duchess was on her way at last, Swaddell intensified his efforts to prise more information about Dutch Jane from Eliza and Sarah before the great lady arrived, but Chaloner could tell he was wasting his time. Eliza was too distressed about her missing husband, while Sarah was disinclined to be helpful. Eventually, the Duchess swept in. Chaloner had the sangfroid to bow in order to mask his consternation, but Swaddell just stood and gaped.

The Duchess had donned the costume she was alleged to have worn to the theatre. It was bright blue, and the neckline plunged well below her ample bosom, which had been daubed thickly with red and white powder. The ensemble was completed with a pair of heavy riding boots and what appeared to be a bishop's mitre. Chaloner supposed she had designed it herself, as no dressmaker would have dared.

'My God!' he heard Sarah breathe. 'I thought the rumours about her wardrobe were exaggerated, but there *is* such an outfit.'

'Eliza, my poor friend,' said the Duchess gently, and opened her arms. 'I am sure Topp will return soon. Come, let me comfort you.'

Eliza ran to her mistress and sobbed against her

259

shoulder. Sarah watched for a moment with jealous eyes, then marched out. She did not bother to acknowledge the Duchess, but if the noblewoman noticed, she gave no indication. She patted the distraught Eliza on the back, murmuring that she had summoned Clayton, and aimed to ask him if he knew where Topp had gone. Then she addressed Chaloner, who was careful to keep his eyes fixed on her face.

'I know you asked for an audience with the Duke, but he is getting ready to visit White Hall with my stepson. They could not go there yesterday, because some vile rogue organised cruel games involving foxes. They remained here, in protest against such disgusting sport.'

'They were here all day, Your Grace?' asked Chaloner, thinking that if so, then neither could have killed Tooley, who was dead by seven o'clock.

'Until eight, when my stepson went out for "important business", although I doubt it was anything of the kind. The boy likes to think that all he does is of great significance, but . . .'

She ended with a disdainful sniff, while Chaloner recalled that Mansfield had been outside the Red Bull with the Cockpit Club by nine. His stepmother was right to be suspicious of his self-aggrandising claims, as his 'business' had been the cowardly attack on Eliza's school – one that had faltered under her brother's withering dressing-down.

'Were you with them, Your Grace?' asked Chaloner innocently, thinking he might as well make sure he could eliminate her, too, although he could think of no reason why she would want to dispatch the worthless rogues of the Cockpit Club.

'For some of the time,' replied the Duchess airily. 'But

I had an errand in the early evening. I returned here at eight, which is how I am able to state with certainty when my stepson left – our paths crossed just as the clocks were striking the hour.'

'What errand?' fished Chaloner, but it was a question too far.

'One of a *personal* nature,' she replied, and before the spy could ask more, she sat Eliza on a bench and strode to the window, where she proceeded to treat the gardeners to a fine view of her frontage. Once her back was to him, Swaddell was able to regain his composure.

'So the Duke and Mansfield are in the clear for whatever happened to Tooley,' he murmured to Chaloner. 'The Duchess, on the other hand . . .'

Chaloner fretted impatiently while Swaddell furnished her broad back with an account of Dutch Jane's demise. He was eager to leave, and was sorry he had agreed to the detour. Then Clayton arrived, obviously irked at being summoned by the Duchess he despised. He had brought Booth and Liddell, perhaps with the intention of intimidating her by force of numbers.

'You wanted to see me?' he asked, insolence not only in his brusque tone, but also by his neglecting to address her properly.

'Topp appears to be missing,' replied the Duchess, still gazing out of the window. 'Have you done him any harm?'

'No, I have not!' declared Clayton, wrong-footed by the blunt question. 'I have not seen him since he proved to be so useless during the crisis with poor Henrietta Florence yesterday. If it had not been for me, the Duke would have lost a valuable animal.'

Eliza leapt to her husband's defence. 'Francis's skills

lie in other areas,' she said sharply. 'But do you swear, by all you hold holy, that you have not seen him since then?'

'I do,' said Clayton, and his expression turned sly. 'Perhaps he has absconded. I do not know why everyone trusts him with—'

The Duchess whipped around to face him, and the sight of her bare breasts caused the words to freeze in his throat. Liddell gulped his astonishment, while Vicar Booth gave a low whimper of horror and scuttled out of the ballroom as fast as his spindly legs would carry him.

'Topp's loyalty is incontestable,' she declared icily. 'Although I am yet to be convinced of yours. I found more irregularities in your accounts yesterday, so I hope you have a credible explanation. If not, I shall urge my husband to dismiss you.'

'You cannot oust me!' cried Clayton, panic jolting him from his shock at her costume. 'I am His Grace's most dedicated servant, whereas Topp is all slippery manners and ineptitude. You cannot keep him in preference to me.'

'I can if I want to,' flashed the Duchess, and came to stare intently at him. He attempted to meet her eyes, but her presence at such close quarters was too disconcerting, and his gaze dropped to the floor.

'I swear,' he mumbled. 'I have not seen Topp. I do not know where he is.'

The Duchess glared at him a while longer, then returned to the window. 'I suppose I believe you. However, if it transpires that you are lying, I shall have you executed for treason.'

Clayton was unsettled by the threat, even if it was one

262

she could never carry out within the bounds of the law. 'I *am* telling the truth!'

'Good,' said the Duchess, then turned to address Chaloner and Swaddell. 'Have either of you two heard about a certain letter sent anonymously to my husband?'

'What letter is this?' asked Clayton, although the question had not been aimed at him. 'And why would this pair—'

'I am not supposed to say,' interrupted the Duchess curtly. 'He swore me to secrecy.'

Not very effectively, thought Chaloner, if she was going to ask questions about it of anyone who happened past. Then it occurred to him that she suspected Clayton of sending the missive, and this was her way of seeing if she could force a confession from him.

'If it is something that can harm the Duke, then you must tell me,' said Clayton sternly. 'He trusts me to look to his interests and—'

'A better man than you is exploring the matter,' interrupted the Duchess. 'One who is assiduous and crafty, and who will leave no stone unturned. He will find the truth. But if you cannot help us with Topp, Clayton, you may go. I have no further use for you at the moment.'

Enraged by the curt dismissal, but not in a position to do much about it, Clayton turned and stalked out. Liddell followed.

'Now, let us discuss Dutch Jane,' said the Duchess when they had gone. 'I suppose you want us to pay for her funeral, but the answer is no. She is not deserving of our charity.'

'I think we must,' said Eliza tiredly. 'Or we shall lay ourselves open to accusations of unkindness. Besides, she was not really bad. Just dishonest, greedy, disloyal and cruel.'

Humour glinted in the Duchess's eyes. 'Small failings, I am sure. But my mind is made up. I will not pay, and nor will you, Eliza. I forbid it. Jane read all my husband's letters and told the Dutch what was in them. We are under no obligation to bury a traitor.'

Swaddell regarded her in astonishment. 'You knew?'

'Of course I knew.' The Duchess smiled superiorly. 'I provided all manner of additional snippets for her to blab, each one carefully designed to mislead and confound. Why do you think we won the Battle of Lowestoft? It was all because of me.'

Chaloner had been at that particular skirmish, and felt that at least some of the credit belonged to the brave seamen who had risked their lives to fight it, but he held his tongue.

'So why did you dismiss her then?' demanded Swaddell, exasperated. 'It was inconvenient for the intelligence services to lose such a valuable tool.'

'Because her paymasters were beginning to distrust her reports, so her value was diminishing,' replied the Duchess. 'Besides, she disobeyed an express order about my poultry and she was unkind to little Molly. I do not tolerate defiance or deliberate cruelty.'

'I do not suppose you know who killed her, do you?' asked Swaddell.

'The Dutch, of course. They did not want to spend money on buying her passage home, but nor did they want her roaming around London blabbing about what she had done. Her fate was sealed the moment she agreed to play the spy.'

By the time Chaloner and Swaddell emerged from Newcastle House, their hackney driver had tired of

264

waiting and had disappeared. They hired another on Holborn, with a lively horse that galloped most of the way to White Hall, so that when they arrived, Chaloner felt as though every bone in his body was thrumming from the jolts they had received. He settled the bill, and then heard someone call his name. It was Kersey, hailing him from a private coach – a new one that was all shiny black paint and gold trimmings. He sat next to a woman who was young, buxom and wore the best clothes money could buy.

'My wife,' said Kersey, patting her knee with a fond smile.

Chaloner felt like asking which one, but the charnel-house keeper's domestic arrangements were none of his business. 'It is not often we see you outside your domain,' he said conversationally. 'Where are you going?'

'To Newcastle House,' replied Kersey. 'A body was delivered to me an hour ago, drowned in the Thames, and items in its pockets reveal it to be one Francis Topp. I did hear he was missing, and now it seems he is found. Here. See for yourselves.'

He handed over a bundle of soggy papers – receipts and other mundane documents that bore Topp's signature. There was also a letter to Eliza, begging her forgiveness for leaving her a widow, but stating that it was best for all concerned: if he was in his grave, no one could accuse him of behaving improperly towards the Duchess, and the malicious lies about their alleged affair would fade away. He then assured her that he loved her very much, and asked her to explain his death to their employers.

'Topp and the Duchess?' breathed Swaddell. 'Lovers? I do not believe it!'

'Nor did the Duke,' said Chaloner. 'He would have stood by Topp, so there was no need for him to dispatch himself.' He glanced at Kersey. 'Are you sure it was suicide? He was not killed by someone else?'

'It was definitely suicide. However, the stench of ale on the body suggests that Topp's capacity for clear thinking was almost certainly impaired.'

'He was a fool then,' declared Swaddell. 'He should have stayed to prove his innocence.'

'Such allegations are easy to make, but difficult to dispel,' Chaloner said quietly. 'Maybe he knew he would never be free of them.'

'But what about the Duchess?' asked Swaddell indignantly. 'His self-murder makes it look as though they *did* have an affair, but he would rather die than be forced to admit it. He has done her a serious disservice by tossing himself in the river.'

Kersey tapped the letter with a beautifully manicured fingernail. 'This suggests he was trying to act in his employers' best interests. Maybe he *was* a little in love with his Duchess.'

'Of course, there is another explanation for his despair,' said Swaddell. 'Namely that his wife had taken a lover in the form of Sarah Shawe.'

'I shall never understand why folk find that so upsetting,' said Kersey, shaking his head in incomprehension. 'It is quite possible to love more than one person at a time.'

Well, a bigamist should know, thought Chaloner.

Chapter 10

Chaloner felt acutely uncomfortable as he walked through White Hall later that day. It was partly because he was with Swaddell, and the assassin was chatting away as if they were old friends, but mostly because it quickly became apparent that many courtiers believed the Earl was responsible for the recent spate of murders. People he barely knew eyed him warily as he passed, then began to whisper to each other the moment he was out of earshot. All in all, he was glad when they reached the chapel, although he baulked when Wiseman emerged, hands stained with blood.

'Poison,' the surgeon declared. 'In both men. I knew Clarke could not be trusted to give a reliable verdict and I was right. It was the same henbane-based toxin that killed Chiffinch, although delivered boldly this time, not hidden in capsules.'

'In oysters?' asked Chaloner.

'Probably in wine,' replied Wiseman. 'Both corpses reeked of it. They must have gulped it down very fast, or they would have noticed something amiss with the taste.'

'I imagine Tooley swallowed his at the drinking contest

267

that followed the fox-tossing,' surmised Chaloner. 'That would have entailed gulping, almost certainly by a man who was already drunk.'

'And Ashley?' asked Swaddell.

'He was a sot – the killer could have plied *him* with wine at any time and he would have accepted it. However, I suspect it happened at Bunhill, as I cannot see anyone lugging a body around for no obvious purpose.'

'And where better than that cemetery to commit such a crime?' mused Swaddell. 'Big, dark, isolated and devoid of witnesses – Tyndal and his lads cannot possibly monitor all of it.'

'There was soil under Ashley's fingernails,' put in Wiseman. 'In my professional opinion, the poisoner gave him the tainted wine, then shoved him into a grave when it began to take effect. Drunk and dying, Ashley tried to claw his way out, but failed.'

Chaloner winced at the image. 'How long before the poison took effect? If it was instantly, all we have to do is find out who gave Tooley his last drink.'

'Unfortunately, it is not that simple,' said Wiseman, and adopted the pompous tone he used on his students. 'There is no way to tell how much of the substance Tooley imbibed, which means I cannot say with certainty when the symptoms began. It may have been in his last cup, but it may equally well have been in his first.'

'The drinking contest was in a tavern,' said Swaddell, 'which was poorly lit and crowded. It was not a private affair for Cockpit Club men only. Ergo, the culprit might be anyone.'

'Not Baron Lucas,' averred Wiseman. 'He was with me then, having his bunions filed.'

'Is there anything else you can tell us?' Chaloner

asked, feeling that Wiseman's testimony so far posed more questions than answers.

'Only that you must hurry to get to the bottom of the matter,' replied Wiseman. 'These rumours about the Earl being responsible are dangerous, because his enemies now circle like bees around a wounded hippopotamus.'

And with that, he strode away, muttering about prescribing a tonic for the King, who had also enjoyed the drinking competition and had woken with a headache. Chaloner supposed they should be grateful that it was not His Majesty who had downed the poison.

He went into the chapel and stared down at the two bodies, wondering who had wanted them – and Chiffinch – dead. He reviewed his original list of suspects.

First, the Cockpit Club. He was sure Widdrington would stoop to poison, and so would Bess. Then there was the fickle but ruthless Captain Rolt, conveniently to hand when Chiffinch's body had been found, and Cobbe with his clever mind and contrived manners. There were others, too, such as young Legg, eager to impress his new and influential friends, and the spotty Richard Pamphlin, a silly fop with too much time on his hands.

Next was Will, who had gained so much from his brother's death. Had Tooley and Ashley helped him with the oysters, but as neither could be trusted to keep quiet, Will had decided to get rid of them, too? Chaloner knew for a fact that there was a hard core of ambition under the Pimp-Master General's dissipated exterior.

Then there were the people from Newcastle House, although most of those had now been exonerated. The Duke and his son had been at home when Tooley had died, while Lucas had an alibi in Wiseman. That left the Duchess, although Chaloner could not see her lurking in a dark cemetery with a flask of toxic wine. And if she had, not even Ashley would have accepted a drink under such circumstances.

Finally, there were Timothy and Fanny Clarke, although Chaloner knew of no reason why Fanny would kill three courtiers, while Clarke lacked the intelligence for so sly a crime. Yet the physician had tried to pass off all three deaths as natural, and as a medical man, he would know better than most how to kill with poison. So would a medical man's wife.

Of course, given that Tooley and Ashley had been poisoned in public places, the list now had to be expanded to include the entire population of London. Was the culprit a servant, perhaps one who had been shabbily treated by those particular men? Or someone who deplored the ruling elite and aimed to pick them off one by one? Chaloner grimaced as he realised that the possibilities were endless.

'There is only one way forward that I can see,' he said to Swaddell, who was standing silently at his side, respecting his need to gather his thoughts. 'We must return to the oysters – try to ascertain exactly who slipped into the larder and tampered with them.'

'But we have both tried that already,' objected Swaddell in exasperation. 'And learned that security is so appallingly lax that virtually anyone could have done it.'

'Do you have a better idea?' asked Chaloner.

Swaddell admitted that he did not.

As they left the chapel, they met Legg, who was carrying a massive bunch of flowers. Without being asked, the young man explained that they were for Ashley and Tooley.

'A nice gift might help me if these prophecies of walking corpses come true,' he elaborated. 'I do not want my dead friends vexed with me for not paying their mortal remains proper respect. They were bigger than me, you see.'

'Very prudent,' drawled Swaddell. 'But since you are here, tell us what duties Tooley and Ashley performed at Court – other than engaging in the kind of behaviour that might see the King toppled from his throne.'

'Not much,' replied Legg. 'That is why such posts are popular – it is money for nothing. They were Yeomen of the Larder, so all they had to do was hang around that place for a couple of hours each week and chat to the staff.'

'When was the last time they performed this arduous task?'

Legg considered. 'Well, Tooley worked on Thursday, which I know because he was late coming to the Shield Gallery that evening. I am not sure about Ashley.'

'Thursday,' mused Swaddell. 'That was when Chiffinch's oysters were poisoned – he ate them in the small hours of Friday morning. Is Tooley our culprit then?'

'Not unless he then went out and poisoned himself,' said Chaloner. 'However, it is time we had another word with the larder guards. Are you coming?'

The assassin was not very keen, but followed Chaloner anyway. Unfortunately, they arrived only to be informed that all four guards who had been on duty that night were now on furlough, so were not available for questioning. The clerk who supplied the information – his name was Abraham Hubbert – added that all had left the city to visit their families.

'How convenient,' said Chaloner, regarding him through narrowed eyes. 'Almost as if someone arranged for them to be out of the way.'

'You see plots where there are none,' said Hubbert, shoving a ledger at him. 'Our rotas are arranged weeks in advance. Look for yourself. You can see that nothing has been changed.'

'Then perhaps *you* can explain how Chiffinch's oysters came to be poisoned in your domain,' said Chaloner coldly. 'And then two of your Yeomen murdered within days.'

Hubbert swallowed hard. 'I cannot – I rarely leave this office, and it is the Yeomen of the Larder who supervise the guards . . .'

'Then how do you explain all the pilfering that takes place here?' demanded Swaddell, growing angry by their lack of progress, so lashing out at the man. 'You are the larder's clerk: you, of all people, must be aware of how much goes missing.'

Hubbert's expression was a combination of fear and defiance. 'What pilfering? I assure you that everything is in order. You cannot prove such a vile accusation.'

'*We* cannot,' acknowledged Chaloner. 'But Spymaster Williamson will. We shall report our suspicions to him, and he will examine all your accounts.'

He turned on his heel and stalked out, leaving Hubbert white-faced with terror.

'Williamson will refuse to do it,' said Swaddell in a low voice as he hurried after him. 'He is too busy with the Dutch war. Besides, he is in Dover.'

'I know,' sighed Chaloner, then grinned. 'But the threat gave Hubbert a good fright, and perhaps it will serve to turn the place honest, if only for a little while.'

'So now what?' asked Swaddell, disheartened.

'Back to the kitchens, I suppose,' sighed Chaloner. 'Perhaps the Master Cook will have remembered something new to help us.'

As usual, the palace kitchens were frantically busy, and the portly William Austen was harried. He swallowed hard when he saw Chaloner and Swaddell, resentful of the interruption when he had so much to do and alarmed that he was to be interrogated again.

'I have already told you all I know about the night that Chiffinch died,' he gulped, looking from one to the other with uneasy eyes. 'And I thought we had agreed that any blame for what happened to the oysters lies with the larder, not the kitchens.'

'It does,' said Swaddell. 'But we wondered if anything else has occurred to you in the interim. After all, I am sure you want to help us in any way you can.'

The look that accompanied these words was so full of venomous warning that the hapless Austen immediately gave the matter some serious thought.

'Well, you have already questioned the page who took the oysters from here to the Shield Gallery. The only other thing I can suggest is that you speak to the boy who fetched them from the fish market.'

The 'boy' transpired to be one Millicent Lantravant, a girl of eleven or twelve, who Austen said was stronger, more efficient and a faster learner than any of her male counterparts.

'It was four o'clock by the time Mr Austen realised that he had forgotten to order the oysters,' she piped, delighted to be the centre of attention. 'So he sent me to Lower Thames Street to buy some at once. But it was so late in the day that our usual traders had sold out.'

Austen regarded her in alarm. 'You did not mention this to me.'

'Because there was no need,' she replied with a proud toss of her head. 'I solved the problem myself. I was standing there, wondering what to do, when the Duchess of Newcastle happened past. She told me to try the oyster-seller on Clerkenwell Green.'

'Not Sarah Shawe?' asked Chaloner, startled.

Millicent nodded, and his mind raced with questions. Did this mean Sarah was the culprit? But how could she be? It was unlikely that she had happened to have poisoned capsules to hand when an opportunity arose to sell her wares to a servant from White Hall. And why would she want to harm Chiffinch anyway – a man she was unlikely to have met?

'Why did a duchess deign to talk to a child?' he asked, not sure what to think, although Austen's horror at the revelations made it clear that *he* had known nothing of what Millicent had done. 'Were you in your palace livery? Is that why?'

Millicent nodded sheepishly. 'And because I was crying. The boys would have taunted me about coming back empty-handed, you see, so I was upset. They are jealous of me, because Mr Austen says I am better than them, and they would love to see me in disgrace.'

'So you went to Clerkenwell. What then?'

'I found the oyster-seller on the green, just where the Duchess said she would be. When the woman saw my uniform, she tried to charge me a fortune, so I told her a lie about White Hall looking for a regular purveyor of shellfish. She dropped the price when she thought we might become one of her regular customers.'

Austen goggled at her. 'My word, child! You have some gall.'

Millicent preened. 'Then I hurried back here, and put them in a bucket of water in the larder, just like we always do. I fetched them just before midnight, when Mr Austen sent for them, and I watched him give them a light sprinkling of lemon and salt.'

'Lemon,' mused Chaloner, recalling that Tooley had claimed to be an expert on the fruit, on the basis of him being a Yeoman of the Larder. 'Are they in season now?'

'Mr Austen grows them in his hothouse,' explained Millicent. 'Shall I take you there?'

'Another time, perhaps. Is there anything else you can tell us?'

Millicent considered. 'When I took the oysters to the larder, someone watched me – a woman, whose face was covered by a scarf. I remember, because the day was mild, so she had no need to wrap herself up so.'

'How can you be sure it was a woman if you did not see her face?'

'Because I can tell the difference,' replied Millicent confidently. 'Of course, the larder is always being watched by people who want to get inside. It contains lots of lovely things, see – sugar, butter, raisins, fruit from Spain . . .'

'What else did you notice about . . . her?'

'That she had very nice shoes – black ones with silver buckles.'

'What of her clothes? Were they the kind worn by servants or courtiers?'

'Servants, although her shoes were of fine quality. I suppose a generous mistress *could* have given them to her, but she looked comfortable in them, as if they had been made for her.'

'But you do not know her name?'

'No, but Michael Mushey might. He was on guard duty that evening and he knows everyone. Ask him.'

'Unfortunately, he is on furlough and has left the city.'

Millicent's expression was scornful. 'Mushey will not have gone anywhere. The other three guards might, but he will still be here.'

'You seem very sure,' said Chaloner warily.

'I *am* sure. He will never leave White Hall, because he wants to be rich, and would be too worried about missing an opportunity. He is only a sentry, but he makes friends with important people, because he has a high opinion of himself.'

'What important people?' asked Swaddell, astonished by her candour.

'Well, he liked to drink with the Yeomen of the Larder, including the two who died.'

'Tooley and Ashley,' put in Austen helpfully. 'And Millicent is right – Mushey does think himself a cut above his fellows. Perhaps he can throw light on what happened to the oysters, although you will have to treat what he says with caution. The man is a born trickster.'

Chaloner thanked them for their help, and walked outside, glad to leave the steam, noise and chaos of the kitchens.

'I wish we had spoken to her days ago,' said Swaddell. 'She probably saw the killer, disguised and waiting for a chance to slip inside the larder. And her opinion of Mushey the guard seems uncannily astute. The only question is: can we trust the testimony of a child?'

'I think we can,' said Chaloner. 'I wonder if the woman outside the larder was the same one who told Millicent to buy the oysters in Clerkenwell. After all, if the Duchess had not intervened, Millicent would have returned to White Hall empty-handed, and Chiffinch would never have eaten the capsules of poison.'

'He would not have eaten them *that night*,' corrected Swaddell. 'I rather suspect they would have been fed to him eventually, given the trouble someone took to make the things. Shall we pay a visit to Mushey now?'

All the palace guards lived in a large building overlooking Scotland Yard, so Chaloner and Swaddell began to walk there at once. They were just passing the larder offices again when Swaddell stopped and pointed to a staircase.

'Tooley's quarters are up there. Perhaps we should spend a moment looking around them. Who knows? It is where he died, so perhaps his killer left some clues.'

'He did not leave any with Ashley,' muttered Chaloner ruefully. 'I spent an age exploring the cemetery, but there was nothing to find.'

Tooley's chambers were surprisingly neat and tidy, other than the bed, which was a tangle of blankets, suggesting that he had flopped there and writhed in his final moments. It quickly became apparent that Chaloner and Swaddell were not the first to have visited, because there was a suspicious absence of anything valuable.

Then Tooley's manservant appeared, and said he had found his master at seven o'clock the previous evening, not long after he had heard thumps coming from the bedchamber. Such sounds were not unusual, as Tooley had been a heavy man with a lumbering tread, and the servant had only thought to check on him when things had gone oddly quiet.

'I saw at once that something was wrong, so I ran for help,' he went on. 'Dr Clarke came, and said he died of a fever. Fearing the plague, I kept my distance. His friends were not worried, though. They came and took his best things – said he would have wanted it.'

'Which friends?' asked Chaloner.

'Colonel Widdrington, his wife and Mr Pamphlin. But it was a lie, because Mr Tooley would *not* have wanted it. He told me that his sister was his only heir.'

Chaloner was disgusted, feeling it was one thing for the Cockpit Club not to grieve for a fellow member, but another altogether to race to his quarters and steal his possessions.

'We will have a word with that cabal again later,' he told Swaddell. 'About raiding Tooley's quarters *and* the drinking game that saw him dead. One of them must have seen the killer tamper with the wine. Or perhaps these three did it together, and they are all guilty.'

'If so, we will find out,' said Swaddell, 'because one will break and betray his fellows.'

They left Tooley's chambers and hurried across Scotland Yard. On their way, they met Clarke and Fanny, who were coming from the opposite direction. The couple were quarrelling.

'It is horrible,' declared Fanny, angry and tearful. 'Bess should not have done it. You demean yourself by being there.'

'I have no choice,' the physician snapped back defensively. 'How else can I win more wealthy clients? Besides, it will be fun, and I have never—' He stopped speaking abruptly when he realised Chaloner and Swaddell were listening.

'Two more of your verdicts were overturned today,' Swaddell informed him icily. 'Tooley did not die of a fever and Ashley did not die of grief.'

'*Hush!*' hissed Clarke, glancing around to make sure no one else had heard. 'And for your information, I never gave an opinion about Ashley, while Tooley *did* die of a fever. You cannot trust Wiseman. He is a mere barber–surgeon, whereas I am a university-trained physician.'

'Where were you on Sunday evening?' asked Chaloner. 'Between six and seven o'clock, and then between nine o'clock and midnight?'

Clarke glowered at him. 'That is none of your business. And you had better not be accusing me of these deaths. I *like* the Cockpit Club men. Indeed, I am on my way to join them now. Being with them is much nicer than being at home.'

He shot Fanny an unpleasant look and stalked away. Chaloner was about to follow and quiz him further when Swaddell homed in on Fanny like a vulture.

'We know you and Bess visited the Red Bull together,' the assassin began, 'so why did you lie about it?'

Chaloner grimaced his impatience. The women's excursion to a tavern was not relevant to the murders, so why was Swaddell wasting their time with it? Or was he just tired of dishonesty, and aimed to take someone to task for it because he could?

'Captain Rolt should not have gossiped,' said Fanny bitterly. 'He is no gentleman.'

'I shall take that as a confession,' said Swaddell. 'So why did you deny going there?'

'Because you asked me in front of my husband,' replied Fanny defiantly, 'and I did not want him to know that I . . . He frequents it himself, you see, and Captain Rolt

279

said it is a. . .' she lowered her voice prudishly, 'a house of ill repute. I had to know the truth.'

'You could not have sent someone else to find out?' demanded Swaddell.

Fanny regarded him askance. 'You mean ask a friend or a servant to determine whether my husband uses ladies of the night?'

She had a point: it would make her a laughing stock, and her sewing circle friends would likely shun her for it. She would become like Barbara Chiffinch – a decent woman struggling to make the best of life married to a disreputable rake. Clarke, on the other hand, would rise in the estimation of his fellow debauchees.

'You need not have worried,' Swaddell told her. 'The Red Bull is not a brothel.'

'No,' acknowledged Fanny. 'However, it *is* frequented by prostitutes – the unhappy ladies who think that learning to read, write and philosophise will raise them from the gutter.'

'You do not approve of women trying to better themselves?' asked Chaloner.

'Of course, but only in *suitable* subjects. Needlework is best. It is very important to be able to judge the quality of pins, cloth and thread, and then to learn how and when to apply specific stitches.'

Her mood lifted as she warmed to her theme, although her voice remained a monotonous drone, and Chaloner understood why so many people described her as 'dull'.

'Reading and writing could be useful to these women,' he said, cutting across a detailed exposition of the virtues of running backstitch.

'Wrong!' she flashed angrily. 'It will only encourage

discontent. They will expect an improvement in their lot after their hard work, but they will never get it.'

'They might,' argued Chaloner. 'It will qualify them for better posts.'

'Which they will never win,' said Fanny, exasperated. 'That is my point. These posts will go to the same people who always get them – folk from the *respectable* classes. Your educated prostitutes will resent it and there will be trouble. And I do not want more upheaval and chaos. I want everything to be safe and stable again.'

'Easy for you to say,' muttered Swaddell. 'You are wealthy, born into a comfortable life. The Red Bull women should not be held back by—'

'Much as I would love everyone to live in nice houses and do rewarding jobs, it will never happen,' interrupted Fanny, shortly and with passion. 'Our world is unjust, and it is cruel to raise the hopes of these women.'

'So what did you do at the Red Bull?' asked Chaloner, unwilling to waste time by debating social ethics with her. 'Stand outside and spy?'

Fanny grimaced. 'I suppose you could describe it so. There was a crack in the window shutter, so we took it in turns to peep through.'

'I cannot see you and Bess Widdrington having much in common,' remarked Swaddell. 'Why choose to go with her?'

'You mean because I am uninteresting and she is full of fun?' asked Fanny archly. 'Well, for your information, there is one thing upon which we both agree: that our country cannot endure more upheaval. We are tired of it.'

'Then why does she encourage the Cockpit Club's asinine antics?' asked Chaloner. 'She must see that they are turning the people against the King.'

281

Fanny winced. 'Unfortunately, she sees that as the only way to win her husband's affections. She adores him, and wants him to feel the same way about her.'

And Fanny was fond of Clarke, so that was something else the two women shared – being cursed with spouses who did not love them back. Sensing it was a sensitive subject, Chaloner brought the discussion back to the Red Bull by asking what she had overheard there.

'Baron Lucas giving a talk about some experiment involving the weather,' she replied. 'After which Mother Broughton announced that all London's wicked will die by Easter Sunday.' A pained expression suffused her face.

'I doubt you will be one of them,' said Swaddell, although it did not sound like a compliment, and Chaloner saw he had taken a dislike to this prim woman and her officious determination to prevent the advancement of her sex.

'Perhaps not, but what about Timothy? He thinks that joining the Cockpit Club will enhance his standing at Court, and will not listen when I say it may do him harm.'

'He has the right of it,' said Swaddell. 'The King prefers sinners to saints, so they are the ones who prosper in White Hall.'

'It is not Timothy's prosperity that concerns me,' said Fanny unhappily. 'It is his *soul*. I do not want him corrupted, but look at him now – racing off to watch goose-pulling!'

'What is goose-pulling?' asked Swaddell.

Fanny's eyes filled with tears. 'Riding horses at a tethered bird to see who can yank its head off. Have you ever heard anything more vile? Perhaps *this* is why there will be a great calamity on Good Friday – we torture God's creatures in the name of sport.'

282

'Will you try to stop it?' asked Chaloner. 'Like you did the fox-tossing?'

Fanny looked away. 'But I failed with that, and now everyone laughs at me.'

'Not everyone,' said Chaloner quietly. 'I applaud what you did. So, I imagine, does the Duchess of Newcastle. She also champions animals.'

Fanny sniffed. 'Your approval is acceptable to me, but hers is not. She is a lunatic, and I do not want my name associated with hers in any way. From now on, I shall confine my palace activities to sewing with Lucy Bodvil and Mary Robartes. They are *decent* company. But speaking of decent company, your Earl tells me that you have cousins staying with you.'

Chaloner nodded. 'Until Easter, when Lady Clarendon will take them.'

Fanny nodded approvingly. 'There is no better person to teach them courtly manners. Until then, he has asked me to entertain them for a few hours each day. He is uneasy with the notion of them having no other company but you and Wiseman.'

Chaloner was indignant. 'What does he think we will do? Teach them spying and dissection?'

'I doubt you will manage that before Easter,' said Fanny, a twinkle in her eye. 'But he has their interests at heart, so bring them to me if you like. I shall ensure their needlework is up to scratch, as you will never find them husbands if they cannot ply a needle or a lucet.'

Chaloner's first instinct was to decline, but the worst anyone could say about Fanny was that she was boring, which, as the Earl had pointed out, was no bad thing in a chaperone. Besides, releasing Veriana and Ursula into her care would put them out of Swaddell's reach, and that was no small consideration.

He was in the process of accepting her offer when Bess Widdrington strutted past on the arm of the spotty Pamphlin. She immediately began to brag about the goose-pulling contest that she had organised.

'But it is cruel, Bess,' objected Fanny, distressed. 'You must cancel it. Besides, Londoners will object to such "sport" in Holy Week.'

'Who cares what they think?' shrugged Bess, and gave a smirk of satisfaction. 'My husband is excited by it, and that is all that matters as far as I am concerned.'

Seeing she would not be convinced, Fanny nodded towards Chaloner and Swaddell. 'They know we were at the Red Bull, Bess. Captain Rolt told them.'

Bess's eyes flashed dangerously as she glared at Chaloner and Swaddell. 'Fanny and I were *right* to investigate the place. It is a hotbed of insurrection, which you two would know if you were any good at your jobs.'

'Women learning to read?' asked Chaloner. 'That is hardly revolutionary.'

'Oh, yes, it is! How do you think rebellions begin? By educating the masses! It is dangerous to let them think for themselves, as then they imagine that they have rights.'

'I agree,' said Pamphlin languidly, scratching one of his pimples. 'We should keep women where they belong, under the thumbs of men who know what is best for them. Current company excepted, of course. Noblewomen are different from the rabble.'

'Other than the Duchess of Newcastle,' spat Bess. 'She shames her husband with her eccentric capers, and he should take her in hand before her example encourages others.'

'I hardly think—' began Chaloner.

'But as for the Red Bull,' Bess forged on, 'because no one else had the sense to end what is happening there, *I* took charge of the situation.'

'What did you do?' asked Swaddell, while Chaloner regarded her uneasily.

'I sent the Cockpit Club to teach those harlots a lesson. Unfortunately, Baron Lucas drove my boys off.' Bess sneered. 'Well, he is the Duchess of Newcastle's brother, so what do you expect? They are as deranged as each other. Did you know that she wrote letters to dozens of courtiers, telling them to boycott our fox-tossing? How dare she!'

'She was right, Bess,' said Fanny quietly. 'It was very cruel and rather coarse.'

'It was *amusing*,' countered Bess, and turned her ire on Chaloner and Swaddell again. 'But why are you two here, pestering your betters? You should be off rounding up whores and others whose lives do not matter.'

'Bess!' cried Fanny, shocked. 'It is hardly—'

'And if *you* had any sense of decorum, you would not be talking to them,' snapped Bess, eyeing her frostily. 'They are beneath you in every way.'

She flounced away, dragging Pamphlin with her.

'Does she ever visit your house?' asked Chaloner, thinking that if the answer was yes, his cousins would go nowhere near it.

'No,' replied Fanny, understanding exactly why he had asked. 'We are acquaintances, not friends, although I shall take steps to avoid her unless she learns some better manners.'

Before Chaloner and Swaddell could resume their journey to Mushey's room, they were distracted by a commotion. A few people were hurrying towards it, but more were walking in the opposite direction, muttering disapprovingly.

'The goose-pulling is revolting enough to repel even White Hall's jaded tastes,' said Swaddell, watching them go.

'It will not be its grisly nature that horrifies them,' predicted Chaloner, 'but the fact that it is popular in Holland. Bess has seriously miscalculated by foisting it on White Hall.'

'Then we should make sure it does not lead to trouble,' said Swaddell. 'Come on.'

Reluctantly, Chaloner trailed after him to the Privy Garden. This was a pleasant area of grass and trees, bordered on three sides by buildings and on the fourth by a wall that separated it from King Street. A wide gravelled path ran down the centre, and they saw a wooden structure had been assembled at one end of it – two upright posts connected by a crossbar. A goose was tied by its feet to the middle of the crossbar, and a servant was in the process of slathering grease over its head and neck, to render it slippery and therefore more of a challenge to hold.

Members of the Cockpit Club watched in gleeful anticipation, although only half a dozen of them had elected to take part in the exercise. These included Widdrington and Pamphlin, and grooms waited nearby with their horses.

'Pamphlin is a Page of the Presence,' remarked Swaddell, eyeing the pimpled courtier with distaste. 'A page – at his age! If I were him, I would be too ashamed to prance about attracting attention.'

A number of spectators had also gathered, but the atmosphere among them was tense. One or two bawled

286

for the fun to start, but a much bigger faction led by Bishop Morley – the man Swaddell claimed as a friend – called for an end to it. The censure only exhilarated Bess, who delighted in the role of flamboyant rebel. She raised her hands and a reluctant silence fell.

'The object of the game,' she announced in a voice that was shrill with excitement, 'is for the competitors to ride full pelt at the goose and grab its head as they pass. The winner is the one who rips it off. Now place your bets. I shall start by wagering five guineas on my husband.'

Widdrington ignored her adoring look as he mounted up. Struggling to conceal her hurt, Bess took a handkerchief and allowed it to flutter to the ground, the signal for him to begin. A murmur of relief rippled through Morley's party when the rider misjudged the distance and veered away too soon. Pamphlin was next, but came no closer to success than Widdrington.

'This is disgraceful,' declared the Duke of Buckingham, who stood with his hands on his hips and an expression of contempt on his dissipated features.

'The King is furious,' agreed Lady Castlemaine. 'Goose-pulling is popular with Dutchmen, and he does not want Londoners thinking his Court apes their filthy habits. Someone should tell Bess that she has done him great harm with this caper.'

'As long as her husband enjoys himself, she will not care,' predicted Buckingham. 'But we should not linger here, lest the King assumes we condone it.'

When they and their coterie had gone, there was a lull in the proceedings while the competitors clustered around the bird to discuss strategies for laying hold of something that was slippery and that struggled. Chaloner walked towards them, Swaddell at his heels.

'Not you two again,' snapped Widdrington irritably. 'Can a man not even pull the head off a goose without being bombarded with impertinent questions?'

'Your friends Ashley and Tooley were poisoned last night,' said Chaloner, repelled enough by them and their antics to engage in a frontal assault. 'Which one of you did it?'

Widdrington laughed, so his cronies did, too. 'If you expect us to remember anything about last night, you are as mad as the Duchess of Newcastle! I still have an aching head from the amount of wine we sank.'

'A killer sat in your midst, yet none of you are worried,' said Chaloner coldly. 'That means one of two things: that you are either too stupid to appreciate the danger you are in, or that you know more about the murders than you are willing to admit.'

Widdrington regarded him with dislike. 'Watch your tongue or I will—'

'Perhaps you can explain why you looted Tooley's room with such indecent haste, too,' Chaloner forged on. 'Surely, such behaviour should be beneath your dignity?'

'Do not single us out for censure,' objected Pamphlin angrily. 'Will Chiffinch ransacked his brother's quarters within an hour. We waited six.'

'We visited Ashley's lair, too,' said Widdrington, and smirked. 'I got a lovely wig-comb. Do you want to see it?'

'Why are you willing to engage in this vile display?' asked Chaloner, glancing at the goose and hating to see its terror. 'It will only encourage Bess to organise more of the same.'

Widdrington declined to reply, leaving Chaloner to

surmise that he *wanted* her to be in trouble, so that no one would object when he packed her off to Ireland. Before he could ask more, she called the competitors to order. They trotted back to the starting point, and Chaloner looked at the goose again. It was a pretty white creature with coal black eyes, and he fancied it was regarding him pleadingly.

Then Bess's handkerchief fluttered to the ground, and Widdrington kicked his horse into a trot. Bishop Morley leapt into its path, and stood with his arms folded and his face pale but determined. Widdrington only just managed to veer away.

'Move!' he bellowed angrily. 'I will not swerve a second time.'

Morley opened his mouth to reply, but was stopped by a sudden babble of voices. The Duchess of Newcastle had arrived with her usual enormous entourage. She was clad in what appeared to be her husband's nightgown and a massive cavalier-style hat, although her servants were more conventionally attired in matching suits of blue satin.

'I disapprove of bloodsport,' she announced importantly. 'It is nasty.'

She marched towards Morley and stood at his side, striking a rather bizarre pose, like a sailor gazing out to sea. Nothing else happened for a moment, then there was a rush as others hurried to join her. Chaloner was touched that so many people should unite to save a bird until he noticed that the King was watching from a window, and as His Majesty had expressed disapproval of the event, everyone wanted to be seen helping to disrupt it.

Dismayed, Bess screeched at them to mind their own

business, but Widdrington had seen the dark expression on the King's face and opted for a tactical retreat. His friends hastened after him. While she watched them disappear, Chaloner cut the goose free, not caring that it smeared grease over his coat. He was just wondering what to do with it when someone tugged his sleeve. It was Molly the chicken girl. She gave him a shy smile and held out her arms.

'I will take her to your house. Where do you live?'

Chaloner told her and she hurried away, the bird hidden inside her cloak.

'That was reckless,' admonished Swaddell. 'She works for the Duchess, who heads our list of murder suspects – well, mine at least – by virtue of her peculiar alibi for when Chiffinch's oysters were poisoned. Alone in blind John Milton's parlour indeed!'

Chapter 11

It was evening by the time Chaloner and Swaddell finally knocked on Michael Mushey's door. There was no reply, and unwilling to waste time, Chaloner picked the lock. They entered a room that was dark because the window shutters were closed, but Chaloner did not need Swaddell to fling them open to tell him what natural light would reveal.

'Dead,' he said, staring down at the body on the bed. 'Is it Mushey?'

'Yes,' replied Swaddell, and scowled. 'We should not have gone to the Privy Garden. Then we might have reached him before the killer did.'

'He has been dead for hours,' said Chaloner. 'Probably since last night. It suggests that he knew exactly who poisoned Chiffinch's oysters – the person *he* allowed inside for a few coins.'

'Was he poisoned, too?'

'We will ask Wiseman, but I imagine so.' Chaloner picked up the half-empty wine jug that sat on the table, and sniffed it. 'He can test this, too, as I suspect it will contain the toxin.'

'Should we discount the Duchess as a suspect then?' asked Swaddell. 'I cannot see her entering a servant's bedchamber to ply him with drink.'

'She has minions who will do anything for her.'

'Does she, now that Topp is dead? Or do you think Eliza did it? Of course, it may have been the Duchess demanding this particular favour that led Topp to drown himself – it was one duty he felt he could not perform for her.'

'Having met Topp, I think he would have found a way to do it if she asked – assassins can be hired by those who do not want to stain their own hands. Just ask Williamson.'

Swaddell ignored the barb. 'Yet I have the sense that all four deaths – Chiffinch, Ashley, Tooley and now Mushey – have their roots in the Cockpit Club. Tooley and Ashley were members, and the kitchen girl claims that Mushey was their friend . . .'

'And Chiffinch?' asked Chaloner. 'He was not a member or a crony.'

'No,' acknowledged Swaddell. 'But he was poisoned, like the others, so we must be looking at a single killer.'

Chaloner was about to reply when a sound made him glance towards the door. He had a fleeting glimpse of two engraved metal tubes before he dived at Swaddell, sending the assassin crashing to the floor. Two sharp cracks followed as the twin pistols discharged.

Swaddell lay still, eyes closed, and Chaloner lost valuable moments searching for a wound before concluding that the assassin was just knocked senseless by the fall. He dashed outside, but there was no sign of their would-be killer, and no indication as to which way he had gone. He did his best, racing down alleys and across

292

courtyards, but the task was hopeless. Defeated, he returned to Mushey's room.

The shots had attracted attention, and people were clustered around the door, demanding explanations. Swaddell had recovered his senses, and was questioning them about the man who had lived there. No one admitted to knowing anything useful, although Mushey's nearest neighbour – a cook named Stephen Bacon – had heard Mushey singing drunkenly at about two in the morning. He had stopped soon afterwards.

'I was glad, because he was keeping me awake,' Bacon gulped. 'But now I realise he went quiet because he was dying, not because he was asleep . . .'

'Was he singing alone or with company?' asked Swaddell.

'Alone,' Bacon grimaced. 'He was paid to guard the larder, but he let anyone in for a price. The stuff that disappeared from that place! He should have been arrested, but the courtiers in charge were getting their cut . . .'

'Which courtiers?'

'Tooley and Ashley mostly. It is a pity they will never answer to their treachery – and it *is* treachery to cheat the King out of his food.'

Chaloner wrote a note to Wiseman, asking him to examine Mushey and the wine as soon as possible, and asked Bacon to deliver it. Then he arranged for the body to be taken to the chapel. Meanwhile, Swaddell explored the room, and discovered a large sum of money hidden under a floorboard, suggesting that Mushey had grown rich by allowing folk to steal the King's victuals. The assassin wrapped it in a handkerchief and handed it to the chaplain, who was among the onlookers, with an order that it was to be given to the poor.

'Do not eye me askance, Tom,' he said huffily. 'You

think that because Williamson views such windfalls as perks of the job, I will follow his example. Well, for your information, I happen to be a very honest man.'

He fingered the dagger at his side, reminding Chaloner that while Swaddell might be averse to theft, he was very much attached to the slitting of throats.

'So, we know one thing for certain,' said Chaloner. 'We would not have been shot at if we posed no risk. Someone is worried that we are on the right track.'

'You think the poisoner and the shooter are one and the same?'

'Well, the poisoner is the one who will most want us to stop prying, so yes. Regardless, we can surmise that the culprit is wealthy, because handguns are expensive.'

'Then perhaps we should look harder at the Duchess.' Swaddell grimaced. 'Williamson will not be very pleased with that solution.'

Nor would the Earl, thought Chaloner.

White Hall was no place to review the possibility that one of the country's highest ranking noblewomen might be a murderer, so Chaloner suggested a nearby tavern. Swaddell argued that Covent Garden would be better, as it would exclude the possibility of eavesdroppers. The gleam in his eye revealed that it was not fear of being overheard that led him to suggest it, but the prospect of seeing Veriana and Ursula.

'It must be nearly ten o'clock,' said Chaloner, determined to prevent it. 'Far too late to disturb Wiseman's household.'

Swaddell grimaced. 'I suppose we had better go to my house then. It is just around the corner, and I have a blood pudding that we can eat while we talk.'

Chaloner was disinclined to step into the assassin's lair, especially to consume something that contained blood, but he could think of no way to refuse without causing offence. He dragged his feet all the way down King Street. Eventually, Swaddell turned into a short but respectable lane called Dean's Yard.

His cottage had a sturdy door and heavy window shutters – natural precautions for a man in his profession. Inside, all was a bleakly functional, with a parlour and a kitchen below, and two sleeping chambers above. The furniture was basic – items that could be abandoned without a backwards glance should their owner ever be obliged to leave at short notice. Everything was neat and clean, though, and an effort had been made to render it more homely with some brightly coloured cushions.

'My mother made those,' said Swaddell, seeing Chaloner look at them. 'I shall take you to meet her soon. It is an honour I have not even afforded Williamson or Bishop Morley.'

'Crikey!' gulped Chaloner, not sure whether to be flattered or alarmed.

He was glad when the blood pudding slipped Swaddell's mind and he was offered a cup of wine instead. Then the assassin got down to business.

'The killer planned Chiffinch's demise very carefully,' he began. 'The capsules were prepared in advance by someone who knew exactly how the victim would consume the oysters – whole, without chewing. The culprit was also sure that no one else would want one.'

Chaloner took up the tale. 'The plan almost came to nothing when the Master Cook forgot to buy them, and it was fortunate that the Duchess was on hand to tell the

295

kitchen girl where else they might be purchased. So, was it coincidence that she suggested going to Sarah Shawe, or was she ensuring that all her preparations were not in vain?'

Swaddell was thoughtful. 'Even if the oysters had been bought from the usual supplier, the killer would still have needed to bribe her way inside the larder, then insert the capsules into the shellfish. It must have been a painstaking process, because it had to deceive the Master Cook and the man who ate them.'

'Was the culprit the woman who Millicent saw waiting outside? The one who kept her face hidden, but who wore fine shoes with her servant's garb, which is an elementary mistake in our trade. People don disguises, then realise they cannot walk or run in unfamiliar foot-wear, so they keep their own, expecting no one to notice.'

'I think we can conclude that this loitering lady was up to no good. Of course, she may just have been waiting to steal some food. Bacon did say that it happens a lot, and the money I found suggests that Mushey made a princely living from looking the other way.'

'But if the Duchess *is* our culprit, why did she want Chiffinch dead? He criticised her, but so do lots of people. And while we mooted the possibility that he plotted against her, there is nothing to suggest that he actually did anything.'

'Perhaps we shall learn something at her soirée. While she is busy with her other guests, one of us will slip away and search her rooms. But what shall we do in the interim? I confess I am out of ideas.'

'Chiffinch's funeral is at midnight,' said Chaloner. 'We should be there – perhaps the killer will be, too. And tomorrow we will try to learn more about the four victims. Perhaps we will uncover something that links them to her, and we can confront her with the evidence.'

'Very well,' said Swaddell, and glanced at the hour candle. 'Before we pay our last respects to Chiffinch, there is just enough time for a nice piece of blood pudding.'

An enormous crowd assembled in Westminster Abbey to watch Thomas Chiffinch interred in the south transept that night. Although the ceremony was due to begin at twelve o'clock, word came that the King had pressing business, so there would be a delay. Having heard a terrific rumpus emanating from the Banqueting House earlier, Chaloner suspected that the 'pressing business' involved wine and a ribald play. There was nothing for it but to wait, although the mourners' patience began to evaporate as time ticked past.

Bored, Chaloner slipped away to prowl darker parts of the abbey, while Swaddell moved among the mourners in the hope of overhearing incriminating conversations. Kings and queens slept on their marble beds, and every crook and cranny was filled with memorials to the great and the good. Chaloner found the place where Oliver Cromwell had rested before his bones were dug up and dangled from a scaffold. As he looked at it, he heard a scraping sound above his head and glanced up in alarm. There was nothing to see, so he supposed a bird was roosting there. Then he recalled that Mother Broughton had predicted walking corpses in the abbey for Tuesday – and it was Tuesday now, as the bell had just chimed one o'clock.

Eventually, the King and his favourites arrived, most unsteady on their feet. The organ thundered out an incongruously jaunty fugue, and Chaloner abandoned his wanderings to return to the nave, looking around to see else who had turned out.

The Earl was there with an enormous contingent from Clarendon House, evidently feeling there was safety in numbers, although Chaloner thought he would have been wiser to stay at home. The Chiffinch family was nearby, so he went to speak to them, although Barbara was the only one who deigned to acknowledge him. She looked old and tired: her brother-in-law's death, coupled with the strain of keeping Will under control, were taking their toll.

'I thought you would have had a solution by now,' she said, rather accusingly. 'It cannot be that difficult – it is not as if Thomas had lots of enemies wanting him dead.'

'He had more than you might think.' Chaloner looked pointedly at Will, who was dabbing his eyes with a satin handkerchief, although there were no tears to dry.

'My husband is not the culprit,' said Barbara firmly, and winced. 'We lead mostly separate lives, as you know, and as I was unable to vouch for his whereabouts at the salient time, I made some enquiries for my own peace of mind.'

'And?' asked Chaloner.

'He was in Chelsea all last week, procuring new prostitutes for the King. He did not return until late on Thursday night, so he had no time to poison his brother's oysters. Upwards of a dozen women will confirm it.'

'Then why did he not tell me this when I asked?' demanded Chaloner, exasperated.

'To see the Earl's investigation founder, I suppose.'

'But I am looking for his brother's killer. Surely that is more important than scoring petty points over an enemy?'

'He thinks he will have a solution from the inquiry he has commissioned himself. I told him that yours is more likely to succeed, but he does not share my faith in you.'

'Who did he hire?'

'The outrageous Cobbe, so if you see *him* acting suspiciously, that is why. Cobbe was with Will in Chelsea when the killer struck, which is why Will chose him as an investigator: Cobbe is the one man in White Hall whose innocence is beyond question.'

Chaloner realised he should have guessed this when Cobbe had been able to say exactly when Ashley and Tooley had died – his precise replies revealed more than a passing interest in the affair. He had also eavesdropped on private conversations in White Hall, as evidenced by the one he had overheard between Ambassador van Goch and his minions.

'Does he have a list of suspects?' he asked.

'Yes, but I imagine it is the same as yours: Dr Clarke, who lied about the cause of death; the Duchess of Newcastle, who should be in Bedlam; and various members of the Cockpit Club, particularly Captain Rolt, who found the body.'

'Fanny Clarke found the body. Rolt was second on the scene.'

'But Fanny was with the Queen all day on Thursday, so had no opportunity to tamper with oysters. Nor did she have a reason to kill Thomas, as her acquaintance with him was no more than a passing one.'

'So which of these suspects do you favour?'

'Someone in the Cockpit Club,' replied Barbara at once. 'Because Cobbe found some letters proving that Thomas had been in the process of discrediting the entire cabal. Once they had been banished in disgrace, Cobbe thinks Thomas would then have turned his attention to others he disliked – such as your Earl and the Duchess.'

'I wish you had told me this sooner,' said Chaloner irritably. 'It would have been helpful.'

'I have only just found out myself – a few minutes ago, when I overheard Cobbe reporting his findings to Will. So if you have any more questions, ask them, not me.'

Chaloner decided he would, at the first opportunity.

The rite that saw Chiffinch laid to rest might have been beautiful had it not been attended by courtiers, who muttered, shuffled and fidgeted like badly behaved children. The Cockpit Club were the worst offenders. Widdrington could not stop yawning, while Bess whispered and giggled animatedly to Pamphlin, clearly hoping to make her husband jealous. It did not work, and if anything, Widdrington looked relieved that she had found someone else to fawn over.

Chaloner wanted to corner Cobbe at once, but the man had contrived to sit between Rolt and young Legg, making him difficult to reach without attracting attention. Clarke lounged nearby, while Fanny knelt with her head bowed, although she did glance up from time to time to ensure that her piety was noticed by those whose opinions she valued.

The deputation from Newcastle House included everyone from the Duke down to Molly. The Duchess wore a long, black cloak, breeches and a wide-brimmed hat that made her look like a Puritan divine. She had brought a book, which she evidently found a lot more interesting than the ceremony, because she did not look up from it once. She attracted a lot of attention. Some was plain curiosity for a famous eccentric, but more was contemptuous, and one whispered conversation mocked her vanity – her expectation that everyone would want to buy her books.

Eliza sat at her side, pale, drawn and full of grief for her husband. The Duchess did not notice her distress, so it was left to Molly to comfort her. Baron Lucas stood next to Mansfield until he saw some of his Royal Society friends, at which point he went to inform them – loudly – that they were mistaken in their theories pertaining to the density of the air in Tenerife.

'Gentlemen, please!' snapped the Duke of York, glaring over at them. 'I am all for scientific enquiry, but this is a funeral, and some of us are trying to sleep.'

Chagrined, the learned gentlemen slunk away, other than Lucas, who looked around for someone else to corner. His eye lit on Chaloner.

'Have you heard about Topp?' he asked in a whisper. 'Steward Clayton was right to question his character, because it transpires that he stole three hundred pounds before drowning himself in a fit of remorse.'

Chaloner raised his eyebrows. 'I knew about his suicide, but not the money. Was it found with his body?'

'The corpse was discovered by river urchins, so what do you think? But Topp's guilt is unequivocal: he was a rogue, and that is all there is to it. Poor Eliza is devastated, of course.'

Chaloner looked across at her white, strained face, and his heart went out to her. The Duchess remained oblivious to her agonies, though, and was still engrossed in her reading.

'Have you heard the rumours that say your sister killed Chiffinch?' Chaloner asked, somewhat baldly.

Lucas snorted his derision. 'Some folk will bray anything to hurt a clever woman, but they are drooling idiots who could not find their arses in the dark. You should set no store by their asinine claims, especially if the accusations come from that worthless Mansfield.'

Hearing his name, the Viscount came to see what was being said about him.

'I suppose you are discussing the fact that I was right about Topp,' he said smugly. 'He is a filthy thief – and my stepmother's lover into the bargain.'

Lucas clipped him smartly around the ear. 'My sister has no lover, you loathsome little maggot. And even if she had decided to experiment with an amour, it would not have been with Topp, who was old enough to be her father.'

'The *Duke* is old enough to be her father,' flashed Mansfield, hand to his ear; he was careful to stay out of Lucas's reach as he went on sneeringly, 'She has always favoured Topp and Eliza over her own family.'

'Yes – Topp *and Eliza*,' said Lucas between gritted teeth. 'The beloved friend she would never betray. You are a fool, boy.'

'We should dismiss Eliza,' sniffed Mansfield sulkily. 'She was obviously Topp's accomplice, and everyone knows that criminals stick together.'

'If you refer to that letter you found,' said Lucas dangerously, 'you had better shut your mouth before I clout your other ear.'

'What letter?' asked Chaloner.

'The one informing my stepmother that Chiffinch was plotting against her,' replied Mansfield, stepping away, lest the Baron made good on his threat. 'The one that *proves* she had a motive for wanting him dead.'

302

'Chiffinch could have plotted all he liked, but he could never have hurt my sister,' declared Lucas stoutly. 'She has done nothing wrong. Now, I wonder what grubby little worm sent that poisonous piece of nonsense.'

'It was not me,' declared Mansfield indignantly, and pretended not to hear Lucas's disbelieving snort as he turned to Chaloner. 'You will interrogate her if you have any sense, before she turns her murderous attentions on anyone else. You have been warned.'

'Ignore him,' ordered Lucas, as Mansfield strutted away. 'The boy is an idiot.'

'May I see the letter?' asked Chaloner.

'I burned it. Chiffinch was *not* plotting against her, and my sister would never hurt a fly, let alone a person.'

Chaloner thought he should be the judge of that.

The ceremony drew to a close eventually, and Chiffinch's coffin was lowered into its allotted space. The moment it settled, there was a loud crash, followed by an explosion of dust – a carving had dropped off one of the nearby monuments. The dead man was forgotten as everyone hurried to see what had happened.

The fault lay with William Camden, author and anti-quary, whose memorial arch included not only a marble bust of himself, but several carvings of grinning Death. One of these had toppled off its moorings. Suspicious scratches revealed that it had not fallen naturally, but even so, Chaloner guessed exactly what was coming next.

'Mother Broughton!' exclaimed someone, although it was too dark to see who. 'She predicted that Death would walk in Westminster Abbey on Tuesday, and so it has!'

The tale was taken up by a hundred voices, and

Chaloner knew that by dawn, all London would believe that the second of the seer's prophecies had come true. He tried to determine who was responsible for the hoax, but it was hopeless. There were too many people, all of whom wore hats or veils, and it was dark. Seeing faces was impossible.

When the last of them had filed out, he went to stand by the grave of the man whose murder he was trying to solve. There was no memorial stone yet, but someone had written out what would later be carved, and had pasted it on the nearest wall. Chaloner translated the Latin in his mind:

> *Here lies Thomas Chiffinch, from his tenderest years a faithful servant, in good fortune and bad, to His Most Serene Majesty Charles II, and thence appointed Comptroller to the Royal Excise, a man of notable honesty and probity. Died 8th April 1666.*

As far as Chaloner was aware, the only true words were the first four and the last four.

Chapter 12

It was almost too late to go to bed by the time Chaloner arrived home, but he tried to sleep anyway, and managed two hours before he was wakened by the gathering daylight and the racket from the market in the piazza outside. He donned clean clothes and went to let his hens out, startled when a goose emerged with them – he had forgotten that Molly had delivered it to his house. It had been carefully degreased, revealing snowy white feathers and a pretty face. How anyone could want to tear its head off was beyond his understanding.

He sat for a moment, enjoying the birds' contented chatter, then set off for the gentleman's club in Hercules' Pillars Alley. It had served him well in the past as a source of useful information, so perhaps its bubbling, vivacious ladies would oblige him now – and he was so desperate for answers that he was willing to look for them anywhere.

The club was owned by Temperance North, Wiseman's paramour. She had once been a demure Puritan maid, and Chaloner was not the only one who had been astounded by the speed and extent of her transformation into a wealthy businesswoman. She had never been slim, but unlimited access to fine food and wine had turned her portly. Unfortunately, none of her friends dared tell her that the dresses she liked to wear were unsuitable for the fuller figure.

Although most of the city was just waking, Temperance was about to go to bed: a contingent of courtiers had visited her once the ceremony in Westminster Abbey was over, so she had been busy. She was in the cosy parlour she used as an office, bagging up the night's takings – such a great pile that Chaloner wondered if Wiseman was right to say that Veriana and Ursula would earn more as courtesans than they ever would from respectable marriages. Temperance seemed to read his mind, and her smile turned mischievous.

'Are you here about your cousins? Bring them to me. I will teach them the ways of the world and find them rich husbands at the same time.'

'Unfortunately, none of your customers are the sort of match my family will want me to make for them,' he said wryly. 'Besides, most are already married.'

'True, so what will you do? Ask some pompous dullard – such as Lucy Bodvil, Mary Robartes or Fanny Clarke – to find the sort of bore you aim to foist on these hapless girls?'

'We shall see,' replied Chaloner vaguely.

'I met Veriana and Ursula in Covent Garden yesterday. They are vivacious young women with a sense of fun. You cannot turn them into prim little dolls, their spirits crushed by the burden of respectability. You should let them *live*.'

Chaloner agreed, but thought there were better ways to do it than by enrolling them in a brothel. Prudently, he changed the subject.

'Did you attend Thomas Chiffinch's funeral last night? I did not see you.'

'I was at the back. I saw the statue of Death come crashing down, though, fulfilling Mother Broughton's prophecy. Before I could escape, I was cornered by Fanny Clarke, who urged me to close the club. She thinks it is evil, and believes I will perish on Good Friday.'

'She threatened you?'

'On the contrary, she was genuinely concerned for my safety, and wants me to repent before it is too late. But what is wicked about making men happy? Indeed, we provide a valuable service, as London is much better being ruled by cheerful men than miserable ones.'

Chaloner was disinclined to argue. 'Have you met the Duchess of Newcastle?'

'Not yet, although she has invited us to her house next month. Do not look so startled! We are often hired to enliven elite gatherings, because we are good at breaking the ice.'

Even if the Duchess did want her soirées to go with a bang, Chaloner was sure she would not knowingly recruit *filles de joie* to do it. It was someone's idea of a joke.

'Who recommended you?' he asked.

'Dr Clarke, who is one of our regulars. He is her near neighbour.'

'He is on my list of suspects for killing Chiffinch,' said Chaloner without thinking.

Temperance gaped. 'Do not be ridiculous, Tom! There is no harm in him. All he wants is a little fun, which he cannot have as long as his tedious little wife is there to drone on about needlework, decency and other such nonsense.'

'Yes,' said Chaloner ambiguously, and returned to the matter in hand. 'So have you heard any rumours about Chiffinch? I know you believe all courtiers are as gentle as lambs, but someone killed him.'

'The only tales to come to me are ones that claim you did it,' replied Temperance tartly. 'However, if you want my opinion, the culprit will be someone in the Cockpit Club. I admire high spirits, but theirs are a little *too* selfishly exuberant. To be frank, Widdrington and Bess frighten me. They are so cold and ruthless . . .'

'Cold and ruthless enough to kill a man who criticised them?' asked Chaloner, thinking that if Temperance considered them too hedonistic, they were probably beyond redemption.

She nodded. 'Their club is based on the principle that nothing matters except enjoyment, so they do not care who they hurt in order to get it. They are dangerous, because their antics damage the King, although they refuse to acknowledge it, especially their elite inner circle.'

'Their elite inner circle,' echoed Chaloner, and began to list them. 'Widdrington, Bess, Pamphlin . . . who else?'

'I am not sure. However, it is not Legg who is too young, or Captain Rolt who is too poor.' Temperance was thoughtful. 'And yet White Hall is unpopular for abandoning the city to the plague, so perhaps Widdrington and his friends are innocent, and some disenchanted Londoner killed Chiffinch.'

'Chiffinch died because someone poisoned his oysters – someone who knew that he liked them *and* that he swallowed them whole. Only courtiers have access to that information.'

'Do they?' asked Temperance quietly. 'I knew it and

308

so do my staff. He dined on them here, and I imagine he ate them in taverns across the city, too.'

With disgust and a crushing sense of defeat, Chaloner saw his list of suspects expand from a handful into thousands.

The discussion had lowered Chaloner's spirits, as it underlined just how far he was from answers. He was also fuzzy-brained from lack of sleep, so he stopped at the Rainbow in the hope that a dish of Farr's best would sharpen his wits.

'What news?' called Farr, but his expression hardened when he saw it was Chaloner. 'Oh, it is you. I am not sure I should serve you, given that your Earl has been killing courtiers. You should leave him and work for someone decent.'

'Unfortunately, decency is in short supply at White Hall,' said Rector Thompson sagely. 'And I do not believe Clarendon dispatched Chiffinch anyway.'

'No, not if the deadly oysters came from Clerkenwell,' put in Stedman. 'He would never go there, because it is where the Duchess of Newcastle lives. She is quite mad, and who wants to risk running into a lunatic?'

'Were these oysters from Sarah Shawe?' asked Farr curiously. 'I buy from her myself. It is a long way to go, but she makes the journey worthwhile. She is a striking lass.'

'She is,' agreed Stedman. 'Although Speed the bookseller told me that she publishes seditious pamphlets, so I would keep your distance if I were you.'

'Seditious pamphlets?' asked Chaloner, sipping the coffee and trying not to wince at the bitter taste. Thompson pushed a plate of sugar towards him, but

309

Chaloner shook his head. He never took it, as a silent but useless protest against the abuse of plantation slaves.

'About women being equal to men, animals having feelings, and whores being more respectable than courtiers,' elaborated Stedman. 'Perhaps she got these wild notions from the Duchess of Newcastle, who is also determined to turn the world upside down again.'

'Then she is succeeding,' sighed Thompson. 'Because the world *is* turning upside down. We have tiny dogs killing bears, a hen slaughtering packs of foxes, geese unseating men from their saddles, while a thousand robins have united to drive people from a church.'

'Goodness!' breathed Chaloner, amazed by how fast fact had been lost to fiction.

'If all that has happened already, imagine what it will be like on Good Friday – the thirteenth day of the month in sixteen sixty-six,' said Stedman darkly. 'Perhaps we should leave the city while we can.'

'Women should not be allowed to say whatever they please,' said Farr, off on a tangent. 'There is a reason why they are banned from coffee houses.'

'What reason?' asked Chaloner archly. 'That they might spout views that are narrow-minded, hypocritical, uninformed or stupid?'

Rector Thompson laughed, although the barb missed its mark with everyone else. After a moment, Farr took up the reins of the discussion again.

'I blame her husband, personally. The Duke should tell her that we do not want to buy her peculiar ramblings, and he should toss them on the fire, where they belong.'

'My wife bought *Philosophical Opinions*,' said Thompson. 'She enjoyed it, so I read it myself. It contained many

310

interesting snippets, which I have used as a basis for sermons.'

'Then it is a good thing none of us ever listen to you,' said Farr, 'because I do not want to be tainted by the ravings of a madwoman, thank you very much. Of course, the Duchess is not nearly as objectionable as that Cockpit Club. One member – the spotty fellow – was riding so fast this morning that he knocked me down.'

'Pamphlin?' asked Chaloner keenly. 'Was he drunk?'

'No, he was in a hurry. His horse was loaded with saddlebags, and I was under the impression that he was making an escape. Regardless, he should have stopped to see if I was injured, but he cantered off without so much as a backward glance.'

'He is a Yeoman of the Larder, you know,' said Stedman. 'One of the best sinecures in White Hall, as you get the pick of all the surplus delicacies. Dates, figs, marchpanes, pies . . .'

Chaloner frowned, recalling what Swaddell had told him about Pamphlin. 'He is a Page of the Presence, not a Yeoman of the Larder.'

'He *was* a page,' said Stedman. 'But he was promoted a couple of weeks ago, which I know because he told me when we were ringing the bells at the cathedral together.'

Chaloner grimaced, realising that he had been remiss to accept information without question. And now it transpired that a third member of the Cockpit Club been in a position to join Ashley, Tooley and Mushey in depriving the King of his victuals.

'How many Yeomen of the Larder are there?' he asked, aware even as he spoke that the question revealed a disgraceful lack of knowledge about the place where he worked.

'Three,' replied Stedman. 'Although the other two have died recently, so His Majesty will be looking for more. Perhaps he will consider me for the honour.'

He laughed and the others joined in, leaving Chaloner to suppose he would have to track Pamphlin down and find out what had prompted his sudden flight. Was he fleeing the scene of his crime – not just murder but stealing from the larder? Or was he just afraid that he might join his two fellow yeomen and Mushey in their graves?

'Speaking of the Duchess,' said Farr, 'I heard that her steward stole three hundred pounds from her, then drowned himself in a fit of remorse.'

'You should know better than to believe gossip, Farr,' said Thompson pompously, 'because Topp is no more drowned than you are. I spoke to him not an hour ago.'

'You did?' asked Chaloner, startled. 'Where?'

'In my church,' replied the rector. 'I confess he gave me a fright, what with all these rumours about walking corpses, but he had only come in to shelter from the rain.'

'Did you speak to him?'

'Yes, once I had satisfied myself that he was no cadaver. He denied being Topp at first, but relented when I reminded him that he and I have been acquainted for years. To be frank, I suspect he started this tale of suicide himself.'

'To make sure no one looks for him,' surmised Chaloner. 'Or the money he is said to have stolen. Still, it is a cruel thing to have done to his wife. She grieves for him.'

'It is unkind,' agreed Thompson. 'And I said so, which is probably why he stormed off in a huff. No one likes to hear that he is a selfish rogue.'

Chaloner was thoughtful. He had never considered

312

Topp as a suspect for Chiffinch's murder, but perhaps he should have done in light of what he had just been told. Topp knew his way around White Hall, and it would not be difficult to don women's clothing and lurk outside the larder, waiting to bribe his way inside. But why would he want Chiffinch dead? Because he really did love his Duchess, and he had heard that Chiffinch was plotting against her? And had he then poisoned Tooley, Ashley and Mushey to cover his tracks?

Chaloner decided to visit Newcastle House at once, to see what more could be learned about the steward and the money he was alleged to have stolen – money that had been suspiciously missing from 'his' corpse. Then he would track down Pamphlin, and find out what had prompted him to flee, especially if it pertained to his post as Yeoman of the Larder and three dead colleagues.

It was still early when Chaloner returned to Covent Garden, aiming to ask Wiseman if he had examined Mushey and the wine. The surgeon had already gone to White Hall, but had left a note detailing his findings. Chaloner was not surprised to learn that the wine had indeed contained the same henbane-based potion that had killed Chiffinch, Ashley and Tooley, or that drinking some of it had ended Mushey's life.

As soon as he had finished reading the message, he sent for a hackney and took Veriana and Ursula to Chaloner Court. They were excited by the prospect of visiting a house that had once belonged to their father, but when they arrived, they were disappointed, finding it wholly unfamiliar to them.

'I remember it being dark and rather gloomy,' said Ursula, as they waited in the hall for a servant to announce them to Fanny. 'With a roof that leaked and mould on the walls. Now there is a new roof, and the walls are beautifully clean.'

'They might be clean, but they are no longer straight,' countered Veriana, less easily impressed. 'The new roof has caused them to bow, and the plaster is flaking off.'

'Well, I like it more now,' declared Ursula. 'Do the Clarkes have sons? I could live here very happily.'

The maid returned at that point, and indicated that they were to follow her to where Fanny was waiting. As they walked through the door into the stylish but impractical orangery, Veriana pointed at the crack in the lintel.

'This place is all style and no substance,' she whispered to Chaloner with smug superiority. 'It was a better house when *we* owned it.'

They weaved through the potted trees to where Fanny sat on her favourite bench. Two of her rescued cockerels were with her, and appeared to have made themselves very much at home. She came to greet the cousins with a sweet smile of welcome.

'We shall spend the day darning my husband's old stockings, so we can give them to the poor,' she informed them. 'And later, I shall send for my milliner to see about new hats. Those will not do – you need something in brown or grey.'

As his cousins' current headwear was pink, blue and festooned with ribbons, Chaloner was not surprised when this news was not greeted with enthusiasm. Ursula contrived to accompany him to the door when he left.

'You cannot leave us here,' she hissed. 'She wants to turn us into younger versions of herself. How can we attract interesting men if we are forced to become drab little ducklings?'

'It is only for a few days,' he whispered back. 'And it is good of Fanny to take the trouble. Then you can go to Lady Clarendon.'

Ursula groaned. 'She will be even worse. We shall end up married to vicars!'

'Would that be so bad?'

'Not if they are rich,' conceded Ursula, then pouted again. 'But we had hoped to have some fun first, which does *not* mean sewing with boring old ladies. It is not fair!'

Chaloner could see her point: he would not appreciate being parcelled off to mend stockings either. Unfortunately, none of them had a choice if they wanted to secure the kind of matches that would save her family from fiscal oblivion.

'Just do it,' he said tiredly, 'and then, if Fanny has no objections, I will take you to Newcastle House with me tomorrow.'

Ursula gave a whoop of delight, and stood on tiptoe to kiss his cheek before scampering away to tell her sister. He smiled, shaking his head, then pushed his domestic travails from his mind, wondering instead how Eliza would react to learning that she was not a widow.

He left Chaloner Court and began to walk across the green to Newcastle House. It started to rain when he was halfway over, forcing him to break into a run. He knocked on the door, which was opened by the butler, who had one of his mistress's books clapped to his head to protect it from the leaking ceiling.

'I would not mind if it was just water,' he confided crossly. 'But those seagulls are up there, and their mess is all mixed up in it. I do not want *that* in my lovely new wig.'

He disappeared to tell Eliza that she had a visitor,

315

leaving Chaloner standing in a place that was no drier than outside. The rain hammered on the glass above, and there were at least twenty buckets scattered around the floor, placed to catch the worst of the drips. A red-faced, panting footman was struggling to empty them before they overflowed.

'The butler will not find Eliza, because she has gone to White Hall with the Duchess,' whispered a voice from the shadows. It was Molly, cuddling one of her hens. 'To spend the day with the Queen.'

'Goodness!' muttered Chaloner, not liking the notion of one of his murder suspects being in company with the woman who would – if she recovered from her latest miscarriage – provide the country with its next monarch.

'What are you doing in here, child?' came Baron Lucas's booming voice. 'You know you are not supposed to take shortcuts through the house with your birds.'

He was coming down the stairs with the Duke, who appeared frail and unsteady next to him. Glancing up, Chaloner saw Mansfield leaning over the banister on the top floor, clearly aiming to eavesdrop on what his father and step-uncle had to say to each other.

'I wanted to show everyone how I can curtsy,' explained Molly, and gave a rather ungainly demonstration. 'Eliza taught me last night, so as to be ready for tomorrow, when so many people of quality will visit.'

'Run along now, girl,' ordered Lucas. 'And do not bring chickens into the house again. My sister might defend them against those who think they are stupid, but that does not mean she wants their droppings all over her floors.'

Molly scuttled away, giving Chaloner a quick smile as she went.

'You have made a friend,' said the Duke to Chaloner. 'Now you will enjoy her affection for ever. Being kind to servants is wise, because you get better service from happy staff than ones who cannot bear the sight of you.'

Chaloner knew the advice was really intended for the listening Mansfield, and wondered if the son and heir was clever enough to heed it. He suspected not.

'I came to report that Topp was seen this morning,' he said. 'Alive.'

The Duke gaped, then gave a whoop of delight. 'I *knew* he was not a man for suicide!'

'So where is he?' demanded Lucas, who seemed less pleased by the news. 'Tell him to report to us at once and explain what the devil is going on.'

'I will, if I see him,' promised Chaloner. 'Although if he really did make off with three hundred pounds, he may be reluctant to oblige.'

The Duke's merry grin faded. 'I am sure he will have a good explanation for that.'

'He will: he stole it,' said Lucas shortly. 'I was fooled by him, too – considered him an honest and loyal fellow. But we were both wrong. He was . . . he *is* a rogue.'

On the landing above, Mansfield murmured heartfelt agreement.

'But he was also accused of seducing my wife,' countered the Duke. 'And we know *that* to be a lie. What if the missing money is just another sly plot against him? If so, I do not blame him for making an escape.'

'He did not "make an escape",' argued Lucas. 'He pretended to be dead, and Eliza and my sister have been distraught. How could he do that to them? Or to you, for that matter?'

The Duke had no answer, and mumbled something

about fetching a warmer hat. He turned to walk back up the stairs. With a hiss of alarm, Mansfield tried to duck out of sight before he was spotted. Unfortunately, he had leaned so far forward that his wig had snagged on the chandelier, and he was obliged to leave it swinging there as he scuttled away.

'I had better take your news to my sister and Eliza in White Hall,' said Lucas to Chaloner, smirking when he saw what had happened. 'Will you come with me?'

While Chaloner and Lucas waited for the Baron's personal coach to be readied – a time-consuming process that meant it would have been quicker to walk – the spy took the opportunity to slip away and question Sarah Shawe about the oysters she had sold to White Hall. She was on the green with her barrow, huddled under the tarpaulin that protected her wares from the rain.

Rather than launch straight into an interrogation, which was unlikely to secure the cooperation of so prickly an individual, he told her about Topp being seen alive.

'I knew *he* would never have hurt himself,' she spat, clearly disappointed. 'He is not a remorseful man. So what did he do? Buy a corpse to stand in for him? There are people who trade in such things – not from choice, but to put food on the table.'

Before he could be steered into a conversation about social injustice, Chaloner asked, 'Were you aware that your oysters were used to kill Chiffinch?'

Sarah glared at him. 'I did hear something to that effect. However, they were perfectly wholesome when they left me. I sold dozens of them that day, and even ate some myself. None of my other customers had a problem.'

'Did you follow the girl – Millicent – back to White Hall to see what she did with them?'

Sarah regarded him askance. 'Why would I do that? My time is too precious to waste on pointless errands. I sold the child my last two dozen oysters, then went home to prepare myself for an evening of teaching and debating in the Red Bull.'

'Did you—'

'I repeat,' interrupted Sarah angrily, 'the oysters left me in perfect health. However, that was hours before they were devoured by the man who died, so investigate what happened to them at the palace. Do not pester *me* with your impertinent questions.'

On that note, Chaloner returned to Newcastle House to see if the coach was ready.

As they swayed towards White Hall in Lucas's over-sprung carriage, Chaloner asked about Topp, hoping to learn something that would point to the steward as the White Hall poisoner – it would be a far more convenient solution than most of the other suspects on the list. Unfortunately, all Lucas could say was that Topp had appeared to be loyal and honest, and the family had left most of their financial and business affairs in his hands.

'They deserve better,' he growled. 'The Duke and my sister are good people, but what does fate hand them? Treacherous servants and the snivelling Mansfield as an heir.'

They alighted at White Hall, and were immediately aware of an atmosphere. The falling statue of Death in Westminster Abbey had convinced many courtiers that Mother Broughton was a genuine prophet, and there were now serious concerns about what would happen in three days' time. More than a few had discovered pressing business at their country estates. Thus if Friday the thirteenth 1666 did presage a great weeping and gnashing of teeth in London they would not be part of it.

The moment Chaloner and Lucas started walking across the Great Court, two men hailed them. The first was Samuel Pepys, an ambitious navy clerk, who nodded to Chaloner, then began to press Lucas for his opinion about a new weave of canvas. The second was Swaddell.

'You told me that Pamphlin was a Page of the Presence,' began Chaloner accusingly. 'But I learned – in my coffee house, of all places – that he is a Yeoman of the Larder. That is the same post that Tooley and Ashley held.'

Swaddell's surprise was quickly replaced by frustration. 'I looked him up in Williamson's files, but our record-keeping has been less assiduous since our clerks have been busy with the Dutch war. Damn it! If we had known . . .'

'I was also told that he raced away in a great hurry this morning.'

'He did – I saw him myself.' Swaddell was thoughtful. 'Which means that either he is the killer and feels the net tightening, or he knows the culprit's identity and elected to vanish before he could follow his friends to the grave.'

'Either way, we need to find him. Do you have any idea where he went?'

'I asked around, but the only person to venture an opinion was Captain Rolt. He said that Pamphlin has parents in Woolwich, but no other kin and no friends outside White Hall.'

Chaloner determined to ride to Woolwich as soon as he had made sure that the Duchess was not left alone with the Queen all day. And if Pamphlin proved to be a waste of time, he would hurry back and concentrate on Topp. He told Swaddell his plan, along with all he had learned since they had last met.

'Do not worry about the Queen,' said the assassin. 'Barbara Chiffinch has vowed not to leave her side until she is completely well again. She is appalled that Her Majesty learned the news of her mother's death from a careless-tongued courtier, and has promised to stay and protect her. You know you can trust her to keep the Queen safe – from the Duchess and everyone else.'

'Yes,' said Chaloner, relieved. 'Now we need to tell Eliza that she is not a widow.'

'Lucas will get there first,' said Swaddell, and Chaloner saw that the Baron had escaped from Pepys and was already entering the Queen's apartments. 'Not that the likes of us would have been allowed in there anyway. Still, it is a pity we shall not witness Eliza's reaction to the news ourselves. It occurs to me that she was Topp's accomplice.'

'Her grief seemed genuine to me.' Chaloner turned towards the palace stables. 'So now we ride to Woolwich.'

'I will stay here and make enquiries about Topp,' said Swaddell. 'I know I said we would be more efficient working together, but time is short, and we are no nearer to finding the truth now than we were when we started. We have no choice but to separate.'

'Of course we have a choice,' countered Chaloner, suspicious of the assassin's sudden desire to ditch him. Had he decided that Topp was indeed the culprit, and aimed to find the steward and slit his throat, to avoid the inconvenience of a public trial?

'Not if you want to make good time to Woolwich,'

321

said Swaddell sheepishly. 'I am not a skilled rider. I will slow you down. Go now, Tom. I will be here when you return.'

Unsettled and unhappy, Chaloner hurried to the stables and used the Earl's authority to requisition a horse, aware as he did so of the grooms' unfriendly stares. They looked away when he glared back.

'Where are you going?' came a familiar voice. It was Barker, although Chaloner took a second glance to be sure, as the Earl's clerk was unshaven, grey-faced and oddly rumpled.

'Woolwich.' Chaloner regarded him in concern. 'Are you ill?'

'Just worn out from the strain of working for a man who is rumoured to be a killer,' replied Barker. 'I keep wondering if there is any truth to the claims – that he really did order the deaths of three critics. Four, if Mushey is to be included.'

'You should know him better than that,' chided Chaloner. 'Besides, who would oblige him? You know it was not me, because you proved my alibi for when Chiffinch died.'

'I did,' acknowledged Barker. 'But that was before I learned that the oysters were poisoned on Thursday night, which means your whereabouts on Friday morning are irrelevant.'

Chaloner had wondered how long it would be before someone worked that one out. 'So you believe me to be an assassin,' he said heavily.

'Of course not! You would have done a much better job at concealing your handiwork.'

Chaloner felt this was no compliment. 'So who is the culprit?'

'That is what unnerves me,' replied Barker, glancing around in agitation. 'I do not know, and I find myself regarding everyone with terrified suspicion.'

At that point, Chaloner realised that the grooms were saddling his horse in such a way that he would be thrown the moment he urged it into a trot, revealing that *they* did not consider the murders too clumsy to be laid at his door. He drove them off with an irritable scowl, and buckled the straps himself. Barker came to watch, so Chaloner continued to quiz him.

'A few days ago, you told me that Tooley caught a fatal fever in the Red Bull. However, not only had he never been there, but nor did he die of a sickness.'

Barker shrugged. 'Blame Bess Widdrington – I got that tale from her. I have never been to the Red Bull either, so how was I to know it was false? I only mentioned the gossip because I thought you might find it helpful.'

'Have you heard that Pamphlin has fled the city?'

'Him and two dozen others. More will follow as Good Friday looms, particularly as the King has expressed a sudden desire to visit Dover. The Queen is too ill to travel with him, but he will not mind abandoning her to whatever fate lies in store for London.'

'Easy!' breathed Chaloner, aware that the grooms had not gone far, and that sort of remark from one of the Earl's retainers to another was dangerous.

'I shall resign today,' whispered Barker. 'The Earl will fall from grace soon, whether innocent of murder or not, and when he does, his staff will share his fate. I recommend that you look for another employer, too, before it is too late.'

And with that, he hurried away, leaving Chaloner staring after him worriedly. Did the clerk know more about the looming crisis than he was willing to admit? Such knowledge would certainly explain his sudden attack of anxiety. Chaloner started after him to ask, but the horse began to fuss, and by the time he had quietened it, Barker had disappeared into the maze of alleys near the kitchens.

Before Chaloner could mount up, he was approached by a courtier named Cotton, who was distantly related to him by virtue of his second marriage.

'You should be wary of Barker,' Cotton muttered. 'He has some odd friends.'

'Any you are willing to name?' asked Chaloner.

'Ask in the Red Bull,' replied Cotton, glancing around to make sure no one else was listening. 'And do not believe him when he says he has never been there, because he has.'

Chaloner clattered out of White Hall, aware that he needed to ride hard if he wanted to find Pamphlin and return home with answers the same day. It was a round journey of roughly twenty miles, mostly on good roads, although there was always the risk of delays from floods, defective bridges, fallen trees or broken-down carts. Even so, he reined in on King Street when he saw Kersey, feeling that the charnel-house keeper owed him an explanation.

Kersey was looking especially trim that morning. He was with a woman he introduced as his wife, although she was different from the last one. She was taller, older and more refined, leading Chaloner to suppose she was a gentlewoman, perhaps one whose family had been beggared by the wars, who had been delighted to forge an alliance with a wealthy man.

'There may have been a mistake,' conceded Kersey, when Chaloner informed him that Topp had been seen alive that morning. 'I based my identification on the papers found in the fellow's pockets, which is usually good enough.'

Chaloner rubbed his eyes, wishing he had taken the trouble to look at the corpse himself. 'So do we have yet another murder to investigate? The "Topp" in your care was dispatched to provide a body?'

'Wiseman examined him, and his verdict was drowning by accident or suicide – there is nothing to suggest foul play. Ergo, if Topp did stage his own death, he probably bought a corpse for the purpose. Then he dressed it in his own clothes, careful to leave "identifying" documents in the pockets. It has been done before.'

'Has it? You should have said so.'

Kersey smiled patiently. 'Why would I? There was no reason to suspect anything amiss, and there are limits to what I can be expected to do.'

'Did anyone come to view the body? His wife? The Duchess?'

'Both, but I advised against it, as the river had not been kind to their loved one's face. The Duchess left money for a coffin, and I was to have delivered the corpse to Clerkenwell today. Obviously, that will no longer be necessary, so she may have a refund.'

'Do you think they are party to the deception?' Chaloner still thought Eliza's grief was genuine, but Swaddell's remarks had sown a seed of doubt, and he wanted the opinion of a man who dealt with bereavement on a daily basis.

'I could not read the Duchess, but Eliza's distress was real.' Kersey's usually amiable face turned stern. 'It is a terrible, selfish thing to have done. I hope he is ashamed of himself.'

Chaloner rode at a rapid clip towards London Bridge, recalling how eerily silent it had been at the height of the plague. He was glad to see it busy again, and to hear the familiar cacophony of curses as drivers bulled their rattling vehicles down a road that was not really wide enough to accommodate traffic in both directions. Above it all was the roar of the river, swollen with recent rains as it thundered through the arches below.

He ignored the grisly sight of the traitors' heads that adorned the entrance to the Southwark end, then turned along the Woolwich road. It was not long before he left the city behind, and was cantering through open country.

It was a miserable journey, with rain slanting into his face the whole way. It was a slow one, too, as churned mud made the road treacherously slick, and he did not want to injure the horse. He reached Woolwich eventually, only to be told that the Pamphlins had moved away during the plague.

'To Deptford,' elaborated the vicar he had hailed. 'Near the dockyards.'

Chaloner rode on, acutely aware of the passing time, even though the sun was hidden behind a bank of thick grey clouds. The rain grew harder still, so he was thoroughly drenched by the time he arrived in the village and found the right house. But his efforts were for nothing, because although the family was happy to co-operate, they had not seen Pamphlin in weeks.

'He prefers his lively friends at Court, and we are not good enough for him now,' confided the father bitterly.

'He has just been made a Yeoman of the Larder, you know.'

'Yes, I do,' growled Chaloner. 'And it was in this larder that another courtier's food was poisoned. It is a serious matter, so if you see him, tell him to return to White Hall at once.'

There was no more to be said, so Chaloner began to ride back to London, disgusted to discover that the wind had changed direction, and was in his face for the homeward journey as well. By the time he reached White Hall, he was cold, wet and weary, and day was turning to night. He stabled the horse, and jumped when Swaddell materialised at his side.

'I learned nothing about Topp, no one told me anything useful about Pamphlin, and our killer remains at large,' reported the assassin glumly. 'You?'

'It was a waste of time,' replied Chaloner dolefully. 'Did you say it was Captain Rolt who told you that Pamphlin had gone to Woolwich?'

Swaddell nodded. 'And there he is now, strutting across the Great Court like a pheasant. Shall we put a blade to his throat, and see if his memory serves him any better?'

Rolt started to run when he spotted Chaloner and Swaddell bearing down on him, but quickly realised this looked suspicious, so he stopped and pretended to be pleased to see them.

'You are very wet, Chaloner,' he remarked, all friendly concern. 'Has it been raining? I would not know, as I have been with the King all day, helping him pack for Dover.'

'You and a hundred others,' muttered Swaddell, thus telling Chaloner that the cosy image of His Majesty and

Rolt sorting through stockings and nether-garments together was a gross misrepresentation. 'Why did you send Tom on a wild-goose chase to Woolwich? You knew Pamphlin would not be there.'

Rolt regarded him askance. 'I knew no such thing! Besides, you did not ask where I thought Pamphlin might be – you asked if he had family or friends outside the city. The fault lay in the question, not the answer.'

'So where is Pamphlin now?' asked Chaloner, fighting the urge to punch him.

Rolt shrugged. 'I have not seen him since early this morning. However, I can tell you that something upset him, because I have never seen a man look more frightened.'

'Perhaps he was afraid of you,' said Swaddell coldly. 'After all, you head our list of suspects for the crime of murder.'

Rolt gaped at him. 'Me? On what grounds?'

Swaddell began to list them. 'The deaths of Tooley and Ashley mean you rise higher in the Cockpit Club hierarchy. You belong to a cabal that Chiffinch threatened to suppress. And you were suspiciously fast on the scene when his body was found. I do not believe you were there looking for a button.'

'Well, I was,' stated Rolt shortly. 'It belonged to my father, and so was of sentimental value. I have explained this to you already.'

But Chaloner recalled what he had read about Rolt in the report that Dutch Jane had left for her paymasters. 'Your father was a Puritan divine. Such men consider buttons sinful fripperies, and refuse to use them.'

'Hah!' exclaimed Swaddell triumphantly. 'You are caught in a lie! The button never existed, and your purpose in visiting the cockpit was to ensure that you had left nothing incriminating at the scene of the murder *you* committed. It was unfortunate that Fanny Clarke decided to rescue cockerels that morning and caught you.'

'You are mistaken!' cried Rolt, beginning to be alarmed. 'The button *does* exist. And if you must know why I was so keen to have it back, it is because it was gold.'

Chaloner regarded him thoughtfully. 'And you could not afford to lose such a thing, because you have no money.'

'Nonsense!' blustered Rolt. 'I am a wealthy man, like all my friends here.'

Chaloner summarised why he knew this to be untrue. 'You live in shabby Kensington, and you walk everywhere because you cannot afford to replace the horse that was killed. But you dare not admit your indigence, lest you are ousted from the Cockpit Club.'

'And it is through your Cockpit Club connections that you hope to land a lucrative post,' finished Swaddell. 'Without them, you will fade into impoverished oblivion.'

Rolt eyed them with dislike. 'So now you know. What are you going to do about it? Tell everyone? Obviously, I have no money to buy your discretion.'

'The name of the killer will ensure our silence,' said Swaddell silkily.

'But I do not know it!' cried Rolt, agitated. 'If I did, I would have informed you already. I do not want a murderer loose in White Hall, as it makes everyone wary of everyone else, and no one will hire me in an atmosphere of unease. The best I can do is tell you who is *not* responsible. I have been helping Cobbe look into the matter, you see.'

He proceeded to list some forty or so courtiers who had alibis for one or more of the murders, thus revealing that Cobbe's list of suspects had been a lot longer than Chaloner and Swaddell's, and that he had been working extremely diligently on the case.

'You can discount Widdrington and Bess as well,' Rolt finished. 'They were with me during the drinking game where Tooley was poisoned. We were discussing a task that Widdrington wants me to conduct on his Cornish estates. Neither slipped away to poison wine.'

'What task?' asked Swaddell disbelievingly.

Rolt eyed him with dislike. 'A review of his stables, if you must know. I am to travel there soon, stopping several places en route to deliver letters to his Devonshire farms. When I hand my finished report to his Cornwall steward, I shall be paid a handsome commission.'

He could tell them no more, so Swaddell indicated that he could leave. There was a nasty gleam in the assassin's eye.

'He will spend the last of his own money delivering all these missives, but will gain nothing in return,' he said, 'because Widdrington owns no Cornish estates.'

'Then why did you not warn him?' asked Chaloner curiously. 'It is a long way down there, and he may never raise the funds to come back again.'

'Almost certainly not,' agreed Swaddell smugly. 'But it serves him right. Have you noticed that people regard you with unease? Well, it is because of him. He smiles to your face, but all the while he whispers that you are the Earl's assassin.'

Chaloner was bemused. 'Why would he do such a thing? I barely know him.'

'Because maligning the Earl's retainers is an easy way

to ingratiate himself with his Cockpit Club cronies. I doubt it is anything personal.'

Chaloner pushed the treacherous captain from his mind. 'So our most likely suspects for the murders are now narrowed down to the Duchess, Topp and Clarke.'

'And the Cockpit Club,' said Swaddell. 'We may have eliminated Widdrington, Bess, Rolt, Cobbe and two dozen more, but Pamphlin and several others remain.'

As he was cold, wet, tired and dispirited, Chaloner was grateful when Swaddell offered to remain in White Hall alone that evening, to question their remaining suspects.

'And if you learn nothing new, we will go to the soirée in Newcastle House tomorrow,' he said. 'The Duchess will be there, and perhaps Topp will have slunk home by then, too, now that his nasty ruse has been exposed.'

'Do not hold your breath,' muttered Swaddell sourly.

Chapter 13

Despite being worn out by his hard ride to Woolwich and back, Chaloner slept poorly, kept awake by worry and the rain that pounded on the roof all night. He rose early, sluiced away the muck of travel in a bucket of warm water, and donned his favourite grey long-coat, feeling that if its drab colour made him look like an assassin, then that was too bad.

In the garden, he tended his poultry, pleased when the goose trustingly ate grain from his hand. Then he went to the parlour, where Wiseman, dressed in his best scarlet doublet, was entertaining Veriana and Ursula with the story of how he had heroically removed a cake of soap that had lodged in the Earl of Bristol's throat. Chaloner had heard the tale before, but still failed to understand what Bristol had been doing to land himself in such a predicament. While the spy helped himself to coddled eggs, Wiseman segued to his plans for the near future.

'The King is going to Dover tomorrow, so I shall join him there in a day or two. He says he does not believe these prophecies about the wicked getting their comeuppance, but he is also cognisant of the fact that one can never be too careful.'

'So His Majesty considers himself sinful?' breathed Ursula, wide-eyed.

'He *knows* he is sinful,' corrected Wiseman with a wink. 'But he does not want to change his ways, so he aims to be well away from the capital until the danger is over.'

'Leaving tomorrow will not make him very popular with Londoners,' remarked Chaloner. 'It is Maundy Thursday, when the monarch always distributes money to the poor.'

'He will fling a few handfuls to the milling masses before he goes,' said Wiseman with a careless wave of his hand. 'It will suffice.'

Chaloner hoped he was right. He finished his eggs and addressed his cousins. 'Are you ready to go to Fanny Clarke?'

'Must we?' groaned Ursula. 'Yesterday, she made us mend stockings with a lot of tedious ladies whose notion of excitement is discussing hems and gussets. I thought I would *die* of boredom. Fanny may be respectable, but she is about as interesting as a dead fish.'

'Besides, we have heard that Clerkenwell will be at the centre of Good Friday's trouble,' put in Veriana slyly. 'You do not want us in such a place, surely?'

'True,' acknowledged Chaloner. 'Which means you had better not go to Newcastle House this afternoon either.'

Ursula's face fell, and she shot her sister an exasperated glance. 'Nothing will happen until the day after tomorrow,' she said hastily. 'However, you will want us to look our best when we meet these wealthy nobles today, so we must stay here this morning, preparing.'

'Let us do that, and in exchange, we will endure Mrs

Boring with no complaints until we go to Lady Clarendon,' promised Veriana. 'We even swear not to laugh when she informs us that the secret of a happy marriage is to ensure our husbands always have clean underwear.'

Feeling he had just been manipulated in ways he could not begin to fathom, Chaloner nodded, then walked to Muscat's Coffee House, where he had arranged to meet Swaddell.

Much of the talk on the streets was of the crisis that would strike the city – starting in Clerkenwell – in less than forty-eight hours. There was no particular sense of fear, as most people seemed to think they were among the godly, and that it was everyone else who would be in trouble. Chaloner met William Prynne on Fleet Street, where the pamphleteer informed him that he was looking forward to the wicked getting their just deserts, as he expected to play a major role in running the country once they had been eradicated.

'But the last time we met,' Chaloner pointed out archly, 'you were dismissive of Mother Broughton's predictions, because she was a woman.'

'She still is a woman,' said Prynne with a moue of distaste. 'However, she was right about the walking corpses, so I have chosen to give her the benefit of the doubt.'

'Has she predicted anything else?'

'Just that tomorrow – Maundy Thursday – will be full of tears, a messenger will die, and the Fleet River will run red with blood. Then on Good Friday, there will be a rain of fire, followed by darkness all over the city, and a lot of wailing and gnashing of teeth.'

'I know about those. Has she said anything new?'

'There was something about the rain of fire coming from a clear blue sky, but I think she may have been

334

drunk at that point. I went to hear her in person last night, you see, and her supporters had been rather generous with the ale. But do not worry about it, Chaloner. By Easter Day, we shall all be in Paradise, and the Sun itself will dance for joy.'

Grumpily, Chaloner retorted that the Sun was not supposed to dance, and that he would far rather it stayed put.

Swaddell was waiting when Chaloner arrived at Muscat's, and although time was short they stayed long enough to down two dishes of coffee apiece, both feeling they needed the mental stimulation the beverage was alleged to provide.

'I loitered in White Hall until well past midnight,' said Swaddell, stifling a yawn. 'It was all but deserted. I think everyone was tired after Chiffinch's funeral feast, which went on well into the small hours of yesterday morning.'

'Did it?' asked Chaloner, signalling for Muscat to bring more coffee.

'Did you hear that halfway through it Will distributed three hundred mourning rings? It was to remind everyone who received one that his brother was a great man. Hypocrite! It is a pity he is no longer a suspect, because I have never liked him.'

Chaloner agreed. 'But of our remaining ones, three live in Clerkenwell: the Duchess, Clarke and Topp, who may or may not have had help from Eliza. And Clerkenwell seems to be where all this trouble will start – trouble that you, as the Spymaster's man, should prevent.'

'Then I suggest we go there now. We will concentrate on Clarke until it is time for the Newcastle House soirée, at which point we will turn our attention to the Duchess and Topp. And if we have no luck with them, we will consider the others on our list.'

'What list?' asked Chaloner with asperity. 'Of the Cockpit Club, we have eliminated everyone except one or two lesser members and Pamphlin, who has disappeared. Of course, it was not just them that Chiffinch alienated with his harsh tongue. Most of White Hall came under attack, too, so where do we start?'

'Perhaps we are wrong to assume Chiffinch was killed because he was critical of other people. He – and then the others – may have been dispatched because someone is unhappy with courtiers in general. So, I repeat: we shall tackle Clarke first, then see what we can learn at Newcastle House. If we are still floundering after, we shall turn our eyes to the palace servants.'

It seemed hopeless to Chaloner, but he hurried to Clerkenwell, aware that Mother Broughton was not the only soothsayer who had things to say about Good Friday. Others were also out in force, although none commanded audiences as large as hers, and traffic around the green came to a standstill when she stood on her box to hold forth. She was still tipsy from the previous night, and her disciples had to hold her arms to prevent her from toppling off.

While Swaddell went to hear what she had to say in the hope of learning something to stop it, Chaloner knocked on Clarke's door, only to be told that the physician was at White Hall and Fanny was out buying thread. Unwilling to waste time waiting for them to return, he trotted to the Red Bull, desperate enough to hope that its patrons might gossip to him about the looming crisis. There were no guards on the door this time, and the budding scholars within glanced up uneasily when he entered. Some recognised him from his previous visit and relaxed, murmuring to the rest that he was a friend of Eliza.

'Mr Barker speaks highly of him, too,' added Joan Cole the tobacco-seller, jerking a thick thumb at Chaloner. 'They work together at Clarendon House, see.'

'Barker comes here?' pounced Chaloner.

'Joan!' cried one of her friends. 'He begged our silence in exchange for free Latin lessons, and we agreed. You have broken his trust!'

So Cotton was right to suggest asking about Barker in the Red Bull, thought Chaloner, and here were the clerk's 'odd' friends – women determined to educate themselves.

'But Mr Barker likes *him*, Mary,' argued Joan, pointing at Chaloner again. 'He will not mind *him* knowing how he helps us with our grammar. Besides, he says he is tired of lying about visiting his mother, because too many people know she is dead.'

'Perhaps so, but he said his Earl would dismiss him if it ever became known that he was teaching us the language of religion and the law,' argued Mary. 'So we cannot—'

'His Earl no longer matters, because Mr Barker has resigned,' interrupted Joan, all smug triumph. 'He does not want to work for a man who cannot see that women are important members of society.'

'He is a saint, coming here to educate us,' said Mary. 'Especially after Bess Widdrington threatened to destroy anyone who teaches us things she thinks we should not know.'

'She is a hypocrite,' spat Joan. '*She* has these skills, but she cannot bear the thought of us having them too. She wants us tied down at home, having babies and toiling over the cooking fire. Pah! As if she ever does a lick of work!'

'Have you come to talk to Sarah?' asked Mary of Chaloner, once the chorus of angry indignation had died down. 'She said you quizzed her about poisoned oysters yesterday, and she has been pondering the matter ever since. She has some theories, and plans to share them with you today.'

Chaloner brightened. 'Where does she live?'

Joan heaved herself to her feet. 'Come. I will show you. It is not far.'

Sarah lived near Mother Broughton. There was no reply to their knock, but Joan had a key. She opened the door and stepped inside. Chaloner wrinkled his nose as he followed: the place was a pit. Discarded clothes and dirty plates sat on every available surface, and there was an eye-watering stench of rancid fat. On the table and in boxes on the floor were glass bottles with bulbous bottoms.

'Those are for pickling cockles,' said Joan, seeing him look at them. 'Now, where is she? Hah! Here she comes. Where have you been, Sarah? You said you would be home all morning.'

'Newcastle House,' replied Sarah smugly. 'I demanded an audience with that wretched little Mansfield, and when he slunk in, I ordered him to put things right with our Duchess.'

'What things?' asked Chaloner, surprised the servants had allowed her anywhere near the Viscount.

'The Duchess agreed to fund a *respectable* gathering of women,' explained Joan, 'but nasty old Mansfield told her that the Red Bull is a brothel and we are all harlots. Shocked, the Duchess immediately withdrew her support.'

Sarah scowled. 'So I went to tell him that he had better tell her the truth, or else.'

'Or else what?' pressed Chaloner, astounded by her audacity.

'I reveal a secret about him.' Sarah made a moue of disdain. 'He capitulated, of course.'

'What secret?'

Sarah's expression turned haughty. 'If I told you, it would not be a secret, and he would then be free to encourage the Duchess to end her affiliation with our school.'

The determined jut of her chin told Chaloner that convincing her to confide in him would be a waste of time, so he let the matter drop. 'It is good of her to help you,' he said instead.

Sarah sniffed. 'Yes and no. She is very rich, so could easily give us more, but she would rather spend it on books for herself. I wish Eliza had a different mistress. She deserves better.'

'You do not like the Duchess?'

'Eliza is worth ten of her. Moreover, she is not half as clever as she thinks she is. Her logic is poor, she has no idea of grammar, and her spelling is as eccentric as her dress.'

It did not take a genius to see that Sarah was deeply jealous of the friendship between Eliza and her mistress. He changed the subject, aware that time was passing.

'Joan said you might have some theories about the poisoned oysters.'

Sarah frowned, evidently having relegated such an unimportant matter to the back of her mind. Then her expression cleared. 'Oh, yes. Your visit prompted me to reflect on it, and I remembered something I had forgotten – namely that someone was watching the girl who came to buy them. I do not believe she noticed, and I assumed at the time that it was some kindly soul who aimed to make sure she came to no harm in deadly Clerkenwell.'

'And now?'

'And now it occurs to me that this someone might have watched her with a view to poisoning the oysters the moment they were left unattended.'

'Can you describe this person?'

'Not really. All I can say is that it could have been a woman.'

'Thank you,' said Chaloner, although he was troubled. Did this mean the Duchess was the culprit after all?

As the Newcastle House soirée was likely to be a stylish affair, Chaloner hurried home and donned black breeches, white stockings and a pearl-grey vest – a loose, collarless, silk-lined garment with short sleeves, gathered at the waist with a belt. Then he borrowed a dark-red long-coat that no longer fitted Wiseman and grabbed his best hat.

When he was dressed, he went to the parlour, and found Ursula and Veriana talking to Temperance. They were so excited about visiting Newcastle House that they had been ready since breakfast, their hair crimped into the corkscrew curls that were currently popular at Court.

Unfortunately, Temperance had lent them some clothes that her prostitutes no longer needed, and Chaloner recoiled when he saw what she considered to be suitable attire. Ursula's neckline was so low-cut that she would have to keep very still or risk an embarrassing spillage, while Veriana's close-fitting bodice left nothing to the imagination. And both had used so many black face-patches that they looked diseased.

'They are perfect,' announced Temperance. 'Do not look horrified, Thomas. I know a lot more about fashion than you do.'

'They are here to find husbands, not clients,' objected Chaloner. 'And I am *not* taking them looking like that.'

There followed a spat of the kind with which Chaloner, who had three older sisters and Puritan parents, was very familiar: his cousins declared they had the right to dress as they pleased, while he maintained that they would not leave the house until they had put on something more appropriate. Eventually, a compromise was reached: the dresses remained, but both girls wore shawls to protect their modesty, kept firmly in place with strong-pinned brooches. The face-patches were reduced to two apiece.

He was about to send Wiseman's groom for a hackney when there was a knock on the door and Swaddell was ushered in. The assassin had also been to some trouble with his toilette, and Chaloner had never seen him look so elegant. He had exchanged his trademark black for a long-coat of pale blue, complemented by an apricot falling-band. His shirt frothed with French lace and matching ribbons, and his slick black hair was concealed under a fine blond wig.

Chaloner gazed at him in surprise, not sure he would have recognised him, although the beady eyes were something of a giveaway. These were fixed unblinkingly on Ursula.

'I have borrowed Williamson's personal coach,' the assassin said before Chaloner could suggest he ogled someone else. 'I thought the ladies should arrive in style. After all, first impressions are important, are they not?'

Ursula gave an excited squeal before darting over to Swaddell and kissing his cheek. Swaddell's pallid face flushed red and he dropped his gloves in a fluster. Temperance smirked.

Chaloner started to point out that it would do his cousins – or him, for that matter – no good whatsoever if they rolled up outside Newcastle House in a carriage emblazoned with the arms of the Spymaster General, but Ursula had already raced out to see it. Veriana was hot on her heels. When he followed, more sedately, Chaloner was relieved to note that the vehicle was tastefully understated, and although there was a crest on the door, it was very small. No one would recognise it unless they looked closely.

'Do not bother fetching your viol, Tom,' advised Temperance, coming to see them off. 'There will be no playing for you today, because if you take your eyes off your wards for an instant, there will be trouble. They are sweet girls, but unversed in the ways of the world.'

'I am not so sure about that,' muttered Chaloner, watching Ursula simper at Swaddell; this time the assassin dropped his peach-coloured handkerchief. 'I have a bad feeling that I have underestimated them.'

Temperance laughed. 'I doubt Mr Swaddell has been on the receiving end of this sort of attention before, and he will propose to one of them unless you take steps to prevent it. And you do not want him in the family. It is bad enough having a lot of regicides, but you will be doomed for certain if you are related to Williamson's creature.'

During the journey from Covent Garden to Clerkenwell, Chaloner pondered the best way to gain access to the

342

Duchess's private quarters, surprised to find himself looking forward to the challenge. His only concern was whether Swaddell was equal to keeping watch for him and monitoring Veriana and Ursula at the same time.

While Chaloner planned, Swaddell entertained the girls. He told them about the omens and portents of doom predicted for two days' hence, and Ursula responded by declaring an intention to enjoy every moment of the coming afternoon, lest it was her first and only foray into high society. Then Veriana began to talk about Chiffinch and the poisoned oysters.

'It was the Duchess of Newcastle who urged him to gobble them all up,' she announced. 'He had had enough after a dozen, but she insisted that he finish them all, on the grounds that if they were going to die on his behalf, then the least he could do was eat them.'

'How do you know?' asked Chaloner, tearing his thoughts from spying.

'Because Lucy Bodvil told us while we were sewing in Chaloner Court,' replied Veriana. 'She disapproved, because gluttony is a sin, and she thinks that if Mr Chiffinch had eaten enough, he should not have been encouraged to overindulge.'

'Did Lucy Bodvil hear this conversation herself?'

'No, she had the tale from some other Court lady. It was unfortunate that these shellfish happened to be poisoned, though, as it looks as if the Duchess is involved in a murder.'

'Not as unfortunate for her as it was for the victim,' murmured Swaddell, and turned the discussion to the latest fashion in wigs.

They rattled along Holborn at a decent lick, but as they turned north, the number of private carriages increased, until there were so many that there was a jam all along Clerkenwell Road. They inched towards the green, at which point Chaloner realised that every one of the vehicles was aiming for Newcastle House.

'I thought this was to be a small gathering,' he said, peering out of the window and recognising coaches belonging to four earls, a bishop and six high-ranking courtiers.

'So did I,' said Swaddell. 'But a large one is better, as it will be easier for us to work.'

'But what about the music?' objected Chaloner, who had been looking forward to hearing the Duchess's matching viols a lot more than invading her boudoir and making sure his cousins did not attract the wrong kind of attention.

'You said you would not be playing anyway,' shrugged Swaddell. 'Which is good news for the rest of us. as you tend to rate technical difficulty above a good tune, which means you are not much fun to listen to. I much prefer a pretty jig to a complex fugue.'

'Lucy Bodvil was shocked that the Duchess should hold a party in Holy Week,' gossiped Ursula, thus preventing Chaloner from calling Swaddell a philistine. 'She thinks we should all refuse to attend. Fortunately, Fanny said that would be rude – that we *should* come, but that we should make a point of behaving with proper decorum.'

She could barely conceal her excitement as they inched closer to the gate, although Veriana strove for an air of worldly indifference. Eventually, it was their turn to alight, and liveried footmen came to open the coach door. Chaloner and his party walked up the steps to the main door, where the Duke and his Duchess stood to greet their guests. The ducal couple had positioned themselves at either end of what appeared to be a horse trough. Then Chaloner saw it *was* a horse trough, set to catch the drips from the leaky ceiling.

The Duke had evidently decided that, as he was at home, he could wear what was most comfortable, so was clad in muddy riding boots and a tatty old coat. By contrast, the Duchess had donned attire more suitable for a coronation. Together, they appeared bizarre.

To enliven the task of welcoming a lot of people he did not know, the Duke was amusing himself by quizzing his guests on the pedigree of their horses. He gaped his disbelief when Swaddell informed him that one nag looked much like another, with four legs and two ends that were equally dangerous. Then he forced a polite smile because, even in his finery, Swaddell was obviously not a man to offend.

Meanwhile, the Duchess embraced Ursula and Veriana like long-lost friends, causing them to gaze pleadingly at Chaloner for guidance on how to respond. Then she returned Chaloner's bow, which was an odd thing for a lady to do, while Swaddell was treated to a smacking kiss on the cheek that made him reach for his dagger.

'We shall eat an olio later,' she informed them with an unnerving grin. 'Which is a stew containing a fine mixture of items. I banned certain spices, though, as they are known to inflame fierce passions. Do you know why I chose an olio as our fare today?'

'Because you wrote a book with "olio" in the title?' suggested Chaloner, although he knew he could not be right, as no one would be that self-serving.

'Yes!' she exclaimed, clapping her hands in girlish delight. '*The World's Olio*. It is clever of me, do you not think?'

'Oh, very,' said Swaddell, when Chaloner was too taken aback to reply.

'Now, Chiffinch's poisoner,' she said, sobering abruptly and regarding both men with disconcerting intensity. 'Have you found him yet?'

'No,' replied Chaloner, and as she had broached the subject, he seized the opportunity to ask some questions of his own. 'But we understand that you told one of the kitchen children where to buy the oysters. Is it true?'

The Duchess nodded. 'I happened to spot the child weeping, because White Hall's usual supplier had sold out, so I stepped in to save the day. The brat was very grateful, and deeply impressed that I, a lady of noble birth, should know about shellfish.'

Chaloner could not read her at all. Was she the cunning killer, toying with the dim-witted investigator? Or was she genuinely careless of the fact that she had played a role – inadvertent or otherwise – in a murder?

'Do you eat Sarah Shawe's wares yourself?'

She regarded him in distaste. 'Oysters are for commoners, so no. Besides, I feel for the creatures. How would you like to be swallowed alive, to die in someone else's stomach?'

'Then why did you facilitate the demise of two dozen of them by sending the child to Sarah?' Chaloner was aware that the question was insolent, and was glad the Duke was busily holding forth on dressage to Ursula and Veriana, sure he would object if he heard.

'I did not think of that at the time,' shrugged the Duchess. 'I regretted it later.'

'But you urged him to eat the ones on his plate, even though he said he was full.'

The Duchess's gaze did not waver. 'I did no such thing.

However, as they had been doused in lemon and salt, the least he could do was put the poor things out of their misery.'

'You must be pleased to learn that Topp is alive,' said Chaloner, in a final, desperate effort to shake her from her exasperating equanimity. 'That he is a thief but not a suicide.'

'I am glad for Eliza. I do not care for myself.'

At that point, the next guests bustled forward to make their obeisance. Chaloner was uncomfortably aware of the Duchess watching him as they gabbled polite nonsense, and he was under the impression that she would have liked to spar a little longer.

Newcastle House was full to bursting and very noisy. Fanny came to whisk Ursula and Veriana away to join her sewing circle, much to their dismay, leaving Chaloner and Swaddell to mingle. The first person to hail them was Clayton, resplendent in a set of new clothes. Viscount Mansfield was with him.

'You and your viol will not be needed today,' the steward said apologetically. 'Once I found out how many people were coming, I had to hire the entire troupe of the King's Private Musick instead.'

'But even they cannot make themselves heard over the rumpus,' sniggered Mansfield. 'My stepmother has invited half of London to share her stupid olio.'

He slithered away into the throng, where he began to murmur disparaging remarks about the Duchess to anyone who would listen. Clayton followed dutifully.

After a while, when the public rooms had become hotter and even more crowded, Chaloner went in search of his cousins. He tracked them down to a quiet antechamber, where a group of middle-aged ladies were admiring the stitches on each other's lace. Ursula's face was a mask of despair, as every time she attempted to slip away, one of the matrons contrived to stop her. Veriana had given up trying, and sat with her arms folded and a pout on her face.

'*Please*, Thomas,' begged Ursula, leaping up to hiss desperately in his ear. 'We cannot stay in here all afternoon. If we are to find good husbands, we must be *noticed*.'

But Chaloner did not want them noticed by the Newcastles' guests. True, the gathering was mostly free of rakes, but there were still enough there to make it dangerous. Baron Lucas had brought friends from the Royal Society, who included several earls of dubious moral reputation, while Cobbe, clad in an eye-catching outfit of purple silk, had also contrived to get inside, despite his affiliation with the Cockpit Club.

The olio was served soon after, and did not induce 'fierce passions' as much as a fierce desire for water. Lucas spat his on the floor with a roar of shock, although others were more genteel and used handkerchiefs or disappeared behind curtains to get rid of theirs. Ursula and Veriana wanted a taste, but Fanny forbade it after her husband, who had gamely taken a very large mouthful, was compelled to glug a pint of wine to soothe the resulting burning.

'Do not touch it,' he gasped, tears running down his cheeks. 'It is toxic – and that is my professional medical opinion.'

'It is very nice,' countered Swaddell, and proceeded to devour an entire bowl without so much as a wince. It was a tactical mistake, as whispers began almost immediately that Satan and his familiars were partial to highly

348

spicy food. Then Chaloner's attention was taken by Brodrick, who bustled up angrily.

'There will be no decent music,' he snarled. 'And that is the only reason I came. I am tempted to don a disguise and go to the cockpit instead, where Bess has organised a bear-fight.'

'You enjoy that sort of thing?' asked Chaloner in distaste.

'Not really, but it is better than being plied with inedible olios here. Or reading law books in Clarendon House, which is my cousin's idea of light entertainment. And at least I would be among my own kind at the cockpit, because look around at who is here – physicians, dowdy matrons, natural philosophers, horse-traders, the rougher kind of cleric . . .'

'True,' agreed Chaloner.

'Worse, I think the Newcastles have let the servants bring their friends,' Brodrick went on in a shocked whisper. 'Because I am sure the ladies next to the refreshments are common traders.'

Chaloner looked to where a small, uncertain gaggle of women from the Red Bull stood. Sarah was in their midst, tall, proud and defiant, as if daring anyone to challenge her right to be there. No one did, so she and her cronies began to help themselves to wine, tentatively at first, then with increasing enthusiasm. Eliza arrived soon after, and Sarah strode forward to greet her, not caring that she jostled other guests as she went. Eliza looked haggard, worn out by the emotional upheavals of a husband missing, then dead, then alive again.

'We shall not stay long,' declared Sarah in a loud, self-important voice. 'We are busy women with hectic lives. But we wanted you to know that you have friends.'

'Er . . . yes,' said Eliza, flustered and embarrassed in

349

equal measure. 'Thank you. Yet I am surprised to see you here . . .'

'I told Molly to let us in,' explained Sarah. 'We thought you might need our support while you are obliged to move among . . . these individuals.' She gazed around in distaste.

'You see what happens when the established order of things is flouted?' Chaloner heard Fanny whisper to her friends. 'Boundaries are blurred, and no one knows where they stand.'

At that point, Baron Lucas swept the Red Bull contingent away to meet his Royal Society cronies, but the company suited neither party, so it was not long before they went their separate ways. Sarah led her coterie to the door, pausing just long enough to murmur something to Eliza, and any discomfiture she might have caused her friend was clearly forgiven, as the glance that she received was one of deep affection.

Eventually, Swaddell sidled up to Chaloner. 'I have just ascertained that the Duchess's boudoir is on the first floor, second door on the right. While you have a poke around, I will pretend to be watching the soirée over the banister. If anyone comes up the stairs, I will rap on it three times with my ring.'

Chaloner could see a lot wrong with that plan, not least of which was that he would be unlikely to hear such a sound once he was where he needed to be. But with luck, the Duchess would be too busy with her guests to return to her private quarters, so the warning would not be needed. He waited until he was sure no one was looking, then ran quickly up the staircase.

The Duchess's half of the house was decorated with an eclectic collection of artwork, and the furniture had been chosen for comfort, rather than style. Her boudoir was a messy, cluttered room, dominated by hanging picture frames. A glance told him that all held enlarged copies of the frontispieces in her books. Clearly, false modesty was not one of her vices.

As the room was so chaotic – table, chairs and floor were covered in papers and books – Chaloner realised a full search would be impossible, so he decided to concentrate on the desk, in the feeble hope that she had been careless enough to leave something incriminating lying out.

The first thing he saw was a list of Mother Broughton's prophecies, accompanied by notes outlining what the Duchess planned to do about them. For example, she aimed to neutralise Good Friday's rain of fire by gathering nice people under her roof, so that their combined virtue would render them all safe. She was also of the opinion that the joy scheduled for Easter Day would be the delight that would burst forth when she announced the publication of her next book.

Aware that folk might need some persuading before they agreed to fall in with her schemes, she had turned to tomes on religion to 'prove' that she was right. One lay open at a page depicting the motifs assigned to various saints. Chaloner frowned at one of the symbols – it was familiar, but he could not recall why. As he puzzled over it, he heard a sound from the closet in the corner. He whipped around, hand on his sword, but before he could draw it, the door flung open and someone jumped out with a gun.

It was Topp.

'Do not come any closer,' the steward hissed. 'If you do, I will shoot you.'

351

Chapter 14

There was silence in the Duchess's boudoir as Topp pointed the gun at Chaloner. The steward was so frightened by the situation in which he found himself that his hands shook violently, and Chaloner knew he was in more danger of being shot by accident than deliberately.

'Put it down,' he ordered. 'Before you hurt yourself.'

'I will hurt you,' blustered Topp, struggling to keep the tremor from his voice. 'You should not have come here. You are trespassing.'

'So are you,' retorted Chaloner. 'You stole three hundred pounds from people who trusted you, then you staged your own death. I cannot see you being welcomed back with open arms.'

Topp swallowed hard. 'I had no choice. That anonymous letter to the Duke . . . Thirty years of faithful service, destroyed by one spiteful pen. And it was lies! I *do* love the Duchess, but as a father loves a daughter. I would never take her as a lover. The very idea is repulsive.'

'The Duke knows that. He did not believe the accusations for a moment.'

'No?' asked Topp, startled and hopeful in equal measure.

'He charged one of the best investigators in the country to find out who wrote it – a man who is visiting the posthouse from which it was sent as we speak. Your employer remained loyal to you, and you repaid him by stealing.'

'I stole nothing,' countered Topp, licking his lips nervously. 'The three hundred pounds was mine – money I am owed for purchases made on his behalf. I am not a thief.'

'Is that so,' said Chaloner, before darting forward to grab the gun. As Topp's pockets and coat bulged suspiciously, he gave the man a shake, and was disgusted but not surprised when all manner of valuable items showered down on to the floor. 'I suppose these are your brooches, necklaces and jewels, then, are they?'

Even with the evidence of his perfidy scattered around his feet, Topp continued to bleat his innocence: the Duchess had promised him these things; he had just taken what was rightfully his; he had only availed himself of a fraction of what she had said he might have . . .

'Enough!' snapped Chaloner, tiring of the self-justifying tirade. 'You are a thief and a killer, and it is time for you to accept responsibility for what you have done.'

Topp regarded him in horror. 'A killer? What are you talking about? I accept that I might have been a little zealous in claiming what I am owed, but I have never hurt anyone.'

Chaloner indicated the gun. It had a distinctively engraved barrel, and he recalled it vividly from White Hall, when it and its partner had poked around the door to Mushey's room and blasted at him and Swaddell.

353

'You are the White Hall killer, who poisoned Chiffinch's oysters, then dispatched Mushey to ensure he never revealed that *you* were the one he let into the palace larder.'

The blood drained from Topp's face. 'No, Your Honour! I have never been inside the larder and I never met this Mushey. I swear on my mother's grave.'

'Then explain how you come to be in possession of this particular handgun.'

'I found it right there.' Topp pointed to a table. 'And there is a matching one under that copy of *The World's Olio*. I snatched it up when I heard you coming, because I thought I might have to protect myself. I had no choice but to wave it at you, although I would never have used it. You *must* believe me, Your Magnificence.'

A quick check revealed that the gun was unloaded, but as the steward seemed unaware of the fact, Chaloner was willing to accept that the weapons did not belong to him. So whose were they? The Duchess's, and it had been she who had shot at him and Swaddell in White Hall? He thought about Sarah's testimony that someone had watched Millicent buy the oysters from her; and Millicent's claim that a woman had lurked outside the larder that same day. Then there was the Duchess's peculiar request to watch Chiffinch dissected. She had been a suspect from the start, so did the pistols prove her guilt?

Topp saw Chaloner's hesitation and sought to capitalise on it. 'On the day the oysters were poisoned, I was off trying to purchase a corpse. It took hours, as I kept being offered ones that were unsuitable. Half were the wrong sex, for a start.'

Chaloner believed him, feeling that no one would admit to buying cadavers unless it was true. And if Topp

354

had not poisoned Chiffinch, then he had not killed the others either.

'So your Duchess murdered Chiffinch,' he said, purely to see if Topp would defend the lady he claimed to love. 'She must have done, given that the guns are hers.'

Topp licked his lips, and Chaloner could almost hear the wheels turning in his head as he pondered how blaming her might benefit himself. 'It is possible, Your Worship,' he hedged eventually, 'but there are far better suspects. Clayton, for example, who is a vile rogue.'

'He certainly does not like you. Indeed, I am surprised you have not accused him of sending that slanderous missive to the Duke.'

'I assumed he had, but when I looked at the Bishop-mark to see when it was posted, it transpires that he was with me at the time. Moreover, I know his handwriting as well as my own. He is not responsible for the letter.'

Answers to that particular mystery were beginning to form in Chaloner's mind, but while he was sure that Thurloe would be pleased to see it solved – assuming the ex-Spymaster had not already done it himself, of course – it was irrelevant to the more pressing matter of murder.

'What is your evidence for accusing Clayton of being the White Hall killer?' he asked.

'I do not have any, Your Worship,' admitted Topp wretchedly. 'But I will find some if you let me go. I will just gather up these baubles, and send word once I have what you need.'

Chaloner laughed. 'I do not think so! But why did you not leave the city after staging your "death"? No one questioned it, and you could have escaped scot-free.'

Topp pulled a disagreeable face. 'Because I realised I would need more than three hundred pounds to build a new life, so I had to come back to see what else was available. It is not theft, though – it is compensation for all the agony and inconvenience I have endured.'

'*You* have endured?' echoed Chaloner, amazed by the unabashed selfishness. 'What about Eliza, who mourned you?'

Topp had the grace to blush. 'I am sorry for that, but she is a loyal wife, and I have explained why I had to do it. She will forgive me eventually. Now, if there is nothing else, Your Eminence, I shall see about getting you some evidence to see Clayton hanged.'

'Stop,' ordered Chaloner, as the steward began to scoop up handfuls of jewellery from the floor. 'I imagine the Duke would like a word with you. Then he can decide how to proceed.'

Finding Topp had put Chaloner in an awkward situation, as he could hardly reveal that he had caught the steward while he had been searching the Duchess's private chambers for evidence that she was a murderer. He had just decided to say that he had met Topp in the hall – the steward would denounce the lie, but who would believe him? – when the door was flung open.

Chaloner's hand tightened around the gun as Eliza and Sarah walked in. Both women stopped dead in their tracks when they saw him, then Eliza turned to her husband with a muted whimper of distress.

'You promised to stay out of sight! Now you will be accused of terrible things, and I shall have to bear the pain of losing you all over again.'

'Do not worry,' said Sarah, who had drawn a dagger. 'I will not allow you to suffer a second time.' She addressed Topp. 'Has anyone else seen you since your "suicide"?'

'Just the Rector of St Dunstan-in-the-West,' replied Topp miserably. 'It was raining, and I ducked into his church for shelter. I did not think he would notice me, but he did.'

'Then I shall put it about that he was drunk at the time.' Sarah regarded Chaloner appraisingly, fingering her knife. 'That just leaves you.'

'You cannot stab him here,' gulped Eliza. 'The Duchess likes these rugs.'

'I will clean up the blood,' offered Topp, while Chaloner wondered why they thought they could best him, when he was not only bigger and stronger, but likely far better armed. 'This man means to destroy me, and I will pay you handsomely if you . . . dissuade him.'

'Pay her with what?' asked Chaloner archly. 'The Duchess's jewellery? If you do, she will be caught and hanged the moment she tries to exchange it for money.'

'My husband would *never* touch the Duchess's things,' declared Eliza stoutly. 'He is her most loyal servant – or he was, until someone wrote that nasty letter. It has destroyed our lives, because things have spiralled out of control since, and now he must leave the country.'

'You will miss him, I am sure,' muttered Chaloner, glancing at Sarah, who was looking delighted by the prospect of the steward being out of the way.

'I will.' Eliza's expression was anguished. 'And I shall spend every waking moment persuading the Duchess of his innocence. Then he can come home.'

'I am afraid his sticky fingers have destroyed all hope of a pardon,' said Chaloner. 'It is a pity he could not control them, because all might have ended well otherwise.'

'We shall return the money Francis *borrowed*,' said Eliza with quiet dignity, 'and I will find a way to exonerate him. Clayton will not win this war – and I am sure he *did* send that letter, no matter what the Bishop-mark says.'

'Clayton is the White Hall killer,' Topp declared confidently, and then indicated Chaloner. 'He accused me of it at first, but I convinced him that he was mistaken.'

'You *are* mistaken,' Eliza told Chaloner firmly. 'Francis was out buying a corpse when the oysters would have been poisoned, and has witnesses to prove it. And do not accuse Sarah or me of the crime either, because we were here in Newcastle House with the Duke, Mansfield and a hundred others. Baron Lucas gave a talk on air pressure that evening, you see, and he locked the doors to make sure no one sneaked out.'

'Although a few people managed to escape regardless,' put in Sarah. 'Namely Clayton and his two unsavoury friends. And the Duchess, of course, who went to visit John Milton, before heading for White Hall to defeat Chiffinch at backgammon. When Baron Lucas and Mansfield arrived there later – they travelled together, so have alibis in each other – she was already in the Shield Gallery. Lucas told me so himself.'

Eliza gave her an irritable glance, then glared at Chaloner. 'But do not even think of accusing My Lady. She is an angel, who has never hurt anyone in her life.'

Chaloner appreciated her loyalty, but dogged devotion was not proof. He said so.

Eliza was silent for a moment, thinking. Gradually, she began to smile, first with relief, then in jubilation. 'But Francis is right – Clayton *is* the White Hall killer! And I can prove it. Sarah, go and make sure no one is listening. We cannot risk eavesdroppers, because I do not want what I am about to say made public, twisted and embellished with every telling.'

'I would rather stay here,' countered Sarah, irked by what was effectively a dismissal. 'You need me to protect you. In case you have not noticed, Chaloner holds a gun.'

'He would have used it by now if he meant us harm,' said Eliza. 'So do as I ask.'

Sarah slouched, very reluctantly, through the door, while Topp looked from Chaloner to Eliza and back again, frightened and anxious about what was about to be revealed.

'When that anonymous letter arrived,' began Eliza, 'the first thing the Duke did was show it to Chiffinch.'

'Why would he do that?' asked Chaloner sceptically.

'Because Chiffinch received lots of applications from people wanting Court posts, so was familiar with their handwriting. He said he could not help, and sent the Duke to a man called William Prynne, who also deals with lots of official correspondence. Prynne did not recognise the writing, but he introduced the Duke to a man who promised to investigate.'

'Who?' asked Topp suspiciously, while Chaloner held his breath.

'The Duke refused to say,' replied Eliza.

Thank God for that, thought Chaloner in relief. 'So there is a link between the letter and one of the murder victims. That is interesting, but it does not prove Clayton is the killer.'

'You are not *listening*. Chiffinch said he "could not help" – he did not say the handwriting was unknown to him. I later overheard him gossiping to Widdrington, and I was under the impression that he *had* recognised it, but had decided to keep the information from the Duke. Perhaps he aimed to blackmail the culprit. Regardless, a few hours later, he was dead.'

'So you think the killer and the author of the letter are one and the same?' asked Chaloner. 'Then it cannot be Clayton, because he was with your husband when the letter was mailed from Grantham.'

Eliza smiled. 'But *you* know that alibi is meaningless – I can see it in your face. Clayton is a clever man, who not only disguised his handwriting – although there are experts who will see past that sort of thing – but sent someone to post the letter in his stead.'

She was right. The culprit would not have taken his missive to the posthouse in person, as Thurloe was likely to discover when he questioned its officials. But Clayton had two good friends: Booth and Liddell. One of them might do his bidding.

'Unfortunately, that is not evidence either,' warned Chaloner.

'It will be if Widdrington tells you what Chiffinch said about it,' argued Eliza. 'Or at least, enough to arrest Clayton for formal questioning.'

Chaloner doubted Widdrington would cooperate, and thought Eliza was clutching at straws. 'It is a fine theory, but I cannot see Clayton perpetrating such an elaborate scheme.'

'I can, Your Worship,' put in Topp eagerly. 'He hates the Duchess and he hates me. He always has, ever since we first met, and I saw through his sly, greedy manners.'

'I understand why he dislikes you,' said Chaloner. 'But why the Duchess?'

'Because he has thrown his eggs in Mansfield's basket, and aims to be sole steward when Mansfield inherits his father's estate,' explained Eliza earnestly. 'The Viscount loathes his stepmother, but would never dare plot against

360

her while the Duke is alive. However, he will not object to someone else doing it on his behalf . . .'

Chaloner was far from convinced, but he had no other leads to follow, and Eliza's suggestion was better than nothing.

'I will look into Clayton,' he said eventually. 'But on two conditions: Topp will return everything he stole – including the three hundred pounds – and he will leave the country tonight.'

'He will,' promised Eliza, sagging in relief. 'You can trust us.'

Her, perhaps, thought Chaloner, but not her devious husband.

The soirée was in full swing when Chaloner rejoined Swaddell on the stairs. The assassin was dismayed, because Fanny's defences had been breached by the flamboyant Cobbe and the handsome young Earl of Lincoln. The pair sat next to Ursula and Veriana, who were delighted to have attracted such charming company, while Fanny fretted and flapped uselessly to one side, openly distressed by her failure to send the manly invaders packing.

Meanwhile, the ballroom was full of people trying to dance, although there were too many even for that great space, and the music was impossible to hear over the roar of lively conversation and laughter.

'You took your time,' said Swaddell accusingly. 'I hope you have something to show for it, because it kept me here when I should have been driving those peacocks from your cousins.'

'You might as well have gone for all the use you were,' retorted Chaloner curtly. 'You let Eliza and Sarah past, and they caught me.'

Swaddell blinked. 'Did they? They told me they were going to fetch some books.'

'They probably were,' said Chaloner acidly. 'From the Duchess's boudoir.'

'Oh,' said Swaddell guiltily. 'I suppose that should have been obvious. But my attention was on our ladies, and how I might save them from those two devious rakes.'

There was no point in berating him further, so Chaloner confined himself to recounting what had happened in the Duchess's rooms. Swaddell was unimpressed.

'You should not have let Topp go! He is a thief and should pay for his crimes.'

'Then you can pursue him later,' said Chaloner shortly. 'But first, we must prove that Clayton was responsible for the anonymous letter and that Chiffinch knew it. Then we can charge him with poisoning Chiffinch, and ask about the other victims once we have him in custody.'

'I hope you are sure about this,' grumbled Swaddell, 'because time is running out. It is Maundy Thursday tomorrow, after which Good Friday will be upon us. We will be too busy ducking rains of fire and gnashing our teeth to investigate murder.'

'Clerkenwell,' mused Chaloner. 'Everything comes back to Clerkenwell. The disasters will begin here, the prophet who predicted them lives here, our prime suspect works here . . .'

'So does our second: the Duchess,' put in Swaddell. 'And if Clayton transpires to be innocent, we shall have to look at her. Eliza is fiercely loyal to her mistress, and may have misled you deliberately. However, before we do anything else, we must remove your cousins from the clutches of those swaggering lotharios.'

Chaloner agreed that a dalliance with Cobbe was not

to be to encouraged, although he had no objection to the Earl of Lincoln. But before he could say so, the Duchess blew three long, shrill blasts on a ceremonial hunting horn that had been hanging on the ballroom wall. Startled, the musicians faltered into silence, the dancers tottered to a standstill, and the bellow of conversation faded away.

'It is time for you all to go home,' she announced, and Chaloner might have laughed at the astonished expressions on her guests' faces if he had not been so taken aback himself. 'This gathering has achieved its purpose, and your presence here is no longer required. Besides, it is Holy Week, so you should not be jigging about like monkeys anyway.'

'But it was you who provided the facilities, ma'am,' objected Brodrick, the only one bold – or drunk – enough to say what everyone else was thinking.

'I did,' acknowledged the Duchess. 'But it was a test, to see who would avail themselves of them, even though dancing is inappropriate for such a solemn day in the Church year. Those people will *not* be invited back again. However, those who restrained themselves will be expected to join me here any time after ten o'clock on Good Friday morning.'

'I do not understand,' snapped Brodrick waspishly. 'What—'

'You must have heard that a great calamity will befall London the day after tomorrow,' interrupted the Duchess, 'after which all evil will be wiped from the face of the Earth. However, the godly will be spared this destruction, so it makes sense for all us righteous types to gather in one place. Then we can enjoy the spectacle together.'

'Goodness!' breathed Swaddell, while the guests –

revellers and sobersides alike – exchanged glances of disbelief. 'I always thought the Almighty would have the task of weighing our souls. Since when did it become the role of the aristocracy?'

'So go home,' the Duchess continued. 'If you are among the fortunate few who will come on Friday, I shall see you then. As for the rest, all I can do is warn you to mend your debauched ways before it is too late.'

'I would not come back here anyway,' muttered Brodrick, as he plonked his glass down hard enough to break it. 'She belongs in Bedlam, and is not fit for proper society.'

Most guests agreed, especially when she elected to stand at the door and inform each person individually whether or not they had won her approbation.

'What manner of gathering will it be on Friday?' asked the Earl of Lincoln, who had passed the test only because Fanny had refused to let him whisk Ursula on to the dance floor.

'We shall read my books until the rain of fire begins, then we will watch the display through the upstairs windows,' replied the Duchess. 'Do not worry – you will be in no danger, and when you are old, you can tell your grandchildren about the Day the World Changed.'

The young nobleman bowed and left, although it was clear that he had no intention of spending what might be his last few hours with the eccentric Duchess of Newcastle.

'*You* may return,' she decreed, as Chaloner, Swaddell, Veriana and Ursula filed past. 'I commend you on your sobriety. I predicted you would fail, but I was wrong.'

Before they could respond, she had turned to inform Brodrick that *he* need not darken her doors again.

Chaloner began to laugh once they were outside, although he was the only one who did. All around, people were outraged that she should dare pass judgement on others, especially as news of the anonymous letter had seeped out, so there were rumours that she strayed outside the marriage bed.

'And she has pronounced her disgusting brother as one of the godly,' hissed Lady Muskerry furiously. 'The man who pawed shamelessly at me all afternoon. His Royal Society cronies qualified, too, but only because they were too busy arguing to dance.'

It was some time before Swaddell's coach arrived, because the Duchess's decision to end the soirée so abruptly meant that all the carriages were needed at once, causing a huge jam.

'Will you come here on Good Friday, Thomas?' asked Fanny, as they waited.

She was standing with the ladies from her sewing circle, all reeling from the news that they were not invited back. Apparently, being staid was not the same as being righteous, and the Duchess had decided to lump them in with the wicked. Dr Clarke was similarly condemned, because he had been spotted making a pass at Lady Muskerry.

'I doubt it,' replied Chaloner. 'What will you do?'

'Go to church,' replied Fanny with a shrug. 'Then invite my friends to sit with me while this rain of fire destroys the sinful.'

Chaloner regarded her askance. 'Surely you do not really believe that will happen?'

'I do not know what to think,' sighed Fanny unhappily. 'But perhaps the King has the right idea, and we should all go to Dover, just in case. But here is my coach at last. Good evening to you.'

Swaddell's carriage appeared eventually, but it was dark by the time it reached Covent Garden. Swaddell inveigled an invitation to stay for a cup of wine, and Wiseman was there to entertain everyone with an account of the King's bowels, so Chaloner decided to leave Clayton until the following day. He wrote a note to Kersey at the charnel house, asked one of Wiseman's servants to deliver it, and went to bed.

Chapter 15

It was just growing light when Chaloner rose the next morning. He went to the garden to let out the hens and the goose, then roused his cousins and told them to prepare for a day with Fanny. They grumbled bitterly, both about the early start and the prospect of such dull company, but they did as they were told.

He was just availing himself of bread and boiled eggs in the parlour when Swaddell was shown in. The assassin had reverted to his trademark black, although there were dark rings under his eyes – Chaloner was not the only one who had been kept awake by churning thoughts the previous night.

'What first?' Swaddell asked, craning his neck to see if he could spot Ursula or Veriana coming down the stairs. 'We must catch the killer today, Tom, because there will be no time tomorrow. I have offered to stay with Ursula then, lest she needs my protection from walking corpses or rains of fire.'

Chaloner would allow neither cousin to spend Good Friday with Swaddell, but it was no time to say so. He hailed a hackney, bundled his still-protesting kinswomen inside, and delivered them to Chaloner Court. Swaddell was at his most charming during the journey, but not even his promise of a visit to the cherry trees at Rotherhithe could distract them from the horrors of a day with middle-aged ladies whose idea of fun was comparing bone and metal pins.

Fanny was waiting for them, and Chaloner experienced a pang of guilt when she informed the girls that, as a change from needlework, they would read the Bible all morning, then cut up old newsbooks for compost in the afternoon.

'We may not be safe with her,' Ursula whispered in a last, desperate attempt to escape the ordeal. 'Not when terrible things will start in Clerkenwell tomorrow – things that will change the world for ever.'

'I shall be with you,' promised Swaddell gallantly. 'Do not worry.'

Veriana nodded polite thanks, but Ursula was much more effusive, and Chaloner saw that he needed to keep the two apart, lest Swaddell took warm-heartedness as a sign of affection. He did not fancy dealing with a Swaddell spurned in love.

He climbed back into the carriage and told the driver to take them to Westminster. While they lurched along the rutted streets, he told Swaddell his plans for the day.

'First, we must visit the charnel house, where I believe we will find proof that Clayton wrote the anonymous letter accusing the Duchess of adultery. Afterwards, we will speak to Widdrington, and ask what Chiffinch told *him* about it. Between the two, I think we might have answers at last.'

'And if Widdrington refuses to cooperate?' asked Swaddell.

'Oh, I am sure you can persuade him,' replied

Chaloner, feeling the time for gentleness was past now that Good Friday was almost upon them.

They travelled the rest of the way in silence, Chaloner thinking about the murders and the solutions that were emerging at last, while Swaddell smiled rather dreamily. They reached the charnel house at the same time as Kersey, who rolled up in his private carriage. Chaloner glanced inside and saw a woman there, although she was neither of his two wives. Kersey alighted, then poked his head back through the window to murmur thanks for a wonderful night.

'You are bold,' Swaddell told him admiringly. 'I would never dare.'

'Never dare what?' asked Kersey blandly.

Secrets and favours, thought Chaloner, reflecting on how many there were in his current investigation. Swaddell knew something about Bishop Morley that meant the prelate was willing to lie for him, while the Duchess had once done Thurloe such an important favour that the ex-Spymaster had gone to Grantham on her behalf. Chiffinch had whispered something to Widdrington that might have a bearing on his murder, and Chaloner himself had done the Topps a favour by letting the steward go in exchange for information.

He followed Kersey inside the charnel house, aware of a mounting sense of unease about the whole affair. There were connections he still did not understand, and he had the sense that if he pulled too hard on one thread, the lot would come crashing down around him. Perhaps *that* was what Mother Broughton thought was about to happen in Clerkenwell – one strand of discontent tweaked, beginning a chain of events that would not stop until the world was upside down again.

'I wonder if the messenger will come to me today,' said Kersey conversationally, and elaborated when Chaloner and Swaddell looked blank. 'Mother Broughton predicted that a "messenger" will die on Thursday and the Fleet River will run red with blood. Or have you taken steps to prevent that from happening?'

'How?' asked Swaddell wearily. 'We do not know who the prediction is for. However, I can tell you that it will not be Ambassador Downing. He has decided to stay in Dover until the danger is past.'

'Wise man,' said Kersey. 'But how may I help you today? I received the note you sent me last night, and did what you asked, but it made no sense.'

'When I was last here,' began Chaloner, 'you showed me the body of a man who had walked around after his brain had stopped working, along with items you had recovered from his pockets. You hoped he might be identified from them, so you could inform his family.'

Kersey inclined his head. 'There was a book by the Duchess of Newcastle, annotated with unflattering remarks, along with some coded messages and a few illegally clipped coins. I was going to send the messages to Spymaster Williamson, but your note arrived just in time, so they are still here. Do you want to see them?'

Chaloner nodded. 'I saw a list of saints' symbols in the Duchess's boudoir last night. One was familiar, although it took me a while to remember why.'

'It was in the messages?' asked Kersey, as he led the way inside, where the box containing the dead man's effects was waiting on the desk in his office.

Chaloner unfolded one of the pieces of paper. 'Yes, here it is – the broken wheel, which appears to be how the sender addresses the recipient.'

'So the dead man identified himself with a saint?' asked Swaddell warily. 'Which one?'

'A broken wheel signifies St Quentin, who was pinned to one during his martyrdom.' Chaloner waited for Swaddell to make the connection, but the assassin remained perplexed, obliging him to spell it out. 'Booth is the vicar of St *Quentin's* near Nottingham.'

'Yes, he did say that is where he has his living,' acknowledged Swaddell. 'He mentioned that it had caught fire recently . . .'

'Which is why he was so angry when he was attacked,' said Chaloner, watching understanding dawn on the assassin's face. 'He cannot afford to lose money to thieves.'

'This Vicar Booth was robbed?' asked Kersey, intrigued.

'A thief ambushed him and ran off with his purse,' explained Chaloner. 'He gave chase, and pursued the culprit into Newcastle House's stables – into the stall occupied by the high-spirited Henrietta Florence. She lunged at Booth when he tried to lay hold of the villain, which allowed him to escape. But the robber later went back – I suspect he had dropped his loot, and thought it would be easy to retrieve. Unfortunately, Henrietta Florence is dangerous . . .'

'My guest's head could have been damaged by a flying hoof,' mused Kersey. 'Indeed, it would explain the injury perfectly.'

'I saw the letter that accused the Duchess of infidelity,' said Chaloner, although he was not about to confide that Thurloe had shown it to him. 'The sender had tried to disguise his hand, but he neglected to change his distinctive *f*s. Now, look at the annotations in the book.'

'The *f*s are unusual,' said Kersey, fascinated.

'They are identical to the ones in the letter, which

means its author and the owner of this book are one and the same. A person whose identifying mark is St Quentin's broken wheel. There cannot be many churches dedicated to St Quentin in England . . .'

'So my guest is not a rebel dealing in coded letters,' surmised Kersey. 'He is just a common thief, and everything in his pockets came from Vicar Booth?'

'Yes,' said Chaloner. 'Now consider the clipped coins. If the thief stole the book and the letters from Booth, the chances are that the money came from Booth, too. Coin-clipping is a capital offence, which is why Booth risked haring after the thief – he *had* to get them back.'

'So Booth is guilty not only of devaluing the King's currency, but also of sending libellous letters to the Duke,' concluded Swaddell. 'Interesting. But I thought we were hoping for evidence that would prove *Clayton's* guilt.'

Chaloner could only assume that Swaddell was muddle-headed from a poor night's sleep, because he was not usually slow-witted. 'Booth is Clayton's friend – they are in it together. Indeed, I wager anything you please that St Quentin's is near Grantham, where the letter was posted. Booth will be the easier nut to crack, so I suggest we tackle him first.'

'No,' said Swaddell. 'We should speak to Widdrington before going to Newcastle House. We need to find out exactly what Chiffinch said to him about the anonymous letter. *Then* we will corner this criminal cleric, because if you are right about these connections, whatever Chiffinch said was what drove Clayton to poison his oysters.'

In the event, they were obliged to follow Chaloner's suggestion, because they arrived at White Hall only to discover that Widdrington had gone to buy a horse in

Hampstead, and was not expected back until the evening. Swaddell wanted to go after him, but Chaloner refused, remembering the hours he had squandered chasing Pamphlin.

'Booth, then,' conceded Swaddell, flagging down a hackney to take them to Clerkenwell. 'But you had better hope we have enough to force a confession, because otherwise all we will do is warn Clayton that we are closing in on him.'

Again, the journey was made in silence, with the assassin staring out of the window, one hand playing idly with his dagger. When they were stopped by a jam on Fleet Street, they heard passers-by talking in excited voices about Good Friday. Most seemed to be looking forward to it, on the grounds that they, as righteous individuals, would be spared. Folk were irked anew with the King, though. He had discharged his Maundy Thursday obligations by giving away coins, but had started – and finished – so early that most people had missed it. Then he had set out for Dover without a backward glance.

Eventually, Chaloner and Swaddell reached Newcastle House, which was busy, as an army of servants laboured to put all back to rights after the Duchess's soirée. Wine stains were being scrubbed from tables, scuff marks polished off floors, and goblets and jugs collected for washing. Chaloner wondered why it had not been done sooner, but had his answer from Molly, who told him that, after most of the guests had gone home, Baron Lucas had taken over the public rooms for an experiment with his Royal Society cronies. She had been his assistant.

'But it did not go according to plan, and everyone ended up covered in chicken muck,' she finished. 'He and I laughed our heads off, but his friends were cross.'

'What kind of experiment?' asked Chaloner, unable to imagine one that entailed manure being brought inside the house. He glanced up, and saw the glass ceiling high above was spattered with brown goo, and as there was no easy way to reach it, it might be there to stay.

'One involving explosions,' replied Molly, not very helpfully. 'They were only little ones, but Baron Lucas said he could easily make them much bigger.'

'Explosions?' asked Swaddell sharply. 'Why would he do such a thing?'

'It is called al-chem-y,' explained Molly, speaking the word slowly to ensure she got it right. 'Learning how things can be mixed up to make loud noises and nasty smells. He loves it, and wanted to show his friends what he can do with droppings, oil and some other stuff.'

Chaloner and Swaddell exchanged an uneasy glance, but before they could question her further, there was a commotion as some of her feathered charges invaded the hall. She scampered away to round them up, amid angry grumbles from the other servants who felt the birds were getting out of control.

'Dutch Jane has a lot to answer for,' muttered the butler. 'If she had not tried to steal one, the Duchess would never have given Molly sole control over the wretched things. Molly is wholly unequal to the task of keeping them in the garden.'

'What a mess!' muttered a cook, looking around in despair. 'And to think we shall have to clean up all over again tomorrow, after the Duchess hosts her next gathering.'

'It will not be as bad then,' predicted the butler, 'because she has only invited the godly. *They* will not spill wine or spoil the floor by dancing.'

As everyone was busy, Chaloner and Swaddell went in search of Vicar Booth themselves. They walked through the hall and into the ballroom, where Eliza was giving instructions to a carpenter – one of Lucas's experiments had involved a hot cauldron, which had burned a black circle on the beautiful oak floorboards. She looked pale and tired, although there was a sparkle in her eye that had been missing when she thought she was a widow. When she saw Chaloner, she came to greet him.

'Thank you for what you did last night,' she said in a low voice. 'The money and jewels have been returned, and my husband is already sailing down the Thames. He will live in France until I have convinced the Duke and Duchess to forgive him. But we all make mistakes, and I am grateful to you for allowing us to put this one right.'

'You are welcome,' mumbled Chaloner, aware of Swaddell's disapproving glare.

'Of course,' Eliza went on wryly, 'Francis will have to work hard to win back *my* good graces. It will not be easy to forget the distress he caused me by pretending to be dead.'

'Perhaps he thought you would be happier with Sarah,' said Swaddell baldly.

Eliza blushed. 'I am fond of Sarah, but Francis is my husband, and will always claim the best part of my heart. Him and my Duchess.'

'We need to talk to Booth,' said Chaloner, feeling the press of time upon him. 'Where might we find him?'

'Hiding in the church next door, lest he is put to work. Personally, I suspect he set fire to his own parish church himself, to give him licence to abandon his flock and loaf about with Clayton and Liddell.'

'We shall ask him,' said Swaddell crisply. 'Because that is entirely possible.'

Clerkenwell's church was peaceful after the busy bustle of Newcastle House, and they found Booth fast asleep on one of its pews. Swaddell woke him with a prod of his dagger. The vicar's eyes were bleary at first, but they snapped into alertness at the sight of the assassin looming over him with a blade.

'What do you want?' he gulped. 'I have done nothing wrong!'

'An interesting way to begin a conversation,' mused Swaddell. 'And one that reveals a guilty conscience as far as I am concerned. Now, time is of the essence, so do not waste mine with pointless denials. We want the truth about the letter you sent to the Duke.'

'What letter?' demanded Booth, although his terrified face revealed the truth.

'We know you wrote it,' said Swaddell. 'You see, we have the thief who relieved you of your purse – the purse that held an annotated book and notes addressed to a man who identifies himself with St Quentin.'

'Many people do,' objected Booth, struggling for defiance. 'He is a popular martyr.'

'Not in this country,' said Chaloner. 'It is an unusual dedication for an English church.'

'So why did you burn it down?' asked Swaddell, quietly menacing. 'In order to come to London and help Clayton malign the Duchess? It seems an extreme way to escape your pastoral duties, but—'

'It was struck by lightning,' bleated Booth. 'I was not even there when it happened! I was in Grantham.'

'Grantham?' pounced Chaloner. 'That is where this

letter was posted. So which crime will you admit – arson or mailing the slanderous missive?'

'Neither!' cried Booth, frightened. 'I am a man of God, not a criminal.'

'Oh, you are a criminal,' countered Swaddell softly, 'and the clipped coins in your purse will see you hanged, drawn and quartered. Debasing the King's currency is treason, and I will make sure you face the full extent of the law.'

The blood drained from Booth's face. 'Those coins are not mine! The thief must have robbed someone else before attacking me.'

'So if we search your lodgings, we will no find more of them?' asked Chaloner.

Booth deflated before their eyes. 'Damn that thief! This is his fault, and if I hang, he will dangle next to me.'

'He is beyond any vengeance of yours,' said Swaddell. 'Henrietta Florence saw to that.'

'The horse killed him?' asked Booth, and his expression turned vindictive. 'Good! But I did not clip those coins for my own benefit. I did it for my parishioners.'

'Really,' said Chaloner flatly. 'And why would you break the law for them?'

Booth hung his head. 'Because they blame me for the loss of their church. You see, it was not lightning that caused the fire, but the candle I forgot and left burning in the vestry when I went to Grantham. To pacify them, I agreed to provide a certain sum . . .'

'Which you decided to raise by shaving the silver from the King's shillings,' finished Swaddell in distaste. 'Very noble.'

Booth licked dry lips. 'I will tell you everything about

the letter if you agree to overlook the coins. Then I will disappear and you will never see me again.'

'You will tell us what you know and I will recommend leniency from the judge,' said Swaddell indignantly. 'Which is more than you deserve.'

Booth opened his mouth to argue, but a glance at the assassin's face warned him against it. He sagged in defeat.

'It was Clayton's idea,' he began wretchedly. 'He hates the Duchess, because she has started to check his accounts, which means he can no longer adjust them to his advantage. It has cost him hundreds of pounds a year. It is bad for Liddell, too, as he is obliged to pay full rent on his stud farm, rather than the half that Clayton always charged him.'

'Does her diligence affect you as well?' asked Chaloner.

Booth nodded miserably. 'Clayton sent me a little bonus each quarter for running a school that does not exist, but she put a stop to that, too. Rather than let her impoverish us, we decided to get rid of her.'

'You mean you plotted her death?' Swaddell's voice was cold and angry.

'No, not that!' gulped Booth. 'Clayton said we should get the Duke to divorce her for adultery. He picked Topp as her fictitious lover, because he wants to be sole steward. Two birds with one stone.'

'Fine behaviour for a cleric,' said Swaddell in distaste.

Booth managed to bristle. 'You no doubt think that Topp is charming, with all his "Your Worships" and "Your Honours". But beneath that oily exterior lies a very sly individual.'

Chaloner wanted to tell him that Topp's unctuousness was not charming at all, but the floodgates were open, and Booth could not stop talking – about how Clayton had asked him to pen the letter because he knew how to disguise his handwriting; how he, Clayton and Liddell had pondered long and hard over the wording; and how he had gone to Grantham to post it, because it was a place where no one knew him.

'And now,' said Swaddell, when the vicar eventually faltered into silence, 'you can tell us why Clayton – no doubt with help from you – murdered Chiffinch. Was it because Chiffinch recognised your distinctive *f*s, and guessed who sent this poisonous tirade?'

Booth gaped at him. 'You cannot lay *that* at my door! I am an innocent man!'

'Of course you are,' muttered Chaloner, 'as long as we overlook coin-clipping, libel, forgery and theft.'

When they had finished with Booth, Chaloner marched him to the stables, and shut him in the stall with Henrietta Florence. The vicar scuttled to the furthest corner and cowered, hands over his head as he wailed his terror. The horse was eating and ignored him, although her ears flicked every time Booth released a fresh howl.

'Do not annoy her by making an unseemly racket,' advised Swaddell, 'or we may return to discover you dead of a crushed skull, too.'

Booth went silent at once. Chaloner ordered a groom to stand guard over him, then he and Swaddell went in search of Clayton. The steward was in the tack room with Liddell. The horse-trader guessed at once that something was amiss, and bolted. Chaloner hared after him, chasing him clear across Clerkenwell Green to the Fleet River. He marched him back to Newcastle House, where they arrived to find Clayton slumped in a chair in defeat and Swaddell leaning against a wall, paring his fingernails with one of his sharp little daggers.

'Clayton has something he would like to tell you, Tom,' the assassin said mildly.

Chaloner had no idea what Swaddell had said or done, but the steward immediately gabbled a confession. It was almost identical to Booth's, the only difference being that it was Liddell who had masterminded the plan, while he and Booth were unwilling helpmeets. Naturally, Liddell objected to this version of events.

'Lies!' he cried. 'It is *you* who devised this—'

'The plan was yours,' snarled Clayton. 'Every last detail of it.'

'You are all in it together,' interrupted Chaloner, tired of their treachery. 'And you will all suffer the consequences. So, now we have dealt with the letter, we can discuss murder. First, you poisoned Chiffinch. We know you have access to White Hall, because I met you there myself. Then you dispatched Tooley, Ashley and Mushey—'

'No!' shouted Clayton, thoroughly rattled. 'I had never even heard of Mushey before Mr Swaddell mentioned him to me just now.'

'Moreover, two of the courtiers died on Sunday,' put in Liddell quickly, 'and we have an alibi for then. It was the day of the fox-tossing, and the Duke remained here in protest. He kept us busy all day with his horses. The Viscount was with us, too.'

Chaloner knew the Duke and his son had stayed home all day, because the Duchess had said so. However, no mention had been made of Clayton and Liddell.

'Then you shot at us in Mushey's room,' Swaddell forged on. 'You—'

'How can we have shot at you?' interrupted Clayton,

terrified. 'We have no guns. And if we had, we would not have needed to resort to poison. Your logic is flawed.'

'But you three, alone of everyone at Newcastle House, were not listening to Lucas's lecture when the toxin was added to Chiffinch's oysters,' argued Chaloner, although he was beginning to fear that he might have made a mistake in accepting Eliza's assumption that the authors of the letter and the White Hall killer were one and the same.

'We did manage to avoid his dull monologue,' acknowledged Liddell, 'but we did not use the time to kill a courtier we had never met. We were in our coffee house – ask anyone at Myddleton's. They will remember us there, because we had a fine debate on chocolate.'

'He is right,' said Clayton, and cunning flared in his eyes. 'We have a solid alibi. The Duchess, however, does not – at least, not one that can be proved. Ask *her* these questions.'

Chaloner experienced a bitter sense of defeat as he finally accepted that the unsavoury trio had nothing to do with Chiffinch's murder, and that he and Swaddell had wasted valuable time solving a crime that was irrelevant. Thurloe would be pleased to know the libellers had been caught, but that was the only positive outcome from their efforts that morning.

Swaddell pulled him to one side. 'There are still other Newcastle House connections to unravel,' he murmured. 'Namely, the Duchess. And her brother – perhaps Baron Lucas persuaded some of his Red Bull friends to go to White Hall and kill on his behalf.'

'But how will we prise answers from that pair?' asked Chaloner dejectedly. 'You cannot sit two nobles down and wave sharp knives at their throats. The only way to catch them is with hard evidence, which we do not have.'

'Widdrington,' said Swaddell, unwilling to concede defeat. 'We can ask him—'

'His testimony is irrelevant,' snapped Chaloner. 'We do not need to know if Chiffinch told him who wrote the libellous letter, because we have worked it out for ourselves. We are back right where we started.'

'Not quite,' said Swaddell. 'We have exposed this rabble, and that counts for something.'

'Unfortunately, that pales into insignificance when compared to a poisoner at large and a city that will descend into chaos tomorrow.'

While Swaddell went to report their findings to the Duke, then summon soldiers to march Clayton and his helpmeets to the nearest gaol, Chaloner stood guard over the prisoners. He resented the wasted time, but dared not delegate the duty to anyone else, sure their slippery tongues would see them escape. Booth wept and pleaded, Liddell brayed threats, and Clayton opted for bribery. Chaloner was glad when Swaddell returned and the unpalatable trio were bundled away. He and the assassin were about to leave themselves when Eliza hailed them.

'I am in your debt more deeply than ever,' she said sincerely. 'You have thwarted this horrible plan to hurt my Duchess and Francis. Now everyone will know that they are the victims of a wicked lie.'

'Yes,' acknowledged Swaddell. 'Although our real purpose in coming here today was to catch whoever killed the courtiers.'

'Perhaps *that* is what Chiffinch and Widdrington were discussing when I saw them in White Hall on Thursday,' said Eliza. 'I assumed it was the letter, as the Duke had approached Chiffinch for help that day, but perhaps it was something else . . .'

'Regardless, it is unlikely to have been the murders,' Chaloner pointed out glumly, 'given that none of the four victims were dead when this conversation took place.'

Eliza frowned. 'Yet it was about something important, because they kept looking around to make sure no one else could hear. They did not consider me a threat, because I am effectively a servant. I still think you should speak to Widdrington about it.'

'Perhaps,' said Chaloner, although he was not about to squander more time following irrelevant leads. He changed the subject. 'The pair of handguns we found in the Duchess's boudoir last night – have you ever seen them before?'

Eliza blinked her surprise. 'You cannot have found them there, because she does not allow firearms in the house. You were holding one, so I assumed they were yours.'

'But Topp told me that he picked it up from her table,' said Chaloner. 'And I believe him, because if it had been his, he would have known it was not loaded when he threatened to shoot me with it. Ergo, it belongs to her.'

'It does not,' insisted Eliza. 'I told you: they are banned. The Duke has a palsy, and she is afraid that he might seize one and have an accident. There have been no guns of any description in their houses for years.'

Chaloner was about to retort that the Duchess had been wearing a brace of pistols when he had first met her, when he remembered that they had been wooden replicas. 'Then how did they get into her private quarters?'

Eliza shrugged. 'Planted there by someone who means her harm, I suppose. And you know there are plenty of those, because you have just arrested three of them. Clearly, someone left the things in the hope that they would see her accused of a crime she did not commit.'

'Well, it was not Clayton and his helpmeets,' averred Swaddell. 'They confined their malice to venomous missives.'

'Then the culprit will be someone she invited to her soirée,' persisted Eliza. 'God knows, there were enough rogues among them. Very few were asked to come back tomorrow, meaning that the majority are sinners and debauchees. You are spoiled for choice.'

'Where was the Duchess on Sunday?' Chaloner's fists were clenched in agitation, as he felt a solution slip further away with every word Eliza spoke. 'We know the Duke stayed here with Mansfield, because he disapproved of the fox-tossing . . .'

'We all did. The Duchess and I were here all morning, sometimes with the Duke, sometimes in the garden with the other ladies. We rode to White Hall in the afternoon to visit the Queen. And in the evening, she and I went to church, returning here about eight o'clock, just as the Viscount was leaving. If you want witnesses, I can provide dozens – for both of us, for every moment of the day. But why do you want to know?'

'Just a routine question,' replied Swaddell smoothly, when Chaloner was too disgusted to speak. In an earlier conversation, the Duchess had intimated that a mysterious errand had taken her out in the evening, but now it transpired that she had just gone to her devotions. Why could she not just have said so, instead of playing games to keep them guessing?

'Mother Broughton!' came a wail, and they turned to see Molly the chicken girl running towards them, her face wet with tears. 'She is dead!'

Clerkenwell's soothsayer was indeed dead. She lay on the bank of the River Fleet, not far from her cosy home. Blood seeped from a gash in her throat while her face was caked in mud. There was a strong smell of ale around her, and Chaloner noticed that her hands were clean, but that there was a deep skid-mark in the silt near her feet.

'I suspect she was walking home from a tavern when she slipped and fell,' he said to Swaddell, who was inspecting the neck wound with the disdain of a man who would have done it much more neatly. 'Her throat was cut when she was unconscious or drunk.'

'How do you know?' asked Swaddell curiously.

'Because there is no blood on her hands. She did not try to staunch the flow – which she certainly would have done, had she known what was happening to her.'

'True,' acknowledged Swaddell. 'People always scrabble at their necks when I apply my blade, although they waste their time. I should have deduced this for myself.'

'So that prophecy came true,' mused Chaloner, trying to dispel the image of Swaddell calmly watching his victims bleed to death. 'She predicted that the Fleet would run red with blood today and it has, although I doubt she thought she would be the one supplying it.'

'The *bank* is stained,' corrected Swaddell, 'but I would not say the river ran red, although I imagine her fanatical disciples will argue the point.'

'She also said a "messenger" would die. *She* is the

messenger – a person who informs others about what is going to happen. However, again, I doubt she thought she would be the one to perish. She told me that she expected to be part of the new government.'

'She was not a very good seer,' agreed Swaddell, and smirked, 'although I shall revise my opinion if you ever embark on a career in cheese.'

Chaloner ignored his levity. 'I think we can safely conclude that Mother Broughton was killed by someone who wants folk to think her projections about tomorrow will come true as well. We had the dead walking in Bunhill and Westminster Abbey – they did no such thing, but that is not what folk believe. Now we have the dead messenger and the blood.'

'And tomorrow we shall have a rain of fire, darkness and gnashing of teeth,' mused Swaddell. 'Followed by an Easter Sunday when the Sun will dance for joy. However, if all this does come to pass, it will have nothing to do with God. A human hand will have directed it and we need to make it stop. It is rebellion of the most insidious kind.'

Idly, Chaloner thought of the many other plots he had helped to thwart since entering the Earl's employ. Most were the King's own fault. If he at least tried to be upright, hardworking and just, his subjects would be less inclined to want him replaced.

'It is Holy Week,' he said, 'a time of sobriety and reflection. But the Court has organised fox-tossing, goose-pulling and dog-racing. Such secularism makes people uneasy. Good Friday falls on the thirteenth day of the month in the year with three sixes. It is superstitious claptrap, but folk are worried by it. The Court should not poke a hornets' nest.'

'Well, it has,' said Swaddell, 'and we must deal with the consequences.'

'No, our remit is to catch Chiffinch's killer,' said Chaloner. 'So I suggest we go to White Hall as we agreed and—'

'Forget Chiffinch,' interrupted Swaddell. 'Preventing a coup is far more important. We *must* prevent these insurgents from harming our city. If we allow them to succeed, it will not matter whether we have caught the killer or not.'

'But we do not know where to begin,' objected Chaloner. His head ached from tension, and he could not recall when he had last enjoyed a full night's sleep.

'By investigating *her* death,' replied Swaddell, nodding down at Mother Broughton. 'Someone will have seen something, because there are dozens of houses overlooking this part of the river. We shall question the residents of every one, and if that yields no results, we shall trawl the taverns. And pray we learn something, because otherwise . . .'

But it was hopeless. Not only were the people who lived in the hovels along the Flect unwilling to talk to strangers, particularly ones from the government, but enquiries at the Red Bull told them that Mother Broughton had left in the small hours of the morning when it had been pitch dark. Ergo, it would have taken a miracle for anyone to have seen more than shadows anyway. Even so, Chaloner and Swaddell persisted until they were bone-weary and their voices were hoarse from asking questions.

'I just heard the nightwatchman call three o'clock,' said Swaddell eventually. 'It is Good Friday, Tom.'

Chaloner rubbed his eyes, which were sore and gritty

from being in so many smoky taverns. 'And we have learned nothing to help us stop whatever is going to happen.'

'I have never felt so helpless in my life,' sighed Swaddell. 'It is like trying to stem the flow of the Fleet. *Think*, Tom! There must be something we can do to prevent our city from erupting into flames around us.'

But Chaloner's mind was blank.

Chapter 16

Neither Chaloner nor Swaddell felt like going home when the Clerkenwell crisis loomed so close, so they went to the Red Bull, where they bought bread, cold meat and breakfast ale. Chaloner's stomach churned, and he kept coming back to the conviction that there *was* something they could do to prevent trouble – he just had to work out what it was. Unfortunately, he was too tired to think clearly, and he wondered if he and Swaddell should have opted for a good night's sleep, rather than wear themselves out with futile enquiries.

He dashed off a note to his cousins, ordering them to stay inside with Wiseman until further notice, politely declining Swaddell's offer to deliver it for him. Instead, he paid John Milton to do it – the blind Puritan poet was desperate for money, and could be trusted to place the letter in their hands. He felt better when it was done, knowing that at least they would be safe from whatever happened that day.

'I promised Ursula my protection,' said Swaddell worriedly. 'I should go to Covent Garden and sit with her, or she will see me as a man whose word cannot be trusted.'

'Your duty lies here,' said Chaloner tiredly, not about to stand by while the assassin foisted himself on his cousins all day. 'She will understand.'

'I did not expect to find you here,' came a voice from behind him. Chaloner leapt up with his hand on his sword, but Widdrington laughed derisively. 'If I had meant you harm, Earl's man, you would be dead already. I could have run you through where you sat.'

'No, you could not,' countered Swaddell in his most dangerous hiss.

'Oh,' gulped Widdrington, unsettled. 'I did not see you in the shadows, Swaddell.'

'Why are you here?' asked Chaloner, aware that he needed to be more careful if he wanted to see the Sun dance on Sunday.

'Pamphlin told me to come,' replied Widdrington, sitting uninvited at their table. 'Before he died, of course. I do not commune with corpses.'

'Pamphlin is dead?' blurted Chaloner, shocked. 'When?'

'Probably on Tuesday,' replied Widdrington, and smirked. 'The day you raced off to Woolwich in the hope of interrogating him, although the truth is that he never left London. He hid in my attic, and might still be alive if he had done what I advised and stayed put.'

'So why didn't he?' asked Swaddell shortly, irked by the gloating.

'Because Bess found out he was there, and he was afraid she would give him away. She is not very good with secrets. He decided to move in with Rolt instead, but he never got there and died on Piccadilly. Near Clarendon House, in fact.'

'Died of what?' asked Chaloner, hating to imagine

what his employer's enemies would make of that unfortunate happenstance.

'Poison, like the others, according to Wiseman. He had a wine-flask with him, and the toxin must have been in that. My guess is that he took a gulp from it, to give him the courage to pass Clarendon House, and that was the end of him.'

'If he was hiding in your attic, then the likelihood is that his wine-flask was filled before he left,' said Swaddell coldly. 'Which means you or Bess killed him.'

Widdrington shrugged. 'We both assumed he was with Rolt until news came last night that his body had been found in a ditch. Naturally, we were horrified to hear it. However, before he left my house, he told me to come here on Good Friday morning. So here I am.'

'If you aim to add to the mayhem,' said Swaddell coldly, 'you will be stopped.'

'Oh, use your wits, man,' snapped Widdrington irritably. 'Do I look like a rabble-rouser to you? I am here to *prevent* trouble – in my capacity as a member of the Artillery Company. My soldiers are outside, ready to swing into action and keep the King's peace.'

Chaloner regarded him incredulously. 'And Pamphlin suggested you do this?'

'Not quite. I told him my plan to mobilise the men today, ready to defend the King from any bother, and *he* said that if there is trouble, it will start in this tavern. He thought it would be the best place to nip anything untoward in the bud.'

'And how would he know?' demanded Swaddell, eyes narrowed.

'Because we decided to monitor it after we failed to get it shut down last Sunday, which we would have succeeded in doing if Baron Lucas had not interfered. Pamphlin took spying duty on Monday night, and heard something that terrified him. Indeed, it was what drove him to take refuge in my attic.'

'What did he hear?' asked Chaloner sceptically.

'That the rain of fire predicted for today is not figurative but literal. In other words, someone aims to bombard the city with fireballs.'

Chaloner gestured around him. 'I see no fireballs. I cannot smell them either, and I would if they were here, because gunpowder reeks.'

Widdrington settled himself more comfortably. 'Then perhaps whoever aims to lob them will bring them here later. If they do, I shall be waiting.'

'But Cockpit Club members are not welcome here,' said Chaloner, and nodded to where the other patrons were glaring in their direction. 'Ergo, Pamphlin cannot have heard anything terrifying here on Monday, because he would not have been allowed inside. Just as Tooley was not, no matter what Bess later claimed.'

'He donned a disguise – we all did when it was our turn to spy. And do not regard *me* in distaste, Chaloner. We did what was right. You may be willing to look the other way while whores are taught to read seditious broadsheets, but we are not. The very idea is anathema.'

'You sound like your wife,' said Swaddell coolly, and Chaloner saw he was not the only one whose dislike of the courtier had intensified during the discussion.

'Bess will not be in a position to bray her opinions soon,' said Widdrington with enormous satisfaction. 'She sails for Ireland in two days, and while the Sun may not dance for joy at her departure, I certainly shall. I am tired of her cloying, clinging presence.'

'You will break her heart,' said Chaloner reproachfully.

'So what? I do not love her and I never will.'

It was no time to discuss Widdrington's marital problems, so Chaloner returned to the matter of the Red Bull. 'Who started the tale that Tooley died of a fever that he caught here?'

'I did, but I believed it was true until Wiseman said otherwise. We were all afraid of catching the plague, especially the time when we tried to get this place shut down by starting a fracas. Why do you think we wore masks?'

'Is that why Baron Lucas was able to order you away so easily?' asked Chaloner. 'Because you were all frightened of catching a fatal fever? None of you really wanted to be here, so when he told you to go . . .'

'We were only too glad to take our leave,' finished Widdrington sheepishly. 'Yes, it was cowardly, but only a fool does not fear the plague.' He forced a smile. 'But Wiseman assures me that Clerkenwell has seen no new cases in months, so I am terrified no longer. And you need not worry about any other trouble erupting here today, because I will prevent it.'

'Will you indeed?' said Chaloner sceptically. 'And why should we believe you?'

The smug arrogance left Widdrington's face. 'You may not think much of me, but I am a patriot. I *will* protect London from whatever is brewing around here.'

'Very honourable,' sneered Swaddell. 'So where are your Cockpit Club friends? Are they ready to defend the King's peace, too?'

Widdrington looked away uncomfortably. 'The only one brave enough to rally to my call is Cobbe. He is outside with the troops. The remainder prefer to see the blood of animals spilled than risk their own. Are you still interested in catching the White Hall killer, by the way?'

'Why?' asked Chaloner suspiciously. 'Do you know who it is?'

'I might,' replied Widdrington smoothly. 'I certainly have a theory to share with you.'

'Does this theory stem from whatever Chiffinch whispered to you on Thursday?' Chaloner shrugged at Widdrington's bemused frown. 'Eliza Topp saw the two of you together.'

Widdrington waved an impatient hand. 'Yes, Chiffinch did accost me, but only to relate some infantile gossip about the Duchess of Newcastle sleeping with her steward. No, my thesis concerns Dr Clarke, who comes here a lot. I assumed it was to ogle the women, but then Pamphlin told me something interesting . . .'

'Yes?' asked Chaloner warily, wondering if Widdrington's sudden burst of helpfulness was intended to keep him and Swaddell occupied while the rest of the Cockpit Club ignited the very trouble he claimed he was there to prevent.

'He saw Clarke buy a phial of poison from another Red Bull customer – a substance that the seller assured him would kill quickly and cleanly.'

Chaloner did not believe him. 'Clarke is a physician with powerful potions of his own. He has no need to buy more in taverns. And who sold it to him anyway?'

Widdrington shrugged. 'These are questions to ask Clarke, not me. There is something else, too: you may recall that Chiffinch was in the Shield Gallery the night he died, after which he went to his apartments. He remained there from four o'clock until shortly before six

'– I saw him emerge myself, and a few of us walked across the Great Court with him.'

'What of it?'

'Cobbe has discovered that Chiffinch was not alone during those two hours – *Clarke* was with him. Now, should you decide to act on my information, you can start in Newcastle House. I saw Clarke go in there not half an hour ago.'

It was still dark outside, although dawn was not far off, and there was enough light for Chaloner and Swaddell to see where they were going. Shadows showed where Cobbe sat with Widdrington's soldiers, waiting for orders, while in the street there was an air of anticipation as folk whispered about what would happen that day. Chaloner wondered how many of them would be alive at the end of it, or if their families would be wailing over their broken bodies.

Cobbe came to exchange polite greetings as they passed, so despite the urgency of the situation, Chaloner took the opportunity to ask something that had been niggling at him ever since he had learned that Cobbe and Will had alibis in each other for Chiffinch's murder.

'I know you and Will were together in Chelsea last week,' he began. 'But he returned to the city on Thursday evening, whereas you did not arrive back until Friday morning. Why did you not travel together?'

Cobbe winced. 'You may have noticed that Will is not the most considerate of men. He rattled off in his private carriage without a backward glance, leaving me to make my own way home. It was nothing malicious – it just never occurred to him that not everyone keeps his own coach and four. And the next public coach was not until the following day.'

'You told Widdrington that Clarke followed Chiffinch into his apartments on the morning Chiffinch died,' said Chaloner. 'Is it true?'

Cobbe nodded. 'I had the tale from three different witnesses. Why? Do you think he—'

'Tom,' growled Swaddell impatiently. 'We do not have time for this. Come.'

He was right – they would have to speak to Cobbe properly later, should they still be alive. Chaloner hurried after Swaddell without another word, aware of bells tolling in the distance to mark this most sombre day of the Christian calendar. All over the city the faithful entered their parish churches to find the altars stripped, and all statues, paintings and symbols draped in purple cloth. It gave the impression that God had moved out.

'Do you believe Widdrington?' Swaddell asked, as he and Chaloner approached Newcastle House. 'I do – about Clarke, at least. We neglected our incompetent physician as we pursued more promising candidates, but I have a feeling that was a serious mistake.'

Chaloner agreed. 'If anyone knows about poisons, it is a *medicus*. But are you sure you want to challenge him now? You said earlier that we should forget about the killer and concentrate on preventing the crisis.'

'How can we, when we do not know what form it will take?' asked Swaddell bitterly. 'At least by cornering Clarke I shall feel as though we are doing something useful. However, while I *believe* Widdrington, I do not trust him. I doubt he is here for honourable purposes.'

'No,' agreed Chaloner. 'So I will tackle Clarke while you organise some troops of your own. We might need them later.'

Swaddell shot him a pitying glance. 'I did that hours

ago. They are in Bishop Morley's garden, ready to spring into action the moment I send for them. I wanted to impose a curfew on Clerkenwell today, but he said that would ignite a riot for certain.'

With despair, Chaloner saw they were damned whatever they did. The sight of armed men on the streets probably would provoke an angry reaction, but to leave the area unsupervised was an invitation for anyone to do as he pleased.

Chaloner was about to knock on Newcastle House's door, when he saw someone sneaking out through the stable gate, hooded and with a heavy sack over his shoulder. He ran forward and grabbed the culprit by the scruff of his neck. His captive shrieked his outrage, then began to kick and struggle.

'Let me go, you filthy commoner! How dare you lay hands on me!'

Recognising the voice, Chaloner released him. 'Viscount Mansfield. Forgive me. I thought you were a burglar.'

Mansfield clutched the sack to his chest, where a tell-tale clank revealed it was full of silver plate. 'This is mine,' he declared defiantly. 'I am not a thief.'

'Of course not,' said Chaloner, wondering how a bold and charismatic warrior like the Duke had sired such a miserable specimen. 'What are you doing out at such an hour?'

'Leaving,' replied Mansfield, brushing himself down in a feeble attempt to restore his dignity. 'I have a coach waiting in Aldgate, and I shall only return to the city when peace reigns again. My father is quite capable of defending Newcastle House, so my military skills are surplus to requirements.'

'I am sure they are,' said Chaloner ambiguously. 'Have you seen Clarke?'

'Clarke?' squeaked Mansfield, alarmed again. 'Why? He knows nothing that will interest you. Leave him alone. I *order* you to stay away from him on pain of death!'

Chaloner and Swaddell exchanged bemused glances.

'Everything I told him is private,' Mansfield gabbled on. 'You *cannot* ask him about it. But how did you guess?' His eyes narrowed. 'I know! It was *her.*'

'Who?' asked Chaloner warily.

'Sarah Shawe! She promised to keep her mouth shut if the Duchess continues to fund her seditious little school, but she is friends with Eliza, who hates me because she thinks I was behind that anonymous letter. *Sarah* told you my secret!'

'Yes, she did,' lied Chaloner, to see what would emerge. 'So now you are exposed.'

'I made *one* pass at her,' cried Mansfield in agitation. 'I thought she would welcome a fine man like me taking an interest, but she was livid and has never let me forget it.' He looked away. 'She keeps threatening to tell my wife unless I do what she says.'

So that was how Sarah kept him in line, mused Chaloner, recalling that she had forced him to retract his accusation about the Red Bull's pupils being prostitutes, thus ensuring that the Duchess continued to provide them with money and books.

'Do not look at *me* reprovingly,' the Viscount snapped sullenly. 'It was a moment of weakness, and I am a red-blooded man. However, I am sure we can reach an accommodation. If you keep my secret, I will tell you another in return.'

'What secret?' asked Swaddell cautiously.

'It is about Sarah. She does not buy pens and paper with the money that my stepmother gives her, but straw and crates. I saw her doing it with my own eyes.'

'Why would she want those?' asked Chaloner, nonplussed.

'Ask her,' suggested Mansfield, 'although expect untruths in return. And while we are on the subject of untruths, if Clayton tells you that it was my idea to send that letter about my stepmother's infidelity, you should not believe him. He will say anything to save himself.'

'He is not the only one,' muttered Chaloner, watching the Viscount scuttle away.

Despite the early hour, Newcastle House was busy as servants prepared to receive those people the Duchess had deemed worthy of her company on the day that the world would change. The lady herself was still abed, but everyone else was in a whirlwind of activity. Chaloner noted that although the staff were expected to remain, the Duke was arranging for his horses to be sent somewhere safe. He declined to speak to Chaloner and Swaddell on the grounds of being too busy, but Baron Lucas strode over to greet them.

'My sister is in your debt,' he said quietly. 'It beggars belief that Clayton – a man we treated and loved like family – would betray her in so sordid a manner. But you have restored her good name.'

'Yes,' said Chaloner impatiently. 'But we need to—'

'Courtiers are falling over themselves to make amends for gossiping about that letter,' Lucas went on, 'and she is inundated with requests to join her here today. Unfortunately, some are from folk she cannot refuse, such as the Duke of York and half the Privy

Council, although no one could possibly rate them as godly individuals.'

'No,' agreed Swaddell. 'But never mind that. We want—'

'I told her to let them all in.' Lucas waved an expansive arm. 'The servants worked hard to get this place shipshape, so we may as well put it to good use.'

'Is Clarke here?' demanded Chaloner, speaking quickly to make himself heard.

'Yes, he came to tend my nephew.' Lucas sneered. 'The boy was in a dreadful state after Clayton's arrest, and needed medicine to calm his nerves. He is afraid we will think the letter was his idea, although he would be wrong. He has neither the wits nor the courage.'

Chaloner was not so sure about that. 'Clarke,' he prompted urgently.

'Still with Mansfield,' replied Lucas. 'Why? Do you suspect him of something remiss? Hah! I knew it. There had to be some reason why that charlatan has been here all hours of the day and night. Come, I shall take you to them.'

He ran up the stairs so fast that Chaloner and Swaddell had no time to say that Mansfield had already left, which meant that the physician could not be with him. They hesitated, so he bawled at them to follow. When they caught up with him, he was hammering on the door to a first-floor bedchamber.

'The brat has locked himself in,' he growled, grabbing the handle and giving it a vigorous shake. 'Do you have a gun? If so, blast the thing open. We do not lock doors in Newcastle House – it smacks of unsavoury doings.'

Unwilling to wait while Lucas sent a servant out to

400

find one, Chaloner quickly picked the lock, although he hated wasting his time when he knew Clarke was not going to be in there. The moment it was done, Lucas stormed inside – and stopped in astonishment.

The room had been stripped completely bare. Marks on the walls showed where paintings had hung, and every stick of furniture was gone. The window was wide open, and scratches on the sill revealed exactly how everything had been removed with no one noticing.

'Lowered on to a cart below and driven away,' said Swaddell unnecessarily.

'The cowardly dog!' bellowed Lucas furiously. 'He thinks the house will be set alight by rioters, but rather than risk himself by fighting at his father's side, he has fled with everything he could lay his hands on.'

'Not quite everything,' said Chaloner, hearing a sound from inside the closet, and so striding towards it and hauling open the door so quickly that Clarke tumbled out on to the floor. 'He left his accomplice behind.'

'Accomplice?' gulped Clarke, scrambling quickly to his feet. 'I am merely helping a patient in acute mental distress. Mansfield is extremely agitated, so I have been humouring him in an effort to calm him down.'

'And does "humouring him" entail stealing the Duke's property?' demanded Lucas.

'Not steal – protect,' corrected Clarke firmly. 'I am sure he will share it with his father if this place goes up in flames.'

'Do you have any particular reason to think it will?' asked Chaloner anxiously.

'Just the seers' claims, although I hope they are wrong. But to return to Mansfield, I dropped the last bag of silver plate out of the window, and he promised to return and unlock the door once it was safely stowed on his wagon. He will verify my tale when he arrives.'

'He has no intention of coming back,' said Swaddell. 'He left you shut in here so it will appear as if you are the thief. I imagine he will deny any involvement when he is questioned.'

Clarke gaped at him. 'But why would he do such a thing? I have answered his every summons for days, no matter what the hour or inconvenience to myself.'

'Which explains the comings and goings you noticed,' said Chaloner to Lucas, feeling his agitation rise as it became obvious that the physician did not possess the raw cunning to be the White Hall killer, and they should be looking elsewhere. Swaddell was unwilling to give up on Clarke as their culprit, though.

'You have a lot of explaining to do,' he said with soft menace. 'You were alone with Chiffinch in his quarters just before he died, and you bought poison in the Red Bull.'

Clarke's jaw tightened. 'I did not *buy* poison – it was given to me in lieu of payment by a patient. I aim to use it on those wretched cockerels. They let Fanny into the orangery, but whenever I try to follow, they fly at me.'

'You would kill her pet birds?' asked Chaloner, regarding the physician in distaste.

'I have a right to go where I choose in my own home,' flashed Clarke defensively.

'Never mind this,' snapped Swaddell. 'Tell us why you killed Chiffinch.'

Clarke's eyes went wide with alarm. 'I did nothing of the kind! I admit I followed him to his rooms on that fatal morning, but it was to beg a reprieve on the money

I owed him after the backgammon. I offered him free medical treatment instead, but he declined, so I left. He should have accepted – I might have been able to save his life.'

'I doubt it,' said Lucas, eyeing him with disdain. 'You could not save Tooley when I found him sick and reeling in White Hall on Sunday evening. I helped him home and sent for you, but your advice was to let him sleep it off.'

'Wait a moment,' said Chaloner. 'You two were with Tooley when he died?'

Lucas continued to glare at Clarke. 'No, we left before he breathed his last. I suspected something was seriously amiss, but this charlatan said he was just drunk. To my shame, I chose to accept his opinion, because I was eager to join the clever ladies at the Red Bull. It cost Tooley his life.'

'How was I supposed to know he had been poisoned?' demanded Clarke. 'He reeked of wine, his eyes were glazed, and he could not form a coherent sentence. He *was* drunk!'

'I think we can discount this bumbling ass as our sly killer,' murmured Swaddell, and Chaloner saw the defeat in his eyes. 'I have no more suspects left.'

'You want to arrest a killer?' asked Clarke, straining to hear what was being said. 'Then go and talk to Sarah Shawe. I have never liked her, and my wife fears for the safety of Clerkenwell as long as she is in it. She is a menace.'

'And now you shift the blame on to an innocent woman,' sneered Lucas in distaste. 'What kind of man are you?'

'One who aims to be alive on Easter Day,' retorted

Clarke. 'Which means I shall leave the city today. I am sure the King will welcome me in Dover.'

'You will stay here,' countered Lucas dangerously. 'You and those of your ilk claim to be the superior sex, so prove it. Go home and do your duty as a man by defending Fanny from whatever happens today.'

'Goodness!' gulped Clarke, daunted.

Chaloner and Swaddell hurried out of Newcastle House. It was now fully light, and the air of excited anticipation was a palpable thing, visible in the people who strode past with a spring in their step, and in the hordes who flocked to the church next door, hoping that a spell on their knees might make the difference between annihilation and survival.

'Perhaps we should join them,' said Swaddell, hoarse from fatigue. 'Because I cannot think of anything else to do.'

'We should go to see Sarah Shawe.'

Swaddell blinked. 'Surely you do not intend to act on Clarke's testimony? He spoke out of malice – he has no evidence against her.'

'Perhaps,' said Chaloner. 'But there are three other reasons why we should speak to her. First, because she has a large collection of glass bottles in her house. Second, because Mansfield told us that she has been buying crates and straw. And third, because she is one of Mother Broughton's strongest advocates.'

'You are speaking in riddles, and I am too weary to decipher them.'

'She has ensured – through Mother Broughton – that everyone knows there will be a rain of fire today, and what Pamphlin overheard in the Red Bull suggests that it will be a real one. I have a bad feeling that she is the person who intends to provide it.'

'What?' Swaddell was incredulous. 'How in God's name have you deduced that?'

Chaloner struggled to rally his tumbling thoughts. 'Crates and straw are used to transport fragile or dangerous items. And her friend Joan Cole said all those glass jars were for pickling cockles. But who bottles shellfish?'

'I still do not understand.'

'Sarah has made fireballs with them. And I know exactly how she learned to do it.'

'You do?' Swaddell sounded too tired to care, but Chaloner was suddenly imbued with energy as answers came at last.

'I overheard her and Lucas in the Red Bull on Sunday, discussing some aspect of combustion. I assumed it was just an academic debate, but she was actually pumping him for information, although I doubt he was aware of it. He was just delighted to converse with someone intelligent.'

'So you think she has made some bombs?' asked Swaddell warily. 'And will rain them down on those she deems to be unworthy, so that she can establish a new world order? It all sounds very unlikely, Tom.'

'Then we will look inside her house. If the bottles are full of cockles, we will know her intentions are innocent. But if they are gone or contain something else . . .'

They hurried to Sarah's unkempt little home, aware of the tension that permeated the alleys through which they ran. They knocked on the front door. There was no reply, so they trotted to the back one, only to find it was bolted from the inside. Chaloner kicked it down.

'She is not coming back,' said Swaddell unnecessarily, looking around and noting the absence of anything portable.

'Lest her plan fails and she is forced to flee,' agreed Chaloner. 'The bottles are gone, too.'

'And not a cockle in sight. However, I recognise that stench.'

'The last time I was here, this place absolutely reeked of rancid fat,' said Chaloner, 'but now the scent is different . . . sharper and stronger.'

'It is saltpetre,' provided Swaddell, and pointed to an open trapdoor leading to a cellar. 'It was probably stored down there, and your rancid fat was used to disguise the smell of it.'

Chaloner groaned. 'Of course! The Earl told me days ago that a quantity of saltpetre was stolen when *Royal Oak* was moored at Tower Wharf. It is why he wants me to sail with the Fleet on Sunday – to find out what happened to it.'

'Saltpetre is one of the ingredients in gunpowder,' said Swaddell soberly.

'Yes! The one that is most difficult to obtain, especially during a war, when the military needs every grain it can lay its hands on. She will also need brimstone and charcoal, but they are more readily available. I am right: she *has* devised some kind of fireball.'

'So Mother Broughton's prophecy will come true after all,' said Swaddell in despair. 'Because Sarah will see to it.'

'I think I can guess where she will start,' said Chaloner. 'The Duchess invited "godly" people to witness the Good Friday catastrophe with her, but a number of high-ranking courtiers and members of the Privy Council have decided to come, too.'

Swaddell's eyes were huge in his exhausted face. 'Well, blowing up the King's closest advisors will certainly usher in a new world order. We had better stop her before she ignites another civil war.'

Stomach churning as he considered the enormity of what Sarah was planning, Chaloner raced back to Newcastle House, Swaddell panting at his heels. They reached it to find guests arriving in droves, although it transpired that the Duchess was still in bed, while the Duke had elected to accompany his horses to the country. With Mansfield also gone, the only noble available to greet them all was Lucas, but he was more interested in conversing with the erudite Bishop of Oxford. The result was pandemonium, as the visitors – invited and otherwise – took the liberty of wandering wherever they pleased.

'Half the government and most of White Hall have turned up,' breathed Swaddell in horror. 'We must warn them to get out. Now!'

'Tell Lucas to do it,' said Chaloner, knowing that no one would obey orders from the Spymaster's assassin and a retainer of the hated Clarendon. 'I will start looking for Sarah. The servants will help.'

But the servants remembered Dutch Jane being dismissed for disobeying the Duchess's orders, and none were willing to risk the same fate by abandoning their assigned duties that day. His frantic pleas fell on deaf ears, and he saw he was on his own.

Reasoning that Sarah could not launch her attack from the public rooms – she would be seen and stopped – he aimed for the cellars. There were a lot of them, all so full that they were a nightmare to search. Sweat trickled down his back as he scrambled over piles of old wood, broken furniture and disused tools. Above his head, he heard the tap of footsteps on wooden floorboards, telling him that Lucas had not yet started the evacuation.

The cellars were clear, so Chaloner aimed for the kitchens. These were frantic with activity, as the cook and his assistants prepared to feed far more people than they had been told to expect. Chaloner hurried on, aiming for the bedrooms on the first floor.

'What are you doing here?' demanded Eliza indignantly, when Chaloner had finished his search on the Duke's side of the house and was about to begin on the Duchess's. 'My Lady is asleep.'

'Then wake her,' ordered Chaloner. 'And tell her to make everyone leave. The rain of fire will start here – missiles that will ignite an inferno that may spread far beyond Clerkenwell.'

'I hope so,' said Eliza, and he saw she held a handgun, cocked and ready to shoot. 'It is what we have been working towards all these weeks.'

Chapter 17

With a sick sense of defeat, Chaloner realised he should have guessed that Sarah's lover would be involved in the plot. Now it was too late. The gun in Eliza's hand was steady, and there was an air of quiet determination about her. She indicated that he was to disarm.

'You cannot allow this to happen,' he said, feeling every bone in his body burn with fatigue as he unbuckled his sword and dropped three knives next to it. He kept a blade in his sleeve, sure she would never guess it was there, although he would only be able to use it on her if she came within range. 'Innocents may die.'

'Innocents *will* die,' she acknowledged. 'But so will the guilty, and new life will rise from the ashes of the old. We shall unleash our rain of fire on all those who have swarmed here, after which it will sweep through Clerkenwell and then cleanse the rest of the city.'

Chaloner was appalled. 'You will kill the Duke and Duchess? I thought you loved them.'

'I do. That is why he is heading to Hampstead with his horses, while she is racing north in the mistaken belief that the plague is back. I would never put them in harm's way.'

'But that is *exactly* what you are doing,' argued Chaloner. 'If they survive and others perish, they will be accused of organising a massacre – the one that started in *their* home. You must stop this madness before it is too late.'

'It will not matter who accuses who after today, because we shall have a fresh start, with leaders who are just and honest, not vicious hedonists who squander our taxes on themselves.'

'The government *is* flawed,' acknowledged Chaloner desperately. 'But you cannot—'

'I do not have time to debate this with you,' interrupted Eliza. 'Now, you have two choices. I can shoot you here – no one will hear, given the racket they are making downstairs – or you can come up to the roof and sit quietly while we work. Well? Which will it be?'

He was tempted to call her bluff and tell her to shoot him, but had a bad feeling that she might actually do it. Slowly, he turned to the stairs, every fibre in his body tensed to whip around and grab the gun. Unfortunately, she read his mind and stayed out of reach. He had the uneasy sense that she, unlike her husband, was both familiar and comfortable with firearms.

He climbed slowly, playing for time as he wracked his brains for a way out of his predicament, but by the time he reached the top, his mind was still a blank. He opened the door and stepped out on to the paved part of the roof. The glass ceiling with its supporting iron brace lay before him. Rain had pooled on the panes, deeper on the ones that still sagged in their lead frames, and a flock of gulls bobbed about in places, but the roof was otherwise deserted.

He turned to reason with her again, but the birds took off en masse, forcing him to duck. While he staggered, off balance, Eliza slammed the door behind him, trapping him on the roof. He whipped around, but too late. He heard her drop a bar into place on the other side and then her footsteps hammering back down the stairs. Then he saw he was not alone: Swaddell lay in a crumpled black heap nearby, eyes closed.

For a moment, Chaloner was too shocked to move. Then he forced himself into action. He ran to Swaddell and shook his shoulder, relieved when the assassin's eyes flickered open. He helped him to sit up.

'It was Eliza,' whispered Swaddell, raising a tentative hand to a lump on his head. 'I ran into her while I was hunting for Lucas. She said people were more likely to heed an order from the Duchess, who was taking the air on the roof. Like a fool, I followed her up here . . .'

Chaloner had been just as trusting, and was appalled that their gullibility would see the start of a crisis from which the city – even the country – might never recover. He crossed the paved part of the roof, and leaned forward to peer through the glass. The pooled water on the outside – and chicken manure from Lucas's experiment on the inside – distorted his view, but he could still see that the hall and the ballroom were full of people. Indeed, the entire house was packed, and he hated to imagine what carnage would ensue when Sarah swung into action.

'We will smash a hole in the ceiling,' he determined. 'Then we can yell down a warning.'

'The glass is strengthened,' said Swaddell. 'Remember? Clayton told us.'

Chaloner thought fast. 'Then we will kick one of the panes out. A number of their frames are already buckled, which is why the Duchess installed that massive brace.'

He stepped on one and began to stamp on it. But the pooled water was knee deep, which made it difficult to put any power behind the blows. All he did was get himself wet.

'They are stronger than they look,' he said in agitation after trying several different places with no success. 'And the guests are making too much noise to hear me thumping. I think a couple looked up, but I doubt they saw me through the chicken muck.'

He hurried to the knee-high balustrade on his left, which overlooked the street, and yelled at the top of his voice at the people down there, but there was too much noise from the arriving carriages and general traffic, so no one looked up. Then he darted to the opposite wall and peered down into the back garden, but it was deserted due to the inclement weather.

Not yet ready to give up, he waded across to the central brace and studied it carefully. It comprised a towering wall of iron plates, and would be impossible to climb, because there were no hand- or footholds. It was anchored to the roof with cement buttresses, but these jutted out too far for squeezing around to reach the other side. Clayton had been right when he had claimed that the Duchess's brace cut one side of the roof off from the other.

'Hey!' bellowed Swaddell, who had followed him and was peering through a tiny slit between two of the metal plates. 'Stop what you are doing immediately!'

Chaloner joined him, and saw that the far side of the roof was a hive of activity. Sarah was there with four women and three men from the Red Bull, along with Eliza, who had gone down the stairs on the Duchess's half of the house, and up the ones of the Duke's to reach them. Their section was stacked with crates. One was open, revealing bottles nestled among a packing of straw. These had oil-soaked rags protruding from their necks, ready to be set alight and thrown. Sarah did indeed aim to rain fire down on the heads of those below.

'Do you hear me?' shouted Swaddell furiously. 'Stop that at once!'

Sarah glanced in his direction before giving a small, smug smile and turning away. Chaloner clenched his fists in impotent frustration. He and Swaddell could holler all they liked, but there was nothing they could do to prevent what was about to happen.

'Do you have a gun?' he asked tersely. 'If we shoot Sarah, the rest might give up. Or better yet, a bullet will shatter one of these panes, and we can warn everyone to get out.'

'I rarely carry firearms – they are too noisy for my requirements.' Swaddell patted himself down. 'And Eliza must have relieved me of my knives when she stunned me.'

Chaloner produced the blade from his sleeve. 'I managed to keep one, but it is useless. We could have aimed a gun through that gap, but tossing a knife through it is impossible.'

Swaddell's eyes were suddenly agleam as he snatched the weapon. 'Not *through* it, Tom – over it. It will be throwing blind, but I spend hours practising this sort of manoeuvre.'

Chaloner regarded him warily. 'You do?'

Swaddell shrugged. 'A single man with few friends

must find something to while away his free evenings. Pray God it works, because it is the only chance we will get.'

He took a deep breath, and his face went blank as he calculated distances and angles in his mind. Then he stepped back and the knife flew, arcing over the brace towards the rebels on the other side. His aim was true, but one of the men moved suddenly, so the blade that should have hit Sarah thudded into him instead. The fellow staggered and fell. There was immediate consternation among his cronies, all of whom dived behind the crates.

'I *told* you to kill them,' yelled Sarah at Eliza. 'But oh, no, you knew best! And now it transpires that you did not even bother to disarm them properly!'

'They gave Francis a chance, so it is only right that I return the favour,' Eliza snapped back. 'But do not worry. I might have missed one knife, but they will have no more.'

Chaloner did not hear Sarah's reply, but Eliza was the only one who did not crouch behind the boxes for protection as they continued to unpack their deadly creations.

'Now what?' he muttered, heart pounding. 'Do we wait here uselessly while they prepare to murder everyone?'

'I am afraid so,' replied Swaddell tersely. 'Unless you have another plan?'

It was agony for Chaloner to feel so helpless. He returned to the paved area near the stairs – the only part of the roof that was above water – and paced restlessly, stopping every so often to kick the glass, batter at the door, or yell in the hope that someone would look up. No one did. Worse, it was bitterly cold so high up, and he and

Swaddell were wet. Meanwhile, Swaddell bombarded the rebels with reasons to stop before it was too late. All ignored him.

'Why the delay?' the assassin muttered. 'Why not just start and get it over with?'

'I suspect they are waiting for three o'clock,' predicted Chaloner. 'The time of Jesus's death on the cross – a symbolic moment for putting their nasty scheme into action.'

'But that is hours away!' gulped Swaddell. 'We will freeze to death before then.'

Chaloner waded over to the brace again. The rebels had not listened to Swaddell, so he had no real hope that he could do better, but he had to do something.

'Eliza, please!' he called. 'Think of the servants. Will you kill them, too?'

'The decent ones are under orders to leave the house at a quarter to three,' replied Eliza, all brisk efficiency. 'They will come to no harm. As for the rest . . . well, who cares?'

'But you cannot murder *all* the Duchess's guests,' he cried. 'The Bishop of Winchester is among them, and he is a good man.'

'That is regrettable,' said Sarah, although she did not sound sorry at all. 'But you cannot bake a cake without breaking eggs.'

'You will fail,' shouted Swaddell. 'The ceiling is strong and will protect everyone from your fireballs. It—'

'We loosened a few of the panes weeks ago,' interrupted Eliza. 'Which is why the ceiling began to leak, of course. All we need to do today is pull them out and we shall be ready.'

'The house will be alight in no time,' put in Sarah

gloatingly. 'It is full of new, oily wood from its recent refurbishment. And when a building this size burns, it will ignite its neighbours.'

'But why?' asked Chaloner, shocked by her venom. 'Surely you cannot hate everyone who lives around the green?'

'We are tired of the way things are, and it is time for change,' explained Sarah shortly. 'You cannot stop us. You heard Mother Broughton's prophecies – all have come true so far.'

'Only because you made them. You knew Dutch spies were using Bunhill cemetery, so you concocted a tale around them. One of you also toppled the statue of Death at Chiffinch's funeral, and cut Mother Broughton's throat to provide blood for the Fleet River.'

'*You* killed her?' asked Eliza, regarding Sarah uneasily. 'Why? She was harmless.'

'She was dead when I found her,' lied Sarah. 'And we had to get some blood and a "messenger" from somewhere once Ambassador Downing decided to stay in Dover.'

'And Dutch Jane?' called Chaloner, looking around frantically for something – anything – that would help him stop them. 'You cut her throat, too. Your "alibi" for her murder was pickling cockles with your friends – or rather, making fireballs with them – but I imagine you slipped out for a while, and then declined to tell them why.'

'She was a traitor,' barked Sarah, while Eliza's jaw dropped in shock and the other women exchanged uneasy glances, which told Chaloner that his guess was right. 'She sold our country's secrets to the enemy. She deserved to die.'

'How did you know what she was doing?' demanded

416

Swaddell, and added in an undertone to Chaloner, 'Obviously, we knew she passed our false intelligence on, but we never understood how until you pursued her to Bunhill.'

'Sarah must have followed her to the cemetery once,' Chaloner whispered, 'where she saw the red lights used by Ambassador van Goch's spies. Cleverly, she wove it into one of Mother Broughton's prophecies.'

'I take note of what is happening in my city,' Sarah was declaring superiorly. 'Which is why I will make a better leader than those useless nobles. It was *I* who thwarted the Dutch spies.'

'Thwarted, but not caught,' called Swaddell acidly. 'Thanks to you, they were able to escape, which means they still pose a threat to our country.'

Sarah's only reply was a dismissive and unrepentant sniff, although her co-conspirators were unsettled to learn that she had acted without consulting them. The women, in particular, were uncomfortable with what she had done to Dutch Jane and Mother Broughton.

'What about Chiffinch?' Chaloner shouted in the hope of causing dissension in the ranks. 'Did he deserve to die, too?'

Sarah snorted her disdain. 'If I had wanted him dead, I would not have used my own oysters to dispatch him. And before you ask, I did not kill the Cockpit Club men either. They are beneath my notice.'

'Please!' cried Swaddell, his voice cracking as he peered through the ceiling and saw even more people cramming themselves into the rooms below. 'You cannot massacre—'

'Enough talk,' barked Sarah. 'We have work to do.'

Chaloner ignored her and addressed the others in the forlorn hope that one would see reason. 'What you do

417

today will make no difference. The King will still be in charge tomorrow, and if you kill these ministers, he will just appoint more of the same. Nothing will change.'

'It *will* change!' snarled Sarah, and whipped around to her helpmeets. 'Do not listen to him. He is so stupid that he still has not identified the White Hall killer, even though the answer is staring him in the face.'

'You lie!' snapped Swaddell. '*You* are the culprit.'

'Are you, Sarah?' asked Eliza uneasily. 'I had no great fondness for those men, but—'

'Of course it is not me,' spat Sarah impatiently. 'And I can prove it, although I should not have to. My word alone should be enough.'

'It is,' Eliza assured her, and smiled tentatively. 'Although if you do have proof . . .'

Sarah's face was a mixture of hurt, disappointment and scorn. 'Then stay here while I fetch the *real* culprit's accomplice. Then you will hear the truth and we can put this divisive mistrust and suspicion behind us.'

Chaloner and Swaddell exchanged a glance of mystification, and when they looked back through the slit between the plates, Sarah had disappeared down the stairs.

'Climb over, quickly!' whispered Chaloner, making a stirrup of his hands. 'The others are less likely to fight you if Sarah is not here.'

When Swaddell's foot was secure, Chaloner propelled him upwards until the assassin could stand on his shoulders.

'Higher!' hissed Swaddell. '*Lots* higher.'

Chaloner did his best, but even holding Swaddell's feet in his hands with his arms stretched as far as they could go, the assassin was still unable to reach the top and haul himself over. They gave up in defeat, and Swaddell slid back down to the roof. Then there was a commotion on the conspirators' side, and they peered through the gap to see that Sarah was back, dragging someone by the hair.

'She was in your Duchess's bedroom,' she informed Eliza. 'Poking around.'

'What?' cried Eliza. 'She should be nowhere near Newcastle House, let alone in my Duchess's private quarters. She was not invited.'

'Very few people downstairs were,' drawled Sarah. 'But aristocrats sense entertainment like maggots to rotting meat, and they flock to enjoy it whether they are welcome or not.'

'Bess Widdrington!' breathed Swaddell, as Sarah's prisoner freed herself furiously and looked around with haughty eyes. 'Is Sarah about to claim that *she* is the White Hall killer?'

'I was looking for my husband,' Bess declared, all angry defiance. 'He said he plans to spend the day in Clerkenwell, so I assumed he meant in Newcastle House. But what are you doing up here? And what is in those flasks? I demand an explanation!'

'It is you who will provide the explanation,' said Sarah, drawing a dagger. Bess stepped back smartly, unnerved. 'You, who helped a poisoner. Go on, admit it.'

'Her confession is not necessary,' called Chaloner, watching Bess jump when she heard his disembodied voice. 'We know the identity of the killer. We have done for days.'

It was a barefaced lie, but he was not about to give Sarah the satisfaction of revealing that the solution had only snapped into his mind when she had produced Bess.

419

'Liar,' sneered Sarah. 'If you did, you would not have accused me of it.'

'We were testing you,' blustered Chaloner. 'The killer is Fanny Clarke.'

There was a short silence after Chaloner spoke, then Bess began to screech a litany of denials. Her spitting vitriol unsettled Sarah's helpmeets, who stopped unpacking fireballs to watch her in alarm. While they were distracted, Swaddell turned to Chaloner.

'The poisoner cannot be Fanny. She has an alibi for Tooley's death – in the Queen.'

'Her Majesty is ill and sleeps most of the time,' Chaloner murmured back. 'Wiseman told me. She would not know if Fanny was there or not, so the "alibi" is worthless.'

'But Fanny would never forge such an alliance with Bess – a debauchee in her own right and married to the leader of the Cockpit Club.'

'Well, she did,' hissed Chaloner, 'because they ultimately share the same beliefs – that educating women will turn the world upside down again. We know from their own admissions that they went to the Red Bull together.'

'You claim *that* as their motive?' Swaddell was far from convinced.

Chaloner nodded. 'And Bess has the added incentive of wanting to please her husband. He also deplores educating women, and she will do anything to win his approval.'

'Learning to read will not make you people of quality,' Bess was jeering at her listeners. 'You are scum with delusions of grandeur, and I shall see every last one of you hanged. My husband is right to say you are nothing.'

'Poison,' called Chaloner, before her intemperate

tongue could see her shoved off the roof. 'Fanny is married to a physician. Ergo, she knows about the toxins in his medical arsenal and how to put them in ingenious little capsules. *That* is how we guessed she was the culprit.'

'Is that your evidence?' sneered Sarah contemptuously. 'Pah!'

'We suspected her the moment she "found" Chiffinch's body,' bluffed Chaloner. 'You see, Captain Rolt had lost a gold button, and went to the cockpit to look for it, expecting to find the place deserted. He almost caught her with her victim.'

'So she pretended to be shocked and swooning,' put in Swaddell, deciding Chaloner needed help. 'Perhaps Rolt was sceptical, so she invented a tale about trapped wind escaping from the body, aiming to make him sympathetic to this unworldly, vulnerable lady.'

'But physicians' wives are used to corpses, and Fanny rescues injured cockerels,' Chaloner went on, watching Bess fold her arms and look away. 'It was all an act.'

'But why kill Chiffinch?' asked Sarah, her gloating tone suggesting that she thought they would not know the answer.

'It was all about the Duchess,' explained Chaloner. 'Chiffinch aimed to discredit her, because he felt her eccentric behaviour reflected badly on the King. Fanny decided—'

'Eccentric behaviour?' interrupted Eliza, her voice dangerously soft.

'In his eyes,' clarified Chaloner quickly. 'Funding the Red Bull school, dressing how she pleases, publishing books under her own name, considering herself the intellectual equal of men. He deplored it all, and said so.'

'He did more than say so,' interjected Eliza coldly. 'He

wrote letters to influential people claiming that she, the Earl of Clarendon and the Cockpit Club had united to overthrow the King. His first missive – to the Archbishop of Canterbury, no less – was penned five days before his death, and claimed that she planned to rule the country herself, like Cromwell did.'

'It meant the Duchess had a motive for wanting him dead,' Chaloner went on, although he suspected no one had believed such outlandish allegations; Chiffinch had seriously overstepped the bounds of credibility. 'Fanny's plan was to see her accused of the crime.'

'Then it failed,' murmured Swaddell, regarding him uneasily. 'The Duchess as the culprit may have crossed our minds, but I doubt anyone else made the connection.'

'Not yet, but they will,' said Chaloner, 'because Fanny has been leaving "clues" to implicate her. It is only a matter of time before everyone knows about them.'

'What clues?' asked Eliza in the same low, angry voice.

'For a start, she put the guns with the engraved barrels in the Duchess's boudoir,' replied Chaloner, 'although that was a mistake. Clearly, she had no way of knowing that firearms are banned from Newcastle House.'

'It was also Fanny who started the rumour about the Duchess urging Chiffinch to finish the poisoned oysters,' put in Swaddell, beginning to be convinced at last.

'And Fanny who left the letter for Mansfield to find,' finished Chaloner, recalling the discussion between the Viscount and Lucas in Westminster Abbey. 'The one informing the Duchess that Chiffinch was plotting against her. The Duchess probably never saw it, but Mansfield could be relied upon to bray that she had – and thus that she knew Chiffinch had been working against her.'

'Alone, each of these clues might be disregarded,' said

Swaddell. 'But added together . . . well, even loyal friends would begin to question her innocence.'

'Fanny and I are right to try to get rid of her,' spat Bess contemptuously. 'She gives White Hall a bad name.'

'Unlike fox-tossing and goose-pulling then,' muttered Swaddell.

Sarah was scowling, and Chaloner could tell she resented the fact that he and Swaddell had worked out some of the answers, because she wanted her friends to think that *she* was the only one with the intelligence to do it. Sulkily, she flung out another challenge.

'But you do not know *how* Fanny poisoned Chiffinch.'

'Of course we do,' Chaloner shot back. 'She had already prepared her toxic capsules, so when the Master Cook sent the kitchen child – Millicent – to buy oysters, she followed her, hoping for a chance to doctor them outside White Hall. The plan almost came to nothing when the fish market had sold out, but then along came the Duchess . . .'

'She played right into Fanny's hands.' Swaddell took up the tale. 'She told Millicent to come to Clerkenwell, which did two things. First, it ensured that there were oysters to poison; and second, it made it look as though she was involved in the crime. And if you want to know why Fanny elected to use poison as a means to dispatch her victim, that is obvious, too.'

'Is it?' asked Sarah, hands on her hips as she glowered in his direction.

'Her husband is a physician, so she knew exactly what to use and how – she chose a method she was comfortable with. You saw her follow Millicent back to White Hall, and Millicent spotted her loitering outside the larder, waiting for a corrupt guard to let her buy her way inside.'

'So why kill *Chiffinch* to strike at the Duchess?' asked Sarah, desperate to find something they had failed to understand. 'Why not just dispatch the Duchess herself?'

'Because that would have created a martyr,' shrugged Chaloner. 'Her books would have flown off the shelves, and others would have emulated her. The only way to be rid of her permanently was to shame her – to present her as a common criminal.'

'So Fanny and Bess aimed to destroy the Duchess because they disapprove of women who want more than a life of drudgery and servitude,' said Sarah to the others. 'If you harbour any doubts about what we do today, their vile scheme should banish them once and for all.'

Eliza regarded Bess icily. 'You plotted to hurt the cleverest, most generous and brilliant woman alive. We shall ensure that you and your ilk never try such a thing again.'

Hurt and indignation flashed in Sarah's eyes at the revelation that someone else ranked more highly in her lover's affections, but it was quickly masked.

'Her nonconformity encourages free-thinking in the masses, which is dangerous,' declared Bess, and pointed at the helpmeets. 'And *they* prove my point. Fanny and I are right to prevent the spread of radical ideas – notions that set us at each others' throats again.'

Eliza fingered her pistol, and Chaloner watched in despair, wishing Bess had the sense to shut up, and not just for her own sake. Gunning down an unarmed woman, setting Clerkenwell alight, plotting to murder Ambassador Downing . . . all would give blinkered traditionalists like Fanny an excuse to block reform for years to come.

'Their next victim was Tooley,' Sarah was calling to him. 'Do you know why?'

'Lemons,' replied Chaloner, although he was tiring of the game. 'Cobbe made some remark about Fanny's superior knowledge of them, which Tooley heard. I suspect it sparked a train of thought that eventually led him to connect Fanny with the poisoned oysters.'

'Really?' blurted Sarah, surprised. 'I assumed he saw her in the larder. He was working there on Thursday evening, when the killer did her deadly work.'

'No one saw her,' snarled Bess. 'She wore a disguise. And the lemons used on Chiffinch's meal were from the Master Cook's private hothouse, not Fanny's orangery.'

'It does not matter where they came from,' argued Chaloner. 'The point is that Cobbe's remark caused Tooley to *associate* Fanny with Chiffinch's death, and once he started to ponder, he began to see answers.'

It occurred to Chaloner that he should have seen them, too, and was disgusted with himself for failing to spot what had been right in front of his eyes.

'What happened then?' asked Swaddell. 'Did Tooley try to blackmail Fanny?'

Bess nodded reluctantly. 'And he was not very nice about it.'

'He won the fox-tossing,' said Chaloner, taking up the tale again, 'so you suggested a drinking game to celebrate. Did Fanny give you the poison for his wine? Rolt claims you were talking to him, but your husband was making lucrative promises, which would have snagged his undivided attention. I doubt he would have noticed you slip away.'

Bess started to deny it, but Eliza raised the gun threateningly. 'All right! Yes, she convinced me that removing Tooley was in our best interests.'

'Ashley was next,' Chaloner continued. 'I imagine he

saw you tampering with Tooley's cup, so you enticed him to Bunhill cemetery, perhaps with the promise of some Cockpit Club jape. But there was no need to kill him – he never did understand the significance of what he had witnessed.'

Bess narrowed her eyes. 'How do you know?'

'Because if he had, he would not have accepted the wine you offered him. As it was, I suspect he gulped it down without question.'

'And Mushey?' asked Sarah, annoyed that they had answers for everything.

'Killed to make sure he never revealed who bribed her way into the larder that night. But Pamphlin, the third Yeoman of the Larder and Mushey's friend, put some of it together. He fled to Widdrington, not realising Bess's role in the affair. She found him hiding in their attic . . .'

'She poisoned the wine in his flask before he escaped,' finished Swaddell. 'So, Sarah, how did *you* guess that Fanny and Bess were the culprits?'

'I did not *guess*,' replied Sarah loftily. 'I applied logic, based on facts learned from Cobbe, who is also exploring these crimes. He was happy to share them with me in return for a favour.'

'I have heard enough nastiness,' said Eliza curtly. 'No more talking.'

Chaloner had never known a time when he had felt more powerless. He tried again and again to batter open the door, while Swaddell yelled himself hoarse trying to attract the attention of pedestrians in the street below. They took turns stamping on the glass, but all they did was drench themselves in dirty water. Then the wind picked up, making it even less likely that someone would hear them. Eventually, the church bells tolled for two o'clock, and people began to head to church for their Good Friday devotions.

On the other side of the roof, Sarah and her friends worked with a deft efficiency that showed they had practised hard for their moment of triumph. Bess was ordered to stand near the garden-side balustrade, out of the way. She was subdued at first, but her natural belligerence soon returned, and she began to taunt her captors.

'You will not succeed,' she sneered. 'And I will see you hang. You are nothing!'

'You will be dead yourself, woman,' retorted Joan Cole the tobacco-seller, who had just arrived with another crate of fireballs in her powerful arms. 'We will make sure you burn first.'

Bess turned her tongue on Eliza. 'Your Duchess will not thank you for destroying her home. She spent a fortune doing it up. She will hate you for ever.'

'She will never know who was responsible,' said Sarah to Eliza quickly. 'And it will not matter anyway, because we shall be living in a better, fairer world. No one will care about what happened before.' She whipped around to face Bess. 'One more word from you, and I will toss you off the roof myself.'

The Red Bull folk grew increasingly tense as the minutes ticked past. The wind blew harder, chilling them all, and Joan began to mutter about the dangers of delaying. They had been lucky so far, but what if some of the revellers decided to visit the roof? After all, it was common knowledge that the servants gave guided tours.

'Light the fire,' said Eliza, coming to a decision. 'And remove the loose panes. It is time.'

'It is not,' countered Sarah sharply. 'We agreed on three o'clock. We shall wait.'

'Joan is right,' snapped Eliza, and Chaloner saw she was near breaking point, emotionally exhausted by the strain of the plot, her husband's antics, and the revelations about Bess and Fanny. 'I think Lady Muskerry just glanced up here and pointed. Either she spotted something amiss, or she wants to come and admire the view. We must act *now*.'

She stepped forward to wrench up a pane before Sarah could stop her, and her cronies were quick to follow suit, eager for the waiting to be over. Water splattered on to the people below, resulting in a chorus of angry yells. There was an immediate rush for the doors, but howls of indignation turned to cries of alarm when it was discovered that all the exits were barred – the rebels had people below, as well as on the roof.

Meanwhile, Joan lit a fire. She grabbed a bottle, touched its oil-soaked cloth to the flame and ran to one of the newly made holes in the ceiling. Her arm went back to lob the fireball, but there was a dull thump and it exploded in her hand. She screamed in horror and pain.

'Begin the rain of fire!' yelled Sarah, leaping in to take charge before Joan's fate caused her helpmeets' resolve to waver. 'Hurry!'

They hesitated, frightened and shocked, so she shoved past them, and started to lob the missiles herself. Her example forced them to drag their eyes away from the dying Joan and concentrate on the task in hand. Bess was forgotten in the sudden frenzy of activity, and might have reached the door – and freedom – had she resisted the urge to gloat.

'Your plot will fail, because you are stupid, with ideas above your station,' she jeered. 'You will all hang and so will the Duchess. I will make sure of it.'

Eliza snapped. Rage suffused her face as she rushed at Bess, giving her an almighty shove that sent her staggering towards the balustrade.

'You will harm my Duchess, will you?' she snarled. 'The woman I love more than any other? Well, we shall see about *that*!'

She pushed Bess again. Bess's eyes opened wide with terror as the backs of her legs caught on the low wall and she began to topple. She flailed blindly, and snatched at Eliza's dress. Eliza tried to rip it free, but Bess's grip was made strong by fear. Screaming, Bess disappeared over the edge, dragging Eliza with her.

Chapter 18

Appalled, Chaloner ran to the balustrade on his side of the roof and looked down into the garden below. Eliza and Bess lay there, broken and bleeding. Sarah released a keening wail of grief, and for a moment, he thought the whole plot would grind to an abrupt halt. But his hope was short-lived. Eliza's death served to inspire Sarah to an even greater frenzy of rage and revenge. She tore into action, howling frantic orders at her remaining help-meets as she sent fireball after fireball hurtling down to the rooms below.

Chaloner knelt to peer through the glass. Now a lot of water had drained away, he could see more clearly through Lucas's splattering of chicken manure. Dozens of terrified eyes gazed upwards, and there was a huge press around the doors as people tried to batter their way out. He also noticed that the rainwater had formed a thin layer over the floor, so that most of the fireballs fizzled out at once. He jumped up and went to shout through the brace again.

'It is not working,' he bellowed. 'Give this up before—'

'Do you think we have confined our assault to

430

Newcastle House?' screamed Sarah, beside herself with frustration and fury. 'The city will burn today no matter what happens here.'

'What else have you done?' demanded Chaloner, a cold coil of dread beginning to writhe in his innards.

Sarah's face was a mask of bitter malice. 'You will see at three o'clock – if you live that long. Fanny will pay for trying to destroy our hopes and dreams.'

'So you aim to strike at Chaloner Court,' surmised Swaddell heavily. 'What—'

'She considers herself godly,' sneered Sarah, 'and intends to watch the Good Friday crisis from her orangery with her like-minded sewing cronies. They will all die.'

'Lucy Bodvil and the others are not wicked,' objected Chaloner in alarm. 'On the contrary, they speak out against the excesses of—'

'They are Fanny's friends,' hissed Sarah. 'And there is a price to pay for that. The same is true of your silly cousins.'

'They are safe in Covent Garden,' said Swaddell quickly. 'With Wiseman.'

'The Queen summoned him,' said Sarah gloatingly. 'So I told Fanny that they were alone on this most holy of days, and she fetched them in her carriage.'

With an anguished cry, Swaddell raced to the door, and began thumping and kicking it for all he was worth. Chaloner only stared at Sarah in stunned disbelief.

'But why? They have never hurt you. Indeed, they want to teach at your school, because they applaud what you are doing there.'

'They came to London to get husbands,' spat Sarah. 'But they should make their own way in the world, not expect some man to support them. Girls like them are responsible for perpetuating a system that is manifestly unjust.'

'It is not for you to dictate how other women choose to spend their lives,' argued Chaloner, horror giving way to anger at her presumption.

'Then stop me,' taunted Sarah viciously. 'Come on!'

But while she argued with him, her accomplices had realised that their fireballs were having scant effect: there was no serious blaze and no major massacre. They began edging towards the stairs, aiming to flee while they could.

'You will be caught,' Swaddell barked at them. 'But I will arrange for you to escape the noose if you help me rescue Ursula and Veriana.'

'Never!' shrieked Sarah. 'They are doomed. You are *all* doomed!'

'Eliza would not want this,' yelled Chaloner desperately. 'She was going to let us go once the rain of fire was over. She did not approve of cold-blooded murder.'

'Eliza,' sneered Sarah. 'She said she loved me, but it was a lie. She refused to leave her husband, even though he was a selfish coward and a thief, and what was the last thing she said? That she loved her Duchess above all others. Well, she can rot in hell!'

'Sarah,' hissed one of the women. 'We must go or they will catch us.'

Sarah laughed wildly and without humour. 'Of course they will catch us! That has been obvious since our first bomb failed to ignite.'

Her friends exchanged agitated glances. 'But what about our places in government?' demanded one. 'And the new world you promised we would lead?'

'You will not have them now.' Sarah shrugged bitterly.

'Baron Lucas must have given me the wrong formula for our missiles, and I fear all has been lost. Unless . . .'

She looked at the chaos below, then at the place where Eliza had gone over the parapet. The madness in her eyes faded, and was replaced by something darker and more dangerous. She snatched up a fireball, lit it, and allowed the flames to catch her skirts. Then she grabbed a bomb-loaded crate and let herself drop with it through the ceiling. There was a moment when Chaloner thought she had sacrificed herself in vain, but then there was a loud thump, followed by a blinding flash. When his vision cleared, he could see fire licking up the walls and the wooden staircase.

Newcastle House was alight.

Chaloner and Swaddell kicked, hammered and shoulder-charged the door with all their might, but it was no use. Smoke billowed through the roof, and the rooms below were pandemonium. One of the doors had been smashed open, and everyone was fighting to squeeze through it, pushing each other and blocking it shut in their frantic desperation to escape.

The fire spread fast, partly because the wood was new, dry and oily, but also because the holes in the ceiling acted like a chimney, drawing the flames upwards. The roar and crackle told Chaloner that it would not be long before the whole house became an inferno, at which point sparks would dance away to ignite other buildings, just as Sarah had intended.

'So this is how Mother Broughton's prophecy will come true,' whispered Swaddell, clenching his fists in impotent fury. 'Smoke *will* darken the skies, and there *will* be much weeping and gnashing of teeth if the whole city burns.'

Chaloner resumed his assault on the door, even though he knew it was futile. His knuckles were skinned, his shoulders were bruised, and he wondered if he had broken his toes, but he ignored the pain and continued to batter.

'Enough, Tom,' croaked Swaddell, dragging him away as smoke swirled more thickly around them. 'Decide now: a quick death by jumping or a lingering one in the flames.'

'Come this way,' came a familiar voice, and Chaloner spun around to see that the door was open. Molly the chicken girl stood inside it, beckoning. 'Come on!'

'How did you . . .' he began.

'I saw you from the garden,' she explained with one of her sweet but vacant smiles. 'So I came up to say hello. But the door was barred, so I—'

Chaloner shoved her and then Swaddell towards the stairwell. Before he followed, he glanced back to see the roof sag dangerously as the lead frames began to melt. He ran down the steps, only to hear an anguished shout from Swaddell.

'The stairs are alight. We are trapped!'

'Then we must take the *secret* route,' said Molly unperturbed. 'Come with me.'

She took Chaloner's hand and pulled him back up a few steps to where a small gap in the wall gave access to the roof-space. She went through it on all fours, then crawled along a series of rafters. Sincerely hoping she knew what she was doing, Chaloner and Swaddell followed.

She led them over to the eaves, where there was a ladder. It led to a hall in the attic, where there was a servants' staircase down to the kitchens. They arrived to find the cook and his staff throwing pots, pans and other utensils into travelling crates.

434

'What are you doing?' howled Swaddell in disbelief. 'Go and help the people trapped in the ballroom before—'

'We did,' interrupted the cook shortly. 'Everyone is out. Now our task is to save the tools of our trade.'

'Your task is the save the house,' countered Swaddell furiously. 'Fill these vessels with water and—'

'The Duke has a much nicer palace in the country,' interrupted the cook. 'So we hope this one *is* razed to the ground. None of us like it very much.'

'But if you let it blaze out of control, it will take Clerkenwell with it,' hissed Swaddell. 'And if that happens, I shall charge you with treason. Now *fill the vessels with water.*'

Chaloner had never seen him look more deadly, so was not surprised when the cook hastened to obey, calling his assistants to do likewise.

'Not you, Molly,' said Chaloner, afraid the child would be trampled in the commotion. 'Go and see to your birds – keep them safe from smoke and flying cinders.'

She scampered away, and he turned his mind to the choice he had to make: fight the blaze in Newcastle House before it spread to ignite the whole city, or race to Chaloner Court in the hope of rescuing his cousins. An anguished glance at a clock on the mantelpiece told him it was three minutes to three – nowhere near enough time to run across the green, find Ursula and Veriana, and whisk them to safety.

'Stay here and organise this rabble, Tom,' ordered Swaddell briskly. 'I will find Ursula . . . the girls.'

It was clear from his white face that the assassin thought any attempt to enter Chaloner Court now would be fatal. Even so, he was ready to try, to save the woman who had captured his attention.

435

'These people are more frightened of you than of me,' said Chaloner. 'You must make sure they stay and do as they are told. I will go to Chaloner Court.'

'But Sarah has likely set an explosion,' argued Swaddell hoarsely. 'How else could she predict that it would happen at three o'clock precisely?'

'Yes,' acknowledged Chaloner. 'Do your duty here. I will see you later.'

He could tell by Swaddell's touching distress that he did not expect them to meet again.

'Then God's speed, Tom, dear friend.'

Heart hammering, Chaloner tore across Clerkenwell Green, not caring that he collided with the spectators who had gathered there to gape at the fire. He was dimly aware of the murmurs that Mother Broughton was right yet again, and many folk were uneasy, beginning to wonder if they really were godly enough to escape the coming carnage.

Chaloner Court was peculiarly still and quiet compared to the other houses around the green, all of which had people leaning out of the windows, calling desperately for reliable reports on the fire. He reached the front door and hammered on it, but there was no reply.

He picked the lock, but something was wrong with the mechanism, and no amount of hammering and battering could budge it. He sprinted to the back of the house, just in time to see two women haring away at top speed. It did not take a genius to guess that they had just lit fuses and were dashing to safety. Then the church clock struck three.

The pair had left the garden gate swinging open, so he shot through it and aimed for the back door. This

436

had been jammed shut by having a bench braced against it. Terrified howls emanated from the hallway within. Through an adjacent window, he could see the ladies from Fanny's sewing circle, plus half a dozen servants.

'Help us!' screamed Lucy Bodvil. 'Those women . . . they told us we are about to be blown to kingdom come! They had knives . . . *Help us!*'

Chaloner hauled the bench away from the door, and was almost knocked from his feet as the prisoners scrambled out. Veriana and Ursula were not among them, and nor was Fanny. He grabbed Lucy's arm as she hurtled past.

'Where are my cousins?'

'Not with us,' replied Lucy, fighting to pull away from him. 'Ask Fanny.'

'So where is Fanny?' demanded Chaloner in agitation.

'She went to the orangery to save her cockerels. Now, let me *go!*'

She tore free of him and was gone. Chaloner hared along the hallway, aware of a powerful reek of gunpowder. Then there was a boom so loud and powerful that he felt the floor jerk beneath his feet. Sincerely hoping the explosion had not been in the orangery, he raced on, ignoring the dust that showered down from the ceiling. He hauled open the orangery door, then jerked backwards when he found himself at the wrong end of a sword.

'Where are my cousins?' he snarled, reaching for his own weapon before remembering that it was still on the floor in Newcastle House, where Eliza had made him leave it.

The expression on Fanny's face was a combination of resigned detachment and stunned disbelief. She shook

437

her head slowly, and began to talk in a flat whisper, as if she could scarcely credit what she was saying.

'Two women were just here. They informed me that my efforts to prevent our world from being turned upside down again have failed. That all I did was for nothing.'

'Where are Veriana and Ursula?' shouted Chaloner, panic-stricken as another blast rocked the house. Dust pattered down from the cracked lintel under which he stood. 'Please! Just tell me. Then you can escape through the back door.'

'Escape is not an option for me,' said Fanny, in the same oddly faraway voice. 'It would mean standing trial for what Bess and I did to Chiffinch and the others. None were good men, but we will be castigated for dispatching them, even so.'

'You will be castigated even more if my cousins die,' yelled Chaloner, his stomach churning. 'Now *tell me where they are!*'

'I did what I thought was right,' Fanny went on softly, although her hand tightened on the sword when Chaloner took an agitated step towards her. 'I wanted everyone to see the Duchess as a dangerous lunatic. We cannot have noblewomen setting that sort of example, and I am tired of upheaval. My country needs stability.'

'I know,' said Chaloner pleadingly. 'And we can discuss it later, but—'

'I suppose my downfall was impatience,' she interrupted. 'When Chiffinch was still alive hours after eating his first oyster, I grew worried. I enticed him to the cockpit – a place I thought would be deserted – with the intention of giving him poisoned wine. But I should have let him be, as he collapsed moments after arriving. I waited with him while he died.'

438

'It does not matter!' shouted Chaloner, beside himself. 'Tell me where—'

He was interrupted by the loudest boom yet, and he staggered as the blast shook the house. So did Fanny, so he lunged for her weapon. She jerked away, flailing wildly, forcing him to dodge away until their places were reversed – he was in the orangery and she stood in the doorway. He opened his mouth to beg again, but there was a groan from above, and the lintel gave way. Fanny disappeared under a deluge of rubble.

For a moment, Chaloner could only stare in horror. Then he darted forward and began to dig her free, tearing his fingernails in his frantic haste. After a moment, he excavated an arm, but there was no life-beat in it. Fanny was dead.

He looked around wildly. Rubble blocked his way back into the house. There was no door to the garden from the orangery, meaning he was trapped. He ran to the biggest window and kicked it with all his might. The lead frame buckled, so he did it again. And again, until he was able to knock the whole thing out. He scrambled through it, and was followed by an eager flurry of feathers – Fanny's rescued cockerels, flapping through the hole and scattering in all directions across the garden.

He limped after them, then turned to survey the house, assessing it for other ways in. What he saw filled him with despair. Smoke poured from every window, so thick that he doubted anyone could still be alive within. The right side of the building had already collapsed, and even as he watched, more of it toppled inwards with a groan and a great billow of dust.

'No,' he whispered hoarsely. 'No, no, no!'

Then he spotted someone in one of the windows, a vague shape blurred by smoke. The figure raised an arm, and he was sure it was Veriana. He took two steps towards her, but there was a deafening rumble, and the rest of the house fell. One moment, there was a window with a living person standing at it, the next there was nothing but empty sky. Stunned, Chaloner dropped to his knees.

'Tom! Tom!'

Dazed with grief and guilt, Chaloner looked up to see Swaddell running towards him.

'Newcastle House is lost?' he asked dully. 'You abandoned your efforts to save it?'

'What? Oh, no – Widdrington arrived with his troops, and as he transpires to be unexpectedly adept at firefighting, I left him to it. Someone told him that his wife started the blaze, so he is keen to prove his worth by dousing it, lest he is accused of being her accomplice.'

'So it is under control?'

'Not yet, but it will be. There is no trouble on the streets either, because everyone is more interested in watching him do clever things with pumps and firehooks. And the men I hid in Bishop Morley's garden will nip any bad behaviour in the bud, should it be necessary.'

'I was too late,' said Chaloner in a low, exhausted voice.

'Yes,' agreed Swaddell sadly. 'This poor old house is well beyond repair, but at least there is no inferno to contain. London is safe once more.'

'Fanny would not tell me where my cousins were,' said Chaloner bleakly. 'I could not reach them . . .'

Swaddell regarded him in surprise. 'You think Ursula and Veriana were inside? No, Tom! They are on the green, watching Widdrington's heroics with everyone else. Surely you saw them as you ran past?'

Chaloner gaped at him. 'They are alive?'

A beatific grin stole over the assassin's face. 'Yes, and Ursula kissed me when I told her we had been frantic for her safety. She called out to you as you ran past, but you ignored her.'

'I thought they were inside when . . . I saw someone at an upstairs window . . .'

'Clarke, probably. Lucy Bodvil said Fanny contrived to lock him in a bedroom when she caught him packing for Dover.'

Chaloner struggled to make sense of it all. 'But Sarah gloated to us that Fanny collected Ursula and Veriana from Covent Garden this morning . . .'

'She tried, but they had already gone out – with Cobbe.'

'With *Cobbe*?'

'Remember Sarah telling us that Cobbe gave her information about Fanny in exchange for "a favour"? I assumed she meant she lay with him, but that is not the boon he demanded. He wanted to know where your cousins were lodging. Somehow, she managed to find out for him.'

'Perhaps Molly told her – she delivered that rescued goose from White Hall to my home.'

'Yes, most likely. Then this morning, while he was lounging in the Red Bull with Widdrington, he somehow learned that they were home alone, with no guardian to fight him off. He abandoned Widdrington at once, and went to whisk them away for a jaunt.'

'What sort of jaunt?' asked Chaloner weakly.

'A pleasant drive around the city, finishing here to

watch the rain of fire.' Swaddell patted Chaloner's shoulder. 'Do not worry, Tom. All is well.'

At that moment, there was a deep groan that sounded as though it came from the very heart of the house. Then the last wall crumpled on to the orangery, crushing it so completely that nothing recognisable remained.

'I am so sorry,' said Swaddell softly. 'Your beautiful ancestral home . . .'

'It does not matter,' said Chaloner, feeling a sudden weight lifted from his shoulders as he saw the assassin was right: all *was* well. 'I never liked what the Clarkes did to it anyway.'

Epilogue

It was a beautiful morning. The sun shone, the sky was blue, and everywhere were signs that spring was well and truly under way. Lent lilies nodded in a gentle breeze, all pale gold and bright white, and fresh new growth greened the trees. Birds sang, and Chaloner's poultry had provided him with ten fine brown eggs and one huge white one.

He and Thurloe sat on a bench in Wiseman's garden. The ex-Spymaster had arrived back in London an hour earlier, and had hurried straight to Covent Garden to find out what had happened in his absence. He had been regaled with quite a tale.

'So Mother Broughton was wrong,' he said. 'The world did not change irrevocably on Good Friday, and Easter is here with all its promises of renewal and salvation. Yet I do believe the Sun is dancing for joy. She was right about that, at least.'

Chaloner squinted upwards. 'It is not! And the world almost changed irrevocably for my cousins. If Cobbe

443

had not taken a fancy to Veriana, they might have been locked up with Clarke when Fanny's house blew up.'

'True, but look on the bright side: their narrow escape will make other relatives think twice before entrusting their children to your tender care.'

Chaloner was not so sure about that, given that good marriages meant everything to a clan staving off poverty. They might decide the risk of explosions was an acceptable one.

He watched his hens hunting for grain and worms. 'Mother Broughton was a charlatan. The Fleet only ran with blood because Sarah cut her throat after she fell down in a drunken stupor; corpses never walked in Bunhill or Westminster Abbey; and there was no weeping and gnashing of teeth on Good Friday.'

'Actually, there was quite a bit of weeping and gnashing,' countered Thurloe. 'By folk who are disappointed that the wicked still run the country. By Sarah's friends because justice and equality remain an impossible dream. By Fanny and Bess because their scheme to prevent destabilising change had failed. By those injured during the attack on Newcastle House . . .'

'All right, all right,' conceded Chaloner. 'But Mother Broughton was still a fraud.'

'Oh, yes,' agreed Thurloe. 'I charged a couple of my former intelligencers to monitor her while I was away, and they inform me that Sarah told her exactly what to "predict" – in exchange for money.'

'Which explains why she lived in a hovel that was stuffed full of smart new furnishings,' sighed Chaloner. 'I should have guessed that was relevant.'

'You should, although it would have made no difference in the end. Yet I am astonished that Fanny was the White Hall killer. She always seemed so dull and meek.'

'Dull, perhaps, meek no. She poisoned Chiffinch without a qualm; she provided Bess with the wherewithal to kill Tooley, Ashley, Mushey and Pamphlin; and she shot at Swaddell and me in White Hall. Of course, Sarah killed Mother Broughton and Dutch Jane with just as much ruthless indifference . . .'

'Thank you for resolving that anonymous letter business, by the way. My enquiries in Grantham revealed the sender as Vicar Booth, but it would have been difficult to prove the others were involved. I was pleased that you provided the Duke with a full cast of culprits.'

Chaloner regarded him curiously. 'What favour did the Duchess once do you, which saw you race to her rescue? I think I have earned the right to ask, after all the trouble that letter caused me.'

'I was sent to the Tower at the Restoration, as you know, and all my assets were seized. My wife and children were in London at the time, terrified and unprotected. The Duchess arranged for them to travel home to Oxfordshire in her own coach. She had no reason to help a Parliamentarian family, but she did – out of pure Christian charity. I shall always be grateful.'

'Do you know what favour Swaddell did for the Bishop of Winchester?' asked Chaloner. 'It was significant enough that Morley would have lied to give me an alibi. Not that he had to in the end, thankfully.'

'Swaddell used to be Morley's steward, and served him faithfully for years. Then Morley was made a bishop, and as prelates can hardly keep assassins on their staff, it was agreed that he would go to Williamson instead. But the pair remain friends.'

Chaloner regarded him askance. 'But Morley is a good man – ethical and decent. How can he have employed someone like Swaddell?'

'Swaddell is not all bad, and loyal servants do not grow on trees. Morley is fond of him. But you are lucky Swaddell likes you, because you do not want him as an enemy, believe me.'

'I know,' said Chaloner drily.

'Incidentally, Clarke's heirs plan to demolish the ruins of your ancestral home and build ten new houses on the site. It will earn them a fortune, as Clerkenwell is a popular location among the rich. They have plucked triumph out of disaster.'

'Speaking of disasters, I need your help to prevent one. Cobbe wants to marry Veriana. He has been offered the post of Receiver General in Southampton, and claims that while he will never be fabulously wealthy, he can keep her in relative comfort.'

'But you are concerned about his character,' surmised Thurloe. 'Perhaps he will become a better man once away from the tainting influence of White Hall.'

Chaloner was not much comforted by the 'perhaps'. 'But what if he does not? Veriana will be stuck with him for the rest of her life.'

'What does she think?'

'She is delighted by his proposal, and thinks she can make something of him.'

'Then I suggest you let her try. Better she marries someone of her own choosing than someone of yours. Then she cannot blame you if the liaison goes wrong.'

It was a good point, and Chaloner supposed he could always insist on a long betrothal, to ensure both parties knew what they were doing.

Thurloe glanced at him. 'More importantly, how do you feel about Swaddell marrying Ursula? He is head over heels in love with her, and she told me, when I arrived just now, that she is just as enamoured of him.'

'I will not allow it,' said Chaloner firmly. 'Never. And if she continues to insist that she considers him a fine catch, I shall ask Wiseman to examine her for signs of madness. No one in her right mind could want a union with Swaddell.'

'Love is a peculiar thing, Tom, and none of us can control who we fall for. Take yourself, for example. You married two women who were patently unsuitable.'

Chaloner disliked being reminded of this. 'That was different,' he said stiffly.

'How?' asked Thurloe gently.

Chaloner had no answer, and returned to the more pressing matter of Ursula. 'But Swaddell is an assassin, who has murdered more people than we can count, and who enjoys slitting throats.'

'True. However, he did share your revulsion for the bloodsports at White Hall, so perhaps there is hope for him yet. Moreover, he has been a loyal friend to you, while a virtuous bishop thinks the world of him . . .'

'But his eyes still gleam at the prospect of killing, and God only knows what he does for Williamson under cover of state secrecy. I do not want such a man in my family.'

'I appreciate that,' said Thurloe. 'However, it is hardly fair to let your opinions stand between two people and their future happiness. I suggest you send Swaddell to the Isle of Man to woo your aunt. Let her decide whether Ursula should accept him.'

Chaloner seized on the solution with relief, sure she

would take one look at the assassin and forbid the match on the spot. 'Thank you,' he said sincerely. 'I will suggest it when I meet him in Clarendon House this evening.'

'Why will he be there, of all places?'

'Because the Earl is holding a soirée to celebrate the fact that he is no longer suspected of poisoning Chiffinch, and as Swaddell and I unmasked the real culprit, we are invited. I am to play my viol.'

'Which I am sure you will enjoy,' said Thurloe indulgently. 'However, I can tell you one group of people who will have no entertainment tonight: the surviving members of the Cockpit Club. They had a bird fight scheduled, but it was cancelled when all their cocks were stolen.'

'Poor Widdrington,' said Chaloner flatly. 'He will be disappointed.'

'Widdrington is currently on his way to Ireland, on the ship that was to have carried his wife. He aims to lie low until the furore surrounding Bess's crimes dies down. Without him, the Cockpit Club will founder.'

'Good,' said Chaloner. 'London's foxes, geese, bulls, bears, dogs, horses and cockerels can breathe again.'

'Speaking of cockerels, I heard that a girl matching the description of Molly from Newcastle House was seen on a cart loaded with cages outside White Hall this morning. There is a rumour that the Cockpit Club's birds are on their way to a safer life in Buckinghamshire.'

'They should like it there,' said Chaloner serenely. 'I know I would.'

'I am surprised you did not go with them. I imagine your family would like to see you, and as you have already solved the case of the stolen saltpetre, it is no longer necessary for you to sail with *Royal Oak* today.'

Chaloner grimaced. 'Spymaster Williamson raced down to Dover in the belief that he was on the trail of a mysterious saltpetre buyer, but it transpires that the "clues" were left by Sarah – she wanted him out of the way, lest he became inconveniently interested in what she was doing. Swaddell says he is mortified to have been so easily deceived.'

'He should be,' said Thurloe, unimpressed. 'He should have delegated the matter to one of his people, not hared off in person. But you have not answered my question. Why did you not go with Molly to Buckinghamshire?'

'Because the Newcastles have accepted an invitation to stay with my Earl while their own house is being repaired, and the Duke has a great fondness for a particular Somerset cheese. I am to travel there and bring some back for him.'

Thurloe raised his eyebrows. 'Mother Broughton predicted cheese in your future, did she not?'

'Coincidence,' said Chaloner firmly.

Low Sunday, one week later

The Duchess was very happy. She sat in her new quarters in Clarendon House and laughed aloud. All the people who had schemed against her were either dead or discredited, and their antics had given her books a huge amount of publicity. In a few days, sales had gone through the roof, and her printer could not produce copies quickly enough to meet the demand.

She was fêted at White Hall, and other women now emulated her style of dress, claiming the clothes she chose were far more comfortable than the cumbersome skirts and bodices dictated by fashion. And the King had approached her the previous day to solicit her opinion on all manner of subjects, including bloodsports. He had listened carefully to her reasons as to why they should be banned, and promised to raise the matter at the next Privy Council meeting.

But better than all that was the loyalty her husband had shown over the letter accusing her of adultery. He had confided last night that, although Clayton had composed and sent the missive, using Booth and Liddell to help him, the whole scheme had been Mansfield's idea. Mansfield had denied it, of course, but her husband did not believe him.

She laughed again. Poor, stupid Mansfield! Of course it had not been his idea! The plot had been devised by a person of considerable intelligence, who could see beyond the inconvenience such accusations would cause in the short term, to the benefits that would accrue in the long. Relations between the Duke and his heir were irrevocably shattered, and she never need worry that the Duke might take Mansfield's side again. Now he would listen only to her.

Everything had worked out exactly as she had intended.

Historical Note

The story of the anonymous letter, in which the Duchess of Newcastle is alleged to have had an affair with her husband's steward Francis Topp, is true. The Duke did not believe a word of it, and immediately ordered an investigation. It eventually emerged that the letter had been sent by another steward, Andrew Clayton. Clayton was corrupt, and when the Duchess decided to inspect his household accounts, he realised that he needed to get rid of her fast. Clayton recruited two friends to help him: a dodgy clergyman named John Booth and a dishonest horse-breeder called Francis Liddell. Together, they composed the letter, taking care to disguise their hand-writing, and dispatched a servant to mail it from a posthouse in Grantham where none of them were known.

Rather stupidly, Clayton later wrote Booth a note about the plot, but forgot to send it through anonymous channels. It was intercepted, and Booth confessed to everything in order to save himself. Clayton tried to wriggle out of his predicament by accusing Booth of coin-clipping, an offence punishable by death. Booth was actually convicted of this crime, but escaped execution when the Duke intervened on his behalf.

Fortunately for the scheming trio, the Duke did not want his wife's name dragged through the mud in a public trial, so the libel charges were quietly dropped. However, there is some suggestion that the plot may have been instigated by Viscount Mansfield, the Duke's weak and uninspiring son by his first marriage, who disliked his stepmother, and lived in constant fear that she would cheat him out of his inheritance.

The Duchess of Newcastle – Margaret Cavendish – was a remarkable lady. She was a poet, playwright and biographer, and is credited with writing one of the first ever science fiction novels. She was also a philosopher, and had opinions about religion, feminism, social rules and animals. Her academic reputation was such that she was permitted to attend a meeting of the Royal Society, then a men-only organisation. Her older brother, Baron Lucas, was a member of the Royal Society, although he may later have been expelled.

Unfortunately, while the Duchess's intellectual abilities may have impressed some of her contemporaries, there were many more who were terrified by them, as she challenged the precepts of Restoration male-dominated society. Some accused her of insanity, although her behaviour suggests she was eccentric rather than deranged – the eye-catching costume that she really did wear to a public theatre is a case in point. As a result, she suffered much ridicule, particularly from those who were less well endowed in the brain department.

The Duke was also accomplished, and was a playwright, soldier and equestrian. It is possible that he suffered from Parkinson's-like symptoms in his later years, which prevented him from pursuing the outdoor activities that he loved.

For all their cleverness the Newcastles made terrible choices regarding their staff. Not only did they employ the treacherous Clayton, but Francis Topp cheated them for years before he was caught, at which point he absconded with £300 and faked his own death to prevent them from looking for him (he eventually died in 1675). Topp's wife Elizabeth (Eliza) was the Duchess's lady-in-waiting, and perhaps her best friend. It is unclear if she knew what her husband was up to, but she was dismissed in disgrace in 1671. She died at a ripe old age in 1703. The Newcastles also had a maid called Dutch Jane.

Newcastle House, which was on Clerkenwell Green, was originally an H-plan building, started in 1630 on the orders of the Duke himself. It is not to be confused with the Newcastle House in Lincoln's Inn Fields, which still exists. However, the Duchess never designed a transparent ceiling for it, and if she had, reinforced glass would not have been available to her, as this was a much later invention.

Some liberty has also been taken with dates. For example, the chances are that the ducal couple were at their estates in Welbeck in April 1666, as Newcastle House was being renovated. Also, the letter plot took place in the early 1670s. More about the Newcastles and their lives can be found in the excellent *Mad Madge* by Katie Whitaker.

Clerkenwell was a rapidly developing suburb in the 1660s. It was a separate parish, and contained a number of open areas. These included Bunhill Fields, Charterhouse, and the Artillery Ground, not to mention the gardens of several great houses. Perhaps its best known public building was the Red Bull, once famous as a playhouse, but probably just a tavern by 1666.

When the plague of 1665 filled London's graveyards, it was decided to create a civic burial ground in Bunhill Fields. Whether it was ready in time to take the plague dead is not known, although it was provided with a surrounding wall and gates between 1665 and 1666. One Mr Tyndal undertook the cost of this, and the site was then leased to him as a private cemetery. Controversially, some of it was left unconsecrated, so that nonconformists could use it without compromising their religious beliefs. Edward Bagshaw, the quarrelsome nonconformist divine (he had a vicious dispute with George Morley, Bishop of Winchester, among others) was buried here, although not until 1671.

Other notable Clerkenwell worthies included the poet John Milton, the famous physician Dr Goddard, the eccentric philanthropist Erasmus Smith, and Izaak Walton of *The Compleat Angler* fame. More infamous residents include Mistress Shawe, who was charged at the Middlesex assizes for being in possession of fireballs with the intention of using them for seditious purposes; and Mother Broughton, who considered herself a prophet. No doubt she had plenty to say about the year containing three sixes, not to mention the fact that Good Friday in 1666 fell on 13 April. There was also a tobacco-seller named Joan Cole.

Other one-time residents of Clerkenwell include Thomas Chaloner the elder (1521–1565) and Thomas Chaloner the younger (1559-1615). The younger Chaloner was the father of Thomas and James the regicides. His Clerkenwell house seems to have come into

James's possession, but this was forfeit at the Restoration, along with all his other property. James and his wife Ursula had several children, one of whom was named Veriana; she married Thomas Cobbe, the Receiver General of Southampton. James Chaloner died on the Isle of Man shortly after the Restoration, leaving his wife and unmarried children in very straitened circumstances. There is some suggestion that he may have swallowed poison to avoid the horrors of a trial.

Other real people in *The Clerkenwell Affair* include the courtiers. Colonel George Widdrington married Elizabeth (Bess) Bertie, and was a close friend of Viscount Mansfield. Widdrington was an outspoken critic of the Earl of Clarendon, and it is interesting to note that he only rose to real power after Clarendon's fall in 1667. George Ashley was a Sergeant of the Larder who died in April 1666; Richard Pamphlin fades from the records after his appointment as Page of the Presence in 1660; Abraham Hubbert was appointed Clerk of the Larder in 1661; and Henry Barker was Clerk of the Crown in Chancery from the Restoration until 1692. Michael Mushey was a Yeoman of the Kitchen in the 1660s, and Millicent Lantravant was a Child of the Kitchen, although as these were usually appointments for boys, this may be a mistake in the records.

Timothy Clarke was Physician to the Household, and was later promoted as Physician to the Person. His wife was named Frances (called Fanny here to prevent confusion with Francis Topp), of whom the diarist Samuel Pepys wrote in April 1666: 'has grown mighty high, fine and proud'. She was allegedly followed to a brothel in Moor Fields by the lively Captain Edward Rolt. Rolt had been a prominent member of Cromwell's court, and was also related to him, but deftly flipped sides at the Restoration. Richard Wiseman was Surgeon to the Person.

James Tooley was not a courtier, but he was murdered in 1666 by William Legg, although the culprit is unlikely to have been the same William Legg who was Colonel of Artillery and had a son named George.

Finally, Thomas Chiffinch died on 6 April 1666, and was interred in Westminster Abbey four days later. He had been Keeper of the Closet and Keeper of the Jewels, two titles that were then claimed by his less respectable younger brother William. 'Will' Chiffinch was known as the Pimp-Master General, as his duties involved providing the King with female company. He was firmly associated with the less salubrious aspects of Court life – its debauchery, corruption and immorality. One biographer remarked that the unsavoury Will carried 'the abuse of backstairs influence to scientific perfection'.